CW01651449

Sinc ... *eath*, published in 1 ... ards, including the ... gger for 1976's best crime novel with *A Demon in My View*, and the Arts Council National Book Awards – genre friction for *The Lake of Darkness* in 1980.

In 1985 Ruth Rendell received the Silver Dagger for *The Tree of Hands*, and in 1987, writing as Barbara Vine, won her third Edgar from the Mystery Writers of America for *A Dark-Adapted Eye*.

She won the Gold Dagger in 1986 for *Live Flesh* and, as Barbara Vine, for *A Fatal Inversion* in 1987 and for *King Solomon's Carpet* in 1991.

Ruth Rendell won the *Sunday Times* Literary Award in 1990, and in 1991 she was awarded the Crime Writers' Association Cartier Diamond Dagger for outstanding contribution to the genre. In 1996 she was awarded the CBE, and in 1997 was made a Life Peer.

Her books have been translated into twenty-five languages and are also published to great acclaim in the United States.

Ruth Rendell has a son and two grandsons, and lives in London.

Put on by Cunning

AND

An Unkindness of Ravens

Ruth Rendell

WH S

Put on by Cunning

Ruth Rendell

WH S

First published by Arrow Books for WH Smith plc in 2001

Put on by Cunning Copyright © Kingsmarkham Enterprises 1981
An Unkindness of Ravens
Copyright © Kingsmarkham Enterprises 1985

Ruth Rendell has asserted her right under the Copyright, Designs and Patents Act, 1988 to be identified as the author of this work

This novel is a work of fiction. Names and characters are the product of the author's imagination and any resemblance to actual persons, living or dead, is entirely coincidental

This book is sold subject to the condition that it shall not, by way of trade or otherwise, be lent, resold, hired out, or otherwise circulated without the publisher's prior consent in any form of binding or cover other than that in which it is published and without a similar condition including this condition being imposed on the subsequent purchaser

Put on by Cunning first published in Great Britain
by Hutchinson in 1981

An Unkindness of Ravens first published in Great Britain
by Hutchinson in 1985

Arrow Books
The Random House Group Limited
20 Vauxhall Bridge Road, London SW1V 2SA

The Random House Group Limited Reg. No. 954009

WH Smith plc
Greenbridge Road, Swindon SN3 3LD

www.whsmith.co.uk

A CIP catalogue record for this book
is available from the British Library

Papers used by WH Smith are natural, recyclable products made from wood grown in sustainable forests. The manufacturing processes conform to the environmental regulations of the country of origin

ISBN 0 09 943588 8

Printed and bound in Great Britain by
Cox & Wyman Ltd, Reading, Berkshire

For Simon

So shall you hear . . .
Of deaths put on by cunning and forc'd cause;
And, in this upshot, purposes mistook
Fall'n on th'inventors' heads – all this can I
Truly deliver.

Hamlet

Part One

1

Against the angels and apostles in the windows the snow fluttered like plucked down. A big soft flake struck one of the Pre-Raphaelite haloes and clung there, cotton wool on gold tinsel. It was something for an apathetic congregation to watch from the not much warmer interior as the rector of St Peter's, Kingsmarkham, came to the end of the second lesson. St Matthew, chapter fifteen, for 27 January.

'For out of the heart proceed evil thoughts, murders, adulteries, fornications, thefts, false witness, blasphemies. These are the things which defile a man. . . .'

Two of his listeners turned their eyes from the pattern the snow was making on a red and blue and yellow and purple 'Annunciation' and waited expectantly. The rector closed the heavy Bible with its dangling marker and opened an altogether more mundane-looking, small black book of the exercise variety. He cleared his throat.

'I publish the banns of marriage between Sheila Katherine Wexford, spinster, of this parish, and Andrew Paul Thorverton, bachelor, of the parish of St John, Hampstead. This is the first time of asking. And between Manuel Camargue, widower, of this parish, and Dinah Baxter Sternhold, widow, of the parish of St Mary, Forby. This is the third time of asking. If any of you know cause or just impediment why these persons should not be joined together in holy matrimony, ye are to declare it.'

He closed the book. Manuel Camargue resigned himself, for the third week in succession, to the sermon. As the congregation settled itself, he looked about him. The same crowd of old faithfuls came each week. He saw only one newcomer, a beautiful fair-haired girl whom he instantly recognized without being able to put a name to her. He worried about this a good deal for the next half-hour, trying to place her, annoyed with himself because his memory had become so hopeless and glasses no longer did much for his eyes.

The name came to him just as everyone was getting up to leave. Sheila Wexford. Sheila Wexford, the actress. That was who it was. He and Dinah had seen her last autumn in that Somerset Maugham revival, though what the name of the play had been escaped him. She had been at school with Dinah, they still knew each other slightly. Her banns had been called before his but her name hadn't registered because of that insertion of Katherine. It was odd that two people as famous as they should have had their banns called simultaneously in this country parish church.

He looked at her again. She was dressed in a coat of sleek pale fur over a black wool dress. Her eye caught his and he saw that she also recognized him. She gave him a quick faint smile, a smile that was conspiratorial, rueful, gay, ever so slightly embarrassed, all those things expressed as only an actress of her calibre could express them. Camargue countered with a smile of his own, the best he could do.

It was still snowing. Sheila Wexford put an umbrella up and made an elegant dash towards the lychgate. Should he offer her a lift to wherever she lived? Camargue decided that his legs were inadequate to running after her, especially through six-inch deep snow. When he reached the gate he saw her getting into a car driven by a man at least old enough to be her father. He felt a pang for her. Was this the bridegroom? And then the absurdity of such a thought, coming from him, struck him forcefully and with a sense which he often had of the folly of human beings and their blindness to their own selves.

Ted was waiting in the Mercedes. Reading the *News of the World*, hands in woollen gloves. He had the engine running to work the heater and the wipers and the demisters. When he saw Camargue he jumped out and opened the rear door.

'There you are, Sir Manuel. I put a rug in seeing it's got so perishing.'

'What a kind chap you are,' said Camargue. 'It was jolly cold in church. Let's hope it'll warm up for the wedding.'

Ted said he hoped so but the long range weather forecast was as gloomy as per usual. If he hadn't held his employer in such honour and respect he would have said he'd have his love to keep him warm. Camargue knew this and smiled to himself. He pulled the rug over his knees. Dinah, he thought, my Dinah. Towards her he felt a desire as passionate, as youthful, as intense, as any he had known as a boy. But he would never touch her, he knew better than that, and his mouth curled with distaste at the idea of it, of him and her together. It would be enough for him that she should be his dear companion – for a little while.

They had entered the gates and were mounting the long curving drive that led up to the house. Ted drove in the two channels, now filling once more with snow, which he had dug out that morning. From the smooth, pure and radiant whiteness, flung like a soft and spotless cloth over the hillocks and little valleys of Camargue's garden, rose denuded silver birches, poplars and willows, and the spikes of conifers, dark green and slate-blue and golden-yellow, as snugly clothed as gnomes.

The jam factory came into view quite suddenly. Camargue called it the jam factory, or sometimes the shoebox, because it was unlike any of the houses around. Not mock or real Tudor, not fake or genuine Georgian, but a long box with lots of glass, and at one end, dividing the original building from the newer wing, a tower with a peaked roof like an oast house. Perched on the weathervane, a facsimile of a treble clef in wrought iron, was a seagull, driven inland in its quest for food. It looked as white as the snow itself against the cinder-dark sky.

Ted's wife, Muriel, opened the front door. You entered the house at the lower level, where it was built into the hillside. There was a wide hall here which led through an arch into the dining room.

'It's so cold, sir,' said Muriel, 'that I'm cooking you a proper lunch since you said you wouldn't be going to Mrs Sternhold's.'

'Jolly thoughtful of you,' said Camargue, who no longer much cared what he ate. Muriel took his coat away to dry it. She and Ted lived in a house in the grounds, a period piece and as much unlike the jam factory as could be. Camargue liked her to have her afternoons off and all of her Sundays, but he couldn't be always checking her generous impulses. When he was half-way up the stairs the dog Nancy came down to meet him, wide smiling mouth and eager pink tongue and young strong paws capable of sending him flying. She was his fifth alsatian, a rich roan colour, just two years old.

The drawing room, two of its walls entirely glass, shone with the curious light that is uniquely reflected off snow. The phone began to ring as he stepped off the top stair.

'Were they well and truly called?'

'Yes, darling, the third time of asking. And at St Peter's?'

'Yes. My word, it was cold, Dinah. Is it snowing in Forby?'

'Well, it is but not all that heavily. Won't you change your mind and come? The main roads are all right and you know Ted won't mind. I do wish you'd come.'

'No. You'll have your parents. They've met me. Let them get over the shock a bit before Saturday.' Camargue laughed at her exclamation of protest. 'No, my dear, I won't come today. Muriel's cooking lunch for me. Just think, after Saturday you'll have to have all your meals with me, no excuses allowed.'

'Manuel, shall I come over this evening?'

He laughed. 'No, please.' It was strange how his accent became more marked when he talked to her. Must be emotion, he supposed. 'The villages will be cut off from Kingsmarkham by tonight, mark my words.'

He went into the music room, the dog following him. Up inside the cone-shaped roof of the tower it was dark like twilight. He looked at the flute which lay in its open case on the table, and then reflectively, no longer with pain, at his clawed hands. The flute had been exposed like that to show to Dinah's mother and Muriel would have been too much in awe of it to put it away. Camargue closed the lid of the case and sat down at the piano. He had never been much of a pianist, a second-class concert average, so it brought him no frustration or sadness to strum away occasionally with those (as he called them) silly old hands of his. He played *Für Elise* while Nancy, who adored piano music, thumped her tail on the marble floor.

Muriel called him to lunch. He went downstairs for it. She liked to lay the big mahogany table with lace and silver and glass just for him, and to wait on him. Far more than he had ever been or could ever be, she was aware of what was due to Sir Manuel Camargue. Ted came in as he was having coffee and said he would take Nancy out now, a good long hike in the snow, he said, she loved snow. And he'd break the ice at the edge of the lake. Hearing the chain on her lead rattle, Nancy nearly fell downstairs in her haste to be out.

Camargue sometimes tried to stop himself sleeping the afternoons away. He was rarely successful. He had a suite of rooms in the wing beyond the tower; bedroom, bathroom, small sitting room where Nancy's basket was, and he would sit determinedly in his armchair, reading or playing records – he was mad about James Galway at the moment. Galway, he thought, was heaps better than he had ever been – but he would always nod off. Often he slept till five or six. He put on the Flute Concerto, Köchel 313, and as the sweet, bright, liquid notes poured out, looked at himself in the long glass. He was still, at any rate, tall. He was thin. Thin like a ramshackle scarecrow, he thought, like an old junk-shop skeleton, with hands that looked as if every joint had been broken and put together again awry. *Tout casse, tout lasse, tout passe.* Now that he was so old he often thought in one or other of the two languages of his infancy. He sat down in the armchair and listened to the music Mozart wrote for a cantankerous Dutchman, and by the time the second movement had begun he was asleep.

Nancy woke him, laying her head in his lap. She had

been back from her walk a long time, it was nearly five. Ted wouldn't come back to take her out again. Camargue would let her out himself and perhaps walk with her as far as the lake. It had stopped snowing, and the last of the daylight, a curious shade of yellow, gilded the whiteness and threw long blue shadows. Camargue took James Galway off the turntable and put him back in the sleeve. He walked along the passage and through the music room, pausing to straighten a crooked picture, a photograph of the building which housed the Camargue School of Music at Wellridge, and passed on into the drawing room. As he approached the tea tray Muriel had left for him, the phone range. Dinah again.

'I phoned before, darling. Were you asleep?'

'What else?'

'I'll come over in the morning, shall I, and bring the rest of the presents? Mother and Dad have brought us silver pastry forks from my uncle, my godfather.'

'I must say, people are jolly generous, the second time round for both of us. I'll have the drive specially cleared for you. Ted shall be up to do it by the crack of dawn.'

'Poor Ted.' He was sensitive to the slight change in her tone and he braced himself. 'Manuel, you haven't heard any more from – Natalie?'

'From that woman,' said Camargue evenly, 'no.'

'I shall have another go at you in the morning, you know, to make you see reason. You're quite wrong about her, I'm sure you are. And to take a step like changing your will without . . . '

His accent was strong as he interrupted her. 'I saw her, Dinah, not you, and I know. Let's not speak of it again, eh?'

She said simply, 'Whatever you wish. I only want what's best for you.'

'I know that,' he said. He talked to her a little longer and then he went downstairs to make his tea. The tranquillity of the day had been marred by Dinah's raising the subject of Natalie. It forced him to think of that business again when he had begun to shut it out.

He carried the teapot upstairs and lifted the folded napkin from the plate of cucumber sandwiches. That woman, whoever she was, had made the tea and brought the pot up, and it was after that that she had looked at Cazzini's golden gift on the wall and he had known. As is true of all honest and guileless people, Camarge resented attempts to practise deceit on him far more than do those who are themselves deceitful. It had been a hateful affront, and all the worse because it had taken advantage of an old man's weakness and a father's affection. Dinah's plea did not at all alter his feelings. It only made him think he should have told the police or his solicitors, after all. But no. He had told the woman that he had seen through her and he had told her what he meant to do, and now he must do his best to forget it. Dinah was what future he had, Dinah would be his daughter and more than daughter.

He sat by the window with the curtains undrawn, watching the snow turn blue, then glow dully white again as the darkness closed in. The moon was coming up, a full, cold, midwinter's moon, a glowing greenish-white orb. At seven he took the tea things down and fed Nancy a large can of dog meat.

By the light of the moon he could see the lake quite clearly from the drawing-room window. To call it a lake was to flatter it, it was just a big pond really. It lay on the other side of the drive, down a shallow slope and ringed with willow trees and hawthorn bushes. Camargue could see that Ted, as good as his word, had been down to the pond that afternoon and broken the ice for air to get in to the fish. There were carp in the pond, some of them very large and very old. Ted's footprints led down to the water's edge and back up again to the drive. He had cast the ice on to the bank in great grey blocks. The moon showed it all up as well as any arc lamp. Nancy's pawprints were everywhere, and in places in the drifts there were signs of where she had plunged and rolled. He stroked her smooth brown head, drawing her against him, gently pushing her to settle down and sleep at his feet. The moon sailed in a black and shining sky from which all the heavy cloud had gone. He opened his book, the biography of an obscure Romanian composer who had once written an étude especially for him, and read for an hour or so.

When it got to half-past eight he could feel himself nodding off again, so he got up and stretched and stood in the window. To his surprise he saw it was snowing once more, snow falling out of the wrack which was drifting slowly over the clear sky and towards where the moon was. The conifers were powdered again, all but one. Then he saw the tree move. He had often thought that by night and in the half-light and through his failing eyes those trees looked like men. Now he had actually mistaken a man for a tree. Or a woman for a tree. He couldn't tell whether it had been Ted or Muriel that he had seen, a trousered figure in a heavy coat moving up now where the path must be towards the birch copse. It must have been one of them. Camargue decided to postpone letting Nancy out for ten minutes. If Ted saw him he would take over and fuss and probably insist on giving the dog a proper walk which she didn't need after all the exercise she had had. If Muriel saw him she would very likely want to come in and make him cocoa.

The figure in the garden had disappeared. Now the moon was no longer so bright. He couldn't remember that he had ever before seen such snow in all the years he had lived in Sussex. In his youth, in the Pyrenees, the snows had come like this with an even more bitter cold. It was remembering those days that had made him plant in this garden all the little fir trees and yews and junipers. . . .

He could have sworn he saw another tree move. How grotesque was old age when the faculties one took for granted like trusted friends began to play on one malicious practical jokes. He called out:

'Nancy! Time to go out.'

She was there at the head of the stairs long before he was. If he had gone first she would have knocked him over. He walked down behind her, propelling her with his toe when she looked anxiously back and up at him. At the foot of the stairs he switched on the outside light to illuminate the wide court into which the drive led. The snowflakes danced like sparks in the yellow light but when he opened the door the sharp cold of the night rushed in to meet him. Nancy bounded out into the whirling snow. Camargue took his sheepskin coat and gloves and a walking-stick from the cloaks cupboard and followed her out.

She was nowhere to be seen, though her paws had ploughed a path down the slope towards the lake. He fastened his coat and pulled the woollen scarf up around his throat. Nancy, though well aware this outing was no regular walk but merely for the purpose of stimulating and answering a call of nature, nevertheless would sometimes go off. If the weather conditions were right, damp and muggy, for instance, or like this, she had been known to go off for half an hour. It would be a nuisance were she to do that tonight when he felt so tired that even on his feet, even with this icy air stinging his face, he could feel drowsiness closing in on him.

'Nancy! Nancy, where are you?'

He could easily go back into the house and phone Ted and ask him to come over and await the dog's return. Ted wouldn't mind. On the other hand, wasn't that yielding to the very helplessness he was always striving against? What business had he to be getting married, to be setting up house again, even recommencing a social life, if he couldn't do such a little thing for himself as letting a dog out before he went to bed? What he would do was return to the house and sit in the chair in the hall and wait for Nancy to come back. If he fell asleep her scraping at the front door would awaken him.

Even as he decided this he did the very opposite. He followed the track she had made down the slope to the lake, calling her, irritably now, as he went.

The marks Ted had made when he broke the ice at the water's edge were already obliterated by snow, while Nancy's fresh tracks were fast becoming covered. Only the stacked ice showed where Ted had been. The area he had cleared was again iced over with a thin grey crust. The lake was a sombre sheet of ice with a faint sheen on it that the clouded moon made, and the willows, which by daylight looked like so many crouched spiders or daddy-long-legs, were laden with snow that clung to them and changed their shape. Camargue called the dog again. Only last week she had done this to him and then had suddenly appeared out of nowhere and come skittering across the ice towards him.

He began breaking the new ice with his stick. Then he heard the dog behind him, a faint crunching on the snow. But when he turned round, ready to seize her collar in the hook of the walking-stick, there was no dog there, there was nothing there but the gnome conifers and the light shining down on the white sheet of the circular courtyard. He would break up the rest of the thin ice, clear an area a yard long and a foot wide as Ted had done, and then he would go back into the house and wait for Nancy indoors.

Again the foot crunched behind him, the tree walked. He stood up and turned and, raising his stick as if to defend himself, looked into the face of the tree that moved.

2

The music met Chief Inspector Wexford as he let himself into his house. A flute playing with an orchestra. This was one of Sheila's dramatic gestures, he supposed, contrived to time with his homecoming. It was beautiful music, slow, measured, secular, yet with a religious sound.

His wife was knitting, on her face the amused, dry, very slightly exasperated expression it often wore while Sheila was around. And Sheila would be very much around for the next three weeks, having unaccountably decided to be married from home, in her own parish church, and to establish the proper period of residence beforehand in her father's house. She sat on the floor, between the log fire and the record player, her cheek resting on one round white arm that trailed with grace upon a sofa cushion, her pale gold water-straight hair half covering her face. When she lifted her head and shook her hair back he saw that she had been crying.

'Oh, Pop, darling, isn't it sad? They've had this tremendous obituary programme for him on the box. Even Mother shed a tear. And then we thought we'd mourn him with his own music.'

Wexford doubted very much if Dora, a placid and eminently sensible woman, had expressed these extravagant sentiments. He picked up the record sleeve. Mozart, Concerto for Flute and Harp, K 229; the English Chamber Orchestra, conductor, Raymond Leppard; flute, Manuel Camargue; harp, Marisa Roblès.

'We actually heard him once,' said Dora. 'Do you remember? At the Wigmore Hall it was, all of thirty years ago.'

'Yes.'

But he could scarcely remember. The pictured face on the sleeve, too sensitive, too mobile to be handsome, the eyes alight with a kind of joyous humour, evoked no image from the past. The movement came to an end and now the music became bright, liquid, a singable tune, and Camargue, who was dead, alive again in his flute. Sheila wiped her eyes and got up to kiss her father. It was all of eight years since he and she had lived under the same roof. She had become a swan since then, a famous lady, a tele-face. But she still kissed him when he came and went, putting her arms around his neck like a nervous child. Wryly, he liked it.

He sat down, listening to the last movement while Dora finished her row in the Fair Isle and went to get his supper. Andrew's regular evening phone call prevented Sheila from getting full dramatic value out of her memorial to Camargue, and by the time she came back into the room the record was over and her father was eating his steak-and-kidney pie.

'You didn't actually know him, did you, Sheila?'

She thought he was reproaching her for her tears. 'I'm sorry, Pop, I cry so easily. It's a matter of having to learn how, you know, and then not being able to unlearn.'

He grinned at her. 'Thus on the fatal bank of Nile weeps the deceitful crocodile? I didn't mean that, anyway. Let me put it more directly. Did you know him personally?'

She shook her head. 'I think he recognized me in church. He must have known I come from round here.' It was nothing that she should be recognized. She was recognized wherever she went. For five years the serial in which she played the most beautiful of the air hostesses had been on television twice a week at a peak-viewing time. Everybody watched *Runway*, even though a good many said shamefacedly that they 'only saw the tail-end before the news' or 'the kids have it on'. Stewardess Curtis was famous for her smile. Sheila smiled it now, her head tilted reflectively. 'I know his wife-that-was-to-be personally,' she said. 'Or I used to. We were at school together.'

'A young girl?'

'Thank you kindly, father dear. Let's say young to be marrying Sir Manuel. Mid-twenties. She brought him to see me in *The Letter* last autumn but I didn't talk to them, he was too tired to come round afterwards.'

It was Dora who brought them back from gossip to grandeur. 'In his day he was said to be the world's greatest flautist. I remember when he founded that school at Wellridge and Princess Margaret came down to open it.'

'D'you know what its pupils call it? Windyridge.' Sheila mimed the blowing of a woodwind, fingers dancing. Then, suddenly, the tears had started once more to her eyes. 'Oh, to die like that!'

Who's Who is not a volume to be found in many private houses. Wexford had a copy because Sheila was in it. He took it down from the shelf, turned to the C's and read aloud:

'Camargue, Sir Manuel, Knight. Companion of Honour, Order of the British Empire, Chevalier of the Legion of Honour. British fluteplayer. Born Pamplona, Spain, 3 June, 1902, son of Aristide Camargue and Ana Parral. Educated privately with father, then at Barcelona Conservatoire. Studied under Louis Fleury.

'Professor of Flute, Madrid Conservatoire, 1924 to 1932. Fought on Republican side Spanish Civil War, escaped to England 1938. Married 1942 Kathleen Lister. One daughter. Naturalized British subject 1946. Concert flautist, has toured Europe, America, Australia, New Zealand and South Africa. Founded 1964 at Wellridge, Sussex, the Kathleen Camargue School of Music in memory of his wife, and in 1968 the Kathleen Camargue Youth Orchestra. Recreations apart from music: walking, reading, dogs. Address: Sterries, Ploughman's Lane, Kingsmarkham, Sussex.'

'They say it's a dream of a house,' said Sheila. 'I wonder if she'll sell, that one daughter? Because if she does Andrew and I might really consider . . . Wouldn't you like me living just up the road, Pop?'

'He may have left it to your friend,' said Wexford.

'So he may. Well, I do hope so. Poor Dinah, losing her first husband that she *adored* and then her second that never was. She deserves some compensation. I shall write her a letter of sympathy. No, I won't. I'll go and see her. I'll phone her first thing in the morning and I'll . . .'

'I'd leave it a day or two if I were you,' said her father. 'First thing in the morning is going to be the inquest.'

'*Inquest?*' Sheila uttered the word in the loaded, aghast tone of Lady Bracknell. 'Inquest? But surely he died a perfectly natural death?'

Dora, conjuring intricately with three different shades of wool, looked up from her pattern. 'Of course he didn't. Drowning, or whatever happened to him, freezing to death, you can't call that natural.'

'I mean, he didn't do it on purpose and no one did it to him.'

It was impossible for Wexford to keep from laughing at these ingenuous definitions of suicide and homicide. 'In most cases of sudden death,' he said, 'and in all cases of violent death there must be an inquest. It goes without saying the verdict is going to be that it was an accident.'

Misadvanture.

This verdict, which can sound so grotesque when applied to the death of a baby in a cot or a patient under anaesthetic, appropriately described Camargue's fate. An old man, ankle-deep in snow, had lost his foothold in the dark, slipping over, sliding into water to be trapped under a lid of ice. If he had not drowned he would within minutes have been dead from hypothermia. The snow had continued to fall, obliterating his footprints. And the frost, ten degrees of it, had silently sealed up the space into which the body had slipped. Only a glove – it was of thick black leather and it had fallen from his left hand – remained to point to where he lay, one curled finger rising up out of the drifts. Misadventure.

Wexford attended the inquest for no better reason than to keep warm, the police station central heating having unaccountably broken down the night before. The venue of the inquest (Kingsmarkham Magistrates' Court, Court Two, Upstairs) enjoyed a reputation for being kept in winter at a temperature of eighty degrees. To this it lived up. Having left his rubber boots just inside the door downstairs, he sat at the back of the court, basking in warmth, surreptitiously peeling off various disreputable layers, a khaki green plastic mac of muddy translucency, an aged black-and-grey herringbone-tweed overcoat, a stole-sized scarf of matted fawnish wool.

Apart from the *Kingsmarkham Courier* girl in one of the press seats, there were only two women present, and these two sat so far apart as to give the impression of choosing each to ostracize the other. One would be the daughter, he supposed, one the bride. Both were dressed darkly, shabbily and without distinction. But the woman in the front row had the eyes and profile of a Callas, her glossy black hair piled in the fashion of a Floating World geisha, while the other, seated a yard or two from him, was a little mouse, headscarfed, huddled, hands folded. Neither, as far as he could see, bore the remotest resemblance to the face on the record sleeve with its awareness and its spirituality. But when, as the verdict came, the geisha woman turned her head and her eyes, dark and brilliant, for a moment met his, he saw that she was far older than Sheila, perhaps ten years older. This, then, must be the daughter. And as the conviction came to him, the coroner turned his gaze upon her and said he would like to express his sympathy with Sir Manuel's daughter in her loss and a grief which was no less a personal one because it was shared by the tens of thousands who had loved, admired and been inspired by his music. He did not think he would be exceeding his duty were he to quote Samuel Johnson and say that it matters not how a man dies but how he has lived.

Presumably no one had told him of the dead man's intended re-marriage. The little mouse got up and crept away. Now it was all over, the beauty with the black eyes got up too – to be enclosed immediately in a circle of men. This of course was chance, Wexford told himself, they were the escort who had brought her, her father's doctor, his servant, a friend or two. Yet he felt inescapably that this woman would always wherever she was be in a circle of men, watched, admired, desired. He got back into his coverings and ventured out into the bitter cold of Kingsmarkham High Street.

Here the old snow lay heaped at the pavement edges in long, low mountain ranges and the new snow, gritty and sparkling, dusted it with fresh whiteness. A yellowish-leaden sky looked full of snow. It was only a step from the court to the police station, but a long enough step in this weather to get chilled to the bone.

On the forecourt, between a panda car and the chief constable's Rover, the heating engineer's van was still parked. Wexford went tentatively through the swing doors. Inside it was as cold as ever and Sergeant Camb, sitting behind his counter, warmed mittened hands on a mug of steaming tea. Burden, Wexford reflected, if he had any sense, would have taken himself off somewhere warm for lunch. Very likely to the Carousel Cafe, or what used to be the Carousel before it was taken over by Mr Haq and became the Pearl of Africa.

This was a title or sobriquet given (according to Mr Haq) to Uganda, his native land. Mr Haq claimed to serve authentic Ugandan cuisine, what he called 'real' Ugandan food, but since no one knew what this was, whether he meant food consumed by the tribes before colonization or food introduced by Asian immigrants or food eaten today by westernized Ugandans, or what these would be anyway, it was difficult to query any dish. Fried potatoes and rice accompanied almost everything, but for all Wexford knew this might be a feature of Ugandan cooking. He rather liked the place, it fascinated him, especially the plastic jungle vegetation.

Today this hung and trembled in the steamy heat and seemed to sweat droplets on its leathery leaves. The windows had become opaque, entirely misted over with condensation. It was like a tropical oasis in the Arctic.

Inspector Burden sat at a table eating Nubian chicken with rice Ruwenzori, anxiously keeping in view his new sheepskin jacket, a Christmas present from his wife, which Mr Haq had hung up on the palm tree hatstand. He remarked darkly as Wexford walked in that anyone might make off with it, you never could tell these days.

'Round here they might cook it,' said Wexford. He also ordered the chicken with the request that for once potatoes might not come with it. 'I've just come from the inquest on Camargue.'

'What on earth did you go to that for?'

'I hadn't anything much else on. I reckoned it would be warm too and it was.'

'All right for some,' Burden grumbled. 'I could have found a job for you.' Since their friendship had deepened, some of his old deference to his chief, though none of his respect, had departed. 'Thieving and break-ins, we've never had so much of it. That kid old Atkinson let out on bail, he's done three more jobs in the meantime. And he's not seventeen yet, a real little villain.' Sarcasm made his tone withering. 'Or that's what I call him. The psychiatrist says he's a pathological kleptomaniac with personality-scarring caused by traumata broadly classifiable as paranoid.' He snorted, was silent, then said on an altered note, 'Look, do you think you were wise to do that?'

'Do what?'

'Go to that inquest. People will think . . . I mean, it's possible they might think . . .'

'People will think!' Wexford scoffed. 'You sound like a dowager lecturing a debutante. What will they think?'

'I only meant they might think there was something fishy about the death. Some hanky-panky. I mean, they see you there and know who you are and they say to themselves, he wouldn't have been there if it had all been as straightforward as the coroner . . .'

He was saved from an outburst of Wexford's temper by an intervention from outside. Mr Haq had glided up to beam upon them. He was small, smiling, very black yet very Caucasian, with a mouthful of startlingly white, madly uneven, large teeth.

'Everything to your liking, I hope, my dear?' Mr Haq called all his customers 'my dear', irrespective of sex, perhaps supposing it to be a genderless term of extreme respect such as 'excellency.' 'I see you are having the rice Ruwenzori.' He bowed a little. 'A flavourful and scrumptious recipe from the peoples who live in the Mountains of the Moon.' Talking like a television commercial for junk food was habitual with him.

'Very nice, thank you,' said Wexford.

'You are welcome, my dear.' Mr Haq smiled so broadly that it seemed some of his teeth must spill out. He moved off among the tables, ducking his head under the polythene fronds which trailed from polyethylene pots in polystyrene plant-holders.

'Are you going to have any pudding?'

'Shouldn't think so,' said Wexford, and he read from the menu with gusto, 'Cake Kampala or ice cream eau-de-Nil – does he mean the colour or what it's made of? Anyway, there's enough ice about without eating it.' He hesitated. 'Mike, I don't see that it matters what people think in this instance. Camargue met his death by misadventure, there's no doubt about that. Surely, though interest in the man will endure for years, the manner of his death can only be a nine days' wonder. As a matter of fact, the coroner said something like that.'

Burden ordered coffee from the small, shiny, damson-eyed boy, heir to Mr Haq, who waited at their table. 'I suppose I was thinking of Hicks.'

'The manservant or whoever he was?'

'He found that glove and then he found the body. It wasn't really strange but it might look strange the way he found the dog outside his back door and took her back to Sterries and put her inside without checking to see where Camargue was.'

'Hicks's reputation won't suffer from my presence in court,' said Wexford. 'I doubt if there was a soul there, bar the coroner, who recognized me.' He chuckled. 'Or if they did it'd only be as Stewardess Curtis's dad.'

They went back to the police station. The afternoon wore away into an icy twilight, an evening of hard frost. The heating came on with a pop just as it was time to go home. Entering his living room, Wexford was greeted by a large, bronze-coloured alsatian, baring her teeth and swinging her tail. On the sofa, next to his daughter, sat the girl who had crept away from the inquest, Camargue's pale bride.

3

He had noticed the Volkswagen parked in the ruts of ice outside but had thought little of it. Sheila got up and introduced the visitor.

'Dinah, this is my father. Pop, I'd like you to meet Dinah Sternhold. She was engaged to Sir Manuel, you know.'

It was immediately apparent to Wexford that she had not noticed him at the inquest. She held out her small hand and looked at him without a flicker of recognition. The dog had backed against her legs and now sat down heavily at her feet, glaring at Wexford in a sullen way.

'Do forgive me for bringing Nancy.' She had a soft low unaffected voice. 'But I daren't leave her alone, she howls all the time. My neighbours complained when I had to leave her this morning.'

'She was Sir Manuel's dog,' Sheila explained.

A master-leaver and a fugitive, Wexford reflected, eyeing the alsatian who had abandoned Camargue to his fate. Or gone to fetch help? That, of course, was a possible explanation of the curious behaviour of the dog in the night.

Dinah Sternhold said, 'It's Manuel she howls for, you see. I can only hope she won't take too long to – to forget him. I hope she'll get over it.'

Was she speaking of the dog or of herself? His answer could have applied to either. 'She will. She's young.'

'He often said he wanted me to have her if – if anything happened to him. I think he was afraid of her going to someone who might not be kind to her.'

Presumably she meant the daughter. Wexford sought

about in his mind for some suitable words of condolence, but finding none that sounded neither mawkish nor pompous, he kept quiet. Sheila, anyway, could always be relied on to make conversation. While she was telling some rather inapposite alsatian anecdote, he studied Dinah Sternhold. Her little round sallow face was pinched with a kind of bewildered woe. One might almost believe she had loved the old man and not merely been in it for the money. But that was a little too much to swallow, distinguished and reputedly kind and charming as he had been. The facts were that he had been seventy-eight and she was certainly fifty years less than that.

Gold-digger, however, she was not. She appeared to have extorted little in the way of pre-marital largesse out of Camargue. Her brown tweed coat had seen better days, she wore no jewellery but an engagement ring, in which the ruby was small and the diamonds pinheads.

He wondered how long she intended to sit there, her hand grasping the dog's collar, her head bowed as if she were struggling to conquer tears or at least conceal them. But suddenly she jumped up.

'I must go.' Her voice became intense, ragged, charged with a sincerity that was almost fierce. 'It was so *kind* of you to come to me, Sheila. You don't know how grateful I am.'

'No need,' Sheila said lightly. 'I wanted to come. It was kind of *you* to drive me home. I had a hire car, Pop, because I was scared to drive in the snow but Dinah wasn't a bit scared to bring me back in the snow and the dark.'

They saw Dinah Sternhold out to her car. Ice was already forming on the windscreen. She pushed the dog on to the back seat and got to work competently on the windows with a de-icing spray. Wexford was rather surprised that he felt no compunction about letting her drive away, but her confidence seemed absolute, you could trust her somehow to look after herself and perhaps others too. Was it this quality about her that Camargue had needed and had loved? He closed the gate, rubbed his hands. Sheila, shivering, ran back into the house.

'Where's your mother?'

'Round at Syl's. She ought to be back any minute. Isn't Dinah nice? I felt so sorry for her, I went straight over to Forby as soon as the inquest was over. We talked and talked. I think maybe I did her a bit of good.'

'Hmm,' said Wexford.

The phone started to ring. Andrew, punctual to the minute. 'Oh, darling,' Wexford heard Sheila say, 'do you remember my telling you about someone I know who was going to marry . . .' He began picking alsatian hairs off the upholstery.

Father and daughter is not the perfect relationship. According to Freud, that distinction belongs to mother and son. But Wexford, looking back, could have said that he had been happy with his daughters and they with him, he had never actually quarrelled with either of them, there had never been any sort of breach. And if Sheila was his favourite he hoped this was so close a secret that no one but himself, not even Dora, could know it.

Any father of daughters, even today, must look ahead when they are children and anticipate an outlay of money on their wedding celebrations. Wexford realized this and had begun saving for it out of his detective inspector's salary, but Sylvia had married so young as almost to catch him napping. For Sheila he had been determined to be well prepared, then gradually, with wonder and a kind of dismay, he had watched her rise out of that income bracket and society in which she had grown up, graduate into a sparkling, lavish jet set whose members had wedding receptions in country mansions or else the Dorchester.

For a long time it had looked as if she would not marry at all. Then Andrew Thorverton had appeared, a young businessman, immensely wealthy, it seemed to Wexford, with a house in Hampstead, a cottage in the country somewhere that his future father-in-law suspected was a sizeable house, a boat and an amazing car of so esoteric a manufacture that Wexford had never before heard of it. Sheila, made old-fashioned and sentimental by love, announced she would be married from home and, almost in the same breath, that she and Andrew would be paying for the entertainment of two hundred people to luncheon in the banquet room of the Olive and Dove. Yes, she insisted, it must be so and Pop must lump it or else she'd go and get married in a register office and have lunch at the Pearl of Africa.

He was slightly humiliated. Somehow he felt she ought to cut garment according to cloth, and his cloth would cover a buffet table for fifty. That was absurd, of course. Andrew wouldn't even notice the few thousand it would cost, and the bride's father would give her away, make a speech and hang on to his savings. He heard her telling Andrew she would be coming up to spend the weekend with him, and then Dora walked in.

'She won't be supporting her friend at the cremation then?'

Sheila had put the phone down. She was sometimes a little flushed and breathless when she had been talking to Andrew. But it was not now of him that she spoke. 'Dinah's not going to it. How could she bear it? Two days after what would have been their wedding day?'

'At least it's not the day itself,' said Wexford.

'Frankly, I'm surprised Sir Manuel's daughter didn't fix it on the day itself. She's capable of it. There's going to be a memorial service at St Peter's on Tuesday and everyone will be there. Solti is coming and probably Menuhin. Dinah says there are sure to be crowds, he was so much loved.'

Wexford said, 'Does she know if he left her much?'

Sheila delivered her reply slowly and with an actress's perfect timing.

'He has not left her anything. He has not left her a single penny.' She sank to the floor, close up by the fire, and stretched out her long legs. 'Her engagement ring and that dog, that's all she's got.'

'How did that come about? Did you ask her?'

'Oh, Pop darling, of course I did. Wasn't I with her for hours and hours? I got the whole thing out of her.'

'You're as insatiably inquisitive as your father!' cried Dora, revolted. 'I thought you went to comfort the poor girl. I agree it's not like losing a young fiancé, but just the same . . .'

'Curiosity,' quoted Wexford, 'is one of the permanent and certain characteristics of a vigorous intellect.' He chuckled. 'The daughter gets it all, does she?'

'Sir Manuel saw his daughter a week before he died and that was the first time he'd seen her for nineteen years. There'd been a family quarrel. She was at the Royal Academy of Music but she left and went off with an American student. The first Camargue and his wife knew of it was a letter from San Francisco. Mrs Camargue – he wasn't a Sir then – got ill and died but the daughter didn't come back. She didn't come back at all till last November. Doesn't it seem frightfully unfair that she gets everything?'

'Camargue should have made a new will.'

'He was going to as soon as they were married. Marriage invalidates a will. Did you know that, Pop?'

He nodded.

'I can understand divorce would but I can't see why marriage.' She turned her legs, toasting them.

'You'll get scorch marks,' said Dora. 'That won't look very nice on the beach in Bermuda.'

Sheila took no notice. 'And what's more, he was going to cut the daughter out altogether. Apparently, that one sight of her was enough.'

Dora, won uneasily on to the side of the gossips, said, 'I wish you wouldn't keep calling her the daughter. Doesn't she have a name?'

'Natalie Arno. Mrs Arno, she's a widow. The American student died some time during those nineteen years. Dinah was awfully reticent about her, but she did say Camargue intended to make a new will, and since he said this just after he'd seen Natalie I put two and two together. And there's another thing, Natalie only got in touch with her father after his engagement to Dinah was announced. The engagement was in the *Telegraph* on 10 December, and on the 12th he got a letter from Natalie telling him she was back and could she come and see him? She wanted a reconciliation. It was obvious she was scared stiff of the marriage and wanted to stop it.'

'And your reticent friend told you all this?'

'She got it out of her, Dora. I can understand. She's a chip off the old block, as you so indignantly pointed out.' He turned once more to Sheila. 'Did she try to stop it?'

'Dinah wouldn't say. I think she hates discussing Natalie. She talked much more about Camargue. She really loved him. In a funny sort of daughterly, worshipping, protective sort of way, but she did love him. She likes to talk about how wonderful he was and how they met and all that. She's a teacher at the Kathleen Camargue School and he came over last Founder's Day and they met and they just loved each other, she said, from that moment.'

The somewhat cynical expressions on the two middle-aged faces made her give an embarrassed laugh. She seemed to take her mother's warning to heart at last, for she got up and moved away from the fire to sit on the sofa where she scrutinized her smooth, pale golden legs. 'At any rate, Pop darling, it's an ill wind, as you might say, because now the house is bound to be sold. I'd love to get a look at it, wouldn't you? Why wasn't I at school with Natalie?'

'You were born too late,' said her father. 'And there must be simpler ways of getting into Sterries.'

There were.

'You?' said Burden first thing the next morning. 'What do *you* want to go up there for? It's only a common-or-garden burglary, one of our everyday occurrences, I'm sorry to say. Martin can handle it.'

Wexford hadn't taken his overcoat off. 'I want to see the place. Don't you feel any curiosity to see the home of our former most distinguished citizen?'

Burden seemed more concerned with dignity and protocol. 'It's beneath you *and* me, I should think.' He sniffed. 'And when you hear the details you'll feel the same. The facts are that a Mrs Arno – she's the late Sir Manuel's daughter – phoned up about half an hour ago to say the house had been broken into during the night. There's a pane of glass been cut out of a window downstairs and a bit of a mess made and some silver taken. Cutlery, nothing special, and some money from Mrs Arno's handbag. She thinks she saw the car the burglar used and she's got the registration number.'

'I like these open-and-shut cases,' said Wexford. 'I find them restful.'

The fingerprint man (Detective Constable Morgan) had already left for Sterries. Wexford's car only just managed to get up Ploughman's Lane, which was glacier-like in spite of gritting. He had been a determined burglar, Burden remarked, to get his car up and down there in the night.

The top of the hill presented an alpine scene, with dark-green and gold and grey conifers rising sturdily from the snow blanket. The house itself, shaped like a number of cuboid boxes pushed irregularly together and with a tower in the midst of them, looked not so much white as dun-coloured beside the dazzling field of snow. A sharp wind had set the treble-clef weathervane spinning like a top against a sky that was now a clear cerulean blue.

Morgan's van was parked on the forecourt outside the front door which was on the side of the house furthest from the lane. Some attempt had been made to keep this area free of snow. Wexford, getting out of the car, saw a solidly built man in jeans and anorak at work sweeping the path which seemed to lead to a much smaller house that stood in a dip in the grounds. He looked in the other direction, noting in a shallow tree-fringed basin the ornamental water newspapers had euphemistically called a lake. There Camargue had met his death. It was once more iced over and the ice laden with a fleecy coat of snow.

The front door had been opened by a woman of about forty in trousers and bulky sweater whom Wexford took to be Muriel Hicks. He and Burden stepped into the warmth and on to thick soft carpet. The vestibule with its cloaks cupboard was rather small but it opened, through an arch, into a hall which had been used to some extent as a picture gallery. The paintings almost made him whistle. If these were originals . . .

The dining-room was open, revealing pale wood panelling and dark red wood furnishing, and in the far corner

Morgan could be seen at his task. A flight of stairs, with risers of mosaic tile and treads that seemed to be of oak, led upwards. However deferential and attentive Mrs Hicks may have been towards Sir Manuel – and according to Sheila he had been adored by his servants – she had no courtesy to spare for policemen. That 'she' was upstairs somewhere was the only introduction they got. Wexford went upstairs while Burden joined Morgan in the dining room.

The house had been built on various different levels of land so that the drawing room where he found himself was really another ground floor. It was a large, airy and gracious room, two sides of which were made entirely of glass. At the farther end of it steps led down into what must surely be the tower. Here the floor was covered by a pale yellow Chinese carpet on which stood two groups of silk-covered settees and chairs, one suite lemon, one very pale jade. There was some fine *famille jaune* porcelain of that marvellous yellow that is both tender and piercing, and suspended from the ceiling a chandelier of startlingly modern design that resembled a torrent of water poured from a tilted vase.

But there was no sign of human occupation. Wexford stepped down under the arch where staghorn ferns grew in troughs at ground level and a *Cissus antarctica* climbed the columns, and entered a music room. It was larger than had appeared from outside and it was dodecagonal. The floor was of very smooth, polished, pale grey slate on which lay three Kashmiri rugs. A Broadwood grand piano stood between him and the other arched entrance. On each of eight of the twelve sides of the room was a picture or bust in an alcove, Mozart and Beethoven among the latter, among the former Cocteau's cartoon of Picasso and Stravinsky, Rothenstein's drawing of Parry, and a photograph of the Georgian manor house in which the music school was housed at Wellridge. But on one of the remaining sides Camargue had placed on a glass shelf a cast of Chopin's hands and on the last hung in a glass case a wind instrument of the side-blown type which looked to Wexford to be made of solid gold. Under it was the inscription: 'Presented to Manuel Camargue by Aldo Cazzini, 1949'. Was it a flute and could it be of gold? He lifted the lid of a case which lay on a low table and saw inside a similar instrument but made of humbler metal, perhaps silver.

He was resolving to go downstairs again and send Muriel Hicks to find Mrs Arno, when he was aware of a movement in the air behind him and of a presence that was not wholly welcoming. He turned round. Natalie Arno stood framed in the embrasure of the further arch, watching him with an unfathomable expression in her eyes.

4

Wexford was the first to speak.

'Good morning, Mrs Arno.'

She was absolutely still, one hand up to her cheek, the other resting against one of the columns which supported the arch. She was silent.

He introduced himself and said pleasantly, 'I hear you've had some sort of break-in. Is that right?'

Why did he feel so strongly that she was liberated by relief? Her face did not change and it was a second or two before she moved. Then, slowly, she came forward.

'It's good of you to come so quickly.' Her voice was as unlike Dinah Sternhold's as it was reasonably possible for one woman's voice to differ from another's. She had a faint American accent and in her tone there was an underlying hint of amusement. He was always to be aware of that in his dealings with her. 'I'm afraid I may be making a fuss about nothing. He only took a few spoons.' She made a comic grimace, pursing her lips as she drew out the long vowel sound. 'Let's go into the drawing room and I'll tell you about it.'

The cast of her countenance was that which one would immediately categorize as Spanish, full-fleshed yet strong, the nose straight if a fraction too long, the mouth full and flamboyantly curved, the eyes splendid, as near to midnight black as a white woman's eyes can ever be. Her black hair was strained tightly back from her face and knotted high on the back of her head, a style which most women's faces could scarcely take but which suited hers, exposing its fine bones. And her figure was no less arresting than her face.

She was very slim but for a too-full bosom, and this was not at all disguised by her straight skirt and thin sweater. Such an appearance, the ideal of men's fantasies, gives a woman a slightly indecent look, particularly if she carries herself with a certain provocative air. Natalie Arno did not quite do this but when she moved as she now did, mounting the steps to the higher level, she walked very sinuously with a stressing of her narrow waist.

During his absence two people had come into the drawing room, a man and a woman. They were behaving in the rather aimless fashion of house guests who have perhaps just got up or at least just put in an appearance, and who are wondering where to find breakfast, newspapers and an occupation. It occurred to Wexford for the first time that it was rather odd, not to say presumptuous, of Natalie Arno to have taken possession of Sterries so immediately after her father's death, to have moved in and to have invited people to stay. Did his solicitors approve? Did they know?

'This is Chief Inspector Wexford who has come to catch our burglar,' she said. 'My friends, Mr and Mrs Zoffany.'

The man was one of those who had been in the circle round her after the inquest. He seemed about forty. His fair hair was thick and wavy and he had a Viking's fine golden beard, but his body had grown soft and podgy and a flap of belly hung over the belt of his too-tight and too-juvenile fawn cord jeans. His wife, in the kind of clothes which unmistakably mark the superannuated hippie, was as thin as he was stout. She was young still, younger probably than Camargue's daughter, but her face was worn and there were coarse, bright threads of grey in her dark curly hair.

Natalie Arno sat down in one of the jade armchairs. She sat with elegant slim legs crossed at the calves, her feet arched in their high-heeled shoes. Mrs Zoffany, on the other hand, flopped on to the floor and sat cross-legged, tucking her long patchwork skirt around her knees. The costume she wore, and which like so many of her contemporaries she pathetically refused to relinquish, would date her more ruthlessly than might any perm or pair of stockings on another woman. Yet not so long ago it had been the badge of an élite who hoped to alter the world. Sitting there, she looked as if she might be at one of the pop concerts of her youth, waiting for the entertainment to begin. Her head was lifted expectantly, her eyes on Natalie's face.

'I'll tell you what there is to tell,' Natalie began, 'and I'm afraid that's not much. It must have been around five this morning I thought I heard the sound of glass breaking. I've been sleeping in Papa's room. Jane and Ivan are in one of the spare rooms in the other wing. You didn't hear anything, did you, Jane?'

Jane Zoffany shook her head vehemently. 'I only wish I had. I might have been able to *help*.'

'I didn't go down. To tell you the truth I was just a little scared.' Natalie smiled deprecatingly. She didn't look as if she had ever been scared in her life. Wexford wondered why he had at first felt her presence as hostile. She was entirely charming. 'But I did look out of the window. And just outside the window – on that side all the rooms are more or less on the ground floor, you know – there was a van parked. I put the light on and took a note of the registration number. I've got it here somewhere. What did I do with it?'

Jane Zoffany jumped up. 'I'll look for it, shall I? You put it down somewhere in here. I remember, I was still in my dressing gown . . .' She began hunting about the room, her scarves and the fringe of her shawl catching on ornaments.

Natalie smiled, and in that smile Wexford thought he detected patronage. 'I didn't quite know what to do,' she said. 'Papa didn't have a phone extension put in his room. Just as I was wondering I heard the van start up and move off. I felt brave enough to go down to the dining room then, and sure enough there was a pane gone from one of the casements.'

'A pity you didn't phone us then. We might have got him.'

'I know.' She said it ruefully, amusedly, with a soft sigh

of a laugh. 'But there were only those half-dozen silver spoons missing and two five-pound notes out of my purse. I'd left my purse on the sideboard.'

'But would *you* know exactly what was missing, Mrs Arno?'

'Right. I wouldn't really. But Mrs Hicks has been round with me this morning and she can't find anything else gone.'

'It's rather curious, isn't it? This house seems to me full of very valuable objects. There's a Kandinsky downstairs and a Boudin, I think.' He pointed. 'And those are signed Hockney prints. That yellow porcelain . . .'

She looked surprised at his knowledge. 'Yes, but . . .' Her cheeks had slightly flushed. 'Would you think me very forward if I said I had a theory?'

'Not at all. I'd like to hear it.'

'Well, first, I think he knew Papa used to sleep in that room and now poor Papa is gone he figured no one would be in there. And, secondly, I think he saw my light go on before he'd done any more than filch the spoons. He was just too scared to stop any longer. How does that sound?'

'Quite a possibility,' said Wexford. Was it his imagination that she had expected a more enthusiastic or flattering response? Jane Zoffany came up with the van registration number on a piece of paper torn from an exercise book. Natalie Arno didn't thank her for her pains. She rose, tensing her shoulders and throwing back her head to show off that amazing shape. Her waist could easily have been spanned by a pair of hands.

'Do you want to see the rest of the house?' she said. 'I'm sure he didn't come up to this level.'

Wexford would have loved to, but for what reason? 'We usually ask the householder to make a list of missing valuables in a case like this. It might be wise for me to go round with Mrs Hicks . . .'

'Of *course*.'

Throughout these exchanges Ivan Zoffany had not spoken. Wexford, without looking at him, had sensed a brooding concentration, the aggrieved attitude perhaps of a man not called on to participate in what might seem to be men's business. But now, as he turned his eyes in Zoffany's direction, he got a shock. The man was gazing at Natalie Arno, had probably been doing so for the past ten minutes, and his expression, hypnotic and fixed, was impenetrable. It might indicate contempt or envy or desire or simple hatred. Wexford was unable to analyse it but he felt a pang of pity for Zoffany's wife, for anyone who had to live with so much smouldering emotion.

Passing through the music room, Muriel Hicks took him first into the wing which had been private to Camargue. Here all was rather more austere than what he had so far seen. The bedroom, study-cum-sitting-room and bathroom were all carpeted in Camargue's favourite yellow – wasn't it in the Luscher Test that you were judged the best-adjusted if you gave your favourite colour as yellow? – but the furnishings were sparse and there were blinds at the windows instead of curtains. A dress of Natalie's lay on the bed.

Muriel Hicks had not so far spoken beyond asking him to follow her. She was not an attractive woman. She had the bright pink complexion that sometimes goes with red-gold hair and piglet features. Wexford who, by initially marrying one, had surrounded himself with handsome women, wondered at Camargue who had a beautiful daughter yet had picked an ugly housekeeper and a nonentity for a second wife. Immediately he had thought that he regretted it with shame. For, turning round, he saw that Mrs Hicks was crying. She was standing with her hand on an armchair, on the seat of which lay a folded rug, and the tears were rolling down her round, red cheeks.

She was one of the few people he had ever come across who did not apologize for crying. She wiped her face, scrubbing at her eyes. 'I've lost the best employer,' she said, 'and the best friend anyone could have. And I've taken it hard, I can tell you.'

'Yes, it was a sad business.'

'If you'll look out of that window you'll see a house over

to the left. That's ours. Really ours, I mean – he *gave* it to us. God knows what it's worth now. D'you know what he said? I'm not having you and Ted living in a tied cottage, he said. If you're good enough to come and work for me you deserve to have a house of your own to live in.'

It was a largish Victorian cottage and it had its own narrow driveway out into Ploughman's Lane. Sheila wouldn't have wanted it, he supposed, its not going with Sterries would make no difference to her. He put up a show for Mrs Hick's benefit of scrutinizing the spot where Natalie Arno said the van had been.

'There weren't many like him,' said Muriel Hicks, closing the door behind Wexford as they left. It was a fitting epitaph, perhaps the best and surely the simplest Camargue would have.

Along the corridor, back through the music room, across the drawing room, now deserted, and into the other wing. Here was a large room full of books, a study or a library, and three bedrooms, all with bathrooms *en suite*. Their doors were all open but in one of them, standing in front of a long glass and studying the effect of various ways of fastening the collar of a very old Persian lamb coat, was Jane Zoffany. She rushed, at the sight of Wexford, into a spate of apologies – very nearly saying sorry for existing at all – and scuttled from the room. Muriel Hick's glassy stare followed her out.

'There's nothing missing from here,' she said in a depressed tone. 'Anyway, those people would have heard something.' There was a chance, he thought, that she might lose another kind of control and break into a tirade against Camargue's daughter and her friends. But she didn't. She took him silently into the second room and the third.

Why had Natalie Arno chosen to occupy her father's bedroom, austere, utilitarian and moreover the room of a lately dead man and a parent, rather than one of these luxurious rooms with fur rugs on the carpets and duck-down duvets on the beds? Was it to be removed from the Zoffanys? But they were her friends whom she had presumably invited. To revel in the triumph of possessing the place and all that went with it at last? To appreciate this to the full by sleeping in the inner sanctum, the very holy of holies? It occurred to him that by so doing she must have caused great pain to Mrs Hicks, and then he reminded himself that this sort of speculation was pointless, he wasn't investigating any crime more serious than petty larceny. And his true reason for being here was to make a preliminary survey for a possible buyer.

'Is anything much kept in that chest?' he asked Mrs Hicks. It was a big teak affair with brass handles, standing in the passage.

'Only blankets.'

'And that cupboard?'

She opened it. 'There's nothing missing.'

He went downstairs. Morgan and his van had gone. In the hall were Burden, Natalie Arno and the Zoffanys, the man who had been sweeping the path, and a woman in a dark brown fox fur who had evidently just arrived.

Everyone was dressed for the outdoors and for bitterly cold weather. It struck Wexford forcefully, as he descended the stairs towards them, that Natalie and her friends looked thoroughly disreputable compared with the other three. Burden was always well turned-out and in his new sheepskin he was more than that. The newcomer was smart, even elegant, creamy cashmere showing above the neckline of the fur, her hands in sleek gloves, and even Ted Hicks, in aran and anorak, had the look of a gentleman farmer. Beside them Natalie and the Zoffanys were a rag-bag crew, Zoffany's old overcoat as shabby as Wexford's own, his wife with layers of dipping skirts hanging out beneath the hem of the Persian lamb. Nothing could make Natalie less than striking. In a coat that appeared to be made from an old blanket and platform-soled boots so out of date and so worn that Wexford guessed she must have bought them in a secondhand shop, she looked raffish and down on her luck. They were hardly the kind of people, he said to himself with an inward chuckle, that one (or the neighbours) would expect to see issuing from a house in Ploughman's Lane.

That the woman in the fur was one of these neighbours Burden immediately explained. Mrs Murray-Burgess. She had seen the police cars and then she had encountered Mr Hicks in the lane. Yes, she lived next door, if next door it could be called when something like an acre separated Kingsfield House from Sterries, and she thought she might have some useful information.

They all trooped into the dining room where Hicks resumed his task of boarding up the broken window. Wexford asked Mrs Murray-Burgess the nature of her information.

She had seen a man in the Sterries grounds. No, not last night, a few days before. In fact, she had mentioned it to Mrs Hicks, not being acquainted with Mrs Arno. She gave Natalie a brief glance that seemed to indicate her desire for a continuation of this state of affairs. No, she couldn't recall precisely when it had been. Last night she had happened to be awake at five-thirty – she always awoke early – and had seen the lights of a vehicle turning out from Sterries into the lane. Wexford nodded. Could she identify this man were she to see him again?

'I'm sure I could,' said Mrs Murray-Burgess emphatically. 'And what's more, I *would*. All this sort of thing has got to be stopped before the country goes completely to the dogs. If I've got to get up in court and say that's the man! – well, I've got to and no two ways about it. It's time someone gave a lead.'

Natalie's face was impassive but in the depths of her eyes Wexford saw a spark of laughter. Almost anyone else in her position would now have addressed this wealthy and majestic neighbour, thanking her perhaps for her concern and public spirit. Most people would have suggested a meeting on more social terms, on do-bring-your-husband-in-for-a-drink lines. Many would have spoken of the dead and have mentioned the coming memorial service. Natalie behaved exactly as if Mrs Murray-Burgess were not there. She shook hands with Wexford, thanking him warmly while increasing the pressure of her fingers. Burden was as prettily thanked and given an alluring smile. They were ushered to the door, the Zoffanys following, everyone coming out into the crisp cold air and the bright sunlight. Mrs Murray-Burgess, left stranded in the dining room with Ted Hicks, emerged in offended bewilderment a moment or two later.

Wexford, no doubt impressing everyone with his frown and preoccupied air, was observing the extent of the double glazing and making rough calculations as to the size of the grounds. Getting at last into their car, he remarked to Burden – a propos of what the inspector had no idea – that sometimes these cogitations still amazed the troubled midnight and the noon's repose.

5

The owner of the van was quickly traced through its registration number. He was a television engineer called Robert Clifford who said he had lent the van to a fellow-tenant of his in Finsbury Park, north London, a man of thirty-six called John Cooper. Cooper, who was unemployed, admitted the break-in after the spoons had been found in his possession. He said he had read in the papers about the death of Camargue and accounts of the arrangements at Sterries.

'It was an invite to do the place,' he said impudently. 'All that stuff about valuable paintings and china, and then that the housekeeper didn't sleep in the house. She didn't either, the first time I went.'

When had that been?

'Tuesday night,' said Cooper. He meant Tuesday the 29th, two days after Camargue's death. When he returned to break in. 'I didn't know which was the old man's room,' he said. 'How would I? The papers don't give you a plan of the bloody place.' He had parked the van outside that window simply because it seemed the most convenient spot and couldn't be seen from the road. 'It gave me a shock when the light came on.' He sounded aggrieved, as if he had been wantonly interrupted while about some legitimate task. His was a middle-class accent. Perhaps, like Burden's little villain, he was a pathological kleptomaniac with personality-scarring. Cooper appeared before the Kingsmarkham magistrates and was remanded in custody until the case could be heard at Myringham Crown Court.

Wexford was able to give Sheila a favourable report on

Camargue's house, but she seemed to have lost interest in the place. (One's children had a way of behaving like this, he had noticed.) Andrew's house in Keats Grove was really very nice, and he did have the cottage in Dorset. If they lived in Sussex they would have to keep a flat in town as well. She couldn't go all the way back to Kingsmarkham after an evening performance, could she? The estate agents had found a buyer for her own flat in St John's Wood and they were getting an amazing price for it. Had Mother been to hear her banns called for the second time? Mother had.

The day of the memorial service was bright and sunny. Alpine weather, Wexford called it, the frozen snow sparkling, melting a little in the sun, only to freeze glass-hard again when the sun went down. Returning from his visit to Sewingbury Comprehensive School – where there was an alarming incidence of glue-sniffing among fourteen-year-olds – he passed St Peter's church as the mourners were leaving. The uniform men wear disguises them. Inside black overcoat and black Homburg might breathe equally Sir Manuel's accompanist or Sir Manuel's wine merchant. But he was pretty sure he had spotted James Galway, and he stood to gaze like any lion-hunting sightseer.

Sheila, making her escape with Dinah Sternhold to a hire car, was attracting as much attention as anyone – a warning, her father thought, of what they might expect in a fortnight's time. The Zoffanys were nowhere to be seen but Natalie Arno, holding the arm of an elderly wisp of a man, a man so frail-looking that it seemed wonderful the wind did not blow him about like a feather, was standing on the steps shaking hands with departing visitors. She wore a black coat and a large black hat, new clothes they appeared to be and suited to the occasion, and she stood erectly, her thin ankles pressed together. By the time Wexford was driven away by the cold, though several dozen people had shaken hands with her and passed on, four or five of the men as well as the elderly wisp remained with her. He smiled to himself, amused to see his prediction fulfilled.

By the end of the week Sheila had received confirmation from the estate agents that her flat was sold, or that negotiations to buy it had begun. This threw her into a dilemma. Should she sign the contract and then go merrily off on her Bermuda honeymoon, leaving the flat full of furniture? Or should she arrange to have the flat cleared and the furniture stored before she left? Persuaded by her prudent mother, she fixed on the Wednesday before her wedding for the removal and Wexford, who had the day off, promised to go with her to St John's Wood.

'We could go to Bermuda too,' said Dora to her husband.

'I know it was the custom for Victorian brides to take a friend with them on their honeymoon,' said Wexford, 'but surely even they didn't take their parents.'

'Darling, I don't mean at the same time. I mean we could go to Bermuda later on. When you get your holiday. We can afford it now we aren't paying for this wedding.'

'How about my new car? How about the new hall carpet? And I thought you'd decided life was insupportable without a freezer.'

'We couldn't have all those things anyway.'

'That's for sure,' said Wexford.

A wonderful holiday or a new car? A thousand pounds' worth of sunshine and warmth took priority now, he reflected as he was driven over to Myringham and the crown court. The snow was still lying and the bright weather had given place to freezing fog. But would he still feel like this when it was sunny here and spring again? Then the freezer and the carpet would seem the wiser option.

John Cooper was found guilty of breaking into and entering Sterries and of stealing six silver spoons, and, since he had previous convictions, sent to prison for six months. Wexford was rather surprised to hear that one of these convictions, though long in the past, was for robbery with violence. Mrs Murray-Burgess was in court and she flushed brick-red with satisfaction when the sentence was pronounced. Throughout the proceedings she had been eyeing the dark, rather handsome, slouching Cooper in the awed and fascinated way one looks at a bull or a caged tiger.

It occurred to Wexford to call in at Sterries on his way

back and impart the news to Natalie Arno. He had promised to let her know the outcome. She would very likely be as delighted as her neighbour, and she could have her spoons back now.

A man who tried to be honest with himself, he wondered if this could be his sole motive for a visit to Ploughman's Lane. After all, it was a task Sergeant Martin or even Constable Loring could more properly have done. Was he, in common with those encircling men, attracted by Natalie? Could she have said of him too, like Cleopatra with her fishing rod, 'Aha, you're caught'? Honestly he asked himself – and said an honest, almost unqualified no. She amused him, she intrigued him, he suspected she would be entertaining to watch at certain manipulating ploys, but he was not attracted. There remained with him a nagging little memory of how, in the music room at Sterries, before he had ever spoken to her, he had sensed her presence behind him as unpleasing. She was good to look at, she was undoubtedly clever, she was full of charm, yet wasn't there about her something snake-like? And although this image might dissolve when confronted by the real Natalie, out of her company he must think of her sinuous movements as reptilian and her marvellous eyes when cast down as hooded.

So in going to Sterries he knew he was in little danger. No one need tie him to the mast. He would simply be calling on Natalie Arno for an obligatory talk, perhaps a cup of tea, and the opportunity to watch a powerful personality at work with the weak. If the Zoffanys were still there, of course. He would soon know.

It was three o'clock on the afternoon of a dull day. Not a light showed in the Sterries windows. Still, many people preferred to sit in the dusk rather than anticipate the night too soon. He rang the bell. He rang and rang again, was pleased to find himself not particularly disappointed that there was no one at home.

After a moment's thought he walked down the path to Sterries Cottage. Ted Hicks answered his ring. Yes, Mrs Arno was out. In fact, she had returned to London. Her friends had gone and then she had gone, leaving him and his wife to look after the house.

'Does she mean to come back?'

'I'm afraid I've no idea about that, sir. Mrs Arno didn't say.' Hicks spoke respectfully. Indeed, he had far more the air of an old-fashioned servant than his wife. Yet again Wexford felt, as he had felt with Muriel Hicks, that at any moment the discreet speaker might break into abuse, either heaping insults on Natalie or dismissing her with contempt. But nothing like this happened. Hicks compressed his lips and stared blankly at Wexford, though without meeting his eyes. 'Would you care to come in? I can give you Mrs Arno's London address.'

Why bother with it? He refused, thanked the man, asked almost as an afterthought if the house was to be sold.

'Very probably, sir.' Hicks, stiff, soldierly almost, unbent a little. 'This house will be. The wife and me, we couldn't stick it here now Sir Manuel's gone.'

It seemed likely that Natalie had taken her leave of Kingsmarkham and the town would not see her again. Perhaps she meant to settle in London or even return to America. He said something on these lines to Sheila as he drove her up to London on the following morning. But she had lost interest in Sterries and its future and was preoccupied with the morning paper which was carrying a feature about her and the forthcoming wedding. On the whole she seemed pleased with it, a reaction that astonished Wexford and Dora. They had been appalled by the description of her as the 'beautiful daughter of a country policeman' and the full-length photograph which showed her neither as Stewardess Curtis nor in one of her Royal Shakespeare Company roles, but reclining on a heap of cushions in little more than a pair of spangled stockings and a smallish fur.

'Dorset Stores It' was the slogan on the side of the removal van that had arrived early in Hamilton Terrace. Two men sat in its cab, glumly awaiting the appearance of the owner of the flat. Recognition of who that owner was mollified them, and on the way up in the lift the younger man asked Sheila if she would give him her autograph for his wife who hadn't missed a single instalment of *Runway* since the serial began.

The other man looked very old. Wexford was thinking he was too old to be of much use until he saw him lift Sheila's big bow-fronted chest of drawers and set it like a light pack on his shoulders. The younger man smiled at Wexford's astonishment.

'Pity you haven't got a piano,' he said. 'He comes from the most famous piano-lifting family in the country.'

Wexford had never before supposed that talents of that kind ran in families or even that one might enjoy a reputation for such a skill. He looked at the old man, who seemed getting on for Camargue's age, with new respect.

'Where are you taking all this stuff?'

A list was consulted. 'This piece and them chairs and that chest up to Keats Grove and . . .'

'Yes, I mean what isn't going to Keats Grove.'

'Down the warehouse. That's our warehouse down Thornton Heath, Croydon way if you know it. The lady's not got so much she'll need more than one container.' He named the rental Sheila would have to pay per week for the storage of her tables and chairs.

'It's stacked up in this container, is it, and stored along with a hundred others? Suppose you said you wanted it stored for a year and then you changed your mind and wanted to get, say, one item out?'

'That'd be no problem, guv'nor. It's yours, isn't it? While you pay your rent you can do what you like about it, leave it alone if that's what you want like or inspect it once a week. Thanks very much, lady.' This last was addressed to Sheila who was dispensing cans of beer.

'Give us a hand, George,' said the old man.

He had picked up Sheila's four-poster on his own, held it several inches off the ground, then thought better of it. He and the man called George began dismantling it.

'You'd be amazed,' said George, 'the things that go on. We're like a very old-established firm and we've got stuff down the warehouse been stored since before the First War. . . .'

'The Great War,' said the old man.

'OK, then, the *Great* War. We've got stuff been stored since before 1914. The party as stored it's dead and gone and the rent's like gone up ten, twenty times, but the family wants it kept and they go on paying. Furniture that's been stored twenty years, that's common, that's nothing out of the way. We got one lady, she put her grand piano in store 1936 and she's dead now, but her daughter, she keeps the rent up. She comes along every so often and we open up her container for her and let her have a look her piano's OK.'

'See if you can shift that nut, George,' said the old man.

By two they were finished. Wexford took Sheila out to lunch, to a little French restaurant in Blenheim Terrace, a far cry from Mr Haq's. They shared a bottle of Domaine du Parc and as Wexford raised his glass and drank to her happiness he felt a rush of unaccustomed sentimentality. She was so very much his treasure. His heart swelled with pride when he saw people look at her, whisper together and then look again. For years now she had hardly been his, she had been something like public property, but after Saturday she would be Andrew's and lost to him for ever. . . . Suddenly he let out a bark of laughter at these maudlin indulgences.

'What's funny, Pop darling?'

'I was thinking about those removal men,' he lied.

He drove her up to Hampstead where she was staying the night and began the long haul back to Kingsmarkham. Not very experienced in London traffic, he had left Keats Grove at four and by the time he came to Waterloo Bridge found himself in the thick of the rush. It was after seven when he walked, cross and tired, into his house.

Dora came out to meet him in the hall. She kept her voice low. 'Reg, that friend of Sheila's who was going to marry Manuel Camargue is here. Dinah Whatever-it-is.'

'Didn't you tell her Sheila wouldn't be back tonight?'

Dora, though aware that she must move with the times, though aware that Sheila and Andrew had been more or less living together for the past year, nevertheless still made attempts to present to the world a picture of her daughter as an old-fashioned maiden bride. Her husband's accusing look – he disapproved of this kind of Mrs Grundy-ish concealment – made her blush and say hastily:

'She doesn't want Sheila, she wants you. She's been here an hour, she insisted on waiting. She says . . . ' Dora cast up her eyes. 'She says she didn't know till this morning that you were a policeman!'

Wedding presents were still arriving. The house wasn't big enough for this sort of influx, and now the larger items were beginning to take over the hall. He nearly tripped over an object which, since it was swathed in corrugated cardboard and brown paper, might have been a plant stand, a lectern or a standard lamp, and cursing under his breath made his way into the living room.

This time the alsatian had been left behind. Dinah Sternhold had been sitting by the hearth, gazing into the heart of the fire perhaps while preoccupied with her own thoughts. She jumped up when he came in and her round pale face grew pink.

'Oh, I'm so sorry to bother you, Mr Wexford. Believe me, I wouldn't be here if I didn't think it was absolutely – well, absolutely vital. I've delayed so long and I've felt so bad and now I can't sleep with the worry. . . . But it wasn't till this morning I found out you were a detective chief inspector.'

'You read it in the paper,' he said, smiling. ' "Beautiful daughter of a country policeman." '

'Sheila never told me, you see. Why should she? I never told her my father's a bank manager.'

Wexford sat down. 'Then what you have to tell me is something serious, I suppose. Shall we have a drink? I'm a bit tired and you look as if you need Dutch courage.'

On doctor's orders, he could allow himself nothing stronger than vermouth but she, to his surprise, asked for whisky. That she wasn't used to it he could tell by the way she shuddered as she took her first sip. She lifted to him those greyish-brown eyes that seemed full of soft light. He had thought that face plain but it was not, and for a moment he could intuit what Camargue had seen in her. If his looks had been spiritual and sensitive so, superlatively, were hers. The old musician and this young creature had shared, he sensed, an approach to life that was gentle, impulsive and joyous.

There was no joy now in her wan features. They seemed convulsed with doubt and perhaps with fear.

'I know I ought to tell someone about this,' she began again. 'As soon as – as Manuel was dead I knew I ought to tell someone. I thought of his solicitors but I imagined them listening to me and knowing I wasn't to – well, inherit, and thinking it was all sour grapes. . . . It seemed so – so *wild* to go to the police. But this morning when I read that in the paper – you see, I know you, you're Sheila's father, you won't . . . I'm afraid I'm not being very articulate. Perhaps you understand what I mean?'

'I understand you've been feeling diffident about giving some sort of information but I'm mystified as to what it is.'

'Oh, of course you are! The point is, I don't really believe it myself. I can't, it seems so – well, outlandish. But Manuel believed it, he was so sure, so I don't think I ought to keep it to myself and just let things go ahead, do you?'

'I think you'd better tell me straight away, Mrs Sternhold. Just tell me what it is and then we'll have the explanations afterwards.'

She set down her glass. She looked a little away from him, the firelight reddening the side of her face.

'Well, then. Manuel told me that Natalie Arno, or the woman who calls herself Natalie Arno, wasn't his daughter at all. He was absolutely convinced she was an impostor.'

6

He said nothing and his face showed nothing of what he felt. She was looking at him now, the doubt intensified, her hands lifted and clasped hard together under her chin. In the firelight the ruby on her finger burned and twinkled.

'There,' she said, 'that's it. It was something to – to hesitate about, wasn't it? But I don't really believe it. Oh, I don't mean he wasn't marvellous for his age and his mind absolutely sound. I don't mean that. But his sight was poor and he'd worked himself into such an emotional state over seeing her, it was nineteen years, and perhaps she wasn't very kind and – oh, I don't know! When he said she wasn't his daughter, she was an impostor, and he'd leave her nothing in his will, I. . . .'

Wexford interrupted her. 'Why don't you tell me about it from the beginning?'

'Where is the beginning? From the time she, or whoever she is. . . .'

'Tell me about it from the time of her return to this country in November.'

Dora put her head round the door. He knew she had come to ask him if he was ready for his dinner but she retreated without a word. Dinah Sternhold said:

'I think I'm keeping you from your meal.'

'It doesn't matter. Let's go back to November.'

'I only know that it was in November she came back. She didn't get in touch with Manuel until the middle of December – 12 December it was. She didn't say anything about our getting married, just could she come and see him and something about healing the breach. At first she wanted to come at Christmas but when Manuel wrote back that that would be fine and I should be there and my parents, she said no, the first time she wanted to see him alone. It sounds casual, putting it like that, Manuel writing back and inviting her, but in fact it wasn't a bit. Getting her first letter absolutely threw him. He was very – well, excited about seeing her and rather confused and it was almost as if he was afraid. I suggested he phone her – she gave a phone number – but he couldn't bring himself to that and it's true he was difficult on the phone if you didn't know him. His hearing was fine when he could *see* the speaker. Anyway, she suggested 10 January and we had the same excitement and nervousness all over again. I wasn't to be there or the Hickses, Muriel was to get the tea ready and leave him to make it and she was to get one of the spare rooms ready in case Natalie decided to stay.

'Well, two or three days before, it must have been about the 7th, a woman called Mrs Zoffany phoned. Muriel took the call. Manuel was asleep. This Mrs Zoffany said she was speaking on behalf of Natalie who couldn't come on the 10th because she had to go into hospital for a check-up and could she come on the 19th instead? Manuel got into a state when Muriel told him. I went over there in the evening and he was very depressed and nervous, saying Natalie didn't really want a reconciliation, whatever she may have intended at first, she was just trying to get out of seeing him. You can imagine. He went on about how he was going to die soon and at any rate that would be a blessing for me, not to be tied to an old man *et cetera*. All nonsense, of course, but natural, I think. He was *longing* to see her. It's a good thing I haven't got a jealous nature. Lots of women would have been jealous.'

Perhaps they would. Jealousy knows nothing of age discrepancies, suitability. Camargue, thought Wexford, had chosen for his second wife a surrogate daughter, assuming his true daughter would never reappear. No wonder, when she did, that emotions had run high. He said only:

'I take it that it was on the 19th she came?'

'Yes. In the afternoon, about three. She came by train

from Victoria and then in a taxi from the station. Manuel asked the Hickses not to interrupt them and Ted even took Nancy away for the afternoon. Muriel left tea prepared on the table in the drawing room and there was some cold duck and stuff for supper in the fridge.'

'So that when she came Sir Manuel was quite alone?'

'Quite alone. What I'm going to tell you is what he told me the next day, the Sunday, when Ted drove him over to my house in the morning.

'He told me he intended to be rather cool and distant with her at first.' Dinah Sternhold smiled a tender, reminiscent smile. 'I didn't have much faith in that,' she said. 'I knew him, you see. I knew it wasn't in him not to be warm and kind. And in fact, when he went down and opened the front door to her he said he forgot all about that resolve of his and just took her in his arms and held her. He was ashamed of that afterwards, poor Manuel, he was sick with himself for giving way.

'Well, they went upstairs and sat down and talked. That is, Manuel talked. He said he suddenly found he had so much to say to her. He talked on and on about his life since she went away, her mother's death, his retirement because of the arthritis in his hands, how he had built that house. She answered him, he said, but a lot of things she said he couldn't hear. Maybe she spoke low, but my voice is low and he could always hear me. However . . .'

'She has an American accent,' said Wexford.

'Perhaps that was it. The awful thing was, he said, that when he talked of the long time she'd been away he actually cried. I couldn't see it was important, but he was so ashamed of having cried. Still, he pulled himself together. He said they must have tea and he hoped she would stay the night and would she like to see over the house? He was always taking people over the house, I think it was something his generation did, and then . . .'

Wexford broke in, 'All this time he believed her to be his daughter?'

'Oh, yes! He was in no doubt. The way he said he found out – well, it's so crazy. . . . Anyway, he actually told her he was going to make a new will after his marriage, and although he intended to leave me the house and its contents, everything else was to go to her, including what remained of her mother's fortune. It was a lot of money, something in the region of a million, I think.

'He showed her the bedroom that was to be hers, though she did say at this point that she couldn't stay, and then they went back and into the music room. Oh, I don't suppose you've ever been in the house, have you?'

'As a matter of fact, I have,' said Wexford.

She gave him a faintly puzzled glance. 'Yes. Well, you'll know then that there are alcoves all round the music room and in one of the alcoves is a flute made of gold. It was given to Manuel by a sort of patron and fan of his, an American of Italian origin called Aldo Cazzini, and it's a real instrument, it's perfectly *playable*, though in fact Manuel had never used it.

'He and Natalie went in there and Natalie took one look in the alcove and said, "You still have Cazzini's golden flute," and it was at this point, he said, that he knew. He knew for certain she wasn't Natalie.'

Wexford said, 'I don't follow you. Surely recognizing the flute would be confirmation of her identity rather than proof she was an impostor?'

'It was the way she pronounced it. It ought to be pronounced Catzini and this woman pronounced it Cassini. Or so he said. Now the real Natalie grew up speaking English, French and Spanish with equal ease. She learnt German at school and when she was fifteen Manuel had her taught Italian because he intended her to be a musician and he thought some Italian essential for a musician. The real Natalie would never have mispronounced an Italian name. She would no more have done that, he said – these are his own words – than a Frenchman would pronounce Camargue to rhyme with Montague. So as soon as he heard her pronunciation of Cazzini he knew she couldn't be Natalie.'

Wexford could almost have laughed. He shook his head in dismissal. 'There must have been more to it.'

'There was. He said the shock was terrible. He didn't say anything for a moment. He looked hard at her, he studied her, and then he could *see* she wasn't his daughter. Nineteen years is a long time but she couldn't have changed that much and in that way. Her features were different, the colour of her eyes was different. He went back with her into the drawing room and then he said, "You are not my daughter, are you?" '

'He actually asked her, did he?'

'He asked her and – you understand, Mr Wexford, that I'm telling you what he said – I feel a traitor to him, doubting him, as if he were senile or mad – he wasn't, he was wonderful, but. . . .'

'He was old,' said Wexford. A foolish, fond old man, fourscore years. . . . 'He was overwrought.'

'Oh, yes, exactly! But the point is he said he asked her and she admitted it.'

Wexford leaned forward, frowning a little, his eyes on Dinah Sternhold's flushed, intent face.

'Are you telling me this woman admitted to Sir Manuel that she wasn't Natalie Arno? Why didn't you say so before?'

'Because I don't believe it. I think that when he said she admitted she wasn't Natalie and seemed ashamed and embarrassed, I think he was – well, dreaming. You see, he told her to go. He was trembling, he was terribly distressed. It wasn't in him to shout at anyone or be violent, you understand, he just told her not to say any more but to go. He heard her close the front door and then he did something he absolutely never did. He had some brandy. He never touched spirits in the normal way, a glass of wine sometimes or a sherry, that was all. But he had some brandy to steady him, he said, and then he went to lie down because his heart was racing – and he fell asleep.'

'It was next day when you saw him?'

She nodded. 'Next day at about eleven. I think that while he was asleep he dreamt that bit about her admitting she wasn't Natalie. I told him so. I didn't humour him –

ours wasn't that kind of relationship. I told him I thought he was mistaken. I told him all sorts of things that I believed and believe now – that eye colour fades and features change and one can forget a language as one can forget anything else. He wouldn't have any of it. He was so sweet and good and a genius – but he was terribly impulsive and stubborn as well.

'Anyway, he started saying he was going to cut her out of his will. She was a fraud and an impostor who was attempting to get hold of a considerable property by false pretences. She was to have nothing, therefore, and I was to have the lot. Perhaps you won't believe me if I say I did my best to dissuade him from that?'

Wexford slightly inclined his head. 'Why not?'

'It would have been in my own interest to agree with him. However, I did try to dissuade him and he was sweet to me as he always was but he wouldn't listen. He wrote to her, telling her what he intended to do, and then he wrote to his solicitors, asking one of the partners to come up to Sterries on February 4th – that would have been two days after our wedding.'

'Who are these solicitors?'

'Symonds, O'Brien and Ames,' she said, 'in the High Street here.'

Kingsmarkham's principal firm of solicitors. They had recently moved their premises into the new Kingsbrook Precinct. It was often Wexford's lot to have dealings with them.

'He invited Mr Ames to lunch with us,' Dinah Sternhold said, 'and afterwards he was to draw up a new will for Manuel. It must have been on the 22nd or the 23rd that he wrote to Natalie and on the 27th – he was drowned.' Her voice shook a little.

Wexford waited. He said gently, 'He had no intention of coming to us and he wasn't going to confide in his solicitor?'

She did not answer him directly. 'I think I did right,' she said. 'I prevented that. I couldn't dissuade him from the decision to disinherit her but I did manage to stop him going to the police. I told him he would make a – well, a scandal, and he would have hated that. What I meant to do was this. Let him make a new will if he liked. Wills can be unmade and remade. I knew Natalie probably disliked me and was jealous but I thought I'd try to approach her myself a month or so after we were married, say, and arrange another meeting. I thought that somehow we'd all meet and it would come right. It would turn out to have been some misunderstanding like in a play, like in one of those old comedies of mistaken identity.'

Wexford was silent. Then he said, 'Would you like to tell me about it all over again, Mrs Sternhold?'

'What I've just told?'

He nodded. 'Please.'

'But why?'

To test your veracity. He didn't say that aloud. If she were intelligent enough she would know without his saying, and her flush told him that she did.

Without digressions this time, she repeated her story. He listened concentratedly. When she had finished he said rather sharply:

'Did Sir Manuel tell anyone else about this?'

'Not so far as I know. Well, no, I'm sure he didn't.' Her face was pale again and composed. She asked him, 'What will you do?'

'I don't know.'

'But you'll do something to find out. You'll prove she *is* Natalie Arno?'

Or that she is not? He didn't say it, and before he had framed an alternative reply she had jumped up and was taking her leave of him in that polite yet child-like way she had.

'It was very good and patient of you to listen to me, Mr Wexford. I'm sure you understand why I had to come. Will you give my love to Sheila, please, and say I'll be thinking of her on Saturday? She did ask me to come but of course that wouldn't be possible. I'm afraid I've taken up a great deal of your time. . . .'

He walked with her out to the Volkswagen which she had parked round the corner of the street on an ice-free patch. She looked back once as she drove away and raised her hand to him. How many times, in telling her story, had she said she didn't believe it? He had often observed how people will say they are sure of something when they truly mean they are unsure, how a man will hotly declare that he doesn't believe a word of it when he believes only too easily. If Dinah Sternhold had not believed, would she have come to him at all?

He asked himself if he believed and if so what was he going to do about it?

Nothing till after the wedding. . . .

7

The success or failure of a wedding, as Wexford remarked, is no augury of the marriage itself. This wedding might be said to have failed. In the first place, the thaw set in the evening before and by Saturday morning it was raining hard. All day long it rained tempestuously. The expected crowd of well-wishers come to see their favourite married, a youthful joyous crowd of confetti-hurlers, became in fact a huddle of pensioners under umbrellas, indifferently lingering on after the Over-Sixties meeting in St Peter's Hall. But the press was there, made spiteful by rain and mud, awaiting opportunites. And these were many: a bridesmaid's diaphanous skirt blown almost over her head by a gust of wind, a small but dismaying accident when the bride's brother-in-law's car went into the back of a press photographer's car, and later the failure of the Olive and Dove management to provide luncheon places for some ten of the guests.

The Sunday papers made the most of it. Their pictures might have been left to speak for themselves, for the captions, snide or sneering, only added insult to injury. Dora wept.

'I suppose it's inevitable.' Wexford, as far as he could recall it and with a touch of paraphrase, quoted Shelley to her. 'They scatter their insults and their slanders without heed as to whether the poisoned shafts light on a heart made callous by many blows or one like yours composed of more penetrable stuff.'

'And is yours made callous by many blows?'

'No, but Sheila's is.'

He took the papers away from her and burnt them, hoping none would have found their way into the Burdens' bungalow where they were going to lunch. And when they arrived just after noon, escorted from their car by Burden with a large coloured golf umbrella, there was not a newspaper to be seen. Instead, on the coffee table, where the *Sunday Times* might have reposed, lay a book in a glossy jacket entitled *The Tichborne Swindle*.

In former days, during the lifetime of Burden's first wife and afterwards in his long widowerhood, no book apart from those strictly necessary for the children's school work was ever seen in that house. But when he re-married things changed. And it could not be altogether due to the fact that his wife's brother was a publisher, though this might have helped, that the inspector was becoming a reading man. It was even said, though Wexford refused to believe it, that Burden and Jenny read aloud to each other in the evenings, that they had got through Dickens and were currently embarking on the Waverley novels.

Wexford picked up the book. It had been, as he expected, published by Carlyon Brent, and was a reappraisal of the notorious nineteenth-century Tichborne case in which an Australian butcher attempted to gain possession of a great fortune by posing as heir to an English baronetcy. Shades of the tale he had been told by Dinah Sternhold. . . . The coincidence of finding the book there decided him. For a little while before lunch he and Burden were alone together.

'Have you read this yet?'

'I'm about half-way through.'

'Listen.' He repeated the account he had been given baldly and without digressions. 'There aren't really very many points of similarity,' he said. 'From what I remember of the Tichborne case the claimant didn't even look like the Tichborne heir. He was much bigger and fatter for one thing and obviously not of the same social class. Lady Tichborne was a hysterical woman who would have accepted practically anyone who said he was her son. You've almost got the reverse here. Natalie Arno looks very much like the young Natalie Camargue and, far from accepting her, Camargue seems to have rumbled her within half an hour.'

' "Rumbled" sounds as if you think there might be something in this tale.'

'I'm not going to stomp up and down raving that I don't believe a word of it, if that's what you mean. I just don't know. But I'll tell you one thing. I expected you to have shouted you didn't believe it long before now.'

Burden gave one of his thin, rather complacent little smiles. In his domestic circle he behaved, much as he had during his first marriage, as if nobody but he had ever quite discovered the heights of marital felicity. Today he was wearing a new suit of smooth matt cloth the colour of a ginger nut. When happy he always seemed to grow thinner and he was very thin now. The smile was still on his mouth as he spoke. 'It's a funny old business altogether, isn't it? But I wouldn't say I don't believe it. It's fertile ground for that sort of con trick, after all. A nineteen-year absence, an old man on his own with poor sight, an old man who has a great deal of money. . . . By the way, how do you know this woman looks like the young Natalie?'

'Dinah Sternhold sent me this.' Wexford handed him a snapshot. 'Camargue was showing her a family photograph album, apparently, and he left it behind in her house.'

The picture showed a dark, Spanish-looking girl, rather plump, full-faced and smiling. She was wearing a summer dress in the style known at the time when the photograph was taken as 'the sack' on account of its shapelessness and lack of a defined waist. Her black hair was short and she had a fringe.

'That could be her. Why not?'

'A whitely wanton with a velvet brow,' said Wexford, 'and two pitchballs stuck in her face for eyes. Camargue said the eyes of the woman he saw were different from his daughter's and Dinah told him that eyes fade. I've never heard of eyes or anything else fading to black, have you?'

Burden refilled their glasses. 'If Camargue's sight was poor I think you can simply discount that sort of thing. I mean, you can't work on the premise that she's not Natalie Camargue because she looks different or he thought she did. The pronouncing of that name wrong, that's something else again, that's really weird.'

Wexford, hesitating for his figure's sake between potato crisps, peanuts or nothing at all, looked up in surprise. 'You think so?'

The thin smile came again. 'Oh, I know you reckon on me being a real philistine but I've got kids, remember. I've watched them getting an education if I've never had much myself. Now my Pat, she had a Frenchwoman teaching them French from when she was eleven, and when she speaks a French word she pronounces the R like the French, sort of rolls it in her throat. The point I'm making is, it happens naturally now, Pat couldn't pronounce a French word with an R in it any other way and *she never will*.'

'Mm hmm.' While pondering Wexford had absentmindedly sneaked two crisps. He held his hands firmly together in his lap. 'There's always the possibility Camargue *heard* the name incorrectly because of defective hearing while it was, in fact, pronounced in the proper way. What I'm sure of is that Dinah is telling the truth. I tested her and she told the same story almost word for word the second time as she has the first, dates, times, everything.'

'Pass over those crisp things, will you? I don't see what motive she'd have for inventing it, anyway. Even if Natalie were out of the way she wouldn't inherit.'

'No. Incidentally, we must find out who would. Dinah could have had spite for a motive, you know. If Natalie is the real Natalie no one of course could hope to prove she is not, and no doubt she could very quickly prove she *is*, but an inquiry would look bad for her, the mud would stick. If there were publicity about it and there very likely would be, there would be some people who would always believe her to be an impostor and many others who would feel a doubt.'

Burden nodded. 'And there must inevitably be an inquiry now, don't you think?'

'Tomorrow I shall have to pass on what I know to Symonds, O'Brien and Ames,' said Wexford, and he went on thoughtfully, 'It would be deception under the '68 Theft Act. Section Fifteen, I believe.' And he quoted with some small hesitations, 'A person who by any deception dishonestly obtains property belonging to another, with the intention of permanently depriving the other of it, shall on conviction on indictment be liable to imprisonment for a term not exceeding ten years.'

'No one's obtained anything yet. It'll take a bit of time for the will to be proved.' Burden gave his friend and superior officer a dubious and somewhat wary look. 'I don't want to speak out of turn and no offence meant,' he said, 'but this could be the kind of thing you get – well, you get obsessional about.'

Wexford's indignant retort was cut off in mid-sentence by the entry of Jenny and Dora to announce lunch.

Kingsmarkham's principal firm of solicitors had moved their offices when the new Kingsbrook shopping precinct was built, deserting the medieval caverns they had occupied for fifty years for the top floor above the British Home Stores. Here all was light, space and purity of line. The offices had that rather disconcerting quality, to be constantly met with nowadays, of looking cold and feeling warm. It was much the same in the police station.

Wexford knew Kenneth Ames well by sight, though he couldn't recall ever having spoken to him before. He was a thin, spare man with a boyish face. That is, his face like his figure had kept its youthful contours, though it was by now seamed all over with fine lines as if a web had been laid upon the skin. He wore a pale grey suit that seemed too lightweight for the time of year. His manner was both chatty and distant which gave the impression, perhaps a false one, that his mind was not on what he was saying or listening to.

This made repeating Dinah Sternhold's account a rather uneasy task. Mr Ames sat with his elbows on the arms of an uncomfortable-looking metal chair and the tips of his fingers pressed together. He stared out of the window at St Peter's spire. As the story progressed he pushed his lips and gradually his whole jaw forward until the lower part of his face grew muzzle-like. This doggy expression he held for a moment or two after Wexford had finished. Then he said:

'I don't think I'd place too much credence on all that, Mr Wexford. I don't think I would. It sounds to me as if Sir Manuel rather got a bee in his belfry, you know, and this young lady, Mrs – er, Steinhalt, is it? – Mrs Steinhall maybe gilded the gingerbread.' Mr Ames paused and coughed slightly after delivering these confused metaphors. He studied his short clean fingernails with interest. 'Once Sir Manuel was married he'd have had to make a new will. There was nothing out of the way in that. We have no reason to believe he meant to disinherit Mrs Arno.' The muzzle face returned as Mr Ames glared at his fingernails and enclosed them suddenly in his fists as if they offended him. 'In point of fact,' he said briskly, 'Sir Manuel invited me to lunch to discuss a new will and to meet his bride, Mrs – er, Sternhill, but unfortunately his death intervened. You know, Mr Wexford, if Sir Manuel had really believed he'd been visited by an impostor, don't you think he'd have said something to us? There was over a week between the visit and his death and during that week he wrote to me and phoned me. No, if this extraordinary tale were true I fancy he'd have said something to his solicitors.'

'He seems to have said nothing to anyone except Mrs Sternhold.'

An elastic smile replaced the muzzle look. 'Ah, yes. People like to make trouble. I can't imagine why. You may have noticed?'

'Yes,' said Wexford. 'By the way, in the event of Mrs Arno not inheriting, who would?'

'Oh dear, oh dear, I don't think there's much risk of Mrs Arno not inheriting, do you, really?'

Wexford shrugged. 'Just the same, who would?'

'Sir Manuel had – has, I suppose I should say if one may use the present tense in connection with the dead – Sir

Manuel has a niece in France, his dead sister's daughter. A Mademoiselle Thérèse Something. Latour? Lacroix? No doubt I can find the name for you if you really want it.'

'As you say, there may be no chance of her inheriting. Am I to take it then that Symonds, O'Brien and Ames intend to do nothing about this story of Mrs Sternhold's?'

'I don't follow you, Mr Wexford.' Mr Ames was once more contemplating the church spire which was now veiled in fine driving rain.

'You intend to accept Mrs Arno as Sir Manuel's heir without investigation?'

The solicitor turned round. 'Good heavens, no, Mr Wexford. What can have given you that idea?' He became almost animated, almost involved. 'Naturally, in view of what you've told us we shall make the most thorough and exhaustive inquiries. No doubt, you will too?'

'Oh, yes.'

'A certain pooling of our findings would be desirable, don't you agree? It's quite unthinkable that a considerable property such as Sir Manuel left could pass to an heir about whose provenance there might be the faintest doubt.' Mr Ames half closed his eyes. He seemed to gather himself together in order to drift once more into remoteness. 'It's only,' he said with an air of extreme preoccupation, 'that it doesn't really do, you know, to place too much credence on these things.'

As the receiver was lifted the deep baying of a dog was the first sound he heard. Then the soft gentle voice gave the Forby number.

'Mrs Sternhold, do you happen to know if Sir Manuel had kept any samples of Mrs Arno's handwriting from *before* she went away to America?'

'I don't know. I don't think so.' Her tone sounded dubious, cautious, as if she regretted having told him so much. Perhaps she did, but it was too late now. 'They'd be inside Sterries, anyway.' She didn't add what Wexford was thinking, that if Camargue had kept them and if Natalie was an impostor, they would by now have been destroyed.

'Then perhaps you can help me in another way. I gather Sir Manuel had no relatives in this country. Who is there I can call on who knew Mrs Arno when she was Natalie Camargue?'

Burden's Burberry was already hanging on the palm tree hatstand when Wexford walked into the Pearl of Africa. And Burden was already seated under the plastic fronds, about to start on his antipasto Ankole.

'I don't believe they have shrimps in Uganda,' said Wexford, sitting down opposite him.

'Mr Haq says they come out of Lake Victoria. What are you going to have?'

'Oh, God. Avocado with Victorian shrimps, I suppose, and maybe an omelette. Mike, I've been on to the California police through Interpol, asking them to give us whatever they can about the background of Natalie Arno, but if she's never been in trouble, and we've no reason to think she has, it won't be much. And I've had another talk with Dinah. The first – well, the only really – Mrs Camargue had a sister who's still alive and in London. Ever heard of a composer called Philip Cory? He was an old pal of Camargue's. Either or both of them ought to be able to tell us if this is the real Natalie.'

Burden said thoughtfully, 'All this raises something else, doesn't it? Or, rather, what we've been told about Camargue's will does. And in that area it makes no difference whether Natalie is Natalie or someone else.'

'What does it raise?'

'You know what I mean.'

Wexford did. That Burden too had seen it scarcely surprised him. A year or two before the inspector had often seemed obtuse. But happiness makes so much difference to a person, Wexford thought. It doesn't just make them happy, it makes them more intelligent, more aware, more alert, while unhappiness deadens, dulls and stupefies. Burden had seen what he had seen because he was happy, and happiness was making a better policeman of him.

'Oh, I know what you mean. Perhaps it was rather too readily assumed that Camargue died a natural death.'

'I wouldn't say that. It's just that then there was no reason to suspect foul play, nothing and no one suspicious seen in the neighbourhood, no known enemies, no unusual bruising on the body. A highly distinguished but rather frail old man happened to go too near a lake on a cold night in deep snow.'

'And if we had known what we know now? We can take it for granted that Natalie's aim – whether she is Camargue's daughter or an impostor – her aim in coming to her father was to secure his property or the major part of it for herself. She came to him and, whether he actually saw through her and denounced her or thought he saw through her and dreamed he denounced her, he at any rate apparently wrote to her and told her she was to be disinherited.'

'She could either attempt to dissuade him,' said Burden, 'or take steps of another sort.'

'Her loss wouldn't have been immediate. Camargue was getting married and had therefore to make a new will after his marriage. She might count on his not wishing to make a new will at once and then another after his marriage. She had two weeks in which to act.'

'There's a point too that, whereas she might have dissuaded him from cutting her out, she couldn't have dissuaded him from leaving Sterries to Dinah. But there don't seem to have been any efforts at dissuasion, do there? Dinah doesn't know of any or she'd have told you, nor did Natalie come to Sterries again.'

'Except perhaps,' said Wexford, 'on the night of Sunday, 27 January.'

Burden's answer was checked by the arrival of Mr Haq, bowing over the table.

'How are you doing, my dear?'

'Fine, thanks.' Any less hearty reply would have summoned forth a stream of abject apology and the cook from the kitchen as well as causing very real pain to Mr Haq.

'I can recommend the mousse Maherere.'

Mr Haq, if his advice was rejected, was capable of going off into an explanation of how this dish was composed of coffee beans freshly plucked in the plantations of Toro and of cream from the milk of the taper-horned Sanga cattle. To prevent this, and though knowing its actual provenance to be Sainsbury's instant dessert, Burden ordered it. Wexford always had the excuse of his shaky and occasional diet. A bowl of pale brown froth appeared, served by Mr Haq's own hands.

Quietly Wexford repeated his last remark.

'The night of 27 January?' echoed Burden. 'The night of Camargue's death? If he was murdered, and I reckon we both think he was, if he was pushed into that water and left to drown, Natalie didn't do it.'

'How d'you know that?'

'Well, in a funny sort of way,' Burden said almost apologetically, 'she told me so.'

'It was while we were up at Sterries about that burglary. I was in the dining room talking to Hicks when Natalie and the Zoffany couple came downstairs. She may have known I was within earshot but I don't think she did. She and Mrs Z. were talking and Natalie was saying she supposed she would have to get Sotheby's or someone to value Camargue's china for her. On the other hand, there had been that man she and Mrs Z. had met that someone had said was an expert on Chinese porcelain and she'd like to get hold of his name and phone number. Zoffany said what man did she mean and Natalie said he wouldn't know, he hadn't been there, it had been at so-and-so's party *last Sunday evening*.'

'A bit too glib, wasn't it?'

'Glib or not, if Natalie was at a party there'll be at least a dozen people to say she was, as well as Mrs Z. And if Camargue was murdered *we will never prove it*. If we'd guessed it at the time it would have been bad enough with snow lying everywhere, with snow falling to obliterate all possible evidence. No weapon but bare hands. Camargue cremated. We haven't a hope in hell of proving it.'

'You're over-pessimistic,' said Wexford, and he quoted softly, 'If a man will begin with certainties, he shall end in doubts, but if he will be content to begin with doubts he shall end in certainties.'

8

A shop that is not regularly open and manned seems to announce this fact to the world even when the 'open' sign hangs on its door and an assistant can be seen pottering inside. An indefinable air of neglect, of lack of interest, of precarious existence and threatened permanent closure hangs over it. So it was with the Zodiac, nestling in deep Victoriana, tucked behind a neo-Gothic square, on the borders of Islington and Hackney.

Its window was stacked full of paperback science fiction, but some of the books had tumbled down, and those which lay with their covers exposed had their gaudy and bizarre designs veiled in dust. Above the shop was a single storey – for this was a district of squat buildings and wide streets – and behind it a humping of rooms, shapelessly huddled and with odd little scraps of roof, gables protruding, seemingly superfluous doors and even a cowled chimney. Wexford pushed open the shop door and walked in. There was a sour, inky, musty smell, inseparable from secondhand books. These lined the shop like wallpaper, an asymmetrical pattern of red and green and yellow and black spines. They were all science fiction, *The Trillion Project*, *Nergal of Chaldea*, *Neuropodium*, *Course for Umbrial*, *The Triton Occultation*. He was replacing on the shelf a book whose cover bore a picture of what appeared to be a Boeing 747 coated in fish scales and with antennae, when Ivan Zoffany came in from a door at the back.

Recognition was not mutual. Zoffany showed intense surprise when Wexford said who he was, but it seemed like surprise alone and not fear.

'I'd like a few words with you.'

'Right. It's a mystery to me what about but I'm easy. I may as well close up for lunch anyway.'

It was ten past twelve. Could they hope to make any sort of living out of this place? Did they try? The 'open' sign was turned round and Zoffany led Wexford into the room from which he had come. By a window which gave on to a paved yard and scrap of garden and where the light was best, Jane Zoffany, in antique gown, shawl and beads, sat sewing. She appeared to be turning up or letting down the hem of a skirt and Wexford, whose memory was highly retentive about this sort of thing, recognized it as the skirt Natalie had been wearing on the day they were summoned after the burglary.

'What can we do for you?'

Zoffany had the bluff, insincere manner of the man who has a great deal to hide. Experience had taught Wexford that what such a nature is hiding is far more often some emotional disturbance or failure of nerve than guilty knowledge. He could hardly have indulged in greater self-deception than when he had said he was easy. There was something in Zoffany's eyes and the droop of his mouth when he was not forcing it into a grin that spoke of frightful inner suffering. And it was more apparent here, on his home ground, than it had been at Sterries.

'How long have you known Mrs Arno?'

Instinctively, Jane Zoffany glanced towards the ceiling. And at that moment a light footstep sounded overhead. Zoffany didn't look up.

'Oh, I'd say a couple of years, give or take a little.'

'You knew her before she came to this country then?'

'Met her when my poor sister died. Mrs Arno and my sister used to share a house in Los Angeles. Perhaps you didn't know that? Tina, my sister, she died the summer before last, and I had to go over and see to things. Grisly business but someone had to. There wasn't anyone else, barring my mother, and you can't expect an old lady of seventy – I say, what's all this in aid of?'

Wexford ignored the question as he usually ignored such

questions until the time was ripe to answer them. 'Your sister and Mrs Arno shared a house?'

'Well, Tina had a flat in her house.'

'A room actually, Ivan,' said Jane Zoffany.

'A room in her house. Look, could you tell me why you want . . .?'

'She must have been quite a young woman. What did she die of?'

'Cancer. She had cancer in her twenties while she was still married. Then she got divorced, but she didn't keep his name, she went back to her maiden name. She was thirty-nine if you want to know. The cancer came back suddenly, it was all over her, carcinomatosis, they called it. She was dead in three weeks from the onset.'

Wexford thought he spoke callously and with a curious kind of resentment. There was also an impression that he talked for the sake of talking, perhaps to avoid an embarrassing matter.

'I hadn't seen her for sixteen or seventeen years,' he said, 'but when she went like that someone had to go over. I can't think what you want with all this.'

It was on the tip of Wexford's tongue to retort that he had not asked for it. He said mildly, 'When you arrived you met Mrs Arno? Stayed in her house perhaps?'

Zoffany nodded, uneasy again.

'You got on well and became friends. After you came home you corresponded with her and when you heard she was coming back here and needed somewhere to live, you and your wife offered her the upstairs flat.'

'That's quite correct,' said Jane Zoffany. She gave a strange little skittish laugh. 'I'd always admired her from afar, you see. Just to think of my own sister-in-law living in Manuel Camargue's own daughter's house! I used to worship him when I was young. And Natalie and I are very close now. It was a really good idea. I'm sure Natalie has been a true friend to me.' She re-threaded her needle, holding the eye up against the yellowed and none-too-clean net curtain. 'Please, why are you asking all these questions?'

'A suggestion has been made that Mrs Arno is not in fact the late Sir Manuel Camargue's daughter but an impostor.'

He was interested by the effect of these words on his hearers. One of them expected this statement and was not surprised by it, the other was either flabbergasted or was a superb actor. Ivan Zoffany seemed stricken dumb with astonishment. Then he asked Wexford to repeat what he had said.

'That is the most incredible nonsense,' Zofffany said with a loaded pause between the words. 'Who has suggested it? Who would put about a story like that? Now just you listen to me. . . . ' Wagging a finger, he began lecturing Wexford on the subject of Natalie Arno's virtues and misfortunes. 'One of the most charming, delightful girls you could wish to meet, and as if she hasn't had enough to put up with. . . .'

Wexford cut him short again. 'It's her identity, not her charm, that's in dispute.' He was intrigued by the behaviour of Jane Zoffany who was sitting hunched up, looking anywhere but at him, and who appeared to be very frightened indeed. She had stopped sewing because her hands would have shaken once she moved each out of the other's grasp.

He went back into the shop. Natalie Arno was standing by the counter on the top of which now lay an open magazine. She was looking at this and laughing with glee rather than amusement. When she saw Wexford she showed no surprise, but smiled, holding her head a little on one side.

'Good morning, Mr – er, Wexford, isn't it? And how are you today?' It was an Americanism delivered with an American lilt and one that seemed to require no reply. 'When you close the shop, Ivan,' she said, 'you should also remember to lock the door. All sorts of undesirables could come in.'

Zoffany said with gallantry, but stammering a little, 'That certainly doesn't include you, Natalie!'

'I'm not sure the chief inspector would agree with you.' She gave Wexford a sidelong smile. She knew. Symonds, O'Brien and Ames had lost no time in telling her. Jane

Zoffany was afraid but she was not. Her black eyes sparkled. Rather ostentatiously, she closed the magazine she had been looking at, revealing the cover which showed it to belong to the medium hard genre of pornography. Plainly, this was Zoffany's under-the-counter solace that she had lighted on. He flushed, seized it rather too quickly from under her hands and thrust it between some catalogues in a pile. Natalie's face became pensive and innocent. She put up her hands to her hair and her full breasts in the sweater rose with the movement, which seemed to have been made quite artlessly, simply to tuck in a tortoiseshell pin.

'Did you want to interrogate me, Mr Wexford?'

'Not yet,' he said. 'At present I'll be content if you'll give me the name and address of the people whose party you and Mrs Zoffany went to on the evening of 27 January.'

She told him, without hesitation or surprise.

'Thank you, Mrs Arno.'

At the door of the room where Jane Zoffany was she paused, looked at him and giggled. 'You can call me Mrs X, if you like. Feel free.'

A housekeeper in a dark dress that was very nearly a uniform admitted him to the house in a cul-de-sac off Kensington Church Street. She was a pretty, dark-haired woman in her thirties who doubtless looked on her job as a career and played her part so well that he felt she *was* playing, was acting with some skill the role of a deferential servant. In a way she reminded him of Ted Hicks.

'Mrs Mountnessing hopes you won't mind going upstairs, Chief Inspector. Mrs Mountnessing is taking her coffee after luncheon in the little sitting room.'

It was a far cry from the house in De Beauvoir Square to which Natalie had sent him, a latter-day Bohemia where there had been Indian bedspreads draping the walls and a smell of marijuana for anyone who cared to sniff for it. Here the wall decorations were hunting prints, ascending parallel to the line of the staircase whose treads were carpeted in thick soft olive-green. The first-floor hall was wide, milk chocolate with white cornice and mouldings, the same green carpet, a *Hortus siccus* in a copper trough on a console table, a couple of fat-seated, round-backed chairs upholstered in golden-brown velvet, a twinkling chandelier and a brown table lamp with a cream satin shade. There are several thousand such interiors in the Royal Borough of Kensington and Chelsea. A panelled door was pushed open and Wexford found himself in the presence of Natalie Arno's Aunt Gladys, Mrs Rupert Mountnessing, the sister of Kathleen Camargue.

His first impression was of someone cruelly encaged and literally gasping for breath. It was a fleeting image. Mrs Mountnessing was just a fat woman in a too-tight corset which compressed her body from thighs to chest into the shape of a sausage and thrust a shelf of bosom up to buttress her double chin. This constrained flesh was sheathed in biscuit-coloured wool and upon the shelf rested three strands of pearls. Her face had become a cluster of pouches rather than a nest of wrinkles. It was thickly painted and surmounted by an intricate white-gold coiffure that was as smooth and stiff as a wig. The only area of Mrs Mountnessing which kept some hint of youth was her legs. And these were still excellent: slender, smooth, not varicosed, the ankles slim, the tapering feet shod in classic court shoes of beige glacé kid. They reminded him of Natalie's legs, they were exactly like. Did that mean anything? Very little. There are only a few types of leg, after all. One never said 'She has her aunt's legs' as one might say a woman had her father's nose or her grandmother's eyes.

The room was as beige and gold as its owner. On a low table was a coffee cup, coffee pot, sugar basin and cream jug in ivory china with a Greek key design on it in gold. Mrs Mountnessing rose when he came in and held out a hand much be-ringed, the old woman's claw-like nails filed to points and painted dark red.

'Bring another cup, will you, Miranda?'

It was the voice of an elderly child, petulant, permanently aggrieved. Wexford thought that the voice and the puckered face told of a lifetime of hurts, real or imagined. Rupert Mountnessing was presumably dead and gone long ago, and Dinah Sternhold had told him there had been no children. Would Natalie, real or false, hope for an inheritance here? Almost the first words uttered by Mrs Mountnessing told him that, if so, she hoped in vain.

'You said on the phone you wanted to talk to me about my niece. But I know nothing about my niece in recent years and I don't – I don't want to. I should have explained that to you, I realize that now. I shouldn't have let you come all this way when I've nothing at all to tell you.' Her eyes blinked more often or more obviously than most people's. The effect was to give the impression she fought off tears. 'Thank you, Miranda.' She took the coffee cup and listened, subsiding back into her chair as he told her the reason for his visit.

'Anastasia,' she said.

The Tichborne Claimant had been recalled, now the Tsar's youngest daughter. Wexford did not relish the reminder, for wasn't it a fact that Anastasia's grandmother, the one person who could positively have identified her, had refused ever to see the claimant, and that as a result of that refusal no positive identification had ever been made?

'We hope it won't come to that,' he said. 'You seem to be her nearest relative, Mrs Mountnessing. Will you agree to see her in my presence and tell me if she is who she says she is?'

Her reaction, the look on her face, reminded him of certain people he had in the past asked to come and identify, not a living person, but a corpse in the mortuary. She put a hand up to each cheek. 'Oh no, I couldn't do that. I'm sorry, but it's impossible. I couldn't ever see Natalie again.'

He accepted it. She had forewarned him with her mention of Anastasia. If he insisted on her going with him the chances were she would make a positive identification simply to get the whole thing over as soon as possible. Briefly he wondered what it could have been that her niece, while still a young girl, had done to her, and then he joined her at the other end of the room where she stood contemplating a table that was used entirely as a stand for photographs in silver frames.

'That's my sister.'

A dark woman with dark eyes, but nevertheless intensely English. Perhaps there was something of the woman he knew as Natalie Arno in the broad brow and pointed chin.

'She had cancer. She was only forty-five when she died. It was a terrible blow to my poor brother-in-law. He sold their house in Pomfret and built that one in Kingsmarkham and called it Sterries. Sterries is the name of the village in Derbyshire where my parents had their country place. Kathleen and Manuel first met there.'

Camargue and his wife were together among the photographs on the table. Arm-in-arm, walking along some Mediterranean sea front; seated side by side on a low wall in an English garden; in a group with a tall woman so like Camargue that she had to be his sister, and with two small dark-haired smiling girls. A ray of sunlight, obliquely slanted at three on a winter's afternoon, fell upon the handsome moustached face of a man in the uniform of a colonel of the Grenadier Guards. Rupert Mountnessing, no doubt. A litle bemused by so many faces, Wexford turned away.

'Did Sir Manuel go to the United States after your niece went to live there?'

'Not to see *her*. I think he went there on a tour – yes, I'm sure he did, though it must be ten or twelve years since he gave up playing. His arthritis crippled him, poor Manuel. We saw very little of each other in recent years, but I was fond of him, he was a sweet man. I would have gone to the memorial service but Miranda wouldn't let me. She didn't want me to risk bronchitis in that terrible cold.'

Mrs Mountnessing, it seemed, was willing to talk about any aspect of family life except her niece. She sat down again, blinking back non-existent tears, held ramrod stiff by her corset. Wexford persisted.

'He went on a tour. Did he make any private visits?'

'He may have done.' She said it in the way people do when they dodge the direct affirmative but don't want to lie.

'But he didn't visit his daughter while he was there?'

'California's three thousand miles from the east coast,' she said, 'it's as far again as from here.'

Wexford shook his head dismissively. 'I don't understand that for nineteen years Sir Manuel never saw his daughter. It's not as if he was a poor man or a man who never travelled. If he had been a vindictive man, a man to bear a grudge – but everyone tells me how nice he was, how kind, how good. I might say I'd had golden opinions from all sorts of people. Yet for nineteen years he never made an effort to see his only child and allegedly all because she ran away from college and married someone he didn't know.'

She said so quietly that Wexford hardly heard her, 'It wasn't like that.' Her voice gained a little strength but it was full of distress. 'He wrote to her – oh, ever so many times. When my sister was very ill, was in fact dying, he wrote to her and asked her to come home. I don't know if she answered but she didn't come. My sister died and she didn't come. Manuel made a new will and wrote to her, telling her he was leaving her everything because it was right she should have his money and her mother's. She didn't answer and he gave up writing.'

I wonder how you come to know that? he asked himself, looking at the crumpled profile, the chin that now trembled.

'I'm telling you all this,' said Mrs Mountnessing, 'to make you understand that my niece is cruel, cruel, a cruel unfeeling girl and violent too. She even struck her mother once. Did you know that?' The note in her voice grew hysterical and Wexford, watching the blinking eyes, the fingers clasping and unclasping in her lap, wished he had not mentioned the estrangement. 'She's a nymphomaniac too. Worse than that, it doesn't matter to her who the men are, her own relations, it's too horrible to talk about, it's too. . . .'

He interrupted her gently. He got up to go. 'Thank you for your help, Mrs Mountnessing. I can't see a sign of any of these propensities in the woman I know.'

Miranda showed him out. As he crossed to the head of the stairs he heard a very soft whimpering sound from the room he had left, the sound of an elderly child beginning to cry.

9

A birth certificate, a marriage certificate, an American driving licence complete with immediately recognizable photograph taken three years before, a United States passport complete with immediately recognizable photograph taken the previous September, and perhaps most convincing of all, a letter to his daughter from Camargue, dated 1963, in which he informed her that he intended to make her his sole heir. All these documents had been readily submitted to Symonds, O'Brien and Ames, who invited Wexford along to their offices in the precinct over the British Home Stores to view them.

Kenneth Ames, distant and chatty as ever, said he had personally seen Mrs Arno, interviewed her exhaustively and elicited from her a number of facts about the Camargue family and her own childhood which were currently being verified. Mrs Arno had offered to take a blood test but since this could only prove that she was *not* Camargue's daughter, not that she was, and since no one seemed to know what Camargue's blood group had been, it was an impracticable idea. Mr Ames said she seemed heartily amused by the whole business, a point of course in her favour. She had even produced samples of her handwriting from when she was at the Royal Academy of Music to be compared with her writing of the present day.

'Do you know what she said to him?' Wexford said afterwards, meeting Burden for a drink in the Olive and Dove. 'She's got a nerve. "It's a pity I didn't do anything criminal when I was a teenager," she said. "They'd have my fingerprints on record and that would solve everything".'

Burden didn't smile. 'If she's not Natalie Camargue, when could the change-over have taken place?'

'Provided we accept what Zoffany says, not recently. Say more than two years ago but after the death of Vernon Arno. According to Ames, he would seem to have died in a San Francisco hospital in 1971.'

'He must have been young still.' Burden echoed Wexford's words to Ivan Zoffany. 'What did he die of?'

'Leukaemia. No one's suggesting there was anything odd about his death, though there's a chance we'll know more when we hear from the California police. But, Mike, if there was substitution, if this is an assumed identity, it was assumed for some other reason. That is, it wasn't put on for the sake of inheriting from Carmargue.'

Burden gave a dubious nod. 'It would mean the true Natalie was dead.'

'She may be but there are other possibilities. The true Natalie may be incurably ill in some institution or have become insane or gone to live in some inaccessible place. And the impostor could be someone who needed an identity because keeping her own was dangerous, because, for instance, she was some kind of fugitive from justice. That Camargue was rich, that Camargue was old, that Natalie was to be his sole heir, all these facts might be *incidental*, might be a piece of luck for the impostor which she only later decided to take advantage of. The identity would have been taken on originally as a safety measure, even perhaps as the only possible lifeline, and I think it was taken on at a point where the minimum of deception would have been needed. Maybe at the time the move was made from San Francisco to Los Angeles or much later, at the time when Tina Zoffany died.'

Burden, who seemed not to have been concentrating particularly on any of this, said suddenly, looking up from his drink and fixing Wexford with his steel-coloured eyes:

'Why did she come to this country at all?'

'To make sure of the dibs,' said Wexford.

'No.' Burden shook his head. 'No, that wasn't the

reason. Impostor or real, she was in no doubt about what you call the dibs. She'd had that letter from Camargue, promising her her inheritance. She need do nothing but wait. There was no need to re-establish herself in his eyes, no need to placate him. If she'd felt there was she'd have tried it before. After all, he was getting on for eighty.

'And it's no good saying she came back because he was getting married again. No one knew he was getting married till 10 December when his engagement was in the *Telegraph*. She came back to this country in November but she made no attempt to see Camargue until after she read about his engagement. She was here for three or four weeks before that. Doing what? Planning what?'

Admiration was not something Wexford had often felt for the inspector in the past. Sympathy, yes, affection and a definite need, for Burden had most encouragingly fulfilled the function of an Achates or a Boswell, if not quite a Watson. But admiration? Burden was showing unexpected deductive powers that were highly gratifying to witness, and Wexford wondered if they were the fruit of happiness or of reading aloud from great literature in the evenings.

'Go on,' he said.

'So why did she come back? Because she was sentimental for her own home, her ain countree, as you might say?' As Scott might say, thought Wexford. Burden went on, 'She's a bit young for those feelings. She's an American citizen, she was settled in California. If she is Natalie Camargue she'd lived there longer than here, she'd no relatives here but a father and an aunt she didn't get on with, and no friends unless you count those Zoffanys.

'If she's an impostor, coming back was a mad thing to do. Stay in America and when Camargue dies his solicitors will notify her of the death, and though she'll no doubt then have to come here and swear affidavits and that sort of thing, *no one will question who she is*. No one would have questioned it if she hadn't shown herself to Camargue.'

'But she had to do that,' Wexford objected. 'Her whole purpose surely in going to see him was to persuade him not to re-marry.'

'She didn't know that purpose would even exist when she left the United States in November. And if she'd stayed where she was she might never have known of Camargue's re-marriage until he eventually died. What would that announcement have merited in a California newspaper? The *Los Angeles Times*, for instance? A paragraph tucked away somewhere. "Former world-famous British flautist . . ." '

'They say flutist over there.'

'Flautist, flutist, what does it matter? Until we know *why* she came here I've got a feeling we're not going to get at the truth about this.'

'The truth about who she is, d'you mean?'

'The truth about Camargue's death.' And Burden said with a certain crushing triumph, 'You're getting an obsession about who this woman is. I knew you would, I said so. What interests me far more is the murder of Carmargue and who did it. Can't you see that in the context of the murder, who she is is an irrelevance?'

'No', said Wexford. 'Who she is is everything.'

The California police had nothing to tell Wexford about Natalie Arno. She was unknown to them, had never been in any trouble or associated with any trouble.

'The litigation in the Tichborne case,' said Burden gloomily, 'went on for three years and cost ninety thousand pounds. That was in 1874. Think what the equivalent of that would be today.'

'We haven't had any litigation yet,' said Wexford, 'or spent a single penny. Look on the bright side. Think of the claimant getting a fourteen-year sentence for perjury.'

In the meantime Kenneth Ames had interviewed two people who had known Camargue's daughter when she was an adolescent. Mavis Rolland had been at the Royal Academy of Music at the same time as Natalie Camargue and was now head of the music department at a girls' school on the South Coast. In her opinion there was no doubt that Natalie Arno was the former Natalie Camargue. She professed to find her not much changed except for her voice which she would not have recognized. On the other hand,

Mary Woodhouse, a living-in maid who had worked for the Camargue family while they were in Pomfret, said she would have known the voice anywhere. In Ames's presence Mrs Woodhouse had talked to Natalie about Shaddough's Hall Farm where they had lived and Natalie had been able to recall events which Mrs Woodhouse said no impostor could have known.

Wexford wondered why Natalie had not proffered as witnesses for her support her aunt and that old family friend, Philip Cory. It was possible, of course, that in the case of her aunt (if she really was Natalie Arno) the dislike was mutual and that, just as he had feared Mrs Mountnessing would recognize her as her niece to avoid protracting an interview, so Natalie feared to meet her aunt lest animosity should make her refuse that recognition. But Cory she had certainly seen since she returned home, and Cory had so surely believed in her as to cling to her arm in the excess of emotion he had no doubt felt at his old friend's obsequies. Was there some reason she didn't want Cory brought into this?

In the early years of broadcasting Philip Cory had achieved some success by writing incidental music for radio. But this is not the kind of thing which makes a man's name. If Cory had done this at all it was on the strength of his light opera *Aimée*, based on the story of the Empress Josephine's cousin, the French Sultana. After its London season it had been enthusiastically taken up by amateur operatic societies, largely because it was comparatively easy to sing, had a huge cast, and the costumes required for it could double for *Entführung* or even *Aladdin*. This was particularly the case in Cory's own locality, where he was looked upon as something of a pet bard. Driving out to the environs of Myringham where the composer lived, Wexford noted in the villages at least three posters announcing that *Aimée* was to be performed yet again. It was likely then to be a disappointed man he was on his way to see. Local fame is gratifying only at the beginning of a career, and it could not have afforded much solace to Cory to see that his more frivolous work was to be staged by the Myfleet and District Operatic Society (tickets £1.20, licensed bar opens seven-thirty) while his tone poem *April Fire* and his ballet music for the *Flowers of Evil* were forgotten.

Parents can of course (as Wexford knew personally) enjoy success vicariously. Philip Cory might be scarcely remembered outside village-hall audiences, but his son Blaise Cory was a celebrity as only a television personality can be. His twice-weekly show of soul-searching interviews, drumming up support for charities, and professing aid for almost anyone out of a job, a home or a marriage, vied for pride of place with *Runway* in the popularity ratings. The name was as much a household word as Frost or Parkinson; the bland, handsome, rather larger-than-life face instantly familiar.

'But he doesn't live here, does he?' said Burden whose *bête noire* Blaise Cory was.

'Not as far as I know.' Wexford tapped the driver on the shoulder. 'Those are the gates up ahead, I think. On the left.'

It had been necessary to keep an eye out for Moidore Lodge which was in deep country, was three miles from the nearest village and, Cory had told Wexford on the phone, was invisible from the road. The pillars that supported the gates and on which sat a pair of stone wolves or possibly alsatians – they very much resembled Nancy – were, however, unmistakable. The car turned in and, as the drive descended, entered an avenue of plane trees. And very strange and sinister they looked at this season, their trunks and limbs half covered in olive-green bark, half stripped to flesh colour, so that they appeared, or would have appeared to the fanciful, like shivering forms whose nakedness was revealed through rags. At the end of this double row of trees Moidore Lodge, three floors tall, narrow, and painted a curious shade of pale pea-green, glared formidably at visitors.

To ring the front-door bell it was necessary to climb half a dozen steps, though at the top of them there was no covered porch, nothing but a thin railing on each side. The wind blew sharply off the downs. Wexford, accustomed of late, as he remarked to Burden, to moving amongst those in the habit of being waited on, expected to be let in by a man or a maid or at least a cleaning woman, and was surprised when the door was opened by Cory himself.

He was no bigger than the impression of him Wexford had gained from that glimpse outside St Peter's, a little thin old man with copious white hair as silky as floss. Rather than appearing disappointed, he had a face that was both cheerful and peevish. He wore jeans and the kind of heavy navy-blue sweater that is called a guernsey, which gave him a look of youth, or the look perhaps of *a* youth who suffers from some terrible prematurely ageing disease. Before speaking, he looked them up and down closely. Indeed, they had passed through the over-heated, dusty, amazingly untidy and untended hall and were in the over-heated, dusty rubbish heap of a living room before he spoke.

'Do you know,' he said, 'you are the first policemen I've ever actually had in my house. In any house I've ever lived in. Not the first I've ever *spoken* to, of course. I've *spoken* to them to ask the way and so forth. No doubt, I've lived a sheltered life.' Having done his best to make them feel like lepers or untouchables, Cory cracked his face into a nervous smile. 'The idea was distinctly strange to me. I've had to take two tranquillizers. As a matter of fact, my son is coming. I expect you've heard of my son.'

Burden's face was a mask of blankness. Wexford said, Who hadn't? and proceeded to enlighten Cory as to the purpose of their visit. The result of this was that the old man had to take another Valium. It took a further full ten minutes to convince him there was a serious doubt about Natalie Arno's identity.

'Oh dear,' said Cory, 'oh dear, oh dear, how dreadful. Little Natalie. And she was so kind and considerate to me at poor Manuel's memorial service. Who could possibly have imagined she wasn't Natalie at all?'

'Well, she may be,' said Wexford. 'We're hoping you can establish that one way or the other.'

Looking at the distracted little man on whom tranquillizers seemed to have no effect, Wexford couldn't help doubting if the truth could be established through his agency. 'You want me to come with you and ask her a lot of questions? How horribly embarrassing that will be.' Cory actually ran his fingers through his fluffy hair. Then he froze, listening, and looking for all the world like an alerted rabbit. 'A car!' he cried. 'That will be Blaise. And none too soon. I must say, really, he knew what he was about when he insisted on being here to support me.'

If the father was no larger than Wexford had anticipated, the son was much smaller. The screen is a great deceiver when it comes to height. Blaise Cory was a small, wide man with a big face and eyes that twinkled as merrily as those of Santa Claus or a friendly elf. He came expansively into the room, holding out both hands to Wexford.

'And how is Sheila? Away on her honeymoon? Isn't that marvellous?' Forewarned, astute, one who had to make it his business to know who was who, he had done his homework. 'You know, she's awfully like you. I almost think I should have known if I hadn't known, if you see what I mean.'

'They want me to go and look at poor Manuel's girl and tell them if she's really her,' said Cory dolefully.

His son put up his eyebrows, made a soundless whistle. 'You don't mean it? Is *that* what it's about?'

He seemed less surprised than his father or Mrs Mountnessing had been. But perhaps that was only because he daily encountered more surprising things than they did.

'Do you also know her, Mr Cory?' Wexford asked.

'Know her? We took our first violin lessons together. Well, that's an exaggeration. Let me say we, as tots, went to the same master.'

'You didn't keep it up, Blaise,' said Cory senior. 'You were never a *concentrating* boy. Now little Natalie was very good. I remember little Natalie playing so beautifully to me when she was fifteen or sixteen, it was Bach's Chaconne from the D minor Partita and she . . .'

Blaise interrupted him. 'My dear father, it is twelve-thirty, and though I seem to remember promising to take you out to lunch, a drink wouldn't come amiss. With the possible exception of Macbeth, you must be the world's worst host.' He chuckled irrepressibly at his own joke. 'Now surely you have something tucked away in one of these glory holes?'

Once more Cory put his hands through his hair. He began to trot about the room, opening cupboard doors and peering along cluttered shelves as if he were as much a stranger to the house as they were. 'It's because I've no one to look after me,' he said distractedly. 'I asked Natalie – or whoever she is, you know – I asked her if she didn't want those Hickses and if she didn't, would they come and work for me? She was rather non-committal, said she'd ask them, but I haven't heard another word. How do *you* manage?'

Wexford was saved from replying by a triumphant shout from Blaise Cory who had found a bottle of whisky and one of dry sherry. It was now impossible to refuse a drink especially as Blaise Cory, with ferocious twinkles, declared that he knew for a fact policemen did drink on duty. The glasses were dusty and fingermarked, not to be too closely scrutinized. Nothing now remained but to fix a time with Philip Cory for visiting Natalie, and Wexford felt it would be wise, in spite of Burden's prejudice, to invite Blaise too.

'Ah, but I've already seen her. And frankly I wouldn't have the foggiest whether she was the late lamented Sir Manuel's daughter or not, I hadn't set eyes on her since we were teenagers. She said she was Natalie and that was good enough for me.'

'You were also at the memorial service?'

'Oh, no, no, no. Those morbid affairs give me the shivers. I'm a *life* person, Mr Wexford. No, I gave Natalie lunch. Oh, it must have been a good five or six weeks ago.'

'May I ask why you did that, Mr Cory?'

'Does one have to have a reason for taking attractive ladies out to lunch apart from the obvious one? No, I'm teasing you. It was actually Natalie who phoned me, recalled our former acquaintance and asked me if I could get a friend of hers a job, a man, she didn't say his name. I'm afraid it was all rather due to my programme. I don't know if a busy man like you ever has a moment to watch it? A poor thing, but mine own. I do make rather bold claims on it – not, however, without foundation *and* results – to aid people in finding – well, niches for themselves. This chap was apparently some sort of musician. Fancied himself on the box, I daresay. Anyway, I couldn't hold out much hope but I asked her to have lunch with me. Now I come to think of it, it was January 17th. I remember because that was the dear old dad's birthday.'

'I was seventy-four,' said Cory senior in the tone of one intending to astonish nobody, as indeed he had.

'And when you met her that day you had no doubt she was the Natalie Camargue you had once known?'

'Now wait a minute. When it came to it, I didn't meet her that day. She cancelled on account of some medical thing she had to have, a biopsy, I think she said. We made a fresh date for the following Tuesday. She kept that and I must say we had a delightful time, she was absolutely charming, full of fun. I was only sorry to have to say I hadn't anything cooking for this bloke of hers. But, you know, I couldn't actually tell you if she was *our* Natalie. I mean, it obviously never occurred to me.' He let his eyes light on Burden as being closer to his own age than the others. 'Would you recognize a lady you hadn't seen since you were nineteen?'

Burden responded with a cold smile which had no disconcerting effect on Blaise Cory.

'It's all rather thrilling, isn't it? Quite a tonic it must be for the dear old dad.'

'No, it isn't,' said the composer. 'It's very upsetting indeed. I think I'll come back to London with you, Blaise, since I've got to be up there tomorrow. And I think I may stay awhile. I suppose you can put up with me for a couple of weeks?'

Blaise Cory put an arm round his father's shoulders and answered with merry affirmatives. Perhaps it was Wexford's imagination that the twinkle showed signs of strain.

The kind of coincidence that leads to one's coming across a hitherto unknown word three times in the same day or receiving a letter from an acquaintance one has dreamed of the night before was no doubt responsible for the poster in the window of the Kingsbrook Precinct travel agents. *Come to sunny California, land of perpetual spring*. . . . A picture of what might be Big Sur and next to it one of what might be Hearst Castle. Wexford paused and looked at it and wondered what the chief constable would say if he suggested being sent to the Golden West in quest of Natalie Arno's antecedents. He could just imagine Colonel Griswold's face.

Presently he turned away and went back to the police station. He had come from Symonds, O'Brien and Ames. Their handwriting expert had examined the writing of the eighteen-year-old Natalie Camargue and that of the thirty-seven-year-old Natalie Arno and expressed his opinion that, allowing for normal changes over a period of nearly two decades, the two samples had in all probability been made by the same person. Wexford had suggested the samples also be examined by an expert of police choosing. Without making any positive objection, Ames murmured that it would be unwise to spoil the ship with too many cooks.

Wexford thought he saw a better way.

'Mike,' he said, putting his head round the door of Burden's office, 'where can we get hold of a violin?'

10

Burden's wife was something of a paragon. She was a history teacher, she was well-read in English literature, she was an excellent cook and dressmaker and now it appeared she was musical too.

'You never told me Jenny played the violin,' said Wexford.

'As a matter of fact,' said Burden rather shyly, 'she used to be with the Pilgrim String Quartet.' This was a local ensemble that enjoyed a little more than local fame. 'I expect we could borrow her Hills if we were very careful with it.'

'Her *what*?'

'Her Hills. It's a well-known make of violin.'

'If you say so, Stradivarius.'

Burden brought the violin along in the morning. They were going to call for Philip Cory at his son's home and drive him to De Beauvoir Place. It was a bright sunny day, the first since the snow had gone.

Blaise Cory lived on Campden Hill, not far from Mrs Mountnessing, and work seemed to have claimed him, for his father was alone in the big penthouse flat. Although he popped a Valium pill into his mouth as soon as he saw them, a night in London had evidently done him good. He was sprightly, his cheeks pink, and he had dressed himself in a dark suit with a thin red stripe, a pink shirt and a burgundy silk tie, more as if he were going to a smart luncheon party than taking part in a criminal investigation.

In the car he was inclined to be talkative.

'I think I shall write to those Hickses personally. I've no

reason to believe they're not well-disposed towards me. I understand they like the country and the thing about Moidore Lodge is, it's in the real country. Charming as poor Manuel's place is, I always used to think there was something Metroland-ish about it. One might as well be living in Hampstead Garden Suburb. Do you know, I thought it would be quite an ordeal facing little Natalie today, but actually I feel rather excited at the prospect. London is such a stimulus, don't you find? It seems to tone up one's whole system. And if she isn't Natalie, there's nothing to be embarrassed about.'

Wexford had no intention of going into the bookshop. The door to the upstairs flat was at the side of the building, a panelled door with a pane of glass in it, set under a porch with a steep tiled roof. As they walked up the path, Wexford leading and Burden bringing up the rear with the violin, the door opened, a woman came out and it immediately closed again. The woman was elderly and so tiny as to be almost a midget. She wore a black coat and a brightly coloured knitted hat and gloves. Cory said:

'Good gracious me! It's Mrs Woodhouse, isn't it?'

'That's right, sir, and you're Mr Cory.' She spoke with a Sussex burr. 'How have you been keeping? Mustn't grumble, that's what I always say. I see Mr Blaise on the telly last night, he's a real scream, just the same as ever. You living in London now, are you?'

'Oh dear, no,' said Cory. 'Down in the same old place.' His eyes widened suddenly as if with inspiration. 'I haven't anyone to look after me. I don't suppose. . . .'

'I'm retired, sir, and never had so much to do. I don't have a moment for myself let alone other folks, so I'll say bye-bye now and nice to see you after all this time.'

She scuttled off in the direction of De Beauvoir Square, looking at her watch like the White Rabbit as she went.

'Who was that?' said Burden.

'She used to work for poor Manuel and Kathleen when they lived at Shaddough's Hall Farm. I can't think what she's doing up here.'

The door, though closed, had been left on the latch.

Wexford pushed it open and they went up the steep staircase. Natalie had come out on to the landing and was waiting for them at the top. Wexford had thought about her so much, had indeed become so obsessive about her, that since last seeing her he had created an image of her in his mind that was seductive, sinister, Mata Hari-like, corrupt, guileful and serpentine. Before the reality this chimera showed itself briefly for the absurd delusion it was and then dissolved. For here, standing before them, was a charming and pretty woman to whom none of these pejorative expressions could possibly apply. Her black hair hung loose to her shoulders, held back by a velvet Alice band. She wore the skirt Jane Zoffany had been altering and with it a simple white shirt and dark blue cardigan. It was very near a school uniform and there was something of the schoolgirl about her as she brought her face down to Cory's and kissed him, saying with the slightest edge of reproach:

'It's good to see you, Uncle Philip. I only wish the circumstances were different.'

Cory drew his face away. He said in a kind of sharp chirp, 'One must do one's duty as a citizen.'

She laughed at that and patted his shoulder. They all went into a small and unpretentious living room from which a kitchen opened. It was all a far cry from Sterries. The furnishings looked as if they had come down to the Zoffanys from defunct relatives who hadn't paid much for them when they were new. Nothing seemed to have been added by Natalie except a small shelf of paperbacks which could only be designated as non-Zoffany because none of them was science fiction.

There was an aroma of coffee and from the kitchen the sound, suggestive of some large hibernating creature snoring, that a percolator makes.

'Do sit down,' said Natalie, 'Make yourselves at home. Excuse me while I see to the coffee.' She seemed totally carefree and gave no sign of having noticed what Burden had brought into the flat. There's no art, thought Wexford, to find the mind's construction in the face.

The coffee, when it came, was good. 'The secret', said

Natalie gaily, 'is to put enough in.' Uttering this cliché, she laughed. 'I'm afraid the British don't do that.'

She surely couldn't be enjoying herself like this if she was not Natalie, if there was any chance of her failing the test ahead of her. He glanced at Burden whose eyes were on her, who seemed to be studying her appearance and was recalling perhaps newspaper photographs or actual glimpses of Camargue. Having taken a sip of his coffee into which he ladled three spoonfuls of sugar, Cory started at once on his questioning. He would have made a good quizmaster. Perhaps it was from him that Blaise had inherited his talents.

'You and your parents went to live at Shaddough's Hall Farm when you were five. Can you remember what I gave you for your sixth birthday?'

She didn't hesitate. 'A kitten. It was a grey one, a British Blue.'

'Your cat had been run over and I gave you that one to replace it.'

'We called it Panther.'

Cory had forgotten that. But Wexford could see that now he remembered and was shaken. He asked less confidently: 'Where was the house?'

'On the Pomfret to Cheriton road. You'll have to do better than that, Uncle Philip. Anyone could have found out where Camargue lived.'

For answer he threw a question at her in French. Wexford wasn't up to understanding it but he gave Cory full marks for ingenuity. There was more to this old man that at first met the eye. She answered in fluent French and Cory addressed her in what Wexford took to be Spanish. This was something he was sure Symonds, O'Brien and Ames had not thought of. But what a sound test it was. Momentarily he held his breath, for she was not answering, her face had that puzzled foolish look people have when spoken to in a language they know less thoroughly than they have claimed.

Cory repeated what he had said. Burden cleared his throat and moved a little in his chair. Wexford held himself perfectly still, waiting, knowing that every second which passed made it more and more likely that she had been discovered and exposed. And then, as Cory was about to speak for the third time, she broke into a flood of fast Spanish so that Cory himself was taken aback, uncomprehending apparently, until she explained more slowly what it was that she had said.

Wexford drank his coffee and she, looking at him mischievously, refilled his cup. On Burden she bestowed one of her sparkling smiles. Her long hair fell forward, Cleopatra-like, in two heavy tresses to frame her face. It was a young face, Wexford thought, even possibly too young for the age she professed to be. And wasn't it also *too Spanish*? Natalie Camargue's mother had been English, typically English, her father half-French. Would their daughter look quite so much like one of Goya's women? None of the evidence, convincing though it was, was as yet conclusive. Why shouldn't an imposter speak Spanish? If the substitution had taken place in Los Angeles she might even be Mexican. Why not know about the kitten and its name if she had been a friend of the true Natalie and had set out to absorb her childhood history?

'What was the first instrument you learned to play?' Cory was asking.

'The recorder.'

'How old were you when you began the violin?'

'Eight.'

'Who was your first master?'

'I can't remember,' she said.

'When you were fifteen you were living at Shaddough's Hall Farm and you were on holiday from school. It was August. Your father had just come back from a tour of – America, I think.'

'Canada.'

'I do believe you're right.' Cory, having been determined almost from Wexford's first words on the subject to consider her an impostor, grew more and more astonished as the interrogation went on. 'You're right, it was. God bless my soul. Do you remember my coming to dinner with your parents? I and my wife? Can you remember that evening?'

'I think so. I hadn't seen you for about a year.'

'Before dinner I asked you to play something for me and you did and . . .'

She didn't even allow him to finish.

'I played Bach's Chaconne from the D minor Partita.'

Cory was stunned into silence. He stared at her and then turned on Wexford an affronted look.

'It was too difficult for me,' she said lightly. 'You clapped but I felt I'd made a mess of it.' The expressions on the three men's faces afforded her an amused satisfaction. 'That's proof enough, isn't it? Shall we all have a drink to celebrate my reinstatement?' She jumped up, took the tray and went into the kitchen, leaving the door open.

It was perhaps this open door and the sound of their hostess humming lightheartedly that stopped Cory from rounding on Wexford. Instead he raised his whiskery white eyebrows almost into his fluffy white hair and shook his head vigorously, a gesture that plainly said he felt he had been brought here on a wild-goose chase. If she wasn't Natalie, Wexford thought, there was no way she could have known about that piece of music. It was impossible to imagine circumstances in which the true Natalie would have spoken of such a thing to the false. If she had done so it would presuppose her having recounted every occasion on which she had played to a friend, listing every friend and every piece of music, since it could never have been foreseen that this particular piece would be inquired about. That Cory would ask this question, a question that had no doubt come into his mind because of his reference to the Bach Chaconne on the previous day, could only have been guessed at by those who had been present at the time, himself, Burden and Blaise.

So one could almost agree with her and acclaim her reinstated as Camargue's heir. She had passed the test no impostor could have passed. He looked at her wonderingly as she returned to the room, the contents of the tray now exchanged for a couple of bottles and an ice bucket. If she was, as she now seemed undoubtedly to be, Natalie Arno, how had Camargue possibly been deceived in the matter? This woman would never have mispronounced a word or a name in a foreign language known to her. And if Camargue had indeed accused her of doing so, it had been in her power to correct that misapprehension at once and to furnish him with absolute proof of who she was. For now Wexford had no doubt that if Camargue had asked her she would have recalled for him the minutest details of her infancy, of the family, of esoteric domestic customs which no one living but he and she could have known. But Camargue had been an old man, wandering in his wits as well as short-sighted and growing deaf. That tiresome woman Dinah Sternhold had wasted their time, repeating to him what was probably only one amongst several of a dotard's paranoid delusions.

Burden looked as if he was ready to leave. He had reached down to grasp once more the handle of the violin case.

'Would you play that piece of music for us now, Mrs Arno?' Wexford said.

If she had noticed the violin, as she surely must have done, she had presumably supposed it the property of Cory and unconnected with herself, for with his question her manner changed. She had put the tray down and had been about to lift her hands from it, but her hands remained where they were and slightly stiffened. Her face was unaltered, but she was no longer quite in command of the situation and she was no longer amused.

'No, I don't think I would,' she said.

'You've given up the violin?'

'No, I still play in an amateurish sort of way, but I'm out of practice.'

'We'll make allowances, Mrs Arno,' said Wexford. 'The inspector and I aren't competent to judge, anyway.' Burden gave him a look implying that *he* might be. 'If you'll play the violin so as to satisfy Mr Cory I will myself be satisfied that Sir Manuel had – made a mistake.'

She was silent. She sat still, looking down, considering. Then she put out her hand for the violin case and drew it towards her. But she seemed not quite to know how to open it, for she fumbled with the catch.

'Here, let me,' said Burden.

She got up and looked at the tray she had brought it. 'I forgot the glasses. Excuse me.'

Burden lifted out the violin carefully, then the bow. The sight of it restored Cory's temper and he touched one of the strings lightly with his finger. From the kitchen came a sudden tinkle of breaking glass, an exclamation, then a sound of water running.

'You may as well put that instrument away again,' said Wexford quietly.

She came in and her face was white. 'I broke a glass.' Wrapped round her left hand was a bunch of wet tissues, rapidly reddening, and as she scooped the sodden mass away, Wexford saw a long thin cut, bright red across three fingertips.

11

It should have been the beginning, not the end. They should have been able to proceed with a prosecution for deception and an investigation of the murder of Sir Manuel Camargue. And Wexford, calling on Symonds, O'Brien and Ames with what he thought to be proof that Natalie Arno was not who she said she was, felt confident he had a case. She might speak French and Spanish, she might know the most abstruse details about the Camargues' family life, but she couldn't play the violin and that was the crux. She had not dared to refuse so she had deliberately cut her fingers on the tips where they must press the strings. Kenneth Ames listened to all this with a vagueness bordering on indifference which would have alarmed Wexford if he hadn't been used to the man's manner. He seemed reluctant to disclose the address of Mrs Mary Woodhouse but finally did so when pressed.

She lived with her son and daughter-in-law, both of whom were out at work, in a council flat on the Pomfret housing estate. While Wexford talked to her, explaining gently but at some length what he suspected, she at first sat still and attentive, but when the purpose of his visit became clear to her, she pushed her brows together and stuck out her underlip and picked up the work on which she had been engaged before he arrived. This was some sort of bed cover, vast in size, of dead-white cotton crochet work. Mrs Woodhouse's crochet hook flashed in and out as she expended her anger through her fingers.

'I don't know what you're talking about, I don't know what you mean.' She repeated these sentences over and over whenever he paused for a reply. She was a small, sharp-featured old woman whose dark hair had faded to charcoal colour. 'I went to see Mrs Arno because she asked me. Why shouldn't I? I've got a sister living in Hackney that's been a bit off-colour. I've been stopping with her and what with Mrs Arno living like only a stone's throw away, it's only natural I'd go and see her, isn't it? I've known her since she was a kiddy, it was me brought her up as much as her mother.'

'How many times have you seen her, Mrs Woodhouse?'

'I don't know what you mean. Hundreds of times, thousands of times. If you mean been to her place like this past week, just the twice. The time you saw me and two days previous. I'd like to know what you're getting at.'

'Were some of those "hundreds of times" last November and December, Mrs Woodhouse? Did Mrs Arno go and see you when she first arrived in this country?'

'I'll tell you when I first saw her. Two weeks back. When that solicitor, that Mr Ames, come here and asked me the same sort of nonsense you're asking me. Only he knew when he was beaten.' The crochet hook jerked faster and the ball of yarn bounced on Mary Woodhouse's lap. 'Had I any doubt Mrs Arno was Miss Natalie Camargue?' She put a wealth of scorn into her voice. 'Of course I hadn't, not a shadow of doubt.'

'I expect Mrs Arno asked you a great many questions, didn't she? I expect she asked you to remind her of things in her childhood which had slipped her mind. The name of a grey kitten, for instance?'

'Panther,' said Mrs Woodhouse. 'That was his name. Why shouldn't I tell her? She'd forgotten, she was only a kiddy. I don't know what you mean, asking me things like that. Of course I've got a good memory, I was famous in the family for my memory. Mr Camargue – he was Mr Camargue then – he used to say, Mary, you're just like an elephant, and people'd look at me, me being so little and thin, and he'd say, You never forget a thing.'

'I expect you understand what conspiracy is, don't you, Mrs Woodhouse? You understand what is meant by a conspiracy to defraud someone of what is theirs by right of law? I don't think you would want to be involved in something of that kind, would you? Something which could get you into very serious trouble?'

She repeated her formula fiercely, one hand clutching the crochet hook, the other the ball of yarn. 'I don't know what you mean. I don't know what you're talking about.'

Mavis Rolland, the music teacher, was next on his list to be seen. He had the phone in his hand, he was about to dial the school number and arrange an appointment with her when Kenneth Ames was announced.

It was as warm in Wexford's office as it was in the Kingsbrook Precinct, but Ames removed neither his black, waisted overcoat nor his black-and-grey check worsted scarf. He took the chair Wexford offered him and fixed his eyes on the northern aspect of St Peter's spire just as he was in the habit of contemplating its southern elevation from his own window.

The purpose of his call, he said, was to inform the police that Symonds, O'Brien and Ames had decided to recognize Mrs Natalie Kathleen Camargue Arno as Sir Manuel Camargue's rightful heir.

In fact, said Ames, it was only their regard for truth and their horror of the possibility of fraud that had led them to investigate in the first place what amounted to malicious slander.

'We were obliged to look into it, of course, though it never does to place too much credence on that kind of mischief-making.'

'Camargue himself. . . . ' Wexford began.

'My dear chap, according to Mrs Steinbeck, according to *her*. I'm afraid you've been a bit led up the garden. Lost your sense of proportion too, if I may say so. Come now. You surely can't have expected my client to play you a pretty tune on that fiddle when she'd got a nasty cut on her hand.'

Wexford noted that Natalie Arno had become 'my

client'. He was more surprised than he thought he could be by Ames's statement, he was shocked, and he sat in silence, digesting it, beginning to grasp its implications. Still staring skywards, Ames said chattily:

'There was never any real doubt, of course.' He delivered one of his strange confused metaphors. 'It was a case of making a mare's nest out of a molehill. But we do now have incontrovertible proof.'

'Oh yes?' Wexford's eyebrows went up.

'My client was able to produce her dentist, chappie who used to see to the Camargue family's teeth. Man called Williams from London, Wigmore Street, in point of fact. He'd still got his records and – well, my client's jaw and Miss Natalie Camargue's are indisputably one and the same. She hasn't even lost a tooth.'

Wexford made his appointment with Miss Rolland but was obliged to cancel it next day. For in the interim he had an unpleasant interview with the chief constable. Charles Griswold, with his uncanny resemblance to the late General de Gaulle, as heavily built, grave and intense a man as Ames was slight, shallow and *distrait*, stormed in upon him on the following morning.

'Leave it, Reg, forget it. Let it be as if you had never heard the name Camargue.'

'Because an impostor has seduced Ames into believing a pack of lies, sir?'

'*Seduced*?'

Wexford made an impatient gesture with his hand. 'I was speaking metaphorically, of course. *She is not Natalie Arno*. My firm belief is that ever since she came here she's been employing a former servant of the Camargue family to instruct her in matters of family history. As for the dentist, did Symonds, O'Brien and Ames check on him? Did they go to him or did he come to them? If this is a conspiracy in which a considerable number of people are involved. . . . '

'You know I haven't the least idea what you're talking about, don't you? All I'm saying is, if a reputable firm of solicitors such as Symonds, O'Brien and Ames will accept this woman and permit her to inherit a very significant property, we will accept her too. And we'll forget way-out notions of pushing old men into frozen lakes when we have not a shred of evidence that Camargue died anything but a natural death. Is that understood?'

'If you say so, it must be, sir.'

'It must,' said the chief constable.

Not the beginning but the end. Wexford had become obsessional about cases before, and the path these obsessions took had been blocked by just such obstacles and opposition. The feeling of frustration was a familiar one to him but it was none the less bitter for that. He stood by the window, cursing under his breath, gazing at the opaque pale sky. The weather had become raw and icy again, a white mist lifting only at midday and then hanging threateningly at tree height. Sheila was coming back today. He couldn't remember whether she was due in at ten in the morning or ten at night and he didn't want to know. That way he couldn't worry too precisely about what was happening to her aircraft in the fog, unable to land maybe, sent off to try Luton or Manchester, running short of fuel. . . . He told himself sternly, reminded himself, that air transport was the safest of all forms of travel, and let his thoughts turn back to Natalie Arno. Or whoever. Was he never to know now? Even if it were only for the satisfaction of his own curiosity, was he never to know who she was and how she had done it? The switch from one identity to another, the impersonation, the murder. . . .

After what Griswold had said, he dare not, for his very job's sake, risk another interview with Mary Woodhouse, keep his appointment with Mavis Rolland, attempt to break down the obduracy of Mrs Mountnessing or set about exposing that fake dentist, Williams. What could he do?

The way home had necessarily to be via the Kingsbrook Precinct, for Dora had asked him to pick up a brace of pheasants ordered at the poulterers there. Proximity to the premises of Symonds, O'Brien and Ames angered him afresh, and he wished he might for a split moment become a delinquent teenager in order to daub appropriate graffiti on their brass plate. Turning from it, he found himself looking once more into the window of the travel agents.

A helpful young man spread a handful of brochures in front of him. What had been Dora's favourites? Bermuda, Mexico, anywhere warm in the United States. They had discussed it endlessly without coming to a decision, knowing this might be the only holiday of such magnitude they would ever have. The poster he had seen in the window had its twin and various highly coloured siblings inside. He glanced up and it was the skyscraper-scape of San Francisco that met his eyes.

The fog had thickened while he was in there. It seemed to lay a cold wet finger on the skin of his face. He drove home very slowly, thinking once more about Sheila, but as he put his key into the front door lock the door was pulled open and there she was before him, browner than he had ever seen her, her hair bleached pale as ivory.

She put out her arms and hugged him. Dora and Andrew were in the living room.

'Heathrow's closed and we had to land at Gatwick,' said Sheila, 'so we thought we'd come and see you on our way. We've had such a fabulous time, Pop, I've been telling Mother, you just have to go.'

Wexford laughed. 'We are going to California,' he said.

Part Two

12

The will, published in the *Kingsmarkham Courier*, as well as in the national press, showed Sir Manuel Camargue to have left the sum of £1,146,000 net. This modest fortune became Natalie Arno's a little more than two months after Camargue's death.

'I shouldn't call a million pounds modest,' said Burden.

'It is when you consider all the people who will want their pickings,' Wexford said. 'All the conspirators. No wonder she's put the house up for sale.'

She had moved into Sterries, but immediately put the house on the market, the asking price being £110,000. For some weeks Kingsmarkham's principal estate agents, Thacker, Prince and Co., displayed in their window coloured photographs of its exterior, the music room, the drawing room and the garden, while less distinguishable shots of it appeared in the local press. But whether the house itself was too stark and simplistic in design for most people's taste or whether the price was too high, the fact was that it remained on sale throughout that period of the year when house-buying is at its peak.

'Funny to think that we know for sure she's no business to be there and no right to sell it and no right to what she gets for it,' said Burden, 'and there's not a damn thing we can do about it.'

But Wexford merely remarked that summer had set in with its usual severity and that he was looking forward to going somewhere warm for his holiday.

The Wexfords were not seasoned travellers and this would be the farthest away from home either had ever been. Wexford felt this need not affect the preparations they must make, but Dora had reached a point just below the panic threshold. All day she had been packing and unpacking and re-packing, confessing shamefacedly that she was a fool and then beginning to worry about the possibility of the house being broken into while they were away. It was useless for Wexford to point out that whether they were known to be in San Francisco or Southend would make little difference to a prospective burglar. He could only assure her that the police would keep an eye on the house. If they couldn't do that for him, whom could they do it for? Sylvia had promised to go into the house every other day in their absence and he set off that evening to give her a spare key.

Wexford's elder daughter and her husband had in the past year moved to a newer house in north Kingsmarkham, and it was only a slightly longer way round to return from their home to his own by taking Ploughman's Lane. To go and look at the house Camargue had built, and on the night before he set out to prove Natalie Arno's claim to it fraudulent, seemed a fitting act. He drove into Ploughman's Lane by way of the side road which skirted the grounds of Kingsfield House. But if Sterries had been almost invisible from the roadway in January and February, it was now entirely hidden. The screen of hornbeams, limes and planes that had been skeletons when last he was there, were in full leaf and might have concealed an empty meadow rather than a house for all that could be seen of it.

It was still light at nearly nine. He was driving down the hill when he heard the sound of running feet behind him. In his rear mirror he saw a flying figure, a woman who was running down Ploughman's Lane as if pursued. It was Jane Zoffany.

There were no pursuers. Apart from her, the place was deserted, sylvan, silent, as such places mostly are even on summer nights. He pulled into the kerb and got out. She was enough in command of herself to swerve to avoid him but as she did so she saw who it was and immediately recognized him. She stopped and burst into tears, crying where she stood and pushing her knuckles into her eyes.

'Come and sit in the car,' said Wexford.

She sat in the passenger seat and cried into her hands, into the thin gauzy scarf which she wore swathed round her neck over a red and yellow printed dress of Indian make. Wexford gave her his handkerchief. She cried some more and laid her head back against the headrest, gulping, the tears running down her face. She had no handbag, no coat or jacket, though the dress was sleeveless, and on her stocklingless feet were Indian sandals with only a thong to attach them. Suddenly she began to speak, pausing only when sobs choked her voice.

'I thought she was wonderful. I thought he was the most wonderful, charming, gifted, *kind* person I'd ever met. And I thought she liked me, I thought she actually wanted my company. I never thought she'd really noticed my husband much, I mean except as my husband, that's all I thought he was to her, I thought it was *me*. . . . And now he says . . . oh God, what am I going to do? Where shall I go? What's going to become of me?'

Wexford was nonplussed. He could make little sense of what she said but guessed she was spilling all this misery out on to him only because he was there. Anyone willing to listen would have served her purpose. He thought too, and not for the first time, that there was something unhinged about her. You could see disturbance in her eyes as much when they were dry as when they were swollen and wet with tears. She put her hand on his arm.

'I did everything for her, I bent over backwards to make her feel at home, I ran errands for her, I even mended her clothes. She took all that from me and all the time she and Ivan had been – when he went out to California they had a relationship!'

He neither winced nor smiled at the incongruous word, relic of the already outdated jargon of her youth. 'Did she tell you that, Mrs Zoffany?' he asked gently.

'He told me. Ivan told me.' She wiped her face with the handkerchief. 'We came down here on Wednesday to stay, we meant to stay till – oh, Sunday or Monday. The shop's a dead loss anyway, no one ever comes in, it makes no difference whether we're there or not. She invited us and we came. I know why she did now. She doesn't want him but she wants him in love with her, she wants him on a string.' She shuddered and her voice broke again. 'He told me this evening, just now, half an hour ago. He said he'd been in love with her for two years, ever since he first saw her. He was longing for her to come and live here so that they could be together and then when she did come she kept fobbing him off and telling him to wait and now . . .'

'Why did he tell you all this?' Wexford interrupted.

She gulped, put out a helpless hand. 'He had to tell someone, he said, and there was no one but me. He overheard her talking to someone on the phone like he was her lover, telling him to come down once we'd gone but to be discreet. Ivan understood then. He's broken-hearted because she doesn't want him. He told his own wife that, that he doesn't know how he can go on living because another woman won't have him. I couldn't take it in at first, I couldn't believe it, than I started screaming. She came into our room and said what was the matter? I told her what he'd said and she said, "I'm sorry, darling, but I didn't know you then". She said that to *me*. "I didn't know you then," she said, "and it wasn't anything important anyway. It only happened three or four times, it was just that we were both lonely." As if that made it better!'

Wexford was silent. She was calmer now, though trembling. Soon she would begin regretting that she had poured out her heart to someone who was almost a stranger. She passed her hands over her face and dropped her shoulders with a long heavy sigh.

'Oh God. What am I going to do? Where shall I go? I can't stay with him, can I? When she said that to me I ran out of the house, I didn't even take my bag, I just ran and you were there and – oh God, I don't know what you must think of me talking to you like this. You must think I'm out of my head, crazy, mad. Ivan says I'm mad, "If you're going to carry on like that," he said, "a psychiatric ward's the best place for you." ' She gave him a sideways look. 'I've been in those places, that's why he said that. If only I had a friend I could go to but I've lost all my friends, in and out of hospital the way I've been. People don't want to know you any more when they think you've got something wrong with your mind. In my case it's only depression, it's a disease like any other, but they don't realize.' She gave a little whimpering cry. 'Natalie wasn't like that, she knew about my depression, she was *kind*. I thought she was, but all the time. . . . I've lost my only friend as well as my husband!'

Her mouth worked unsteadily from crying, her eyes were red. She looked like a hunted gypsy, the greying bushy hair hanging in shaggy bundles against her cheeks. And it was plain from her expression and her fixed imploring eyes that, because of his profession and his manner and his having caught her the way he had, she expected him to do something for her. Wreak vengeance on Natalie Arno, restore an errant husband or at least provide some dignified shelter for the night.

She began to speak rapidly, almost feverishly. 'I can't go back there, I can't face it. Ivan's going home, he said so, he said he'd go home tonight, but I can't be with him, I can't be alone with him, I couldn't bear it. I've got my sister in Wellridge but she won't want me, she's like the rest of them. . . . There must be somewhere I could go, you must know somewhere, if you could only. . . .'

There flashed into Wexford's mind the idea that he could take her home with him and get Dora to give her a bed for the night. The sheer nuisance this would be stopped him. They were going on holiday tomorrow, their flight went at one p.m, which meant leaving Kingsmarkham for Heathrow at ten. Suppose she refused to leave? Suppose Zoffany arrived? It just wasn't on.

She was still talking non-stop. 'So if I could possibly be with you there are lots of things I'd like to tell you. I feel if I could only get them off my chest I'd be that much better and they'd help you, they're things you'd want to know.'

'About Mrs Arno?' he said sharply.

'Well, not exactly about her, about *me*. I need someone to listen and be sympathetic, that does you more good than all the therapy and pills in the world, I can tell you. I can't be alone, don't you understand?'

Later he was to castigate himself for not giving in to that first generous impulse. If he had done he might have known the true facts that night and, more important, a life might have been saved. But as much as the unwillingness to be involved and to create trouble for himself, a feeling of caution prevented him. He was a policeman, the woman was a little mad. . . .

'The best thing will be for me to drive you back up the hill to Sterries, Mrs Zoffany. Let me. . . .'

'No!'

'You'll very probably find your husband is ready to leave and waiting for you. You and he would still be in time to catch the last train to Victoria. Mrs Zoffany, you have to realize he'll get over this, it's something that will very likely lose its force now he's brought it into the open. Why not try to . . .?'

'No!'

'Come, let me take you back.'

For answer, she gathered up her skirts and draperies and half jumped, half tumbled out of the car. In some consternation, Wexford too got out to help her, but she had got to her feet and as he put out his arm she threw something at him, a crumpled ball. It was his handkerchief.

She stood for a little while a few yards from him, leaning against the high jasmine-hung wall of one of these sprawling gardens. She hung her head, her hands up to her chin, like a child who has been scolded. It was deep dusk now and growing cool. Suddenly she began to walk back the way she had come. She walked quite briskly up the hill, up over the crown of the hill, to be lost amid the soft, hanging, darkening green branches.

He waited a while, he hardly knew what for. A car passed him just as he started his own, going rather fast down the hill. It was a mustard-coloured Opel, and although it was much too dark to see at all clearly, the woman at the wheel looked very much like Natalie Arno. It was a measure, of course, of how much she occupied his thoughts.

He drove home to Dora who had packed for the last time and was watching Blaise Cory's programme on the television.

13

Wexford was driving on the wrong side of the road. Or that was how he put it to himself. It wasn't as bad as he had expected, the San Diego Freeway had so many lanes and traffic moved at a slower pace than at home. What was alarming and didn't seem to get any better was that he couldn't judge the space he had on the right-hand side so that Dora exclaimed, 'Oh, Reg, you were only about an inch from that car. I was sure you were going to scrape!'

The sky was a smooth hazy blue and it was very hot. Nine hours' flying had taken its toll of both of them. Stopped at the lights – traffic lights hung somewhere up in the sky here – Wexford glanced at his wife. She looked tired, she was bound to, but excited as well. For him it wasn't going to be much of a holiday, unless you agreed with those who say that a change is as good as a rest, and he was beginning to feel guilty about the amount of time he would have to spend apart from her. He had tried to explain that if it wasn't for this quest of his they wouldn't be coming here at all, and she had taken it with cheerful resignation. But did she understand quite what he meant? It was all very well her saying she was going to look up those long-lost friends of hers, the Newtons. Wexford thought he knew just how much they would do for a visitor, an invitation to dinner was what that would amount to.

He had just got used to the road, was even beginning to enjoy driving the little red automatic Chevette he had rented at the airport, when the palms of Santa Monica were before them and they were on Ocean Drive. He had promised Dora two days here, staying in luxury at the Miramar, before they set off for wherever his investigations might lead them.

Where was he going to begin? He had one meagre piece of information to go on. Ames had given it to him back in February and it was Natalie Arno's address in Los Angeles. The magnitude of his task was suddenly apparent as, once they had checked in and Dora had lain down in their room to sleep, he stood under the eucalyptus trees, looking at the Pacific. Everything seemed so big, a bigger sea, a bigger beach, a vaster sky than he had ever seen before. And as their plane had come in to land he had looked down and been daunted by the size of the sprawling, glittering, metallic-looking city spread out there below them. The secret of Natalie Arno had appeared enormous in Kingsmarkham; here in Los Angeles it was surely capable of hiding itself and becoming for ever lost in one of a hundred million crannies.

But one of these crannies he would explore in the morning. Tuscarora Avenue, where Natalie had lived for eight years after coming south from San Francisco, Tuscarora Avenue in a suburb called Opuntia. The fancy names suggested to Wexford that he might expect a certain slumminess, for at home Vale Road would be the site of residential elegance and Valhalla Grove of squalor.

The shops were still open. He walked up Wilshire Boulevard and bought himself a larger and more detailed street plan of Los Angeles than the car hire company had provided.

The next morning when he went out Dora was preparing to phone Rex and Nonie Newton. A year or two before she met Wexford Dora had been engaged to Rex Newton; a boy-and-girl affair it had been, they were both in their teens, and Rex had been supplanted by the young policeman. Married for thirty years now, Rex had retired early and emigrated with his American wife to California. Wexford hoped wistfully that they would be welcoming to Dora, that Nonie Newton would live up to the promises she had made in her last letter. But he could only hope for the best.

By ten he was on his way to Opuntia.

The names had misled him. Everything here had an exotic name, the grand and tawdry alike. Opuntia wasn't shabby but paintbox bright with houses like Swiss chalets or miniature French chateaux set in garden plots as lush as jungles. He had previously only seen such flowers in florist's shops or the hothouses of public gardens, oleanders, bougainvilleas, the orange-and-blue bird-of-paradise flower, emblem of the City of the Angels. No wind stirred the fronds of the fan palms. The sky was blue, but white with smog at the horizon.

Tuscarora Avenue was packed so tightly with cars that two drivers could hardly pass each other. Wexford despaired of finding a niche for the Chevette up there, so he left it at the foot of the hill and walked. Though there were side streets called Mar Vista and Oceania Way, the sea wasn't visible, being blocked from view by huge apartment buildings which raised their penthouse tops out of a forest of palm and eucalyptus. 1121 Tuscarora, where Natalie Arno had lived, was a small squat house of pink stucco. It and its neighbours, a chocolate-coloured mini-castle and a baby hacienda painted lemon, reminded Wexford of the confections on the sweets trolley at the Miramar the previous night. He hesitated for a moment, imagining Natalie there, the light and the primary colours suiting her better than the pallor and chill of Kingsmarkham, and then he went up to the door of the nearest neighbour, the chocolate-fudge-iced 1123.

A man in shorts and a tee-shirt answered his ring. Wexford, who had no official standing in California, who had no right to be asking questions, had already decided to represent himself as on a quest for a lost relative. Though he had never before been to America, he knew enough of Americans to be pretty sure that this kind of thing, which might at home be received with suspicion, embarrassment and taciturnity, would here be greeted with warmth.

The householder, whose shirt campaigned in red printed letters for the Equal Rights Amendment, said he was called Leo Dobrowski and seemed to justify Wexford's belief. He asked him in, explained that his wife and children had gone to church, and within a few minutes Wexford found himself drinking coffee with Mr Dobrowski on a patio hung with the prussian-blue trumpets of morning glory.

But in pretending to a family connection with Tina Zoffany he had made a mistake. Leo Dobrowski knew all about Tina Zoffany and scarcely anything about Natalie Arno or any other occupants of 1121 Tuscarora. Hadn't Tina, in the two years she had lived next door, become Mrs Dobrowski's closest friend? It was a pleasure, though a melancholy one, for Mr Dobrowski at last to be able to talk about Tina to someone who *cared*. Her brother, he thought, had never cared, though he hoped he wasn't speaking out of turn in saying so. If Wexford was Tina's uncle, he would know what a sweet lovely person she had been and what a tragedy her early death was. Mrs Dobrowski herself had been made sick by the shock of it. If Wexford would care to wait until she came back from church he knew his wife had some lovely snapshots of Tina and could probably let him have some small keepsake of Tina's. Her brother had brought all her little odds and ends to them, wouldn't want the expense of sending them home, you could understand that.

'You sure picked the right place when you came to us,' said Mr Dobrowski. 'I guess there's not another family on Tuscarora knew Tina like we did. You have ESP or something?'

After that Wexford could scarcely refuse to meet the church-going wife. He promised to come back an hour later. Mr Dobrowski beamed his pleasure and the words on his tee-shirt – 'Equality of rights under the law shall not be denied or abridged by the United States or any state on account of sex' – expanded with his well-exercised muscles.

The occupants of 1125 – this time Wexford was a cousin of Natalie's and no nonsense about it – were new to the district and so were those who lived further down the hill in a redwood-and-stucco version of Anne Hathaway's cottage. He went to 1121 itself and picked up from the man he spoke to his first piece of real information, that the house had not been bought but was rented from Mrs Arno. Who was there in the neighbourhood, Wexford asked him, who might have known Mrs Arno when she lived here? Try 1122 on the opposite side, he was advised. In an ever-changing population, the people at 1122, the Romeros, had been in residence longest.

Natalie's cousin once more, he tried at 1122.

'You English?' said Mrs Donna Romero, a woman who looked even more Spanish than Natalie and whose jet-black hair was wound on to pink plastic rollers.

Wexford nodded.

'Natalie's English. She went home to her folks in London. That's all I know. Right now she's somewhere in London, England.'

'How long have you been living here?'

'I just love your accent,' said Mrs Romero. 'How long have we been here? I guess it'd be four years, right? We came the summer Natalie went on that long vacation up the coast. Must've been the summer of '76. I guess I just thought the house was empty, no one living there, you know, you get a lot of that round here, and then one day my husband says to me, there's folks moved into 1121, and that was Natalie.'

'But she'd lived there before?'

'Oh, sure she lived there before but we didn't, did we?' Donna Romero said this triumphantly as if she had somehow caught him out. 'She had these roomers, you know? There was this guy she had, he was living here illegally. Well, I guess everyone knew it, but my husband being in the Police Department – well, he had to do what he had to do, you know?'

'You mean he had him deported?'

'That's what I mean.'

Wexford decided he had better make himself scarce before an encounter threatened with the policeman husband. He contented himself with merely asking when this deportation had taken place. Not so long ago, said Mrs Romero, maybe only last fall, as far as she could remember.

It was now noon and growing fiercely hot. Wexford

reflected that whoever it was who had first described the climate of California as perpetual spring hadn't had much experience of an English April. He went back across the road.

The presence on the drive of 1123 of a four-year-old manoeuvring a yellow and red truck and a six-year-old riding a blue bicycle told him Mrs Dobrowski was back. She greeted him so enthusiastically and with such glistening if not quite tearful eyes that he felt a thrust of guilt when he thought of her conferring later with the man at 1121 and with Patrolman (Lieutenant? Captain?) Romero. But it was too late now to abandon the role of Tina's uncle. He was obliged to listen to a catalogue of Tina's virtues while Mrs Dobrowski, small and earnest and wearing a tee-shirt campaigning for the conservation of the sea otter, pressed Tina souvenirs on him, a brooch, a pair of antique nail scissors, and a curious object she said was a purse ashtray.

At last he succeeded in leading the conversation to Natalie by saying with perfect truth that he had seen her in London before he left. It was immediately clear that Mrs Dobrowski hadn't approved of Natalie. Her way of life had not been what Mrs Dobrowski was used to or expected from people in a nice neighbourhood. Turning a little pink, she said she came from a family of Baptists, and when you had children you had standards to maintain. Clearly she felt that she had said enough on the subject and reverted to Tina, her prowess as what she called a stenographer, the sad fact of her childlessness, the swift onset of the disease which had killed her. Wexford made a second effort.

'I've often wondered how Tina came to live here.'

'I guess Natalie needed the money after Rolf Ilbert moved out. Johnny was the one who told Tina Natalie had a room for rent.'

Wexford made a guess. 'Johnny was Natalie's – er, friend?'

Mrs Dobrowski gave him a grim smile. 'I've heard it called that. Johnny Fassbender was her lover.'

The name sounded German but here might not be. When Wexford asked if he were a local man Mrs Dobrowski said no, he was Swiss. She had often told Tina that one of them should report him to the authorities for living here without a residence permit, and eventually someone must have done so, for he was discovered and deported.

'That would have been last autumn,' Wexford said.

'Oh, no. Whatever gave you that idea? It was all of three years ago. Tina was still alive.'

There was evidently a mystery here, but not perhaps one of pressing importance. It was Natalie's identity he was primarily concerned with, not her friendships. But Mrs Dobrowski seemed to feel that she had digressed too far for politeness and moved rapidly on to her visitor's precise relationship to Tina. Was he her true uncle or uncle only by marriage? Strangely, Tina had never mentioned him. But she had mentioned no one but the brother who came over when she died. She, Mrs Dobrowski, would have liked Ivan to have stayed at her house while he was in Los Angeles but hadn't known how to broach this as she had hardly exchanged a word with Natalie all the years they had lived there. Wexford pricked up his ears at that. No, it was true, she had never set foot inside 1121 or seen Natalie closer than across the yard.

Wexford noted that what she called the yard was, by Kingsmarkham standards, a large garden, dense with oleanders, peach trees and tall cacti. In order not to offend Mrs Dobrowski, he was obliged to carry off with him the brooch as a keepsake. Perhaps he could pass it on to the Zoffanys.

'It's been great meeting you,' said Mrs Dobrowski. 'I guess I can see a kind of look of Tina about you now. Around the eyes.' She gathered the four-year-old up in her arms and waved to Wexford from the porch. 'Say hello to Ivan for me.'

In the heat of the day he drove back to the Miramar and took Dora out to lunch in a seafood restaurant down by the boardwalk. He hardly knew how to tell her he was going to have to leave her alone for the afternoon as well. But he did tell her and she bore it well, only saying that she would make another attempt to phone the Newtons.

In their room she dialled their number again while he consulted the directory, looking for Ilberts. There was no Rolf Ilbert in the Los Angeles phone book or in the slimmer Santa Monica directory, but in this latter he did find a Mrs Davina Lee Ilbert at a place called Paloma Canyon.

Dora had got through. He heard her say delightedly, 'Will you really come and pick me up? About four?' Considerably relieved, he touched her shoulder, got a wide smile from her, and then he ran out to the lift, free from guilt at least for the afternoon.

It was too far to walk, half-way to Malibu. He found Paloma Canyon without difficulty and encouraged the car up an impossibly steep slope. The road zig-zagged as on some alpine mountainside, opening up at each turn bigger and better views of the Pacific. But otherwise he might have been in Ploughman's Lane. All super residential areas the world over are the same, he thought, paraphrasing Tolstoy, it is only the slums that differ from each other. Paloma Canyon was Ploughman's Lane with palms. And with a bluer sky, daisy lawns and an architecture Spanish rather than Tudor.

She wasn't the wife but the ex-wife of the man called Rolf Ilbert. No, she didn't mind him asking, she would be only too glad if there was anything she could do to get back at Natalie Arno. Would he mind coming around to the pool? They always spent their Sunday afternoons by the pool.

Wexford followed her along a path through a shrubbery of red and purple fuchsias taller than himself. She was a tall thin woman, very tanned and with bleached blonde hair, and she wore a sky-blue terry-cloth robe and flat sandals. He wondered what it must be like to live in a climate where you took it for granted you spent every Sunday afternoon round the pool. It was extremely hot, too hot to be down there on the beach, he supposed.

The pool, turquoise blue and rectangular with a fountain playing at the far end, was in a patio formed by the balconied wings of the lemon-coloured stucco house. Davina Lee Ilbert had evidently been lying in a rattan lounging chair, for there was a glass of something with ice in it and a pair of sunglasses on the table beside it. A girl of about sixteen in a bikini was sitting on the rim of the fountain and a boy a bit younger was swimming lengths. They both had dark curly hair and Wexford supposed they must resemble their father. The girl said 'Hi' to him and slipped into the water.

'You care for iced tea?' Mrs Ilbert asked him.

He had never tasted it but he accepted. While she was fetching it he sat down in one of the cane peacock chairs, looking over the parapet to the highway and the beaches below.

'You want to know where Rolf met her?' Davina Ilbert took off her robe and stretched out on the lounger, a woman of forty with a good if stringy figure who had the discretion to wear a one-piece swimsuit. 'It was in San Francisco in '76. Her husband had died and she was staying with friends in San Rafael. The guy was a journalist or something and they all went into the city for this writers' conference that was going on, a cocktail party, I guess it was. Rolf was there.'

'Your former husband is a writer?'

'Movie and TV scripts,' she said. 'You wouldn't have heard of him. Whoever heard of script writers? You have a serial called *Runway* on your TV?'

Wexford said nothing, nodded.

'Rolf's done some of that. You know the episodes set at Kennedy? That's his stuff. And he's made a mint from it, thank God.' She made a little quick gesture at the balconies, the fountain, her own particular expanse of blue sky. 'It's Natalie you want to know about, right? Rolf brought her back to LA and bought that house on Tuscarora for her.'

The boy came out of the pool and shook himself like a dog. His sister said something to him and they both stared at Wexford, looking away when he met their eyes.

'He lived there with her?' he asked their mother.

'He kind of divided his time between me and her.' She drank from the tall glass. 'I was really dumb in those days, I trusted him. It took me five years to find out and when

I did I flipped. I went over to Tuscarora and beat her up. No kidding.'

Wexford said impassively, 'That would have been in 1976?'

'Right. Spring of '76. Rolf came back and found her all bruised and with two black eyes and he got scared and took her on a trip up the coast to get away from me. It was summer, I don't suppose she minded. She was up there – two, three months? He'd go up and join her when he could but he never really lived with her again.' She gave a sort of tough chuckle. 'I'd thrown him out too. All he had was a hotel room in Marina del Rey.'

The sun was moving round. Wexford shifted into the shade and the boy and girl walked slowly away into the house. A humming bird, no larger than an insect, was hovering on the red velvet threshold of a trumpet flower. Wexford had never seen one before. He said:

'You said "up the coast". Do you know where?'

She shrugged. 'They didn't tell me their plans. But it'd be somewhere north of San Simeon and south of Monterey, maybe around Big Sur. It could have been a motel, but Rolf was generous, he'd have rented a house for her.' She changed her tone abruptly. 'Is she in trouble? I mean, real trouble?'

'Not at the moment,' said Wexford. 'She's just inherited a very nice house and a million from her father.'

'Dollars?'

'Pounds.'

'Jesus, and they say cheating never pays.'

'Mrs Ilbert, forgive me, but you said your former husband and Mrs Arno never lived together again after the summer of '76. Why was that? Did he simply get tired of her?'

She gave her dry bitter laugh. '*She* got tired of him. She met someone else. Rolf was still crazy about her. He told me so, he told me all about it.'

Wexford recalled Jane Zoffany. Husbands seemed to make a practice of confiding in their wives their passion for Natalie Arno. 'She met someone while she was away on this long holiday?'

'That's what Rolf told me. She met this guy and took him back to the house on Tuscarora – it was hers, you see, she could do what she wanted – and Rolf never saw her again.'

'*He never saw her again?*'

'That's what he said. She wouldn't see him or speak to him. I guess it was because he still hadn't divorced me and married her, but I don't know. Rolf went crazy. He found out this guy she was with was living here illegally and he got him deported.'

Wexford nodded. 'He was a Swiss called Fassbender.'

'Oh, no. Where d'you get that from? I don't recall his name but it wasn't what you said. He was English. Rolf had him deported to England.'

'Did *you* ever see her again?'

'Me? No, why would I?'

'Thank you, Mrs Ilbert. You've been very frank and I'm grateful.'

'You're welcome. I guess I still feel pretty hostile towards her for what she did to me and my kids. It wouldn't give me any grief to hear she'd lost that house and that million.'

Wexford drove down the steep hill, noticing attached to a house wall something he hadn't seen on the way up. A printed notice that said 'No Solicitors'. He chuckled. He knew very well that this was an American equivalent of the 'nice' suburb's injunction to hawkers or people delivering circulars, but it still made him laugh. He would have liked to prise it off the wall and take it home for Symonds, O'Brien and Ames.

Dora was out when he got back to the Miramar and there was a note for him telling him not to wait for dinner if she wasn't back by seven-thirty. Rex Newton, whom he had rather disliked in the days when they had been acquaintances, he now blessed. And tomorrow he would devote the whole day exclusively to Dora.

14

From the map it didn't look as if there was much in the way of habitation in the vicinity of Big Sur, and Wexford's idea that Natalie Arno's trail might therefore easily be followed was confirmed by an elderly lady in the hotel lobby. This was a Mrs Lewis from Denver, Colorado, who had spent, it appeared, at least twenty holidays in California. There was hardly a house, hotel or restaurant, according to Mrs Lewis, between San Simeon in the south and Carmel in the north. The coast was protected, Wexford concluded, it was conserved by whatever the American equivalent might be of the National Trust.

The Miramar's enormous lobby had carpet sculpture on the walls. Although it was probably the grandest hotel Wexford had ever stayed in, the bar was so dark as to imply raffishness or at least that it would be wiser not to see what one was drinking. In his case this was white wine, the pleasant, innocuous, rather weak chablis which must be produced here by the millions of gallons considering the number of people he had seen swilling it down. What had become of the whisky sours and dry martinis of his reading? He sat alone – Dora and Mrs Lewis were swapping family snaps and anecdotes – reflecting that he should try to see Rolf Ilbert before he began the drive northwards. Ilbert was surely by now over Natalie and would have no objection to telling him the name of the place where she had stayed in the summer of 1976. Wexford finished his second glass of wine and walked down past the sculptured carpet palms to phone Davina Ilbert, but there was no reply.

In the morning, when he tried her number again, she

told him her ex-husband was in London. He had been in London for two months, researching for a television series about American girls who had married into the English aristocracy. Wexford realized he would just have to trace Natalie on what he had. They drove off at lunchtime and stopped for the night at a motel in Santa Maria. It was on the tip of Wexford's tongue to grumble to Dora that there was nothing to do in Santa Maria, miles from the coast and with Route 101 passing through it. But then it occurred to him that a visitor might say exactly that about Kingsmarkham. Perhaps there was only ever something obvious to do in the centre of cities or by the sea. Elsewhere there was ample to do if you lived there and nothing if you didn't. He would have occupation soon enough and then his guilt about Dora would come back.

Over dinner he confided his theory to her.

'If you look at the facts you'll see that there was a distinct change of personality in 1976. The woman who went away with Ilbert had a different character from the woman who came back to Los Angeles. Think about it for a minute. Camargue's daughter had led a very sheltered, cared-for sort of life, she'd never been out in the world on her own. First there was a secure home with her parents, then elopement with and marriage to Arno, and when Arno died, Ilbert. She was always under the protection of some man. But what of the woman who appears *after* the summer of '76? She lets off rooms in her house to bring in an income. She doesn't form long steady relationships but has casual love affairs – with the Swiss Fassbender, with the Englishman who was deported, with Zoffany. She can't sell the house Ilbert bought for her so she lets it out and comes to England. Not to creep under her father's wing as Natalie Camargue might have done, but to shift for herself in a place of her own.'

'But surely it was a terrible risk to go to Natalie's own house and live there as Natalie? The neighbours would have known at once, and then there'd be her friends. . . .'

'Good fences make good neighbours,' said Wexford. 'There's a lot of space between those houses, it's a shifting population, and if my idea is right Natalie Camargue was a shy, reserved sort of woman. Her neighbours never saw much of her. As to friends – if a friend of Natalie's phoned she had only to say Natalie was still away. If a friend comes to the house she has only to say that she herself is a friend who happens to be staying there for the time being. Mrs Ilbert says Ilbert never saw her after she came back. Now if the real Natalie came back it's almost impossible Ilbert never saw her. Never was alone with her maybe, never touched her, but never saw her? No, it was the impostor who fobbed him off every time he called with excuses, with apologies, and at last with direct refusals, allegedly on the part of the real Natalie, ever to see him again.'

'But, Reg, how could the impostor know so much about the real Natalie's past?'

He took her up quickly. 'You spent most of last evening talking to Mrs Lewis. How much do you know about her from, say, two hours' conversation?'

Dora giggled. 'Well, she lives in a flat, not a house. She's a widow. She's got two sons and a daughter. One of the sons is a realtor, I don't know what that is.'

'Estate agent.'

'Estate agent, and the other's a vet. Her daughter's called Janette and she's married to a doctor and they've got twin girls and they live in a place called Bismarck. Mrs Lewis has got a four-wheel drive Chevrolet for the mountain roads and a holiday house, a log cabin, in the Rockies and . . .'

'Enough! You found all that out in two hours and you're saying the new Natalie couldn't have formed a complete dossier of the old Natalie in – what? Five or six weeks? And when she came to England she had a second mentor in Mary Woodhouse.'

'All right, perhaps she could have.' Dora hesitated. He had had a feeling for some hours that she wanted to impart – or even break – something to him. 'Darling,' she said suddenly, 'You won't mind, will you? I told Rex and Nonie we'd be staying at the Redwood Hotel in Carmel and it so happens, I mean, it's a complete coincidence, that they'll be staying with Nonie's daughter in Monterey at the same time. If we had lunch with them once or twice – or I did – well, you won't mind, will you?'

'I think it's a wonderful idea.'

'Only you didn't used to like Rex, and I can't honestly say he's changed.'

'It's such a stupid name,' Wexford said unreasonably. 'Stupid for a man, I mean. It's all right for a dog.'

Dora couldn't help laughing. 'Oh, come. It only just misses being the same as yours.'

'A miss is as good as a mile. What d'you think of my theory then?'

'Well – what became of the old Natalie?'

'I think it's probable she murdered her.'

The road came back to the sea again after San Luis Obispo. It was like Cornwall, Wexford thought, the Cornish coast gigantically magnified both in size and in extent. Each time you came to a bend in the road another bay opened before you, vaster, grander, more majestically beautiful than the last. At San Simeon Dora wanted to see Hearst Castle, so Wexford drove her up there and left her to take the guided tour. He went down on the beach where shade was provided by eucalyptus trees. Low down over the water he saw a pelican in ponderous yet graceful flight. The sun shone with an arrogant, assured permanence, fitting for the finest climate on earth.

There wasn't much to San Simeon, a car park, a restaurant, a few houses. And if Mrs Lewis was to be believed, the population would be even sparser as he drove north. The Hearst Castle tour lasted a long time and they made no more progress that day, but as they set off next morning Wexford began to feel something like dismay. It was true that if you were used to living in densely peopled areas you might find the coast here sparsely populated, but it wasn't by any means *un*populated. Little clusters of houses – you could hardly call them villages – with a motel or two, a store, a petrol station, a restaurant, occurred more often then he had been led to believe. And when they came to Big Sur and the road wandered inland through the redwood forest, there were habitations and places to stay almost in plenty.

They reached the Redwood Hotel at about eight that night. Simply driving through Carmel had been enough to lower Wexford's spirits. It looked a lively place, a considerable seaside resort, and it was full of hotels. Another phone call to Davina Ilbert elicited only that she had no idea of Ilbert's London address. Wexford realized that there was nothing for it but to try all the hotels in Carmel, armed with his photograph of Natalie.

All he derived from that was the discovery that Americans are more inclined to be helpful than English people, and if this is because they are a nation of salesmen just as the English are a nation of small shopkeepers, it does little to detract from the overall pleasant impression. Hotel receptionists exhorted him on his departure to have a good day, and then when he was still at it after sundown, to have a nice evening. By that time he had been inside every hotel, motel and lobby of apartments-for-rent in Carmel, Carmel Highlands, Carmel Woods and Carmel Point, and he had been inside them in vain.

Rex Newton and his American wife were sitting in the hotel bar with Dora when he got back. Newton's skin had gone very brown and his hair very white, but otherwise he was much the same. His wife, in Wexford's opinion, looked twenty years older than Dora, though she was in fact younger. It appeared that the Newtons were to dine with them, and Newton walked into the dining room with one arm round his wife's waist and the other round Dora's. Dora had given them to understand he was there on official police business – what else could she have said? – and Newton spent most of his time at the table holding forth on the American legal system, American police, the geography and geology of California and the rival merits of various hotels. His wife was a meek quiet little woman. They were going to take Dora to Muir Woods, the redwood forest north of San Francisco, on the following day.

'If he knows so much,' Wexford grumbled later, 'he might have warned you there are more hotels up here than in the West End of London.'

'I'm sorry, darling. I didn't ask him. He does rather talk the hind leg off a donkey, doesn't he?'

Wexford didn't know why he suddenly liked Rex Newton very much and felt even happier that Dora was having such a good time with him.

For his own part, he spent the next day and the next making excursions down the coast the way they had come, visiting every possible place to stay. In each he got the same response – or worse, that the motel had changed hands or changed management and that there were no records for 1976 available. He was learning that in California change is a very important aspect of life and that Californians, like the Athenians of old, are attracted by any new thing.

Nonie Newton was confined to bed in her daughter's house with a migraine. Wexford cut short his inquiries in Monterey to get back to Dora, who would have been deserted by her friends. The least he could do for her was take her on the beach for the afternoon. He asked himself if he hadn't mismanaged everything. The trip wasn't succeeding either as an investigation or as a holiday. Dora was out when he got back, there was no note for him, and he spent the rest of the day missing his wife and reproaching himself. Rex Newton brought her back at ten and, in spite of Nonie's illness, sat in the bar for half an hour, holding forth on the climate of California, seismology and the San Andreas Fault. Wexford couldn't wait for him to be gone to unburden his soul to Dora.

'You could always phone Sheila,' she said when they were alone.

'Sure I could,' he said. 'I could phone Sylvia and talk to the kids. I could phone your sister and my nephew Howard and old Mike. It would cost a great deal of money and they'd all no doubt say hard cheese very kindly, but where would it get me?'

'To Ilbert,' she said simply.

He looked at her.

'Rolf Ilbert. You said he does part of the script for

Runway. He's in London. Even if he's not working on *Runway* now, even if she's never met him, Sheila's in a position to find out where he is, she could easily do it.'

'So she could,' he said slowly. 'Why didn't I think of that?'

It was eleven o'clock on the Pacific coast but seven in London, and he was lucky to find her up. Her voice sounded as if she were in the next room. He knew exactly what her voice in the next room would sound like because his hotel neighbours had had *Runway* on for the past half-hour.

'I don't know him, Pop darling, but I'm sure I can find him. Nothing easier. I'll shop around some likely agents. Where shall I ring you back?'

'Don't call us,' said her father. 'We'll call you. God knows where we'll be.'

'How's Mother?'

'Carrying on alarmingly with her old flame.'

He would have laughed as he said that if Dora had shown the least sign of laughing.

Because it wasn't his nature to wait about and do nothing he spent all the next day covering what remained of the Monterey Peninsula. Something in him wanted to say, forget it, make a holiday of the rest of it, but it was too late for that. Instead of relaxing, he would only have tormented himself with that constantly recurring question, where had she stayed? It was awkward phoning Sheila because of the time difference. All the lines were occupied when he tried at eight in the morning, tea time for her, and again at noon, her early evening. When at last he heard the ringing there was no answer. Next day, or the day after at the latest, they would have to start south and leave behind all the possible places where Natalie Arno might have changed her identity. They had only had a fortnight and eleven days of it were gone.

As he was making another attempt to phone Sheila from the hotel lobby, Rex Newton walked in with Dora. He sat down, drank a glass of chablis, and held forth on Californian vineyards, migraine, the feverfew diet and the gluten-free diet. After half an hour he went, kissing Dora – on the cheek but very near the mouth – and reminding her of a promise to spend their last night in America staying at the Newtons' house. And also their last day.

'I suppose I'm included in that,' Wexford said in a rather nasty tone. Newton was still not quite out of earshot.

She was cool. 'Of course, darling.'

His investigation was over, failed, fruitless. He had rather hoped to have the last two days alone with his wife. But what a nerve he had and how he was punished for it!

'I'm hoist with my own petard, aren't I?' he said and went off to bed.

The Newtons were flying back that morning. It would be a long weary drive for Wexford. He and Dora set off at nine.

The first of the *Danaus* butterflies to float across the windscreen made them both gasp. Dora had seen one only once before, Wexford never. The Milkweed, the Great American Butterfly, the Monarch, is a rare visitor to the cold British Isles. They watched that one specimen drift out over the sea, seeming to lose itself in the blue meeting the blue, and then a cloud of its fellows were upon them, thick as autumnal leaves that strow the brooks in Vallombrosa. And like leaves too, scarlet leaves veined in black, they floated rather than flew across the span of California One, down from the cliffs of daisies, out to the ocean. The air was red with them. All the way down from Big Sur they came, wings of cinnabar velvet, butterflies in flocks like birds made of petals.

'The Spanish for butterfly is *mariposa*,' said Dora. 'Rex told me. Don't you think it's a beautiful name?'

Wexford said nothing. Even if he managed to get hold of Sheila now, even if she had an address or a phone number for him, would he have time to drive back perhaps a hundred miles along this route? Not when he had to be in Burbank or wherever those Newtons lived by nightfall. A red butterfly came to grief on his windscreen, smashed, fluttered, died.

They stopped for a late lunch not far north of San Luis Obispo. He tried in vain to get through to Sheila again and then Dora said she would try. She came back from the phone with a little smile on her lips. She looked young and tanned and happy, but she hadn't been able to reach Sheila. Wexford wondered why she should look like that if she hadn't been talking to anyone. The Newtons would have been back in their home for hours by now. He felt that worst kind of misery, that which afflicts us as the result entirely of our own folly.

The road that returned from inland to the coast wound down through yellow hills. Yuccas pushed their way up through the sun-bleached grass and the rounded mountains were crowned with olives. The hills folded and dipped and rose and parted to reveal more hills, all the same, all ochreish in colour, until through the last dip the blue ocean appeared again. Dora was occupied with her map and guide book.

There was a little seaside town ahead. A sign by the roadside said: Santa Xavierita, height above sea level 50.2 metres, population 482. Dora said:

'According to the book there's a motel here called the Mariposa. Shall we try it?'

'What for?' said Wexford crossly. 'Half an hour's kip? We have to be two hundred miles south of here by eight and it's five now.'

'We don't have to. Our plane doesn't go till tomorrow night. We could stay at the Mariposa, I think we're meant to, it was a sign.'

He nearly stopped the car. He chuckled. He had known her thirty-five years but he didn't know her yet. 'You phoned Newton back there?' he said but in a very different tone from the one he would have used if he had asked that question ten minutes before. 'You phoned Newton and said we couldn't make it?'

She said demurely, 'I think Nonie was quite relieved really.'

'I don't deserve it,' said Wexford.

Santa Xavierita had a wide straggly street with a dozen

side turnings at right angles to it, as many petrol stations, a monster market, a clutch of restaurants and among a dozen motels, the Mariposa. Wexford found himself being shown, not to a room, but to a little house rather like a bungalow at home in Ramsgate or Worthing. It stood in a garden, one of a score of green oases in this corner of Santa Xavierita, and up against its front door was a pink and white geranium as big as a tree.

He walked back between sprinklers playing on the grass to the hotel reception desk and phoned Sheila on a collect call. In London it was two in the morning, but by now he was unscrupulous. Sheila had got Ilbert's address. She had had it for two days and couldn't understand why her father hadn't phoned. Ilbert was staying at Durrant's Hotel in George Street by Spanish Place. Wexford wrote down the number. He looked round for someone to inform that he intended to make a call to London.

There was no sign of the little spry man called Sessamy who had checked them in. No doubt he was somewhere about, watering the geraniums and fuchsias and the heliotrope that smelt of cherries. Wexford went back to find Dora and tell her the news, such as it was. She was in the kitchen of their bungalow, arranging in a glass bowl, piling like an Arcimboldo still life, the fruit they had bought.

'Reg,' she said, turning round, a nectarine in her hand, 'Reg, Mrs Sessamy who owns this place, she's English. And she says we're the first English people to stay here since – a Mrs Arno in 1976.'

15

'Tell me about it,' Wexford said.

'I don't know anything about it. I don't know any more than I've told you. Your Natalie Arno stayed here in 1976. After we've eaten we're to go and have coffee with Mrs Sessamy and she'll enlighten you.'

'Will she now? And how did you account for my curiosity? What did you tell her about me?'

'The truth. The idea of you being a real English policeman almost made her cry. She was a GI bride, I think, she's about the right age. I honestly think she expects you to turn up in a blue uniform and say 'ere, 'ere, what's all this about? and she'd love it!'

He laughed. It was rare for him to praise his wife, almost unknown for him to call her by an endearment. That wasn't his way, she knew it and wouldn't have wanted it. It would have bracketed her with those he loved on the next level down. He put his hand on her arm.

'If something comes of all this,' he said, 'and one of us gets sent back here at the government's expense, can I come too?'

There was, of all things, a Lebanese restaurant in the main street of Santa Xavierita. They walked there and ate delicate scented versions of humous and kebab and honey cake. The sun had long gone, sunk almost with a fizzle into that blue sea, and now the moon was rising. The moonlight painted the little town white as with frost. It was no longer very warm. In the gardens, which showed as dark little havens of lushness in aridity, the sprinklers still rotated and sprayed.

Wexford marvelled at his wife and, with hindsight, at his own ignorant presumption. Instead of allowing herself to be a passive encumbrance, she had made him absurdly jealous and had hoodwinked him properly. By some sixth sense or some gift of serendipity, she had done in an instant what had eluded him for nearly a fortnight – found Natalie Arno's hideout. And like Trollope's Archdeacon of his wife, he wondered at and admired the greatness of that lady's mind.

The Sessamys lived in a white-painted frame building, half their home and half the offices of the motel. Their living room was old-fashioned in an unfamiliar way, furnished with pieces from a thirties culture more overblown and Hollywood-influenced than that which Wexford himself had known. On a settee, upholstered in snow-white grainy plastic, a settee that rather resembled some monstrous dessert, a cream-coated log perhaps, rolled in coconut, sat the fattest woman Wexford had ever seen. He and Dora had come in by way of the open French windows, as she had been instructed, and Mrs Sessamy struggled to get to her feet. Like a great fish floundering to raise itself over the rim of the keeper net, she went on struggling until her guests were seated. Only then did she allow herself to subside again. She gave a big noisy sigh.

'It's such a pleasure to see you! You don't know how I've been looking forward to it ever since Mrs Wexford here said who you was. A real bobby! I turned on the waterworks, didn't I, Tom?'

Nearly forty years' domicile in the United States had not robbed her of a particle of her old accent or given her a hint of new. She was a Londoner who still spoke the cockney of Bow or Limehouse.

'Bethnal Green,' she said as if Wexford had asked. 'I've never been back. My people all moved out to one of them new towns, Harlow. Been there, of course. Like every other year mostly we go, don't we, Tom?'

Her husband made no reply. He was a little brown monkey of a man with a face like a nut. He suggested they have a drink and displayed a selection of bottles ranged behind a small bar. There was no sign of the promised coffee. When Dora had apologetically refused bourbon, rye, chablis, Hawaiian cocktail, Perrier, grape juice and gin, Mrs Sessamy announced that they would have tea. Tom would make it, the way she had taught him.

'It's such a pleasure to see you,' she said again, sinking comfortably back into white plastic. 'The English who come here, mostly they stop up at the Ramada or the Howard Johnson. But you picked the old Mariposa.'

'Because of the butterflies,' said Dora.

'Come again?'

'*Mariposa* – well, it means butterfly, doesn't it?'

'It does?' said Tom Sessamy, waiting for the kettle to boil. 'You hear that, Edie? How about that then?'

It seemed the policy of the Sessamys to question each other frequently but never to answer. Mrs Sessamy folded plump hands in her enormous lap. She was wearing green trousers and a tent-like green and pink flowered smock. In her broad moon face, in the greyish-fair hair, could still be seen traces of the pretty girl who had married an American soldier and left Bethnal Green for ever.

'Mrs Wexford said you wanted to know about that girl who lived here – well, stopped here. Though she must have been here three months. We thought she'd go on renting the chalet for ever, didn't we, Tom? We thought we'd got a real sinecure.'

'I'd heard it was up around Big Sur she stayed,' said Wexford.

'So it was at first. She couldn't stick it, not enough life for her, and it was too far to drive to Frisco. You can get up to San Luis in twenty minutes from here by car. She had her own car and he used to come up in a big Lincoln Continental.'

'Ilbert?'

'That's right, that was the name. I will say for her she never pretended, she never called herself Mrs Ilbert. Couldn't have cared less what people thought.'

Tom Sessamy came in with the tea. Wexford who, while

in California, had drunk from a pot made with one teabag, had seen tea made by heating up liquid out of a bottle or by pouring warm water on to a powder, noted that Tom had been well taught by his wife.

'I never did fancy them bags,' said Edith Sessamy. 'You can get tea loose here if you try.'

'Hafta go to the specialty shop over to San Luis,' said Tom.

Mrs Sessamy put cream and sugar into her cup. 'What more d'you want to know about her?' she said to Wexford.

He showed her the photograph. 'Is that her?'

She put on glasses with pink frames and rhinestone decoration. Mrs Sessamy had become Californian in all ways but for her tea and her speech. 'Yes,' she said, 'yes, I reckon that's her.' Her voice was full of doubt.

'I guess that's her,' said Tom. 'It's kinda hard to say. She kinda wore her hair loose. She got this terrific tan and wore her hair loose. Right, Edie?'

Edith Sessamy didn't seem too pleased by her husband's enthusiastic description of Natalie Arno. She said rather sharply, 'One man wasn't enough for her. She was two-timing that Ilbert the minute he was off to L.A. For instance, there used to be a young fella hung about here, kipped down on the beach, I reckon you'd have called him a beachcomber in olden times.'

'Kinda hippie,' said Tom.

'She carried on with him. I say he slept on the beach, that summer I reckoned he slept most nights in Natalie's chalet. Then there was an English chap, but it wasn't long before she left she met him, was it, Tom?'

'Played the guitar at the Maison Suisse over to San Luis.'

'Why did she leave?' Wexford asked.

'Now that I can't tell you. We weren't here when she left. We were at home, we were in England.'

'Visiting with her sister over to Harlow,' said Tom.

'She was living here like she'd stay for the rest of her life when we left. That'd have been the end of July, I reckon. Tom's cousin from Ventura, she come up to run the place like she always does when we're off on our holidays. She kept in touch, I reckon we got a letter once a week. I remember her writing us about that woman who got drowned here, don't you, Tom? But she never mentioned that girl leaving. Why should she? There was guests coming and going all the time.'

'You weren't curious yourselves?'

Edith Sessamy heaved up her huge shoulders and dropped them again. 'So if we were? There wasn't much we could do about it, six thousand miles away. She wasn't going to tell Tom's cousin why she upped and went, was she? When we come back we heard that's what she'd done, a moonlight flit like. Ilbert come up the next day but the bird was flown. She went off in her car, Tom's cousin said, and she'd got a young chap with her, and she left that poor mug Ilbert to pay the bill.'

Wexford woke up very early the next morning. The sun was perhaps the brightest and the clearest he had ever seen and the little town looked as if it had been washed clean in the night. Yet Edith Sessamy had told him that apart from a few showers the previous December they had had no rain for a year. He bathed and dressed and went out. Dora was still fast asleep. He walked down the narrow straight road bordered with fan palms, feather dusters on long tapering handles, that led to Santa Xavierita state beach.

The sky was an inverted pan of speckless blue enamel, the sea rippling blue silk. Along the silver sand a young man in yellow tee-shirt and red shorts was jogging. Another, in swimming trunks, was doing gymnastic exercises, sit-ups, press-ups, toe-touching. There was no one in the water. In the middle of the beach was a chair raised up high on stilts for the use of the lifeguard who would sit on it and halloo through his trumpet at over-venturesome swimmers.

Wexford's thoughts reverted to the night before. There was a question he ought to have asked, that he had simply overlooked at the time, because of the crushing disappointment he had felt at the paucity of Edith Sessamy's information. Disappointment had made him fail to select from that mass of useless matter the one significant sentence. He recalled it now, picking it out as the expert might pick out the uncut diamond from a handful of gravel.

Two hours later, as early as he decently could, he was waiting in the motel's reception area by the counter. Ringing the bell summoned Tom Sessamy in shortie dressing gown which left exposed hairless white legs and long white feet in sandals of plaited straw.

'Hi, Reg, you wanna check out?'

'I wanted to ask you and your wife a few more questions first if you'll bear with me.'

'Edie, are ya decent? Reg's here ta pick your brains.'

Mrs Sessamy was rather more decent than her husband in an all-enveloping pink kimono printed with birds of paradise. She sat on the white sofa drinking more strong black tea, and on her lap on a tray were fried eggs and fried bacon and hash browns and English muffins and grape jelly.

'It's been such a pleasure meeting you and Dora, I can't tell you.' She had told him at least six times already, but the repetition was somehow warming and pleasant to hear. Wexford returned the compliment with a few words about how much they had enjoyed themselves.

'You wanna cup of Edie's tea?' said Tom.

Wexford accepted. 'You said last night a woman was drowned here. While you were away. D'you know any more than that? Who she was? How it happened?'

'Not a thing. Only what I said, a woman was drowned. Well, it was a young woman, a girl really, I do know that, and I reckon I heard she was on holiday here from the East somewhere.'

'You hafta talk to the cops over to San Luis,' said Tom.

'Wait a minute, though – George Janveer was lifeguard here then, wasn't he, Tom? I reckon you could talk to George.'

'Why don't I call George right now?' said Tom.

He was dissuaded from this by his wife since it was only just after eight. They would phone George at nine. Wexford wasn't pressed for time, was he? No, he wasn't, not really, he had all day. He had a 200 mile drive ahead of him, of course, but that was nothing here. Edith Sessamy said she knew what he meant, it was nothing here.

He walked slowly back. At last a clear pattern was emerging from the confusion. The pieces fluttered and dropped into a design as the coloured fragments do when you shake a kaleidoscope. Camargue too had been drowned, he thought.

Just after nine he went back and paid his bill. Tom said apologetically that he had phoned George Janveer's home and talked to Mrs Janveer who said George had gone to Grover City but she expected him back by eleven.

'Oughta've called him at eight like I said,' said Tom.

Wexford and Dora put the cases in the car and went to explore what they hadn't yet seen of Santa Xavierita. Wouldn't it be best, Wexford asked himself, to head straight for San Luis Obispo and call on the police there and see what facts he could get out of them? But suppose he couldn't get any? Suppose, before they imparted anything to him, they required proof of who he was and what he was doing there? He could prove his identity, of course, and present them with bona fides but it would all take time and he hadn't much left. He had to be at Los Angeles international airport by six in time for their flight home at seven. Better wait for Janveer who would know as much as the police did and would almost certainly talk to him.

Mrs Janveer was as thin as Edith Sessamy was fat. She was in her kitchen baking something she called devil's food and her overweight black labrador was sitting at her feet, hoping to lick out the bowl.

It was after eleven and her husband still hadn't come back from Grover City. Maybe he had met a friend and they had got drinking. Mrs Janveer did not say this in a shrewish or condemnatory way or even as if there were anything to be defensive about. She said it in exactly the same tone, casual, indifferent, even slightly complacent, she would have used to say he had met the mayor or gone to a meeting of the Lions.

Wexford was driven to ask her if she remembered anything about the drowned woman. Mrs Janveer put the tin of chocolate cake mixture into the oven. The dog's tail began to thump the floor. No, she couldn't say she remembered much about it at all, except the woman's first name had been Theresa, she recalled that because it was hers too, and after the drowning some of her relations had come out to Santa Xavierita, from Boston, she thought it was, and stayed at the Ramada Inn. She put the mixing bowl under the tap and her hand to the tap. The dog let out a piteous squeal. Mrs Janveer shrugged, looking upset, and slapped the bowl down in front of the dog with a cross exclamation.

Wexford waited until half-past eleven. Janveer still hadn't come. 'Considering what I know now,' he said to Dora, 'they're bound to send me back here. It's only time I need.'

'It's a shame, darling, it's such bad luck.'

He drove quickly out of the town, heading for the Pacific Highway.

16

The difference between California and Kingsmarkham was a matter of colour as well as temperature. The one was blue and gold, the sun burning the grass to its own colour; the other was grey and green, the lush green of foliage watered daily by those massy clouds. Wexford went to work, not yet used to seeing grass verges instead of daisy lawns, shivering a little because the temperature was precisely what Tom Sessamy had told him it could fall to in Santa Xavierita in December.

Burden was waiting for him in his office. He had on a lightweight silky suit in a shade of taupe and a beige silk shirt. No one could possibly have taken him for a policeman or even a policeman in disguise. Wexford, who had been considering telling him at once what he had found out in California, now decided not to and instead asked him to close the window.

'I opened it because it's such a muggy stuffy sort of day,' said Burden. 'Not cold, are you?'

'Yes, I am. Very cold.'

'Jet lag. Did you have a good time?'

Wexford grunted. He wished he had the nerve to start the central heating. It probably wouldn't start, though, not in July. For all he knew, the chief constable had to come over himself on 1 November and personally press a button on the boiler. 'I don't suppose there've been any developments while I was away?' he said.

Burden sat down. 'Well, yes, there have. That's what I'm doing in here. I thought I ought to tell you first thing. Jane Zoffany has disappeared.'

Zoffany had not reported her missing until she had been gone a week. His story, said Burden, was that he and his wife had been staying at Sterries with their friend Natalie Arno, and on the evening of Friday, 27 June his wife had gone out alone for a walk and had never come back. Zoffany, when pressed, admitted that immediately prior to this he and his wife had quarrelled over an affair he had had with another woman. She had said she was going to leave him, she could never live with him again, and had left the house. Zoffany himself had left soon after, taking the 10.05 p.m. train to Victoria. He believed his wife would have gone home by an earlier train.

However, when he got to De Beauvoir Place she wasn't there. Nor did she appear the next day. He concluded she had gone to her sister in Horsham. This had apparently happened once before after a quarrel. But Friday 4 July had been Jane Zoffany's birthday, her thirty-fifth, and a birthday card came for her from her sister. Zoffany then knew he had been wrong and he went to his local police station.

Where no one had shown much interest, Burden said. Why should they? That a young woman should temporarily leave her husband after a quarrel over his infidelity was hardly noteworthy. It happened all the time. And of course she wouldn't tell him where she had gone, that was the last thing she had wanted him to know. Burden only got to hear of it when Zoffany also reported his wife's disappearance to the Kingsmarkham police. He seemed genuinely worried. It would not be putting it too strongly to say he was distraught.

'Guilt,' said Wexford, and as he pronounced the word he felt it himself. It was even possible he was the last person – the last but one – to have seen Jane Zoffany alive. And he had let her go. Because he was off on holiday, because he didn't want to inconvenience Dora or upset arrangements. Of course she hadn't taken refuge with her sister or some friend. She had had no handbag, no money. He had let her go, overwrought as she was, to walk away into the dusk of Ploughman's Lane – to go back to Sterries and

Natalie Arno.

'I had a feeling we ought to take it a bit more seriously,' Burden said. 'I mean, I wasn't really alarmed but I couldn't help thinking about poor old Camargue. We've got our own ideas about what kind of a death that was, haven't we? I talked to Zoffany myself, I got him to give me the names of people she could possibly have gone to. There weren't many and we checked on them all.'

'And what about Natalie? Have you talked to her?'

'I thought I'd leave that to you.'

'We'll have to drag the lake,' said Wexford, 'and dig up the garden if necessary. But I'll talk to her first.'

The effect of her inherited wealth was now displayed. A new hatchback Opel, mustard-coloured, automatic transmission, stood on the gravel circle outside the front door. Looking at her, staring almost, Wexford remembered the skirt Jane Zoffany had mended, the old blanket coat. Natalie wore a dress of some thin clinging jersey material in bright egg-yellow with a tight bodice and full skirt. Around her small neat waist was tied a belt of yellow with red, blue and purple stripes. It was startling and effective and very fashionable. Her hair hung loose in a glossy black bell. There was a white gold watch on one wrist and a bracelet of woven white gold threads on the other. The mysterious lady from Boston, he thought, and he wondered how you felt when you knew your relatives, parents maybe, and your friends thought you were dead and grieved for you while in fact you were alive and living in the lap of luxury.

'But Mr Wexford,' she said with her faint accent – a New England accent? 'But, Mr Wexford, Jane never came back here that night.' She smiled in the way a model does when her mouth and not her eyes are to show in the toothpaste ad. 'Her things are still in the room she and Ivan used. Would you like to see?'

He nodded. He followed her down to the spare rooms. On the carved teak chest stood a Chinese bowl full of Peace roses. They went into the room where he had once before seen Jane Zoffany standing before the long mirror and fastening the collar of a Persian lamb coat. Her suitcase lay open on the top of a chest of drawers. There was a folded nightdress inside it, a pair of sandals placed heel to toe and a paperback edition of Daphne du Maurier's *Rebecca*. On the black-backed hairbrush on the dressing table and the box of talcum powder lay a fine scattering of dust.

'Has Mrs Hicks left you?'

'In the spirit if not the flesh yet, Mr Wexford. She and Ted are going to Uncle Philip.' She added, as if in explanation to someone who could not be expected to know intimate family usage, 'Philip Cory, that is. He was just crazy to have them and it's made him so happy. Meanwhile this place is rather neglected while they get ready to leave. They've sold their house and I think I've sold this one at last. Well, practically sold it. Contracts have been exchanged.' She chatted on, straightening the lemon floral duvet, opening a window, for all the word as if he too were a prospective purchaser rather than a policeman investigating an ominous disappearance. 'I'm having some of the furniture put in store and the rest will go to the flat I've bought in London. Then I'm thinking of going off on vacation somewhere.'

He glanced into the adjoining bathroom. It had evidently been cleaned before Muriel Hicks withdrew her services. The yellow bath and basin were immaculate and fresh honey-coloured towels hung on the rail. Without waiting for permission, he made his way into the next room, the one Natalie had rejected in favour of using Camargue's very private and personal territory.

There were no immediately obvious signs that this room had ever been occupied since Camargue's death. In fact, it seemed likely that the last people to have slept here were Dinah Sternhold's parents when they stayed with Camargue at Christmas. But Wexford, peering quickly, pinched from the frill that edged one of the green and blue flowered pillows, a hair. It was black but it was not from Natalie's head, being wavy and no more than three inches long.

This bathroom too lacked the pristine neatness and cleanliness of the other. A man no more than ordinarily observant might have noticed nothing, but Wexford was almost certain that one of the blue towels had been used. On the basin, under the cold tap, was a small patch of tide mark. He turned as Natalie came up softly behind him. She was not the kind of person one much fancied creeping up on one, and he thought, as he had done when he first met her, of a snake.

'That night,' he said, 'Mrs Zoffany ran out of the house and then afterwards her husband left. How long afterwards?'

'Twenty minutes, twenty-five. Shall we say twenty-two and a half minutes, Mr Wexford, to be on the safe side?'

He gave no sign that he had noticed the implicit mockery. 'He walked to the station, did he?'

'I gave him a lift in my car.'

Of course. Now he remembered that he had seen them. 'And after that you never saw Mrs Zoffany again?'

'Never.' She looked innocently at Wexford, her black eyes very large and clear, the lashes lifted and motionless. 'It's the most extraordinary thing I ever came across in my life.'

Considering what he knew of her life, Wexford doubted this statement. 'I should like your consent to our dragging the lake,' he said.

'That's just a polite way of saying you're going to drag it anyway, isn't it?'

'Pretty well,' he said. 'It'll save time if you give your permission.'

Out of the lake came a quantity of blanket weed, sour green and sour smelling; two car tyres, a bicycle lamp, half a dozen cans and a broken wrought-iron gate as well as a lot of miscellaneous rubbish of the nuts and bolts and nails variety. They also found Sir Manuel Camargue's missing glove, but there was no trace of Jane Zoffany. Wexford wondered if he had chosen the lake as the first possible place to search because of the other drownings associated with Natalie Arno.

It was, of course, stretching a point to touch the garden

at all. But the temptation to tell the men to dig up the flowerbed between the lake and the circular forecourt was very great. It was, after all, no more than three or four yards from the edge of the lake and the soil in it looked suspiciously freshly turned and the bedding plants as if they had been there no more than a day or two. Who would put out bedding plants in July? They dug. They dug to about three feet down and then even Wexford had to admit no body was buried there. Ted Hicks, who had been watching them for hours, now said that he had dug the bed over a week ago and planted out a dozen biennials. Asked why he hadn't said so before, he said he hadn't thought it his place to interfere. By then it was too late to do any more, nine on a typical English July evening, twilight, greyish, damp and cool.

Wexford's phone was ringing when he got in. The chief constable. Mrs Arno had complained that he was digging up the grounds of her house without her permission and without a warrant.

'True,' said Wexford, because it was and it seemed easier to confess than to get involved in the ramifications of explaining. A scalding lecture exploded at him from the mouthpiece. Once again he was overstepping the bounds of his duty and his rights, once again he was allowing an obsession to warp his judgement. And this time the obsession looked as if it were taking the form of a vindictive campaign against Mrs Arno.

Had her voice on the phone achieved this? Or had she been to Griswold in person, in the yellow dress, holding him with her glowing black eyes, moving her long pretty hands in feigned distress? For the second time he promised to persecute Natalie Arno no more, in fact to act as if he had never heard her name.

What changed the chief constable's mind must have been the systematic searching of the Zodiac. Two neighbours of Ivan Zoffany went independently to the police, one to complain that Zoffany had been lighting bonfires in his garden by night, the other to state that she had actually seen Jane in the vicinity of De Beauvoir Place on the night of Sunday, 29 June.

The house and the shop were searched without result. Zoffany admitted to the bonfires, saying that he intended to move away and take up some other line of work, and it was his stock of science-fiction paperbacks he had been burning. Wexford applied for a warrant to search the inside of Sterries and secured one three days after the dragging of the lake.

17

The house was empty. Not only deserted by its owner but half-emptied of its furnishings. Wexford remembered that Natalie Arno had said she would be going away on holiday and also that she intended having some of the furniture put in store. Mrs Murray-Burgess, that inveterate observer of unusual vehicles, told Burden when he called at Kingsfield House that she had seen a removal van turn out of the Sterries drive into Ploughman's Lane at about three on Tuesday afternoon. It was now Thursday, 17 July.

With Wexford and Burden were a couple of men, detective constables, called Archbold and Bennett. They were prepared not only to search but to dismantle parts of the house if need be. They began in the double garage, examining the cupboards at the end of it and the outhouse tacked on to its rear. Since Sterries Cottage was also empty and had been since the previous day, Wexford intended it to be searched as well. Archbold, who had had considerable practice at this sort of thing, picked the locks on both front doors.

The cottage was bare of furniture and carpets. Like most English houses, old or new, it was provided with inadequate cupboard space. Its walls were of brick but were not cavity walls, and at some recent period, perhaps when Sir Manuel and the Hickses had first come, the floors at ground level had been relaid with tiles on a concrete base. No possibility of hiding a body there and nowhere upstairs either. They turned their attention to the bigger house.

Here, at first, there seemed even less likelihood of being able safely to conceal the body of a full-grown woman. It was for no more than form's sake that they cleared out the cloaks cupboard inside the front door, the kitchen broom cupboard and the small room off the kitchen which housed the central-heating boiler and a stock of soap powders and other cleansers. From the first floor a great many pieces had gone, including the pale green settee and armchairs, the piano and all the furniture from Camargue's bedroom and sitting room. Everywhere there seemed to be blank spaces or marks of discolouration on the walls where this or that piece had stood. The Chinese vase of Peace roses, wilted now, had been stuck on the floor up against a window.

Bennett, tapping walls, discovered a hollow space between the right-hand side of the hanging cupboard and the outside wall in Camargue's bedroom. And outside there were signs that it had been the intention on someone's part to use this space as a cupboard for garden tools or perhaps to contain a dustbin, for an arch had been built into which to fit a door and this arch subsequently filled in with bricks of a slightly lighter colour.

From the inside of the hanging cupboard Bennett set about unscrewing the panel at its right-hand end. Wexford wondered if he were getting squeamish in his old age. It was with something amounting to nausea that he stood there anticipating the body falling slowly forward as the panel came away, crumpling into Bennett's arms, the tall thin body of Jane Zoffany with a gauzy scarf and a red and yellow dress of Indian cotton for a winding sheet. Burden sat on the bed, rubbing away fastidiously at a small powder or plaster mark that had appeared on the hem of his light fawn trousers.

The last screw was out and the panel fell, Bennett catching it and resting it against the wall. There was nothing inside the cavity but a spider which swung across its webs. A little bright light and fresh air came in by way of a ventilator brick. Wexford let out his breath in a sigh. It was time to take a break for lunch.

Mr Haq, all smiles and gratified to see Wexford back, remarked that he was happy to be living in a country where they paid policemen salaries on which they could afford to have holidays in California. With perfect sincerity, he said this made him feel more secure. Burden ordered for both of them, steak Soroti, an innocuous beef stew with carrots and onions. When Mr Haq and his son were out of earshot he said he often suspected that the Pearl of Africa's cook hailed from Bradford. Wexford said nothing.

'It's no good,' said Burden, 'we aren't going to find anything in that place. You may as well resign yourself. You're too much of an optimist sometimes for your own good.'

'D'you think I want the poor woman to be dead?' Wexford retorted. 'Optimist, indeed.' And he quoted rather crossly, 'The optimist proclaims that we live in the best of all possible worlds. The pessimist fears this is true.'

'You want Natalie Arno to be guilty of something and you don't much care what,' said Burden. 'Why should she murder her?'

'Because Jane Zoffany knew who she really is. Either that or she found out how the murder of Camargue was done and who did it. There's a conspiracy here, Mike, involving a number of conspirators and Jane Zoffany was one of them. But there's no more honour among conspirators than there is among thieves, and when she discovered how Natalie had betrayed her she saw no reason to be discreet any longer.' He told Burden what had happened when he encountered Jane Zoffany in Ploughman's Lane on 27 June. 'She had something to tell me, she would have told me then only I didn't realize, I didn't give her a word of encouragement. Instead she went back to Sterries and no doubt had the temerity to threaten Natalie. It was a silly thing to do. But she was a silly woman, hysterical and unstable.'

The steak Soroti came. Wexford ate in silence. It was true enough that he wanted Natalie Arno to have done something, or rather that he now saw that charging her with something was almost within his grasp. Who would know where she had gone on holiday? Zoffany? Philip Cory? Would anyone know? They had the ice cream eau-de-Nil to follow but Wexford left half of his.

'Let's get back there,' he said.

It had begun to rain. The white walls of Sterries were streaked with water. Under a lowering sky of grey and purple cloud the house had the shabby faded look which belongs particularly to English houses built to a design intended for the Mediterranean. There were lights on in the upper rooms.

Archbold and Bennett were working on the drawing room, Bennett having so thoroughly investigated the chimney as to clamber half-way up inside it. Should they take up the floor? Wexford said no, he didn't think so. No one could hope to conceal a body for long by burying it under the floor in a house which was about to change hands. Though, as Wexford now told himself, it wasn't necessarily or exclusively a body they were looking for. By six o'clock they were by no means finished but Wexford told them to leave the rest of the house till next day. It was still raining, though slightly now, little more than a drizzle. Wexford made his way down the path between the conifers to check that they had closed and locked the door of Sterries Cottage.

In the wet gloom the alsatian's face looking out of a ground-floor window and almost on a level with his own made him jump. It evoked strange ideas, that there had been a time shift and it was six months ago and Camargue still lived. Then again, from the way some kind of white cloth seemed to surround the dog's head. . . .

'Now I know how Red Riding Hood felt,' said Wexford to Dinah Sternhold.

She was wearing a white raincoat with its collar turned up and she had been standing behind the dog, surveying the empty room. A damp cotton scarf was tied under her chin. She smiled. The sadness that had seemed characteristic of her had left her face now. It seemed fuller, the cheeks pink with rain and perhaps with running.

'They've gone,' she said, 'and the door was open. It was a bit of a shock.'

'They're working for Philip Cory now.'

She shrugged. 'Oh well, I suppose there was no reason they should bother to tell me. I'd got into the habit of bringing Nancy over every few weeks just for them to see her. Ted loves Nancy.' She took her hand from the dog's collar and Nancy bounded up to Wexford as if they were old friends. 'Sheila said you'd been to California.'

'For our summer holiday.'

'Not entirely, Mr Wexford, was it? You went to find out if what Manuel thought was true. But you haven't found out, have you?'

He said nothing, and she went on quickly, perhaps thinking she had gone too far or been indiscreet. 'I often think how strange it is she could get the solicitors to believe in her and Manuel's old friends to believe in her and the police and people who'd known the Camargues for years, yet Manuel who wanted to believe, who was pretty well geared up to believe anything, saw her on that one occasion and didn't believe in her for more than half an hour.' She shrugged her shoulders again and gave a short little laugh. Then she said politely as was her way, 'I'm so sorry, I'm keeping you. Did you want to lock up?' She took hold of the dog again and walked her out into the rain. 'Has she sold the house?' Her voice suddenly sounded thin and strained.

Wexford nodded. 'So she says.'

'I shall never come here again.'

He watched her walk away down the narrow lane which led from the cottage to the road. Raindrops glistened on the alsatian's fur. Water slid off the flat branches of the conifers and dripped on to the grass. Uncut for more than a week, it was already shaggy, giving the place an unkempt look. Wexford walked back to the car.

Burden was watching Dinah Sternhold shoving Nancy on to the rear seat of the Volkswagen. 'It's a funny thing,' he said. 'Jenny's got a friend, a Frenchwoman, comes from Alsace. But you can't call her an Alsatian, can you? That word always means a dog.'

'You couldn't call anyone a Dalmatian either,' said Wexford.

Burden laughed. 'Americans call alsatians German Shepherds.'

'We ought to. That's their proper name and I believe the Kennel Club have brought it in again. When they were brought here from Germany after the First World War there was a lot of anti-German feeling – hence we used the euphemism "alsatian". About as daft as refusing to play Beethoven and Bach at concerts because they were German.'

'Jenny and I are going to German classes,' said Burden rather awkwardly.

'What on earth for?'

'Jenny says education should go on all one's life.'

Next morning it was heavy and sultry, the sun covered by a thick yellow mist. Sterries awaited them, full of secrets. Before he left news had come in for Wexford through Interpol that the woman who drowned in Santa Xavierita in July 1976 was Theresa or Tessa Lanchester, aged thirty, unmarried, a para-legal secretary from Boston, Massachusetts. The body had been recovered after having been in the sea some five days and identified a further four days later by Theresa Lanchester's aunt, her parents both being dead. Driving up to Sterries, Wexford thought about being sent back to California. He wouldn't mind a few days in Boston, come to that.

Archbold and Bennett got to work on the spare bedrooms but without positive result and after lunch they set about the study and the two bathrooms.

In the yellow bathroom they took up the honey-coloured carpet, leaving exposed the white vinyl tiles beneath. It was obvious that none of these tiles had been disturbed since they were first laid. The carpet was replaced and then the same procedure gone through in the blue bathroom. Here there was a shower cabinet as well as a bath. Archbold unhooked and spread out the blue and green striped shower curtain. This was made of semi-transparent nylon with a narrow machine-made hem at the bottom. Archbold, who was young and had excellent sight, noticed that the machine stitches for most of the seam's length were pale blue but in the extreme right-hand corner, for about an inch, they were not blue but brown. He told Wexford.

Wexford, who had been sitting on a window-sill in the study, thinking, watching the cloud shadows move across the meadows, went into the blue bathroom and looked at the curtain and knelt down. And about a quarter of an inch from the floor, on the panelled side of the bath, which had been covered for nearly half an inch by the carpet pile, were two minute reddish-brown spots.

'Take up the floor tiles,' said Wexford.

Would they find enough blood to make a test feasible? It appeared so after two of the tiles had been lifted and the edge of the one which had been alongside the bath panelling showed a thick dark encrustation.

18

'You might tell me where we're going.'

'Why? You're a real ignoramus when it comes to London.' Wexford spoke irritably. He was nervous because he might be wrong. The chief constable had said he was and had frowned and shaken his head and talked about infringements of rights and intrusions of privacy. If he was wrong he was going to look such a fool. He said to Burden, 'If I said we were going to Thornton Heath, would that mean anything to you?'

Burden said nothing. He looked huffily out of the window. The car was passing through Croydon, through industrial complexes, estates of small red terraced houses, shopping centres, big spreadeagled roundabouts with many exits. Soon after Thornton Heath station Wexford's driver turned down a long bleak road that was bounded by a tall wire fence on one side and a row of sad thin poplars on the other. Thank God there were such neighbours about as Mrs Murray-Burgess, thought Wexford. A woman endowed with a memory and a gimlet eye as well as a social conscience.

'An enormous removal van,' she had said, 'a real pantechnicon, and polluting what's left of our country air with clouds of the filthiest black diesel fumes. Of course I can tell you the name of the firm. I sat down and wrote to their managing director at once to complain. William Dorset and Company. I expect you've seen that slogan of theirs, "Dorset Stores It", it's on all their vans.'

The company had branches in north and south London, in Brighton, Guildford, and in Kingsmarkham, which was no doubt why both Sheila and Natalie Arno had employed them. Kingsmarkham people moving house or storing furniture mostly did use Dorset's.

Here and there along the road was the occasional factory as well as the kind of long, low, virtually windowless building whose possible nature or use it is hard for the passer-by to guess at. Perhaps all such buildings, Wexford thought as they turned into the entrance drive to one of them, served the same purpose as this one.

It was built of grey brick and roofed with red sheet iron. What windows it had were high up under the roof. In the concrete bays in front of the iron double doors stood two monster vans, dark red and lettered 'Dorset Stores It' in yellow.

'They're expecting us,' Wexford said. 'I reckon that's the office over there, don't you?'

It was an annexe built out on the far side. Someone came out before they reached the door. Wexford recognized him as the younger of the two men who had moved Sheila's furniture, the one whose wife had not missed a single episode of *Runway*. He looked at Wexford as if he thought he had seen him somewhere before but knew just the same that he was mistaken.

'Come in, will you, please? Mr Rochford's here, our deputy managing director. He reckoned he ought to be here himself.'

Wexford's heart did not exactly sink but it floundered a little. He would so much rather have been alone, without even Burden. Of course he could have stopped all these people coming with him, he had the power to do that, but he wouldn't. Besides, two witnesses would be better than one and four better than two. He followed the man who said his name was George Prince into the office. Rochford, a man of Prince's age and in the kind of suit which, while perfectly clean and respectable, looks as if it has been worn in the past for emergency manual labour and could be put to such use again if the need arose, sat in a small armchair with an unopened folder on his knees. He jumped up and the folder fell on the floor. Wexford shook hands with him and showed him the warrant.

Although he already knew the purpose of the visit, he turned white and looked nauseous.

'This is a serious matter,' he said miserably, 'a very serious matter.'

'It is.'

'I find it hard to believe. I imagine there's a chance you're wrong.'

'A very good chance, sir.'

'Because,' said Rochford hopefully and extremely elliptically, 'in summertime and after – well, I mean, there's been nothing of that sort, has there, George?'

Not yet, thought Wexford. 'Perhaps we might terminate this suspense,' he said, attempting a smile, 'by going and having a look?'

'Oh yes, yes, by all means. This way, through here. Perhaps you'll lead the way, George. I hope you're wrong, Mr Wexford, I only hope you're wrong.'

The interior of the warehouse was cavernous and dim. The roof, supported by girders of red iron, was some thirty feet high. Up there sparrows flitted about and perched on these man-made branches. The sunlight was greenish, filtering through the tinted panes of high, metal-framed windows. George Prince pressed a switch and strip lighting came on, setting the sparrows in flight again. It was chilly inside the warehouse, though the outdoor temperature had that morning edged just into the seventies.

The place had the air of a soulless and shabby township erected on a grid plan. A town of caravans, placed symmetrically a yard or two apart and with streets crossing each other at right angles to give access to them. It might have been a camp for refugees or the rejected spill-over of some newly constituted state, or the idea of such a place in grim fiction or cinema, a settlement in a northern desert without a tree or a blade of grass. Wexford felt the fantasy and shook it off, for there were no people, no inhabitants of this container camp but himself and Burden and George Prince and Rochford padding softly up the broadest aisle.

Of these rectangular houses, these metal cuboids ranked

in rows, iron red, factory green, camouflage khaki, the one they were making for stood at the end of the topmost lane to debouch from the main aisle. It stood up against the cream-washed wall under a window. Prince produced a key and was about to insert it into the lock on the container door when Rochford put out a hand to restrain him and asked to see the warrant again. Patiently, Wexford handed it to him. They stood there, waiting while he read it once more. Wexford had fancied for minutes now that he could smell something sweetish and foetid but this became marked the nearer he got to Rochford and it was only the stuff the man put on his hair or his underarms. Rochford said:

'Mrs N. Arno, 27a De Beauvoir Place, London, N1. We didn't move it from there, did we, George? Somewhere in Sussex, didn't you say?'

'Kingsmarkham, sir. It was our Kingsmarkham branch done it.'

'Ah, yes. And it was put into store indefinitely at the rate of £5.50 per week starting from 15 July?'

Wexford said gently, 'Can we open up now, sir, please?'

'Oh, certainly, certainly. Get it over, eh?'

Get it over. . . . George Prince unlocked the door and Wexford braced himself for the shock of the foul air that must escape. But there was nothing, only a curious staleness. The door swung silently open on oiled hinges. The place might be sinister and evocative of all manner of disagreeable things, but it was well-kept and well-run for all that.

The inside of the container presented a microcosm of Sterries, a drop of the essence of Sir Manuel Camargue. His desk was there and the austere furnishings from the bedroom and sitting room in his private wing, the record player too and the lyre-backed chairs from the music room and the piano. If you closed your eyes you could fancy hearing the first movement from the Flute and Harp Concerto. You could smell and hear Camargue and nothing else. Wexford turned away to face the furniture from the spare bedrooms, a green velvet ottoman in a holland cover, two embroidered footstools, sheathed in plastic, a pair of golden Afghan rugs rolled up in hessian, and under a bag full of quilts and cushions, the carved teak chest, banded now with two stout leather straps.

The four men looked at it. Burden humped the quilt bag off on to the ottoman and knelt down to undo the buckles on the straps. There was a rattly intake of breath from Rochford. The straps fell away and Burden tried the iron clasps. They were locked. He looked inquiringly at Prince who hesitated and then muttered something about having to go back to the office to check in his book where the keys were.

Wexford lost his temper. 'You knew what we'd come for. Couldn't you have checked where the keys were before we came all the way down here? If they can't be found I'll have to have it broken open.'

'Look here. . . .' Rochford was almost choking. 'Your warrant doesn't say anything about breaking. What's Mrs Arno going to say when she finds her property's been damaged? I can't take the responsibility for that sort of. . . .'

'Then you'd better find the keys.'

Prince scratched his head. 'I reckon she said they were in that desk. In one of the pigeonholes in that desk.'

They opened the desk. It was entirely empty. Burden unrolled both rugs, emptied the quilt bag, pulled out the drawers of the bedside cabinet from Camargue's bedroom.

'You say you've got a note of where they are in some book of yours?' said Wexford.

'The note says there in the desk,' said Prince.

'Right. We break the chest open.'

'They're down here,' said Burden. He pulled out his hand from the cleft between the ottoman's arm and seat cushion and waved at them a pair of identical keys on a ring.

Wexford fitted one key into the lock on the right-hand side, turned it, and then unlocked the left-hand side. The clasps opened and he raised the lid. The chest seemed to be full of black heavy-duty polythene sheeting. He grasped a fold of it and pulled.

The heavy thing that was contained in this cold glossy slippery shroud lurched against the wooden wall and seemed to roll over. Wexford began to unwrap the black stuff and then a horrible thing happened. Slowly, languidly, as if it still retained life, a yellowish-white waxen arm and thin hand rose from the chest and loomed trembling over it. It hung in the air for a moment before it subsided. Wexford stepped back with a grunt. The icy thing had brushed his cheek with fingers of marble.

Rochford let out a cry and stumbled out of the container. There was a sound of retching. But George Prince was made of tougher stuff and he came nearer to the chest with awe. With Burden's help, Wexford lifted the body on to the floor and stripped away its covering. Its throat had been cut and the wound wadded with a bloody towel, but this had not kept blood off the yellow dress, which was splashed and stained with red all over like some bizarre map of islands.

Wexford looked into the face, knowing he had been wrong, feeling as much surprise as the others, and then he looked at Burden.

Burden shook his head, appalled and mystified, and together they turned slowly back to gaze into the black dead eyes of Natalie Arno.

19

'*Cui bono*?' said Kenneth Ames. 'Who benefits?' He made a church steeple of his fingers and looked out at St Peter's spire. 'Well, my dear chap, the same lady who would have benefited had you been right in your preposterous assumption that poor Mrs Arno was not Mrs Arno. Or to cut a tall story short, Sir Manuel's niece in France.'

'You never did tell me her name,' said Wexford.

He did not then. 'It's an extraordinary thing. Poor Mrs Arno simply followed in her father's footmarks. It's no more than a week ago she asked me if she should make a will and I naturally advised her to do so. But, as was true in the case of Sir Manuel, she died before a will was drawn up. She too had been going to get married, you know, but she changed her mind.'

'No, I didn't know.'

Ames made his doggy face. 'So, as I say, the beneficiary will be this French lady, there being no other living relatives whatsoever. I've got her name somewhere.' He hunted in a drawer full of folders. 'Ah, yes. A Mademoiselle Thérèse Lerèmy. Do you want her precise address?'

The transformation of Moidore Lodge was apparent long before the house was reached. The drive was swept, the signboard bearing the name of the house had been re-painted black and white, and Wexford could have sworn the bronze wolves (or alsatians) had received a polish.

Blaise Cory's Porsche was parked up in front of the house and it was he, not Muriel Hicks, who opened the door. They send for him like other people might send for their solicitor, thought Wexford. He stepped into a hall from which all dust and clutter had been removed, which even seemed lighter and airier. Blaise confided, looking once or twice over his shoulder:

'Having these good people has made all the difference to the dear old dad. I do hope you're not here to do anything which might – well, in short, which might put a spanner in the works.'

'I hardly think so, Mr Cory. I have a question or two to ask Mrs Hicks, that's all.'

'Ah, that's what you people always say.' He gave the short, breathy, fruity laugh with which, on his show, he was in the habit of receiving the more outrageous of the statements made by his interviewees. 'I believe she's about the house, plying her highly useful equipment.'

The sound of a vacuum cleaner immediately began overhead as if on cue, and Wexford would have chosen to go straight upstairs but he found himself instead ushered into Philip Cory's living room.

Ted Hicks was cleaning the huge Victorian french windows, the old man, once more attired in his boy's jeans and guernsey, watching him with fascinated approval. Hicks stopped work the moment Wexford came in and took up his semi-attention stance.

'Good morning, sir!'

'Welcome, Chief Inspector, welcome.' Cory spread out his meagre hands expansively. 'A pleasure to see you, I'm sure. It's so delightful for me to have visitors and not be ashamed of the old place, not to mention being able to find things. Now, for instance, if you or Blaise were to require a drink I shouldn't have to poke about looking for bottles. Hicks here would bring them in a jiffy, wouldn't you, Hicks?'

'I certainly would, sir.'

'So you have only to say the word.'

It being not yet ten in the morning, Wexford was not inclined to utter any drink-summoning word but asked if he might have a talk in private with Mrs Hicks.

'I saw in the newspaper about poor little Natalie,' said

Cory. 'Blaise thought it would upset me. Blaise was always a very *sensitive* boy. But I said to him, how can I be upset when I don't know if she was Natalie or not?'

Wexford went upstairs, Hicks leading the way. Moidore Lodge was a very large house. Several rooms had been set aside to make a dwelling for the Hickses without noticeably depleting the Cory living space. Muriel Hicks, who had been cleaning Cory's own bedroom with its vast four-poster, came into her own rooms, drying her newly washed hands on a towel. She had put on weight since last he saw her and her pale red hair had grown longer and bushier. But her brusque and taciturn manner was unchanged.

'Mrs Arno was going away on her holidays. She says to me to see to the moving when the men came next day. It wasn't convenient, we were leaving ourselves and I'd got things to do, but that was all the same to her, I daresay.' Her husband flashed her an admonitory look, implying that respect should be accorded to *all* employers, or else perhaps that she must in no way hint at ill of the dead. Her pink face flushed rosily. 'Well, she said that was the only day Dorset's could do it, so it was no use arguing. She'd had a chap there staying the weekend. . . .'

'A *gentleman*,' said Hicks.

'All right, Ted, a gentleman. I thought he'd gone by the Sunday, and maybe he had, but he was back the Monday afternoon.'

'You saw him?'

'I *heard* him. I went in about six to check up with her what was going and what was staying, and I heard them talking upstairs. They heard me come in and they started talking French so I wouldn't understand, and she laughed and said in English, "Oh, your funny Swiss accent!" By the time I got upstairs he'd hid himself.'

'Did you hear his name, Mrs Hicks?'

She shook her head. 'Never heard his name and never saw him. She was a funny one, she didn't mind me knowing he was there and what he was to her like, but she never wanted me nor anyone to actually see him. I took it for granted they both went off on their holidays that same evening. She said she was going, she told me, and the car was gone.'

'What happened next day?'

'The men came from Dorset's nine in the morning. I let them in and told them what to take and what not to. She'd left everything labelled. When they'd gone I had a good clear-up. There was a lot of blood about in the blue bathroom, but I never gave it a thought, reckoned one of them had cut theirselves.' Wexford remembered the deliberate cutting of Natalie's fingertips in the bathroom in De Beauvoir Place and he almost shuddered. Muriel Hicks was more stolid about it than he. 'I had a bit of a job getting it off the carpet,' she said. 'I saw in the paper they found her at Dorset's warehouse. Was she . . .? I mean, was *it* in that chest?'

He nodded.

She said indifferently, 'The men did say it was a dead weight.'

Blaise Cory walked out to the car with him. It was warm today, the sky a serene blue, the leaves of the plane trees fluttering in a light frisky breeze. Blaise said suddenly and without his usual affected geniality:

'Do you know Mrs Mountnessing, Camargue's sister-in-law?'

'I've seen her once.'

'There was a bit of a scandal in the family. I was only seventeen or eighteen at the time and Natalie and I – well, it wasn't an affair or anything, we were like brother and sister. We were close, she used to tell me things. The general made a pass at her and the old girl caught them kissing.'

'The general?' said Wexford.

Blaise made one of his terrible jokes. 'Must have been caviare to him.' He gave a yelp of laughter. 'Sorry. I mean old Roo Mountnessing, General Mountnessing. Mrs M told her sister and made a great fuss, put all the blame on poor little Nat, called her incestuous and a lot of crap like that. As if everyone didn't know the old boy was a satyr. Camargue was away on a tour of Australia at the time or he'd have intervened. Mrs Camargue and her sister tried to lock Nat up, keep her a sort of prisoner. She got out and hit her mother. She hit her in the chest, quite hard, I think. I suppose they had a sort of brawl over Natalie trying to get out of the house.'

'And?'

'Well, when Mrs Camargue got cancer Mrs Mountnessing said it had been brought on by the blow. I've heard it said that can happen. The doctors said no but Mrs M. wouldn't listen to that and she more or less got Camargue to believe it too. I've always thought that's why Natalie went off with Vernon Arno, she couldn't stand things at home.'

'So that was the cause of the breach,' said Wexford. 'Carmargue blamed her for her mother's death.'

Blaise shook his head. 'I don't think he did. He was just confused by Mrs M. and crazy with grief over his wife dying. The dear old dad says Camargue tried over and over again to make things right between himself and Nat, wrote again and again, offered to go out there or pay her fare home. I suppose it wasn't so much him blaming her for her mother's death as her blaming herself. It was guilt kept her away.'

Wexford looked down at the little stocky man.

'Did she tell you all this when you had lunch with her, Mr Cory?'

'Good heavens, no. We didn't talk about that. I'm a *present* person, Chief Inspector, I live in the moment. And so did she. Curious,' he said reflectively, 'that rumour which went around back in the winter that she was some sort of impostor.'

'Yes,' said Wexford.

It was not a long drive from Moidore Lodge to the village on the borders of St Leonard's Forest. It was called Bayeux Green, between Horsham and Wellridge, and the house Wexford was looking for bore the name Bayeux Villa. Well, it was not all that far from Hastings, there was another village nearby called Doomsday Green, and very likely the name had something to do with the tapestry.

He found the house without having to ask. It was in the centre of the village, a narrow, detached, late nineteenth-century house, built of small pale grey bricks and with only a small railed-in area separating it from the pavement. The front door was newer and inserted in it was a picture in stained glass of a Norman soldier in chain mail. Wexford rang the bell and got no answer. He stepped to one side and looked in at the window. There was no sign of recent habitation. The occupants, at this time of the year, were very likely away on holiday. It seemed strange that they had made no arrangements for the care of their houseplants. Tradescantias, peperomias, a cissus that climbed to the ceiling on carefully spaced strings, a Joseph's coat, a variegated ivy, all hung down leaves that were limp and parched.

He walked around the house, looking in more windows, and he had a sensation of being watched, though he could see no one. The two little lawns looked as if they had not been cut for a month and there were weeds coming up in the rosebed. After he had rung the bell again he went to the nearest neighbour, a cottage separated from Bayeux Villa by a greengrocer's and a pair of garages.

It was a comfort to be himself once more, to have resumed his old standing. The woman looked at his warrant card.

'They went off on holiday – oh, it'd be three weeks ago. When I come to think of it, they must be due back today or tomorrow. They've got a caravan down in Devon, they always take three weeks.'

'Don't they have friends to come in and keep an eye on the place?'

She said quickly, 'Don't tell me it's been broken into.'

He reassured her. 'Nobody's watered the plants.'

'But the sister's there. She said to me on the Saturday, my sister'll be staying while we're away.'

This time he caught her off guard. He came up to the kitchen window and their eyes met. She had been on the watch for him too, creeping about the house, looking out for him. She was still wearing the red and yellow dress of

Indian cotton, she had been shut up in there for three weeks, and it hung on her. Her face looked sullen, though not frightened. She opened the back door and let him in.

'Good morning, Mrs Zoffany,' he said. 'It's a relief to find you well and unharmed.'

'Who would harm me?'

'Suppose you tell me that. Suppose you tell me all about it.'

She said nothing. He wondered what she had done all by herself in this house since 27 July. Not eaten much, that was obvious. Presumably, she had not been out. Nor even opened a window. It was insufferably hot and stuffy and a strong smell of sweat and general unwashedness emanated from Jane Zoffany as he followed her into the room full of dying plants. She sat down and looked at him in wary silence.

'If you won't tell me,' he said, 'shall I tell you? After you left me on that Friday evening you went back to Sterries and found the house empty. Mrs Arno had driven your husband to the station. As a matter of fact, her car passed me as I was driving down the hill.' She continued to eye him uneasily. Her eyes had more madness in them than when he had last seen her. 'You took your handbag but you left your suitcase; didn't want to be lumbered with it, I daresay. There's a bus goes to Horsham from outside St Peter's. You'd have had time to catch the last one, or else maybe you had a hire car.'

She said stonily, 'I haven't money for hire cars. I didn't know about the bus, but it came and I got on.'

'When you got here you found your sister and her husband were leaving for their summer holiday the next day. No doubt they were glad to have someone here to keep an eye on the place while they were gone. Then a week later you got yourself a birthday card. . . .'

'No.' She shook her head vehemently. 'I only posted it. My sister had bought a card for me and written in it and done the envelope and everything. She said, here, you'd better have this now, save the postage. I went out at night and posted it.' She gave a watery vague smile. 'I liked hiding, I enjoyed it.'

He could understand that. The virtue for her would be twofold. To some extent she would lose her identity, that troubling self, she would have hidden here from herself as successfully as she had hidden from others. And there would be the satisfaction of becoming for a brief while important, of causing anxiety, for once of stimulating emotions.

'What I don't see,' he said, 'is how you managed when the police came here making inquiries.'

She giggled. 'That was funny. They took me for my sister.'

'I see.'

'They just took it for granted I was my sister and they kept on talking about Mrs Zoffany. Did I have any idea where Mrs Zoffany might be? When had I last seen her? I said no and I didn't know and they had to believe me. It was funny, it was a bit like . . .' She put her fingers over her mouth and looked at him over the top of them.

'I shall have to tell your husband where you are. He's been very worried about you.'

'Has he? Has he *really*?'

Had she, during her semi-incarceration, watched television, heard a radio, seen a newspaper? Presumably not, since she had not mentioned Natalie's death. He wouldn't either. She was safe enough here, he thought, with the sister coming back. Zoffany himself would no doubt come down before that. Would they perhaps get her back into a mental hospital between them? He had no faith that the kind of treatment she might get would do her good. He wanted to tell her to have a bath, eat a meal, open the windows, but he knew she would take no advice, would hardly hear it.

'I thought you'd be very angry with me.'

He treated that no more seriously than if the younger of his grandsons had said it to him. 'You and I are going to have to have a talk, Mrs Zoffany. When you've settled down at home again and I've got more time. Just at present I'm very busy and I have to go abroad again.'

She nodded. She no longer looked sullen. He let himself out into Bayeux Green's little high street, and when he glanced back he saw her gaunt face at the window, the eyes following him. In spite of what he had said, he might never see her again, he might never need to, for in one of those flashes of illumination that he had despaired of ever coming in this case, he saw the truth. She had told him. In a little giggly confidence she had told him everything there still remained for him to know.

In the late afternoon he drove out to the home of the chief constable, Hightrees Farm, Millerton. Mrs Griswold exemplified the reverse of the Victorian ideal for children; she was heard but not seen. Some said she had been bludgeoned into passivity by forty years with the colonel. Her footsteps could sometimes be heard overhead, her voice whispering into the telephone. Colonel Griswold himself opened the front door, something which Wexford always found disconcerting. It was plunging in at the deep end.

'I want to go to the South of France, sir.'

'I daresay,' said Griswold. 'I shall have to settle for a cottage in north Wales myself.'

In a neutral voice Wexford reminded him that he had already had his holiday. The chief constable said yes, he remembered, and Wexford had been somewhere very exotic, hadn't he? He had wondered once or twice how that sort of thing would go down with the public when the police started screaming for wage increases.

'I want to go to the South of France,' Wexford said more firmly, 'and I know it's irregular but I would like to take Mike Burden with me. It's a little place *inland* – ' Griswold's lips seemed silently to be forming the syllables St Tropez, ' – and there's a woman there who will inherit Camargue's money and property. She's Camargue's niece and her name is Thérèse Lerèmy.'

'A French citizen?'

'Yes, sir, but . . .'

'I don't want you going about putting people's backs up, Reg. Particularly foreign backs. I mean, don't think you can go over there and arrest this woman on some of your thin suspicions and . . .'

But before Wexford had even begun to deny that this was his intention he knew from the moody truculent look which had replaced obduracy in Griswold's face that he was going to relent.

20

From the city of the angels to the bay of the angels. As soon as they got there the taxi driver took them along the Promenade des Anglais, though it was out of their way, but he said they had to see it, they couldn't come to Nice and just see the airport. While Wexford gazed out over the Baie des Anges, Burden spoke from his newly acquired store of culture. Jenny had a reproduction of a picture of this by a painter called Dufy, but it all looked a bit different now.

It was still only late morning. They had come on the early London to Paris flight and changed planes at Roissy-Charles de Gaulle. Now their drive took them through hills crowned with orange and olive trees. Saint-Jean-de-l'Éclaircie lay a few miles to the north of Grasse, near the river Loup. A bell began to chime noon as they passed through an ivy-hung archway in the walls into the ancient town. They drove past the ochre-stone cathedral into the Place aux Eaux Vives where a fountain was playing and where stood Picasso's statue 'Woman with a Lamb', presented to the town by the artist (according to Wexford's guide book) when he lived and worked there for some months after the war. The guide book also said that there was a Fragonard in the cathedral, some incomparable Sevres porcelain in the museum, the Fondation Yeuse, and a mile outside the town the well-preserved remains of a Roman amphitheatre. The taxi driver said that if you went up into the cathedral belfry you could see Corsica on the horizon.

Wexford had engaged rooms for one night – on the

advice of his travel agent in the Kingsbrook Precinct – at the Hotel de la Rose Blanche in the *place*. Its vestibule was cool and dim, stone-walled, stone-flagged, and with that indefinable atmosphere that is a combination of complacency and gleeful anticipation and which signifies that the food is going to be good. The chef's in his kitchen, all's right with the world.

Kenneth Ames had known nothing more about Mademoiselle Lerèmy than her name, her address and her relationship to Camargue. It was also known that her parents were dead and she herself unmarried. Recalling the photograph of the two little girls shown him by Mrs Mountnessing, Wexford concluded she must be near the age of Camargue's daughter. He looked her up in the phone book, dialled the number apprehensively because of his scanty French, but got no reply.

They lunched off seafood, bread that was nearly all crisp crust, and a bottle of Monbazillac. Wexford said in an abstracted sort of voice that he felt homesick already, the hors d'oeuvres reminded him of Mr Haq and antipasto Ankole. He got no reply when he attempted once more to phone Thérèse Lerèmy, so there seemed nothing for it but to explore the town.

It was too hot to climb the belfry. On 24 July Saint-Jean-de-l'Éclaircie was probably at its hottest. The square was deserted, the narrow steep alleys that threaded the perimeter just inside the walls held only the stray tourist, and the morning market which had filled the Place de la Croix had packed up and gone. They went into the cathedral of St Jean Baptiste, dark, cool, baroque. A nun was walking in the aisle, eyes cast down, and an old man knelt at prayer. They looked with proper awe at Fragonard's 'Les Pains et Les Poissons', a large hazy canvas of an elegant Christ and an adoring multitude, and then they returned to the bright white sunshine and hard black shadows of the *place*.

'I suppose she's out at work,' said Wexford. 'A single woman would be bound to work. It looks as if we'll have to hang things out a few hours.'

'It's no hardship,' said Burden. 'I promised Jenny I wouldn't miss the museum.'

Wexford shrugged. 'O.K.'

The collection was housed in a sienna-red stucco building with Fondation Yeuse lettered on a black marble plaque. Wexford had expected it to be deserted inside but in fact they met other tourists in the rooms and on the winding marble staircase. As well as the Sevres, Burden had been instructed to look at some ancient jewellery discovered in the Condamine, and Wexford, hearing English spoken, asked for directions from the woman who had been speaking correctly but haltingly to an American visitor. She seemed to be a curator, for she wore on one of the lapels of her dark red, near-uniform dress an oval badge inscribed Fondation Yeuse. He forced himself not to stare – and then wondered how many thousands before him had forced themselves not to stare. The lower part of her face was pitted densely and deeply with the scars of what looked like smallpox but was almost certainly acne. In her careful stumbling English she instructed him where to find the jewellery. He and Burden went upstairs again where the American woman had arrived before them. The sun penetrating drawn Venetian blinds shone on her flawless ivory skin. She had hands like Natalie Arno's, long and slender, display stands for rings as heavy and roughly made as those on the linen under the glass.

'We may as well get on up there,' said Wexford after they had bought a *flacon* of Grasse perfume for Dora and a glazed stoneware jar in a Picasso design for Jenny. 'Get on up there and have a look at the place.'

The two local taxis, which were to be found between the fountain and the hotel de la Rose Blanche, were not much in demand at this hour. Their driver spoke no English but as soon as Wexford mentioned the Maison du Cirque he understood and nodded assent.

On the north-eastern side of the town, outside the walls, was an estate of depressing pale grey flats and brown wooden houses with scarlet switchback roofs. It was as bad as home. Worse? ventured Burden. But the estate was soon left behind and the road ran through lemon groves. The driver persisted in talking to them in fast, fluent, incomprehensible French. Wexford managed to pick out two facts from all this, one that Saint-Jean-de-l'Éclaircie held a lemon festival each February, and the other that on the far side of the hill was the amphitheatre.

They came upon the house standing alone at a bend in the road. It was flat-fronted, unprepossessing but undoubtedly large. At every window were wooden shutters from which most of the paint had flaked away. Big gardens, neglected now, stretched distantly towards olive and citrus groves, separated from them by crumbling stone walls.

'Mariana in the moated grange,' said Wexford. 'We may as well go to the circus while we're waiting for her.'

The driver took them back. The great circular plain which was the base of the amphitheatre was strangely green as if watered by a hidden spring. The tiers of seating, still defined, still unmistakable, rose in their parallel arcs to the hillside, the pines, the crystalline blue of the sky. Wexford sat down where some prefect or consul might once have sat.

'I hope we're in time,' he said. 'I hope we can get to her before any real harm has been done. The woman has been dead nine days. He's been here, say, eight. . . .'

'If he's here. The idea of him being here is all based on your ESP. We don't know if he's here and, come to that, we don't know who he is or what he looks like or what name he'll be using.'

'It's not as bad as that,' said Wexford. 'He would naturally come here. This place, that girl, would draw him like magnets. He won't want to lose the money now, Mike.'

'No, not after plotting for years to get it. How long d'you reckon we're going to be here?'

Wexford shrugged. The air was scented with the herbs that grew on the hillsides, sage and thyme and rosemary and bay, and the sun was still very warm. 'However long it may be,' he said enigmatically, 'to me it would be too short.' He looked at his watch. 'Martin should have seen

Williams by now and done a spot of checking up for me at Guy's Hospital.'

'Guy's Hospital?'

'In the course of this case we haven't remembered as often as we should that Natalie Arno went into hospital a little while before Camargue died. She had a biopsy.'

'Yes, what *is* that?'

'It means to look at living tissue. It usually describes the kind of examination that is done to determine whether certain cells are cancerous or not.'

Once this subject would have been a highly emotive one for Burden, an area to be avoided by all his sensitive acquaintances. His first wife had died of cancer. But time and his second marriage had changed things. He responded not with pain but only with an edge of embarrassment to his voice.

'But she didn't have cancer.'

'Oh, no.'

He sat down in the tier below Wexford. 'I'd like to tell you what I think happened, see if we agree.' On the grass beside him the shadow of Wexford's head nodded. 'Well, then. Tessa Lanchester went on holiday to that place in California, Santa – what was it?'

'Santa Xavierita.'

'And while she was there she met a man who played the guitar or whatever in a restaurant in the local town. He was living in America illegally and was very likely up to a good many other illegal activities as well. He was a con man. He had already met Natalie Arno and found out from her who her father was and what her expectations were. He introduced Tessa to Natalie and the two women became friends.

'He persuaded Tessa not to go back home to Boston but to remain longer in Santa Xavierita learning all she could about Natalie's life and past. Then he took Natalie out swimming by night and drowned her and that same night left with Tessa for Los Angeles in Natalie's car with Natalie's luggage and the key to Natalie's house. From then on Tessa became Natalie. The changes Natalie's body had undergone after five days in the sea made a true identification impossible and, since Tessa was missing, the corpse was identified as that of Tessa.

'Tessa and her accomplice then set about their plan to inherit Camargue's property, though this was somewhat frustrated by Ilbert's intervening and the subsequent deportation. Tessa tried in vain to sell Natalie's house. I think at this time she rather cooled off the plan. Otherwise I don't know how to account for a delay of more than three years between making the plan and putting it into practice. I think she cooled off. She settled into her new identity, made new friends and, as we know, had two further love affairs. Then one of these lovers, Ivan Zoffany, wrote from London in the autumn of 1979 to say he had heard from his sister-in-law who lived near Wellridge that Camargue was about to re-marry. That alerted her and fetched her to England. There she was once more able to join forces with the man who had first put her up to the idea. They had the support and help of Zoffany and his wife. How am I doing so far?'

Wexford raised his eyebrows. 'How did they get Williams and Mavis Rolland into this? Bribery?'

'Of course. It would have to be a heavy bribe. Williams's professional integrity presumably has a high price. I daresay Mrs Woodhouse could be bought cheaply enough.'

'I never took you for a snob before, Mike.'

'It's not snobbery,' said Burden hotly. 'It's simply that the poorer you are the more easily you're tempted. Shall I go on?'

The shadow nodded.

'They hesitated a while before the confrontation. Tessa was naturally nervous about this very important encounter. Also she'd been ill and had to have hospital treatment. When she finally went down to Sterries she blundered, not in having failed to do her homework – she knew every fact about the Camargue household she could be expected to, she knew them like she knew her own family in Boston – but over the pronunciation of an Italian name. Spanish she knew – many Americans do – French she knew, but it never occurred to her she would have to pronounce Italian.

'The rest we know. Camargue told her she would be cut out of his will, so on the following Sunday she made a sound alibi for herself by going to a party with Jane Zoffany. *He* went down to Sterries, waited for Camargue in the garden and drowned him in the lake.'

Wexford said nothing.

'Well?'

As befitted a person of authority sitting in the gallery of an amphitheatre, Wexford turned down his thumbs. 'The last bit's more or less right, the drowning bit.' He got up. 'Shall we go?'

Burden was still muttering that it had to be that way, that all else was impossible, when they arrived back at the Maison du Cirque. Ahead of them a bright green Citroen 2 CV had just turned into the drive.

The woman who got out of it, who came inquiringly towards them, was the curator of the Fondation Yeuse.

21

The sun shone cruelly on that pitted skin. She had done her best to hide it with heavy make-up, but there would never be any hiding it. And now as she approached these two strangers she put one hand up, half covering a cheek. Close to, she had a look of Camargue, all the less attractive traits of the Camargue physiognomy were in her face, too-high forehead, too-long nose, too-fleshy mouth, and added to them that acne-scarred skin. She was sallow and her hair was very dark. But she was one of those plain people whose smiles transform them. She smiled uncertainly at them, and the change of expression made her look kind and sweet-tempered.

Wexford introduced them. He explained that he had seen her earlier that day. Her surprise at being called upon by two English policemen seemed unfeigned. She was astonished but not apparently nervous.

'This is some matter concerning the *musée* – the museum?' she asked in her heavily accented English.

'No, mademoiselle,' said Wexford, 'I must confess I'd never heard of the Fondation Yeuse till this morning. You've worked there long?'

'Since I leave the university – that is, eighteen years. M. Raoul Yeuse, the Paris art dealer, he is, was, the brother of my father's sister. He has founded the museum, you understand? Excuse me, monsieur, I fear my English is very bad.'

'It is we who should apologize for having no French. May we go into the house, Mademoiselle Lerèmy? I have something to tell you.'

Did she know already? The announcement of the discovery of the body at Dorset's would have scarcely appeared in the French newspapers until three days ago. And when it appeared would it have merited more than a paragraph on an inside page? A murder, in England, of an obscure woman? The dark eyes of Camargue's niece looked merely innocent and inquiring. She led them into a large high-ceilinged room and opened latticed glass doors on to a terrace. From the back of the Maison du Cirque you could see the green rim of the amphitheatre and smell the scented hillsides. But the house itself was shabby and neglected and far too big. It had been built for a family and that family's servants in days when perhaps money came easily and went a long way.

Now that they were indoors and seated she had become rather pale. 'This is not bad news, I hope, monsieur?' She looked from one to the other of them with a rising anxiety that Wexford thought he understood. He let Burden answer her.

'Serious news,' said Burden. 'But not personally distressing to you, Miss Lerèmy. You hardly knew your cousin Natalie Camargue, did you?'

She shook her head. 'She was married. I have not heard her husband's name. When last I am seeing her she is sixteen, I seventeen. It is many years . . . '

'I'm afraid she's dead. To put it bluntly, she was murdered and so was your uncle. We're here to investigate these crimes. It seems the same person killed them both. For gain. For money.'

Both hands went up to her cheeks. She recoiled a little. 'But this is terrible!'

Wexford had decided not to tell her of the good fortune this terrible news would bring her. Kenneth Ames could do that. If what he thought was true she would be in need of consolation. He must now broach the subject of this belief of his. Strange that this time he could be so near hoping he was wrong. . . .

Her distress seemed real. Her features were contorted into a frown of dismay, her tall curved forehead all wrinkles. 'I am so sorry, this is so very bad.'

'Mademoiselle Lerèmy . . . '

'When I am a little girl I see him many many times, monsieur. I stay with them in Sussex. Natalie is, was, nice, I think, always laughing, always very gay, have much sense of ***humeur***. The world has become a very bad place, monsieur, when such things as this happen.' She paused, bit her lip. 'Excuse me, I must not say "sir" so much, is it not so? This I am learning to understand . . . ' She hesitated and hazarded, 'Lately? Recently?'

Her words brought him the thrill of knowing he was right – and sickened him too. Must he ask her? Burden was looking at him.

The telephone rang.

'Please excuse me,' she said.

The phone was in the room where they were, up beside the windows. She picked up the receiver rather too fast and the effect on her of the voice of her caller was pitiful to see. She flushed deeply and it was somehow apparent that this was a flush of intense fearful pleasure as well as embarrassment.

She said softly, 'Ah, Jean. . . . We see each other again tonight? Of course it is all right, it is fine, very good.' She made an effort, for their benefit or her caller's, to establish formality. 'It will be a great pleasure to see you again.'

He was here all right then, he was talking to her. But where was he? She had her back to them now. 'When you have finished your work, yes. *Entends*, Jean, I will fetch – pick up – pick you up. Ten o'clock?' Suddenly she changed into rapid French. Wexford could not understand a word but he understood *her*. She had been speaking English to a French speaker so that her English hearers would know she had a boy friend, a lover. For all her scarred face, her plainness, her age, her obscure job in this backwater, she had a lover to tell the world about.

She put the phone down after a murmured word or two, a ripple of excited laughter. Wexford was on his feet, signalling with a nod to Burden.

'You do not wish to ask me questions concerning my

uncle and my *cousine* Natalie, monsieur?'

'It is no longer necessary, mademoiselle.'

The taxi driver had gone to sleep. Wexford woke him with a prod in his chest.

'La Rose Blanche, *s'il vous plaît.*'

The sun was going down. There were long violet shadows and the air was sweet and soft.

'He's a fast worker if ever there was one,' said Burden.

'The material he is working on could hardly be more receptive and malleable.'

'Pardon? Oh, yes, I see what you mean. Poor girl. It's a terrible handicap having all that pitting on her face, did you notice? D'you think he knew about that? Before he came here, I mean? The real Natalie might have known – you usually get that sort of acne in your teens – but Tessa Lanchester wouldn't have. Unless she picked it up when she was gathering all the rest of her info in Santa Xavierita.'

'Mrs Woodhouse might have known,' said Wexford. 'At any rate, he knew she was unmarried and an heiress and no doubt that she worked in the museum here. It was easy enough for him to scrape up an acquaintance.'

'Bit more than an acquaintance,' said Burden grimly.

'Let's hope it hasn't progressed far yet. Certainly his intention is to marry her.'

'Presumably his intention was to marry that other woman, but at the last she wouldn't have him and for that he killed her.' Burden seemed gratified to get from Wexford a nod of approval. 'Once he'd done that he'd realize who the next heir was and come here as fast as he could. But there's something here doesn't make sense. In putting her body in that chest he seems to have meant to keep it concealed for months, possibly even years, but the paradox there is that until the body was found death wouldn't be presumed and Thérèse Lerèmy wouldn't get anything.'

Wexford looked slyly at him. 'Suppose he intended by some means or other to prove, as only he could, that it was Natalie Arno and not Tessa Lanchester who drowned at Santa Xavierita in 1976? If that were proved Thérèse would become the heir at once and in fact *would have been* the rightful possessor of Sterries and Camargue's money for the past six months.'

'You really think that was it?'

'No, I don't. It would have been too bold and too risky and fraught with problems. I think this was what was in his mind. He didn't want the body found at once because if he then started courting Thérèse even someone as desperate as she might suspect he was after her money. But he wanted it found at some time in the not too distant future or his conquest of Thérèse would bring him no profit at all. What better than that the presence of a corpse in that warehouse should make itself apparent after, say, six months? And if it didn't he could always send the police an anonymous letter.'

'That's true,' said Burden. 'And there was very little to connect him with it, after all. If you hadn't been to California we shouldn't have known of his existence.'

Wexford laughed shortly. 'Yes, there was some profit in it.' They walked into the hotel. Outside Burden's room where they would have separated prior to dressing, or at least sprucing up, for dinner, Burden said, 'Come in here a minute. I want to ask you something.' Wexford sat on the bed. From the window you could see, not the square and the fountain but a mazy mosaic of little roofs against the backdrop of the city walls. 'I'd like to know what we're going to charge those others with. I mean, Williams and Zoffany and Mary Woodhouse. Conspiracy, I suppose – but not conspiracy to murder?'

Wexford pondered. He smiled a little ruefully. 'We're not going to charge them with anything.'

'You mean their evidence will be more valuable as prosecution witnesses?'

'Not really. I shouldn't think any of them would be a scrap of use as witnesses of any kind. They didn't witness anything and they haven't done anything. They all seem to me to be perfectly blameless, apart from a spot – and I'd guess a very small spot – of adultery on the part of Zoffany.' Wexford paused. 'That reconstruction of the case you gave me while we were at the amphitheatre, didn't it strike you there was something unreal about it?'

'Sort of illogical, d'you mean? Maybe, bits of it. Surely that's because they were so devious that there are aspects which aren't clear and never will be?'

Wexford shook his head. 'Unreal. One can't equate it with what one knows of human nature. Take, for instance, their foresight and their patience. They kill Natalie in the summer of 1976 and Tessa impersonates her. Fair enough. Why not go straight to England, make sure Natalie is the beneficiary under Camargue's will and then kill Camargue?'

'I know there's a stumbling block. I said so.'

'It's more than a stumbling block, Mike, it's a bloody great barrier across the path. Think what you – and I – believed they did. Went back to Los Angeles, ran the risk of being suspected by the neighbours, exposed by Ilbert – returned to and settled in what of all cities in the world was the most dangerous to them. And for what?'

'Surely she stayed there to sell the house?'

'Yet she never succeeded in selling it, did she? No, a delay of three-and-a-half years between the killing of Natalie and the killing of Camargue was too much for me to swallow. I can come up with just one feeble reason for it – that they were waiting for Camargue to die a natural death. But, as I say, that's a feeble reason. He might easily have lived another ten years.' Wexford looked at his watch. 'I'll leave you to your shaving and showering or whatever. A wash and brush-up will do me. Laquin won't be here before seven.'

They met again in the bar where they each had a Stella Artois. Wexford said:

'Your suggestion is that Tessa came to England finally because, through Zoffany's sister-in-law, she heard that Camargue intended to marry again. Doesn't it seem a bit thin that Jane Zoffany's sister should come to know this merely because she lives in a village near the Kathleen Camargue School?'

'Not if she was set by the others to watch Camargue.'

Wexford shrugged. 'The others, yes. There would be

five of them, our protagonist and her boy friend, the Zoffanys and Jane Zoffany's sister. Five conspirators working for the acquisition of Camargue's money. Right?'

'Yes, for a start,' said Burden. 'There were finally more like eight or nine.'

'Mary Woodhouse to give Tessa some advanced coaching, Mavis Rolland to identify her as an old school chum, and Williams the dentist.' Wexford gave a little shake of the head. 'I've said I was amazed at their foresight and their patience, Mike, but that was nothing to the trouble they took. That staggered me. All these subsidiary conspirators were persuaded to lie, to cheat or to sell their professional integrity. Tessa studied old samples of Natalie's handwriting, had casts made of her jaw, took lessons to perfect her college French and Spanish – though she neglected to polish up her Italian – while one of the others made a survey of the lie of the land round Sterries and of Camargue's habits. Prior to this Zoffany's sister-in-law was sending a secret agent's regular dispatches out to Los Angeles. Oh, and let's not forget – Jane Zoffany was suborning her neighbours into providing a fake alibi. And all this machinery was set in motion and relentlessly kept in motion for the sake of acquiring a not very large house in an acre of ground and an *unknown sum of money* that, when the time came, would have to be split between eight people.

'I've kept thinking of that and I couldn't believe in it. I couldn't understand why those two had chosen Camargue as their prey. Why not pick on some tycoon? Why not some American oil millionaire? Why an old musician who wasn't and never had been in the tycoon class?'

Burden supplied a hesitant answer. 'Because his daughter fell into their hands, one supposes. Anyway, there's no alternative. We know there was a conspiracy, we know there was an elaborate plan, and one surely simply comments that it's impossible fully to understand people's motivations.'

'But isn't there an alternative? You said I was obsessed, Mike. I think more than anything I became obsessed by the complexity of this case, by the deviousness of the protagonist, by the subtlety of the web she had woven. It was only when I saw how wrong I'd been in these respects that things began to clear for me.'

'I don't follow you.'

Wexford drank his beer. He said rather slowly, 'It was only then that I began to see that this case wasn't complicated, there was no deviousness, there was no plotting, no planning ahead, no conspiracy whatsoever, and that even the two murders happened so spontaneously as really to be unpremeditated.' He rose suddenly, pushing back his chair. Commissaire Mario Laquin of the Compagnies Republicaines de Securité of Grasse had come in and was scanning the room. Wexford raised a hand. He said absently to Burden as the commissaire came towards their table, 'The complexity was in our own minds, Mike. The case itself was simple and straightforward, and almost everything that took place was the result of accident or of chance.'

It was a piece of luck for Wexford that Laquin had been transferred to Grasse from Marseilles some six months before, for they had once or twice worked on cases together and since then the two policemen and their wives had met when M. and Mme Laquin were in London on holiday. It nevertheless came as something of a shock to be clasped in the commissaire's arms and kissed on both cheeks. Burden stood by, trying to give his dry smile but succeeding only in looking astonished.

Laquin spoke English that was almost flawless. 'You pick some charming places to come for your investigations, my dear Reg. A little bird tells me you have already had two weeks in California. I should be so lucky. Last year when I was in pursuit of Honorat L'Eponge, where does he lead me to but Dusseldorf, I ask you!'

'Have a drink,' said Wexford. 'It's good to see you. I haven't a clue where this chap of ours is. Nor do I know what name he's going under while here.'

'Or even what he looks like,' said Burden for good measure. He seemed cheered by the presence of Laquin whom he had perhaps expected to speak with a Peter Sellers accent.

'I know what he looks like,' said Wexford. 'I've seen him.'

Burden glanced at him in surprise. Wexford took no notice of him and ordered their drinks.

'You'll dine with us, of course?' he said to Laquin.

'It will be a pleasure. The food here is excellent.'

Wexford grinned wryly. 'Yes, it doesn't look as though we'll be here to enjoy it tomorrow. I reckon we're going to have to take him at the Maison du Cirque, in that wretched girl's house.'

'Reg, she has known him no time at all, a mere week at most.'

'Even so quickly can one catch the plague. . . . You're right, of course.'

'A blessing for her we're going to rid her of him, if you ask me,' said Burden. 'A couple of years and he'd have put her out of the way as well.'

'She implied he was working here . . .'

'Since Britain came in the European Economic Community, Reg, there is no longer need for your countrymen to have work permits or to register. Therefore to trace his whereabouts would be a long and laborious business. And since we know that later on tonight he will be at the Maison du Cirque . . . '

'Sure, yes, I know. I'm being sentimental, Mario, I'm a fool.' Wexford gave a grim little laugh. 'But not such a fool as to warn her and have him hop off on the next plane into Switzerland.'

After *bouillabaisse* and a fine *cassoulet* with brie to follow and a small armagnac each, it was still only nine. Ten-thirty was the time fixed on by Wexford and Laquin for their visit to the house by the amphitheatre. Laquin suggested they go to a place he knew on the other side of the Place aux Eaux Vives where there was sometimes flamenco dancing.

In the evening there was some modest floodlighting in

the square. Apparently these were truly living waters and the fountain was fed by a natural spring. While they dined tiers of seating had been put up for the music festival of Saint Jean-de-l'Éclaircie, due to begin on the following day. A little warm breeze rustled through the plane and chestnut leaves above their heads.

The flamenco place was called La Mancha. As they passed down the stairs and into a kind of open, deeply sunken courtyard or cistern, a waiter told Laquin there would be no dancing tonight. The walls were made of yellow stone over which hung a deep purple bougainvillea. Instead of the dancers a thin girl in black came out and sang in the manner of Piaf. Laquin and Burden were drinking wine but Wexford took nothing. He felt bored and restless. Nine-thirty. They went up the stairs again and down an alley into the cobbled open space in front of the cathedral.

The moon had come up, a big golden moon flattened like a tangerine. Laquin had sat down at a table in a pavement cafe and was ordering coffee for all three men. From here you could see the city walls, part Roman, part medieval, their rough stones silvered by the light from that yellow moon.

Some teenagers went by. They were on their way, Laquin said, to the discotheque in the Place de la Croix. Wexford wondered if Camargue had ever, years ago, sat on this spot where they were. And that dead woman, when she was a child . . . ? It was getting on for ten. Somewhere in St Jean she would be meeting him now in the little green Citroen. The yellow hatchback Opel was presumably left in the long-term car park at Heathrow. He felt a tautening of tension and at the same time relief when Laquin got to his feet and said in his colloquial way that they should be making tracks.

Up through the narrow winding defile once more, flattening themselves tolerantly against stone walls to let more boys and girls pass them. Wexford heard the music long before they emerged into the Place aux Eaux Vives. A Mozart serenade. The serenade from *Don Giovanni*, he thought it was, that should properly be played on a mandolin.

Round the last turn in the alley and out into the wide open square. A group of young girls, also no doubt on their way to the discotheque, were clustered around the highest tier of the festival seating. They clustered around a man who sat on the top, playing a guitar, and they did so in the yearning, worshipping fashion of muses or nymphs on the plinth of some statue of a celebrated musician. The man sat aloft, his tune changed now to a Latin American rhythm, not looking at the girls, looking across the square, his gaze roving as if he expected at any moment the person he waited for to come.

'That's him,' said Wexford.

Laquin said, 'Are you sure?'

'Absolutely. I've only seen him once before but I'd know him anywhere.'

'I know him too,' said Burden incredulously. 'I've seen him before. I can't for the life of me think where, but I've seen him.'

'Let's get it over.'

The little green 2CV was turning into the *place* and the guitarist had seen it. He drew his hand across the strings with a flourish and jumped down from his perch, nearly knocking one of the girls over. He didn't look back at her, he made no apology, he was waving to the car.

And then he saw the three policemen, recognizing them immediately for what they were. His arm fell to his side. He was a tall thin man in his late thirties, very dark with black curly hair. Wexford steadfastly refused to look over his shoulder to see her running from the car. He said:

'John Fassbender, it is my duty to warn you that anything you say will be taken down and may be used in evidence . . . '

22

They were in the Pearl of Africa, having what Wexford called a celebration lunch. No one could possibly feel much in the way of pity for Fassbender, so why not celebrate his arrest? Burden said it ought to be called an elucidation lunch because there were still a lot of things he didn't understand and wanted explained. Outside it was pouring with rain again. Wexford asked Mr Haq for a bottle of wine, *good* moselle or a riesling, none of your living waters from Lake Victoria. They had got into sybaritic habits during their day in France. Mr Haq bustled off to what he called his cellar through the fronds of polyethylene Spanish moss.

'Did you mean what you said about there having been no conspiracy?'

'Of course I did,' Wexford said, 'and if we'd had a moment after that I'd have told you something else, something I realized before we ever went to France. The woman we knew as Natalie Arno, the woman Fassbender murdered, was never Tessa Lanchester. Tessa Lanchester was drowned in Santa Xavierita in 1976 and we've no reason to believe either Natalie or Fassbender even met her. The woman who came to London in November of last year came solely because Fassbender was in London. She was in love with Fassbender and since he had twice been deported from the United States he could hardly return there.'

'How could he have been deported twice?' asked Burden.

'I wondered that until the possibility of dual nationality occurred to me and then everything about Fassbender became simple. I'd been asking myself if she had two boyfriends, an Englishman and a Swiss. There was a good deal of confusion in people's minds over him. He was Swiss. He was English. He spoke French. He spoke French with a Swiss accent. He was deported to London. He was deported to Geneva. Well, I'll come back to him in a minute. Suffice it to say that it was after he had been deported a second time that she followed him to London.'

He stopped. Mr Haq, beaming, teeth flashing and spilling, was bringing the wine, a quite respectable-looking white medoc. He poured Wexford a trial half-glassful. Wexford sipped it, looking serious. He had sometimes said, though, that he would rather damage his liver than upset Mr Haq by sending back a bottle. Anyway, the only fault with this wine was that it was at a temperature of around twenty-five degrees Celsius.

'Excellent,' he said to Mr Haq's gratification, and just stopped himself from adding, 'Nice and warm.' He continued to Burden as Mr Haq trotted off, 'She had a brief affair with Zoffany during Fassbender's first absence. I imagine this was due to nothing more than loneliness and that she put it out of her head once Zoffany had departed. But he kept up a correspondence with her and when she needed a home in London he offered her a flat. Didn't I tell you it was simple and straightforward?

'Once there, she saw that Zoffany was in love with her and hoped to take up their relationship (to use Jane Zoffany's word) where it had ended a year and a half before. She wasn't having that, she didn't care for Zoffany at all in that way. But it made things awkward. If she had Fassbender to live with her there, would Zoffany be made so jealous and angry as to throw her out? She couldn't live with Fassbender, he was living in one room. The wisest thing obviously was to keep Fassbender discreetly in the background until such time as he got a job and made some money and they could afford to snap their fingers at Zoffany and live together. We know that Fassbender was in need of work and that she tried to get him a job through Blaise Cory. The point I'm making is that Zoffany never knew of

Fassbender's existence until he overheard Natalie talking on the phone to him *last month*.

'I suspect, though I don't know for certain, that there was no urgency on her part to approach Camargue. Probably she gave very little thought to Camargue. It was the announcement of his engagement that brought her to get in touch with him – perhaps reminded her of his existence. But there was no complex planning about that approach, no care taken with the handwriting or the style of the letter, no vetting of it by, say, Mrs Woodhouse. . . .'

Young Haq came with their starter of prawns Pakwach. This was a shocking pink confection into which Burden manfully plunged his spoon before saying, 'There must have been. It may be that the identity of the woman we found in that chest will never be known, but we know very well she was an impostor and a fraudulent claimant.'

'Her identity is known,' said Wexford. 'She was Natalie Arno, Natalie Camargue, Camargue's only child.'

Pouring more wine for them, Mr Haq burst into a flowery laudation of various offerings among the entrées. There was caneton Kioga, wild duck breasts marinated in a succulent sauce of wine, cream and basil, or T-bone Toro, tender steaks *flambés*. Burden's expression was incredulous, faintly dismayed. Fortunately, his snapped 'Bring us some of that damned duck,' was lost on Mr Haq who responded only to Wexford's gentler request for two portions of caneton.

'I don't understand you,' Burden said coldly when Mr Haq had gone. 'Are you saying that the woman Camargue refused to recognize, the woman who deliberately cut her hand to avoid having to play the violin, whose antecedents you went rooting out all over America – that woman was Camargue's daughter all the time? We were wrong. Ames was right, Williams and Mavis Rolland and Mary Woodhouse and Philip Cory were right, but we were wrong. Camargue was wrong. Camargue was a senile half-blind old man who happened to make a mistake. Is that it?'

'I didn't say that,' said Wexford. 'I only said that Natalie

Arno was Natalie Arno. Camargue made no mistake, though it would be true to say he misunderstood.' He sighed. 'We were such fools, Mike – you, me, Ames, Dinah Sternhold. Not one of us saw the simple truth, that though the woman who visited Camargue was not his daughter, she was not his daughter, if I may so put it, for just one day.'

'You see,' he went on, 'an illusion was created, as if by a clever trick. Only it was a trick we played upon ourselves. We were the conjurers and we held the mirrors. Dinah Sternhold told me Camargue said the woman who went to see him wasn't his daughter. I jumped to the conclusion – you did, Dinah did, we all did – that therefore the woman *we* knew as Natalie Arno wasn't his daughter. It never occurred to us he could be right and yet she might still be his daughter. It never occurred to us that the woman he saw might not be the woman who claimed to be his heir and lived in his house and inherited his money.'

'It wasn't Natalie who went there that day but it was Natalie before and always Natalie after that?' Burden made the face people do when they realize they have been conned by a stratagem unworthy of their calibre. 'Is that what you're saying?'

'Of course it is.' Wexford grinned and gave a rueful shake of the head. 'I may as well say here and now that Natalie wasn't the arch-villainess I took her for. She was cruel and devious and spiteful only in my imagination. Mind you, I'm not saying she was an angel of light. She may not have killed her father or plotted his death, but she connived at it afterwards and she had no scruples about taking an inheritance thus gained. Nor did she have any scruples about appropriating other women's husbands either on a temporary or a permanent basis. She was no paragon of virtue but she was no Messalina either. Why did I ever think she was? Largely, I'm ashamed to say, because Dinah Sternhold told me so.

'Now Dinah Sternhold is a very nice girl. If she blackened Natalie's character to me before I'd even met her, I'm sure it was unconscious. The thing with Dinah, you see, is that odd though it undoubtedly seems, she was genuinely in love with that old man. He was old enough to be her grandfather but she was as much in love with him as if he'd been fifty years younger. Have you ever noticed that it's only those who suffer most painfully from jealousy that say, "I haven't a jealous nature"? Dinah said that to me. She was deeply jealous of Natalie and perhaps with justification. For in marrying her, wasn't Camargue looking to replace his lost daughter? How then must she have felt when that lost daughter turned up? Dinah was jealous and in her jealousy, all unconsciously, without malice, she painted Natalie as a scheming adventuress and so angled the tale of the visit to Camargue to make her appear at once as a fraudulent claimant.'

'I'd like to hear your version of that visit.'

Wexford nodded. The duck had arrived, modestly veiled in a thick brown sauce. Wexford took a sip of his wine instead of a long draught, having decided with some soul-searching that it would hardly do to send for a second bottle. He sampled the duck, which wasn't too bad, and said after a few moments:

'The first appointment Natalie made with her father she couldn't keep. In the meantime something very disquieting had happened to her. She discovered a growth in one of her breasts.'

'How d'you know that?'

'A minute scar where the biopsy was done showed at the post-mortem,' said Wexford. 'Natalie went to her doctor and was sent to Guy's Hospital, the appointment being on the day she had arranged to go down to Sterries. She didn't want to talk to her father on the phone – I think we can call that a perfectly natural shrinking in the circumstances – so she got Jane Zoffany to do it. Shall I say here that Natalie was a congenital slave-owner and Jane Zoffany a born slave?

'Well, Jane made the call and a new date for the 19th. Natalie went to the hospital where they were unable to tell her whether the growth was malignant or not. She must come into their Hedley Atkins Unit in New Cross for a biopsy under anaesthetic.

'Now we're all of us afraid of cancer but Natalie maybe had more reason than most of us. She had seen her young husband die of leukaemia, a form of cancer, her friend Tina too, but most traumatic for her, her mother had died of it and died, it had been implied, through her daughter's actions. Moreover, at the time she had only been a few years older than Natalie then was. Small wonder if she was terrified.

'Then – due no doubt to some aberration on the part of the Post Office – the letter telling her she was to go into the Hedley Atkins Unit on 17 January didn't arrive till the morning before. This meant she couldn't go to Kingsmarkham on the 19th. I imagine she was past caring. All that mattered to her now was that she shouldn't have cancer, shouldn't have her beautiful figure spoilt, shouldn't live in dread of a recurrence or an early death. Jane Zoffany could deal with her father for her, phone or write or send a telegram.'

From staring down at his empty plate, Burden now lifted his eyes and sat bolt upright. 'It was Jane Zoffany who came down here that day?'

Wexford nodded. 'Who else?'

'She too is thin and dark and about the right age. . . . But why? Why pose as Natalie? For whatever possible purpose?'

'It wasn't deliberate,' Wexford said a shade testily. 'Haven't I said scarcely anything in this case was deliberate, planned or premeditated? It was just typical silly muddled Jane Zoffany behaviour. And what months it took me to guess it! I suppose I had an inkling of the truth, that wet day in the garden at Sterries, when Dinah said how strange it was Natalie could get the solicitors and Camargue's old friends to believe in her, yet Camargue who wanted to believe, who was longing to believe, saw her *on that one occasion* and didn't believe in her for more than half an hour. And when Jane Zoffany said how the police had taken her for her own sister and then stuck her hand up over her mouth – I knew then, I didn't need to be told any more.'

'But she did tell you more?'

'Sure. When I talked to her last night. She filled in the gaps.'

'Why did she go down to Sterries at all?' asked Burden.

'Two reasons. She wanted to see the old man for herself – she'd been an admirer of his – and she didn't want his feelings hurt. She knew that if she phoned and told him Natalie had yet again to keep a hospital appointment he'd think she was making excuses not to see him and he'd be bitterly hurt. For nineteen years his daughter had stayed away from him and now that she had come back and they were on the brink of a reunion, he was to be fobbed off with a phone call – and a second phone call at that. So she decided to go down and see him herself. But not, of course, with any idea of posing as Natalie, nothing of that sort entered her head. It's just that she's a rather silly muddled creature who isn't always quite mentally stable.'

'You mean,' said Burden, 'that she came down here simply because it seemed kinder and more polite to call in person? She came to explain why Natalie couldn't come and – well, sort of assure him of Natalie's affection for him? Something like that?'

'Something very much like that. And also to get a look at the man who had been acclaimed the world's greatest flautist.' Wexford caught Mr Haq's eye for their coffee. 'Now Camargue,' he said, 'was the first person to cast a doubt on Natalie's identity, it was Camargue who started all this, yet it was Camargue himself who took Jane Zoffany for his daughter because it was *his daughter that he expected to see*.

'He had waited for nineteen years – eventually without much hope. Hope had reawakened in the past five weeks and he was keyed up to a pitch of very high tension. He opened the door to her and put his arms round her and kissed her before she could speak. Did she try to tell him then that he had made a mistake? He was deaf. He was carried away with emotion. She has told me she was so confused and aghast that she played along with him while trying to decide what to do. She says she was embarrassed, she was afraid to disillusion him.

'She humoured him by speaking of the Cazzini gold flute – which Natalie had possibly mentioned to her but which was in any case clearly labelled – and having no knowledge of Italian, she mispronounced the name. We know what happened then. Camargue accused her of imposture. But it was no dream of Camargue's, no senile fantasy, that his visitor confessed. Jane Zoffany freely admitted what she had been longing to admit for the past half-hour – but it did her no good. Camargue was convinced by then this was a deception plotted to secure Natalie's inheritance and he turned her out of the house.

'And that, Mike, was all this so-called imposture ever amounted to, half an hour's misunderstanding between a well-meaning neurotic and a "foolish, fond old man." '

While Burden experimented yet again with ice cream eau-de-Nil, Wexford contented himself with coffee.

'Natalie,' he said, 'came out of hospital on January 20th and she was so elated that the biopsy had shown the growth to be benign that instead of being angry she was simply amused by Jane's activities. As I've said, she had a very lively sense of fun. I think it must have tickled her to imagine the pair of them at cross-purposes, the wretched Jane Zoffany confessing and the irate Camargue throwing her out. What did it matter, anyway? She hadn't got cancer, she was fit and well and on top of the world and she could easily put that nonsense with her father right again. Let her only see if she could get a job out of Blaise Cory for her Johnny and then she'd see her father and patch things up.

'Before she could get around to that Camargue had written to her, informing her she should inherit nothing under the new will he intended to make.'

'Which led her,' said Burden, 'to plan on killing him first.'

'No, no, I've told you. There was no planning. Even

after that letter I'm sure Natalie was confident she could make things smooth with her father. Perhaps she even thought, as Dinah says *she* did, that this could best be effected after the marriage. Natalie was not too concerned. She was amused. The mistake she made was in telling Fassbender. Probably for the first time Fassbender realized just how potentially wealthy a woman his girl friend actually was.'

'Why do you say for the first time?'

'If he'd known it before,' Wexford retorted, 'why hadn't he married her while they were both in California? That would have been a way of ensuring he didn't get deported. She was an American citizen. In those days, no doubt, she would have been willing enough to marry him, so if they didn't it must have been because he couldn't see there was anything in it for him. But now he did. Now he could see there was a very pleasant little sinecure here for the rest of their lives if only she wasn't so carefree and idle as to cast it all away.

'That Sunday Natalie went to a party with Jane Zoffany. She went because she liked parties, she liked enjoying herself, her whole life had been blithely dedicated to enjoying herself. There was no question of establishing an alibi. Nor, I'm sure, did she know Fassbender had taken himself off down to Kingsmarkham to spy out the land and have a look at the house and the affluence Natalie was apparently so indifferent to. It was on the impulse of the moment, in a sudden frenzy of – literally – taking things at the flood, that he seized Camargue and forced him into the water under the ice.'

For a moment they were both silent. Then Burden said: 'He told her what he'd done?'

A curious look came into Wexford's face. 'I suppose so. At any rate, she knew. By the time of the inquest she knew. How much she cared I don't know. She hadn't seen her father for nineteen years, but still he was her father. She didn't care enough to shop Fassbender, that's for sure. Indeed, you might say she cared so little that she was prepared to take considerable risks to *defend* Fassbender.

No doubt, she liked what she got out of it. Life had been a bit precarious in the past four years, hadn't it? Once rid of Ilbert, it was a hand-to-mouth affair, and one imagines that while she was in De Beauvoir Place she was living solely on the rent from her house in Los Angeles. But now she had Sterries and the money and everything was fine. I'd like to think it was his murdering her father that began the process of going off Fassbender for Natalie, but we've no evidence of that.'

'What I don't understand is, since she *was* Natalie Arno, why did she play around half pretending she wasn't? It was a hell of a risk she was taking. She might have lost everything.'

'There wasn't any risk,' said Wexford. 'There wasn't the slightest risk. If she wasn't Natalie there might be many ways of apparently proving she was. But since she was Natalie it could never possibly be proved that she was not.'

'But why? Why do it?'

Burden had never had much sense of humour. And lately, perhaps since his marriage, Wexford thought, this limited faculty had become quiescent. 'For fun, Mike,' he said, 'for fun. Don't you think she got enormous fun out of it? After all, by that time she believed there was no question of our associating Camargue's death with foul play. What harm could she do herself or Fassbender by just ever so slightly hinting she might be the impostor Dinah Sternhold said she was? And it must have been fun, I can see that. It must have been hilarious dumbfounding us by answering Cory's questions and then really giving me hope by nicking her fingers with a bit of glass.

'I said we were fools. I reckon I was an arch fool. Did I really believe an impostor would have had her instructor with her on the very morning she knew we were coming? Did I really believe in such an enormous coincidence as Mary Woodhouse leaving that flat by chance the moment we entered it? What fun Natalie must have got out of asking her old nanny or whatever she was to come round for a cup of coffee and then shooing her out when our car stopped outside. Oh, yes, it was all great fun, and as soon as it had gone far enough she had only to call in her dentist and prove beyond the shadow of a doubt who she was. For Williams is genuinely her dentist, a blameless person of integrity who happens to keep all his records and happens to have been in practice a long time.' Wexford caught Mr Haq's eye. 'D'you want any more coffee?'

'Don't think so,' said Burden.

'I may as well get the bill then.' Mr Haq glided over through the jungle. 'Once,' Wexford said, 'she had proved herself Natalie Arno to the satisfaction of Symonds, O'-Brien and Ames, everything was plain sailing. The first thing to do was sell Sterries because it wouldn't do to have Fassbender show his face much around Kingsmarkham. But I think she was already beginning to go off Fassbender. Perhaps she saw that though he hadn't been prepared to marry her in America, even for the reward of legal residence there, he was anxious to do so now she was rich. Perhaps, after all, she simply decided there was no point in marrying. She hadn't done much of it, had she? Once only and she'd been a widow for nine years. And what would be the point of marrying when she now had plenty of money of her own and was happily independent? Still, this sort of speculation is useless. Suffice it to say that she had intended to marry Fassbender but she changed her mind. They quarrelled about it on the very eve of their going away on holiday together, and in his rage at being baulked of possession of the money he had killed for, had been to prison for, he attacked her and cut her throat.

'The body he put into that chest, which he locked, knowing it would be removed by Dorset's on the following day. Then off he went in the yellow Opel to Heathrow to use one of the two air tickets they had bought for their holiday in the South of France.'

Wexford paid the bill. It was modest, as always. By rights he ought, months ago, to have run Mr Haq in for offences under the Trade Descriptions Act. He would never do that now. They walked out into the High Street where the sun had unaccountably begun to shine. The pavements were drying up, the heavy grey clouds rushing at a great rate away to the horizon. At too great a rate, though, for more than temporary disappearance.

The Kingsbrook tumbled under the old stone bridge like a river in winter spate. Burden leaned over the parapet. 'You knew Fassbender when we came upon him in that place in France,' he said. 'I've been meaning to ask you how you did. You hadn't seen him in America, had you?'

'Of course I hadn't. He wasn't in America while I was. He'd been back here for over a year by then.'

'Then where had you seen him?'

'Here. Back at the very start of this case. Back in January just after Camargue died. He was at Sterries too, Mike. Can't you remember?'

'You saw him too,' Wexford went on. 'You said when we spotted him, "I've seen him somewhere before." '

Burden made a gesture of dismissal. 'Yes, I know I did. But I was mistaken. I couldn't have seen him, I was mixing him up with someone else. One wouldn't forget that name.'

Instead of replying, Wexford said, 'Fassbender's father was a Swiss who lived here without ever becoming naturalized. I don't know what his mother was or is, it hardly matters. John Fassbender was born here and has dual nationality, Swiss and British, not at all an uncommon thing. Ilbert had him deported to this country in 1976 but of course there was nothing to stop him going back into America again on his Swiss passport. When Romero shopped him three years later he was sent back to Switzerland but he soon returned here. Presumably, he liked it better here. Maybe he just preferred the inside of our prisons – he'd seen enough of them.'

'He's got a record, has he?'

Wexford laughed. 'Don't happen to have your German dictionary on you, do you?'

'Of course I don't carry dictionaries about with me.'

'Pity. I don't know why we've walked all the way up here. We'd better take shelter, it's going to rain again heavens hard.'

He hustled Burden down the steps into the Kingsbrook

Precinct. A large drop of rain splashed against the brass plate of Symonds, O'Brien and Ames, a score more against the travel agency's window, blurring the poster that still invited customers to sunny California.

'In here,' said Wexford and pushed open the door of the bookshop. The dictionaries section was down at the back on the left-hand side. Wexford took down a tome in a green-and-yellow jacket. 'I want you to look up a word. It won't be much use to you in your studies, I'm afraid, but if you want to know where you saw Fassbender before you'll have to find out what his name means.'

Burden put the book down on the counter and started on the Fs. He looked up. 'Spelt Fassbinder, a barrel maker, a maker of casks . . .'

'Well?'

'A cooper. . . .' He hesitated, then said slowly, 'John Cooper, thirty-six, Selden Road, Finsbury Park. He broke into Sterries the night after the inquest on Camargue.'

Wexford took the dictionary away from him and replaced it on the shelf. 'His father called himself Cooper during the war – Fassbender wasn't generally acceptable then, on the lines of Beethoven and German Shepherds, one supposes. Fassbender held his British passport in the name of Cooper and his Swiss as Fassbender.

'That burglary was the only bit of planning he and Natalie did and that was done on the spur of the moment. It was a desperate measure taken in what they saw as a desperate situation. What alerted Natalie, of course, was Mrs Murray-Burgess telling Muriel Hicks she'd seen a suspicious-looking character in the Sterries grounds and that without a doubt she'd know him again. The only thing was, she couldn't quite remember which night. Natalie and Fassbender knew which night, of course. They knew it was the night Camargue drowned. So they faked up a burglary. Natalie slept in her late father's room, not to keep away from the amorous marauding Zoffany, still less to wound the feelings of Muriel Hicks, but to be in a room where she could credibly have heard breaking glass and seen the van's number.

'She had to have seen that to facilitate our rapidly getting our hands on Fassbender. Then Mrs Murray-Burgess could do her worst – it was a burglar she had seen and not a killer. In the event, he served four months. He came out in June, with two months' remission for good conduct.'

'I only saw him once,' said Burden. 'I saw him down the station here when we charged him.'

'With nicking six silver spoons,' said Wexford. 'Come on, the rain's stopped.'

They went outside. Once more a bright sun had appeared, turning the puddles into blinding mirrors.

Burden said doubtfully, 'It was a bit of a long shot, wasn't it? I mean, weren't they – well, over-reacting? They were supposing in the first place that Mrs Murray-Burgess would come to us and secondly that if she did we'd connect the presence of a man in the Sterries garden on an unspecified night with an old man's accidental death.'

'There was more to it than that,' said Wexford with a grin. 'She'd seen me, you see.'

'Seen you? What d'you mean?'

'At the inquest. You said at the time people would think things and you were right. Someone must have told Natalie who I was, and that was enough. I only went there because our heating had broken down, I was looking for somewhere to get warm, but she didn't know that. She thought I was there because at that early stage we suspected foul play.'

Burden started to laugh.

'Come,' said Wexford, 'let us shut up the box and the puppets, for our play is played out.'

And in the uncertain sunshine they walked up the street to the police station.

An Unkindness of Ravens

Ruth Rendell

WH S

To Sonia and Jeff

1

She was a neighbour. She was an acquaintance of Dora's and they spoke if they met in the street. Only this time there had been more to it than passing the time of day.

'I said I'd tell you,' Dora said. 'I said I'd mention it. She had that strange look she sometimes has and, to tell you the truth, I was awfully embarrassed.'

'What did she say?' Wexford asked.

' "Rod's missing" or "Rod's disappeared" – something like that. And then she asked me if I'd tell you. Because of who you are, of course.'

Detective chief inspectors have better things to do with their time than waste it listening to the complaints of women whose husbands have run off with other women. Wexford hadn't been in the house five minutes before he decided that was what had happened. But she was a neighbour. She lived in the next street to his. He ought to be glad really, he thought, that it hadn't the makings of a case for him to investigate.

His house and this one had been built at the same time, in the mid-1930s when Kingsmarkham was growing out of being a village. And structurally they were much the same house, three bedrooms, two receptions, kitchen, bathroom and downstairs loo. But his was a home, comfortable and full of lovingly collected things and this was – what? A shelter to keep the rain off, a place where people could eat, sleep and watch television. Joy Williams took him into the front room that she called the lounge. There were no books. The carpet was a square surrounded by mustard yellow vinyl tiles and the furniture a three-piece suite covered in grainy mustard-coloured synthetic leather. The 1935 fireplace, which in his house had been replaced by one of York stone, accommodated an electric fire of complicated design, part Regency, part medieval, and with a portcullis effect at the front. Above it hung a mirror framed in segments of green and yellow frosted glass, a fine specimen of Art Deco if you liked that sort of thing. The only picture was a composition in coloured silver paper of two cats playing with a ball of wool.

'She's rather a colourless person,' Dora had said. 'Doesn't seem interested in anything and always seems depressed. I don't suppose living with Rodney Williams for twenty years has done much for her.'

Joy. Dora had said rather apologetically that it was a misnomer. She was a woman whose whole self had turned grey, not just her hair. Her features had once been good, were probably still good, only her awful complexion, lined, pitted, pinkish-grey, rough and worn, masked them. Apparently she was forty-five but she looked ten years more. Up until his arrival she had been watching television and the set was still on, though with the sound turned off. It was the biggest set Wexford had ever seen, at any rate in a domestic setting. He guessed she spent a fair proportion of her time watching it and perhaps felt uneasy when the screen was blank.

There was no seat in the room that did not face it. He sat on the end of the sofa at an angle, turning his back. Joy Williams's eyes flickered over the flashing figures of skaters taking part in some contest. She sat on the extreme edge of her chair.

'Did your wife tell you what I . . . ?'

'She said something.' He interrupted to save her the embarrassment he could see already mottling her nose and cheeks with dull red. 'Something about your husband being missing.'

Joy Williams laughed. It was a laugh he was to hear often and get to know, a harsh cackle. There was no humour in it, no gaiety, no amusement. She laughed to hide emotion or because she knew no other way of showing it. The hands in her lap stretched and clenched. She wore a very wide, heavily chased platinum or white-gold wedding ring with an even more ornate platinum or white-gold engagement ring containing amid the pits and pyramids a minuscule diamond.

'He went on a trip to Ipswich and I haven't seen him since.'

'Your husband's a sales representative, I think Dora said.'

'With Sevensmith Harding,' she said. 'The paint people.'

She need not have added that. Sevensmith Harding were probably the biggest suppliers to builders' merchants and home decorating retail stores in the south of England. Sevenstar matt and silk emulsion coated a million walls, he thought, between Dover and Land's End. He and Dora had just had their second bedroom done up in it, and if he wasn't much mistaken the paintwork in Mrs Williams's own hall was the newest shade in Sevenshine non-drip high gloss, Wholewheat.

'He covers Suffolk for them.' She began pushing the rings up and down.

'It was last Thursday he went – well, yesterday week. It's the twenty-third now, that must have been the fifteenth. He said he was going to Ipswich to stop the night and start first thing in the morning.'

'What time did he leave?'

'It was evening time. About six. He'd been home all afternoon.'

It was at this point that Wexford had his thought about the other woman. It would be a good three and a half hour run from Kingsmarkham to Ipswich even via the Dartford Tunnel. A salesman who was legitimately going to drive to Suffolk and could have started at four instead of six would surely have done so.

'Where did he stay in Ipswich? At a hotel presumably?'

'A motel. Outside Ipswich, I think.'

She spoke listlessly, as if she knew little about her husband's work and took no interest in it. The door opened and a girl came in. She stopped on the threshold and said, 'Oh, sorry.'

'Sara, what time did Dad go when he left?'

'Around six.'

Mrs Williams nodded. She said, 'This is my daughter Sara,' pronouncing the name so that the first syllable rhymed with 'car'.

'I believe you've a son too?'

'Kevin. He's twenty. He's away at university.'

The girl stood with her arms over the back of the yellow plastic armchair no one was sitting in, her eyes fixed on her mother in a more or less neutral way, though one that tended towards the hostile rather than the friendly. She was very slender, fair, with the face of a Renaissance painter's model, small-featured with a high forehead and a secretive look. Her hair was exceptionally long, reaching almost to her waist, and with the rippling appearance hair has which is usually done up in plaits. She wore jeans and a tee-shirt with a design on it of a raven and the letters ARRIA superimposed over it.

She picked up a photograph in a chrome frame off the only table in the room, a bamboo affair with a glass top almost hidden by the sofa back. Passing it to Wexford, she stuck her thumb at the head of the man sitting on a beach with a teenage boy and a girl who was herself five years before. The man was big, tall, but out of condition and running to fat around his middle. He had a huge domed forehead. His features, perhaps because they were dominated by this bare dome, looked insignificant and crowded together, the mouth a lipless slit stretched into a smile for the camera.

Wexford handed it back to her. She replaced it on the table, let her eyes linger on her mother for a moment, a curious, faintly contemptuous look, and walked out of the room. He heard her feet going upstairs.

'When did you expect your husband to come back?'

'The Sunday night, he said. I didn't think much about it when he didn't. I thought he'd stayed another night and he'd be back Monday, but he wasn't and he never phoned.'

'You didn't phone the motel yourself?'

She looked at him as if he had proposed to her some gargantuan and complex task quite beyond her capacity, writing a fifty-thousand-word thesis perhaps or devising a computer programme.

'I wouldn't do that. I mean, it's a long-distance call. I haven't got the number anyway.'

'Did you do anything?'

She laughed the dry humourless cackle. 'What could I do? Kevin was home for the weekend but he went back to Keele on the Sunday.' She spoke as if action in such a matter could only be taken by a member of the male sex. 'I knew I'd have been let know if he'd had an accident. He's got his name on him, his bank card and his cheque book and ever so many things with his name on.'

'You didn't phone Sevensmith Harding, for instance?'

'What good would that have done? He never went in there for weeks on end.'

'And you haven't heard a word from him since? For – let's see – eight days, you've had no indication where he might be?'

'That's right. Well, five days. I expected him to be gone the first three.'

He would have to ask it. After all, she had called him in. As a neighbour to confide in certainly, but primarily as a policeman. Nothing he had heard so far made him feel even a preliminary inquiry into Rodney Williams's whereabouts was called for. Looking at Mrs Williams, the house, the daughter, the set-up, he could only wonder with an unkindness he would never openly have expressed even to Dora why the man had stayed so long. He had run off with another woman, or run off *to* another woman, and only cowardice was holding him back from writing the requisite letter or making the obligatory phone call.

'Forgive me, but is it possible your husband could be – ' he sought for a word and came out with a mealy-mouthed one he despised ' – friendly with some other woman? Could he have been seeing another woman?'

She gave him a long, cold, unshocked look. Whatever she might say, Wexford could tell his suggestion had already crossed her mind and done more than cross her mind. There was something in that look which told him she was the sort of woman who made a point, a principle almost, of avoiding admitting anything unpleasant. Push it away, suppress it, get out of the habit of thinking, don't wonder or think or speculate, for that will make you unhappy. Don't think, don't wonder, turn on the telly and in mindless apathy stare at the screen until it's time for bed and the doctor's little Mogadon that comes on a permanent prescription you pick up at reception.

Of course, he might be doing her an injustice. All this was only in his imagination. 'It's just a possibility,' he said. 'I'm sorry I had to suggest it.'

'I don't know what he does when he's away days and nights on end, do I? All our married life he's been away selling as much as he's been home. I don't know what floozies he's had and I wouldn't ask.'

The old-fashioned word suited the room and Mrs Williams's grey, Crimplene-clad, scurfy respectability. For the first time he noticed the thick sprinkling of dandruff, like a fall of flour, on the shoulders of her blouse. He had given her a solution which to most women would be the least acceptable, but she, he thought, was relieved. Did she suspect her husband of having been up to something *illegal* so that something *immoral* would be seen as a happier alternative?

You suspect everyone and everything, he told himself. You policeman!

'Do you think we ought to do anything?'

'If you mean by that should you report him as a missing person and the police take steps to find him, no, certainly not. The chances are you'll have word from him in the next few days. If you don't, I think your best course will be to see a solicitor or go to your Citizen's Advice Bureau. But don't do that before you've been on to Sevensmith Harding. The likelihood is you'll find him through them.'

She didn't thank him for coming. He hadn't even been home yet, he had called on her on his way home, but she didn't thank him or apologize for taking up his time. He looked back and saw her still standing on the doorstep holding the door, a very thin angular woman in fawn blouse and unfashionably cut dark green trousers with bell bottoms and a high waist. Her front garden was the only one in Alverbury Road with no spring bulbs out, not a narcissus to relieve the bit of lawn and the dark yew hedge.

It was a cloudy evening, bright as noonday still, April-cool. This little honeycomb of streets was like an orchard in springtime, puffs and clouds of pink and white blossom all over the gardens and drifts of petals already lying on the pavements. A great weeping cherry, pink as ice cream, had taken over his front lawn.

His wife was sitting in an armchair placed in much the same position at the same angle to the fireplace as the chair Joy Williams had sat in, in a room of the same size and proportions to the one he had just left. But there the resemblance ended. A log fire was burning. It had been a cold winter and the spring was cold and protracted, frosts threatening nightly to nip that blossom. Dora was making patchwork, a bedspread in blues and reds, all shades of blues and reds in a multiplicity of patterns, and the finished part covered the long red velvet skirt of the housedress she had taken to wearing in the evenings because of the cold. Her hair was dark and plentiful. Wexford had told her she must be a gipsy to have hair still not grey at nearly sixty.

'Did you see Mike today?'

She meant Detective Inspector Burden. Wexford said no, he had been at court in Myringham.

'Jenny came in to tell me she'd had the results of the amniocentesis. The baby's all right and it's a girl.'

'What's amniocentesis?'

'They stick something through the abdominal wall into the womb and take out a sample of amniotic fluid. The fluid's got cells from the foetus in it and they grow them like a sort of culture, I think. Anyway, the cells divide and they can tell if Down's Syndrome is present and spina bifida too. And of course they can tell the sex by whether the chromosomes come out XY or XX.'

'What a lot you know! Where did you pick up all that?'

'Jenny told me.' She got up and transferred the patchwork to the seat of the chair. 'They can't do an amniocentesis till the sixteenth week of pregnancy and there's always a risk of losing the baby.'

He followed her out into the kitchen. He was more than usually aware this evening of the warmth and light in his own house. It occurred to him that Joy Williams had offered him nothing, not even a cup of tea. Dora had opened the oven door and was looking critically at a steak and kidney pie that was almost ready on the top shelf.

'Do you want a drink?'

'Why not?' she said. 'Celebrate Jenny and Mike's healthy baby.'

'I'm surprised she took any risk,' he said when she had her sherry and he his Bell's and three parts water. 'She's very set on having this child. They've been trying for years.'

'She's forty-one, Reg. At that age there's also a much higher risk of having a mongoloid baby. Anyway, all's well.'

'Don't you want to hear about your Mrs Williams?'

'Poor Joy,' said Dora. 'She was rather pretty when I first knew her. Of course, that was eighteen years ago. I suppose he's gone off with some girl, has he?'

'If you knew that I don't know what you roped me in for.'

Dora laughed. She had a rich throaty giggle. Immediately she said she knew she shouldn't laugh. 'He's such an awful man. You never met him, did you? There's something so secretive and deceitful about him. I used to think no one could be so obviously like that if they really had something to hide.'

'But now you're not so sure.'

'I'll tell you something I was scared to tell you at the time. I thought you might do something violent.'

'Sure,' he said. 'I've always been so wild and free with my fists. What are you on about?'

'He made a pass at Sylvia.'

She said it defiantly. Standing there in the long red dress, holding the sherry glass, her eyes suddenly wide and wary, she looked astonishingly young.

'So?' His elder daughter was thirty, married twelve years, and the mother of two tall sons. 'She's an attractive woman. I daresay men do make passes at her and no doubt she can take care of herself.'

Dora gave him a sidelong look. 'I said I was scared to tell you. She was fifteen at the time.'

The violent feelings she had predicted were there to hand. After all those years. His fifteen-year-old daughter! He resisted the temptation to bellow. Nor did he stamp. He took a sip of his drink and spoke coolly. 'And, like a good little girl, she came to mother and told her?'

Dora said flippantly, 'Sweet of her, wasn't it? I was touched. I think the truth was, Reg, she was scared stiff.'

'Did you do anything?'

'Oh, yes. I went to him and told him what her father was. He didn't know. I don't think there was ever much communication between him and Joy. Anyway, it worked. He made himself very scarce and Sylvia didn't baby-sit for them again. I didn't tell Joy but I think she knew and was disillusioned. Anyway, she didn't adore him any more the way she used to.'

'I was adored once,' Wexford quoted.

'And still are, darling. You know we all adore you. You haven't forfeited our respect, running after little girls. Can I have some more sherry?'

'You'll have to get it yourself,' said Wexford, opening the oven and taking out the pie. 'All this drinking and gossiping. I want my dinner.'

2

The firm of Sevensmith Harding had been founded in 1875 by Septimus Sevensmith who called himself a colourman. He sold artists' materials in a shop in the High Street in Myringham. Paints for exterior- and interior-decorating use came along later. After the First World War in fact, when Septimus's granddaughter married a Major John Harding who left a leg behind him at Passchendaele.

The first great house-building boom of the eighties and nineties was past and gone, the next due to begin. Major Harding got in on it. He began manufacturing in huge quantities the browns and greens dear to the hearts of builders creating the terraces and semidetacheds which were growing in branches and tentacles out of South London. And towards the end of the decade he brought out a daring shade of cream.

Already the company had been renamed Sevensmith Harding. It kept its offices in Myringham High Street, though the factory behind was soon to be moved to sites on distant industrial complexes. With the disappearance of its retail trade the shop as such also disappeared.

The world's paint industry enjoyed a steady growth during the 1960s and early 1970s. It is estimated that close on five hundred companies make paint in the United Kingdom but the bulk of the sales volume is handled by a few large manufacturers. Four of these manufacturers dominate the British Isles and one of them is Sevensmith Harding.

Today their paints, Sevenstar vinyl silk and Sevenstar vinyl matt emulsion, Sevenshine gloss and satin finish, are manufactured at Harlow in Essex, and their wallpapers, borders and coordinating tiles at Crawley in Sussex. The head offices in Myringham, in the centre of the High Street opposite the Old Flag Hotel, have more a look of solicitors' chambers or the establishment of a very refined antique dealer than the seat of paint makers. Indeed, there is scarcely anything to show that they are paint makers. The bow windows with their occasional pane of distorted glass that flank the front door contain, instead of cans of paint and display stands of delighted housewives with brushes in their hands, a *famille noire* vase of dried grasses on one side and a Hepplewhite chair on the other. But over the door, Georgian in style and of polished mahogany, are royal armorial bearings and the legend: 'By appointment to Her Majesty Queen Elizabeth the Queen Mother, Colourists and Makers of Fine Pigments'.

The company chairman, Jeremy Harding-Grey, divided his time between his house in Monte Carlo and his house in Nassau, and the managing director, George Delahaye, though he lived in Sussex, was seldom seen in the vicinity of Myringham. But the deputy managing director was a humbler person and altogether more on the level of ordinary men. Wexford knew him. They had met at the home of Sylvia's father-in-law, an architect, and since then the Gardners had once been guests at a drinks party at the Wexfords' and the Wexfords guests at the Gardners'. But for all that Wexford would not have considered himself on the kind of terms with Miles Gardner to warrant dropping in at Sevensmith Harding when he found himself in Myringham at lunchtime to ask Miles out for a drink and a sandwich.

A fortnight had passed since his talk with Joy Williams and he had virtually forgotten about it. He had dismissed it from his mind before he went to bed that same night. And if he had thought about it at all since then it had only been to tell himself that by now Mrs Williams and her solicitor would be settling things to her satisfaction or that

Williams had returned home, having found like many a man before him that domesticity is the better part of economics.

But even if Williams were still missing there was nothing to justify Wexford's making inquiries about him at Sevensmith Harding. Let Joy Williams do that. He wouldn't be missing as far as his employers were concerned. No matter how complex a man's love life he still has to go to work and earn his bread. Williams earned it on too humble a level though, Wexford reflected, for it to be likely Miles Gardner had ever heard of him.

He and Burden had both been at Myringham Crown Court, witnesses in two separate cases, and the court had adjourned for lunch. Burden would have to go back to watch his case – a rather ticklish matter concerning the receiving of stolen goods – through to the bitter end, but Wexford's day, at least as far as appearing in court went, was over. As they walked towards the hotel Burden was silent and morose. He had been like this since they came out of court. If it had been anyone else Wexford would have supposed his mood due to the dressing down, indeed the scathing tongue-lashing, meted out to him by the alleged receiver's counsel. But Burden was impervious to such things. He had taken that sort of stick too many times to care. This was something else, something closer to home, Wexford thought. And now he came to think of it, this, whatever it was, had been growing on Burden for days now, weeks even, a morose surly misery that didn't seem to affect his work but militated badly against his relations with other people.

He looked the same as ever. There was no sign of anxiety or care in his appearance. He was thin but he had always been thin. Wexford didn't know if it was a new suit he was wearing or last year's cleaned and the trousers nightly pressed in the electric press his wife had given him for Christmas. ('Like those things you get in swish hotels,' Burden had said proudly.) It was a happy marriage,

Burden's second, as happy as his first. But almost any marriage Burden made would be happy, he had a gift for marriage. He was uxorious without making himself ridiculous. There couldn't be anything in his marriage that was bugging him. His wife was pregnant with a longed-for child – longed for by her at any rate. Burden had a grown-up son and daughter by his first marriage. Wexford considered an idea that came to him and then dismissed it as absurd and out of character. Burden was the last man to dread the coming child just because he was now in his mid-forties. That he would take in his stride.

'What's wrong, Mike?' he asked as the silence became oppressive.

'Nothing.'

The classic answer. One of the cases in which a statement means the precise opposite of what it says, as when a man in doubt says he's absolutely certain.

Wexford didn't press it. He walked along, looking about him at the old market town which had changed so much since he had first known it. A huge shopping complex had been built, and since then an arts centre, incorporating theatre, cinema and concert hall. The university term was three weeks old and the place was thronged with blue-jeaned students. But up at this end of the town, where preservation orders proliferated and buildings were listed, things were much the same. Things were even rather better since the local authority had woken up to the fact that Myringham was beautiful and worth conserving and had therefore cleaned and tidied and painted and planted.

He looked into the bow windows of Sevensmith Harding, first at the Hepplewhite chair, then at the vase. Beyond the dried grasses he could see a young girl receptionist talking on the phone. Wexford and Burden crossed the road and went into the Old Flag.

Wexford had been there once or twice before. It was not a place ever to be crowded in the middle of the day. The busy lunch trade went to the cheaper brighter pubs and the wine bars. In the smaller of the lounge bars where food was being served several vacant tables remained. Wexford was making for one of them when he caught sight of Miles Gardner sitting alone.

'Won't you join me?'

'You look as if you're waiting for someone,' Wexford said.

'Any congenial company that offers itself.' He had a gracious warm manner of speaking that was in no way affected. Wexford recalled that this was what he had always liked about him. 'They do a nice prawn salad,' Miles Gardner said. 'And if you can get here before one they'll send up to the butcher for a fillet steak.'

'What happens at one?'

'The butcher closes. He opens at two and then the pub closes. There's Myringham for you.'

Wexford laughed. Burden didn't laugh but sat wearing the sort of stiff polite expression that indicates to even the most insensitive that one would be happier – or less miserable – on one's own. Wexford made up his mind to ignore him. Gardner seemed delighted with their company and, having bought a round of drinks, began to talk in the easy rather elegant way he had about the new house he had just moved into which Sylvia's father-in-law had designed. It was a valuable gift, Wexford thought, to be able to talk to people, one whom you had only just met and the other a mere acquaintance, as if they were old friends whom you conversed with regularly.

Gardner was a small, undistinguished-looking man. His style was in his voice and manner. He had a much taller wife and two or three rather noisy daughters, Wexford remembered. From the new house and the time it had taken to get itself built, Gardner had moved on to talk of work, lack of work and unemployment, eliciting mild sparks of interest from Burden, at least to the extent of extracting monosyllables from him. Sevensmith Harding had battled against laying off workers at their Harlow factory and the battle had been won – allowing for the few redundancies which Gardner insisted had been acceptable to the men and women concerned.

'Yes,' said Burden. 'I daresay.'

Always reactionary, he had until a few years back threatened to become unbearably right wing and Blimpish, but Jenny had reversed the tide. Burden was far more of a moderate now. He did not, as he once would have, launch into a tirade against unemployment benefits, Social Security payments and general idleness. Or perhaps it was only this depression of his that made him forbear.

'The whole attitude towards work and employment and keeping one's job is changing, I find,' Gardner said. He began talking about what he thought gave rise to these new patterns and made it interesting enough. Or so Wexford thought. Burden, eating prawn salad rather too rapidly, kept looking at his watch. He had to be back in court by two. Wexford thought he would be glad to be rid of him for a while.

'Isn't what you're really saying,' he said to Gardner, 'that, in spite of the threat of unemployment and the inadequacy of unemployment benefits, men seem to have lost that craven fear of losing their jobs they had in the thirties?'

'Yes, and to a great extent, at any rate among the middle class, lost the feeling they used to have that they had to stick in a hated job or career for the rest of their lives just because it's the one they went into at twenty.'

'Then what's brought this change about?'

'I don't know. I've thought about it but the answers I come up with don't satisfy me. But I can tell you that just as the fear has gone, and the respect for employers because they were employers, so has pride in one's job and the old loyalty to a company. My marketing manager is a case in point. Time was when you could say a man in that position would also be a responsible person, someone you could trust not to let you down. He'd have been proud – and yes, I'll say it, *grateful* – to be where he was and he'd have had a real feeling for the firm's welfare too.'

'What's he done?' said Burden. 'Decided to change his career in midstream?'

It was said acidulously but Gardner gave no sign of having noticed the edge to Burden's voice and replied pleasantly.

'Not so far as I know. He simply walked out on me. He's on three months' notice, or supposed to be. First we get a phone call from his wife saying he's sick, then not a word until a letter of resignation comes, very clipped and curt, and a note at the bottom – ' Gardner looked almost apologetic – 'quite an *insolent* sort of note, saying he'd be in touch with our accounts department about his superannuation.'

'Had he been with you long?'

'All his working life, I gather, and five years as marketing manager.'

'At least you'll have no difficulty in finding a replacement in these hard times.'

'It's going to be a case of promotion for one of our best reps. That's always been Sevensmith Harding's policy. Promote rather than take in from outside. Only usually, of course, we're given a bit more time.'

Burden got up and said he must get back to court. He shook hands with Gardner and had the grace to mutter something about its having been good to meet him.

'Let me get you another beer,' said Wexford when Burden had left and been described (very much to his surprise) by Gardner as a 'nice chap'.

'Thanks so much. I don't suppose they'll sling us out before two-thirty, will they?'

The beer came, one of the 130 varieties of 'real ale' the Old Flag claimed to stock.

'It's not by any chance my neighbour Rodney Williams you'll be promoting, is it?'

Gardner looked up at him, surprised.

'Rod Williams?'

'Yes. He lives in the next street to me.'

Gardner said in a patient tone, 'Rod Williams is our former marketing manager, the one I was telling you resigned.'

'Williams?'

'Yes, I thought I explained. Perhaps I didn't say the name.'

'Somebody,' said Wexford, 'is getting hold of the wrong end of the stick here.'

'It's you,' said Gardner, smiling.

'Yes, I expect it is. Somebody has given me the wrong end of the stick. Am I to take it then that Williams wasn't one of your reps and didn't cover the Suffolk area for you?'

'He was once. He did once. Up till five years ago. We kept to our customary policy and when our former marketing manager took early retirement due to a heart condition, we promoted Rod Williams.'

'As far as his wife knows he's still a rep. That is, he's still spending half his time selling up in Suffolk.'

Gardner's eyebrows went up. He gave a twisted grin. 'His private life is no affair of mine.'

'Nor mine.'

It was Gardner who changed the subject. He began talking about his eldest daughter who was getting married in the late summer. Wexford finally parted from him with a promise to be in touch, to 'get Dora to give Pam a ring and fix something up'. Driving home to Kingsmarkham, he thought for a while about Rodney Williams. There had been no room in his own marriage for alibis. He wondered what it would be like to have a marriage in which a permanent, on-going, five-year-long alibi existed as an integral part of life. Unthinkable. Unimaginable. He stopped trying to identify and thought about it with detachment.

What had happened perhaps was that five years ago Williams had met a girl with whom he wanted to spend time without ending his marriage. Keeping his promotion a secret from his wife would have been a way of achieving this. Probably the girl lived in Myringham. While Joy Williams believed her husband was staying at a motel outside Ipswich he was in reality seeing this other girl, no doubt sharing her home and doing his nine-to-five job at Sevensmith Harding in Myringham.

It was the sort of situation some men chuckle over. Wexford wasn't one of them. And there was another aspect, one that few men would find funny. If Williams hadn't told his wife about his promotion he presumably also hadn't told her about the considerable increase in salary that went with it. Still, there was no more mystery. Williams had written to the company. Joy had phoned with excuses. Back in Alverbury Road Williams was still perhaps managing to shore up a few fragments of deceit against discovery.

It was nine at night and he was still in his office, going through for the tenth time the statements he had taken for the preparation of a case of fraud against one Francis Wingrave Adams. He still doubted whether they would constitute a watertight case and so did counsel representing the police, though both knew he was guilty. On the final stroke of nine – St Peter's clock had a dead sound too, like St Mary Woolnoth's – he put the papers away and set off to walk homewards.

Lately he had taken to walking to and from work. Dr Crocker recommended it, pointing out that it was less than half a mile.

'Hardly worth it then,' Wexford said.

'A couple of miles' walk a day could make a difference of ten years' life to you.'

'Does that mean that if I walked six miles a day I could prolong my life by thirty years?'

The doctor had refused to answer that one. Wexford, though feigning to scoff, had gone some way towards obeying him. Sometimes his walk took him down Tabard

Road past Burden's bungalow, sometimes along Alverbury Road where the Williams family lived, and there was an occasional longer route along one of the meadow footpaths. Tonight he intended to drop in and see Burden for a final assessment of the Adams business.

But now he began to feel that there was very little left to say about this man who had conned an elderly woman out of £20,000. He wouldn't talk about that. Instead he would try to get out of Burden what was happening in his life to account for his depression.

The Burdens still lived in the bungalow Burden had moved into soon after his first marriage where the garden after twenty years and more still had an immature look and the ivy which tried to climb up the house had been ruthlessly cut back with secateurs. Only the front door changed. It had been all colours – Burden was a relentless decorator – but Wexford had liked the rose pink best. Now it was a dark greenish blue – Sevenshine Oriental Peacock probably. Above the door, now dusk had come, the porch light was on, a lantern of leaded lights in the shape of a star.

Jenny came to let him in. She was halfway through her pregnancy now and 'showing', as the old wives say. Instead of a smock she wore a full-sleeved, square-necked dress with a high waist, like the one the woman is wearing in Vermeer's *The Letter*. She had let her golden-brown hair grow and it hung to her shoulders. But, for all that, Wexford was shocked by her appearance. She looked drawn and dispirited.

Burden, having years ago agreed to stop calling Wexford 'sir', now called him nothing at all. But Jenny called him Reg. She said, 'Mike's in the living room, Reg,' and added in a way quite unlike her usual self, 'I was just going to bed.'

He felt constrained to say he was sorry for calling so late, though it was only twenty past nine. She shrugged and said it didn't matter and she said it in a way which seemed to imply that nothing much mattered. He followed her into the room where Burden was.

On the middle cushion of the three-seater settee Burden sat reading *Police Review*. Wexford would have expected Jenny to have been sitting beside him but she hadn't been. Beside a chair at the far end of the room lay her book face downwards and a piece of white knitting that had a look about it of the knitter's having no enthusiasm for her task. In a glass vase on the windowsill dying wallflowers stood in three inches of water.

'Have a drink,' said Burden, laying down his magazine. 'There's beer. There is beer, isn't there, Jenny?'

'I don't know. I never touch the stuff.'

Burden said nothing. He left the room, went out to the kitchen and came back with two cans on a tray. Burden's first wife would have said, and Jenny once would have said, that they must have glasses to drink the beer out of. Jenny, languidly sitting down, picking up book and knitting but looking at neither, said, 'You can drink it out of the can, can't you?'

Wexford began to feel awkward. Some sort of powerful angry tension that existed between these two seemed to hang in the air like smoke, to get in his throat and give him a choky feeling. He snapped the top off his beer can. Jenny was holding the knitting needles in one clenched hand and staring at the wall. He had no intention of talking about Francis Wingrave Adams in her presence. On other occasions like this he and Burden would have gone into one of the other rooms. Burden sat on the settee, wearing his half-frown. He opened the beer can with a sharp, rough movement and a spurt of froth shot out across the carpet.

Three months before Wexford had seen Jenny soothing and practical when her husband had dropped, not a spoonful of beer, but a bowl of strawberry mousse on the paler newer carpet of the dining room. She had laughed and told him to leave the clearing up to her. Now she gave a cry of real distress and jumped up out of her chair.

'All right,' said Burden. 'All right. I'll do it. It's nothing anyway. I'll get a cloth.'

She burst into tears. She put one hand up to her face and ran out of the room. Burden followed her. That is, Wexford thought he had followed her but he came back almost immediately holding a floorcloth.

'Sorry about that,' he said on his hands and knees. 'Of course it's not the beer. It's just any little thing sets her off. Take no notice.' He lifted an angry face. 'I've made up my mind I'm simply not going to take any notice any more.'

'But if she's not well, Mike . . . '

'She is perfectly well.' Burden got up and dropped the cloth onto the tiled kerb of the fireplace. 'She is having an ideal trouble-free pregnancy. Why, she wasn't even sick. When I remember what Jean went through . . . ' Wexford could hardly believe his ears. For a husband – and such a husband as Burden – to make that comparison! Burden seemed to realize what he had said and a dull flush crept across his face. 'No, honestly, she's perfectly fit, she says so herself. It's simply neurotic behaviour.'

Wexford had sometimes thought in the past that if every instance diagnosed by Burden as neurotic were taken as sound, almost the entire population would have to be tranquillized, not to say confined in mental hospitals. He said, 'The amniocentesis was all right, wasn't it? They didn't tell her something to worry her?'

Burden hesitated. 'Well, as a matter of fact they did.' He gave an ugly humourless laugh. 'That's just what they did. They told her something to worry her. You've hit the nail bang on the head. It doesn't worry *me* and I'm the child's father. But it worries her like hell and I'm the one who has to bear the brunt of it.' He sat down and said very loudly, almost shouting, 'I don't want to talk about it anyway. I've said too much already and I've no intention of saying any more. I feel like learning a formula to explain my wife's conduct and repeating it to people when they first come in the door.'

Wexford said quietly, 'You can do it extempore for it is nothing but roaring.'

He got a glare for that. 'I came to talk about Adams. Or are you too preoccupied with your domestic fracas to care?'

'I told you, I'm simply not going to take any notice any more,' said Burden, and they talked about Adams not very profitably for the next half-hour.

Dora was in bed when he got home, sitting up reading. While he undressed he told her about the Burdens.

'They're too old to have babies,' was all she would say.

'Flying in the face of nature, would you call it?'

'You'd be surprised, my lad. I might. And by the way, Rod Williams hasn't come back. I saw Joy and she hasn't heard a word.'

'But I had the distinct impression she'd phoned Sevensmith Harding,' Wexford began.

'You told her to, you mean. You told her to phone them and find out if they could tell her anything and she's going to.'

That wasn't what he had meant. He got into bed, sure now that he hadn't heard the last of the Williams affair.

3

For more than a couple of weeks now he had been keeping his eye on the dark blue Ford Granada parked outside his house in Arnold Road, Myringham. It had appeared there for the first time soon after Easter. Graham Gee couldn't see it from his front windows nor, because of the tall lonicera hedge, from his front garden. He saw it when he drove his own car out of the entrance to his garage each morning and when he drove it in each afternoon at 5.30.

At first (he told the police) he thought it might have something to do with the boy opposite, the teenage son of the people in the bungalow. But it was too respectable a car for that. Well, it was *then*. Dismissing that theory, he wondered if it belonged to some commuter who was using Arnold Road as a station car park. Arnold Road wasn't very near Myringham Southern Region Station, it was a good quarter of a mile away, but it was probably the nearest street to the station not clogged on both sides with commuters' cars.

Graham Gee began to see the presence of the Ford Granada outside his gate as the thin end of the wedge. Soon there would be a hundred rail travellers' cars parked in Arnold Road. He was not a commuter himself but a partner in a firm of accountants in Pomfret.

Arnold Road was known as a 'nice neighbourhood'. The houses were detached, standing in large gardens. There weren't any rough elements, there wasn't any trouble, except perhaps for the theft of dahlias from someone's front garden the previous autumn. So Graham Gee was surprised to notice one morning that the Granada's hub caps had gone. Perhaps they had always been gone though, he couldn't remember. Still, he knew the wheels hadn't always been gone. The car hadn't always been propped up on bricks. Dirty now, streaked with rain, it sat on its brick supports, looking as if it might after all be the property of the teenager opposite.

He still did nothing about it, though he knew by now that it was there all the time. It wasn't driven there in the morning and taken away in the evening. For a week now it hadn't been drivable. It took the smashing of a rear window to get him to do something.

The rear window had been broken, the front doors opened and the interior stripped. The radio had been removed, the headrests taken off the front seats, and something dug out of the dashboard, a clock perhaps. Though the boot was open, the thieves hadn't thought it worth their while to help themselves to the snow shovel inside. Gee phoned the police.

There was no need for the police to go through the procedure of tracing the driver through the Vehicle Licensing Department in Swansea, for the vehicle registration document was in the Granada's glove compartment along with a road map of southern England, a ballpoint pen and a pair of sunglasses.

Vehicle registration documents have named on them the 'keeper' of the vehicle, not its owner, a fact which was also of assistance to the police. This one listed the keeper as Rodney John Williams of 31 Alverbury Road, Kingsmarkham.

Why had Williams dumped the car in Arnold Road when Sevensmith Harding's own car park was less than a quarter of a mile away behind the company's High Street offices? That car park was never locked. It had no gates, only an opening in the fence and on the fence a nctice requesting 'unauthorized personnel' not to park there.

'I don't understand it,' Miles Gardner said. 'Frankly, we've been wondering what to do about recovering the car but we don't know where Williams is. He didn't mention the car in his letter of resignation. Apparently, wherever he was when he first left, he's no longer with his wife, otherwise we would have tackled her. He's disappeared into thin air. It's a bit much really, isn't it? I gather the car's in a state, not much more than a shell?'

'The engine's still there,' said Wexford.

Gardner made a face. They were in his rather gloomy though luxurious office, a room not so much panelled as lined with oak, the decor dating from those between-wars days when hardwood was plentiful. None of your Sevenstar matt emulsion here, Wexford thought to himself.

There were more framed photographs than in the average elderly couple's living room. On Gardner's desk, placed to catch his eye every time he looked up, was a big one of tall Mrs Gardner and her three girls, all affectionate nestling and entwined arms. The walls were reserved for various groups and gatherings of men at company functions or on sporting occasions. One was of a cricket match with a tall gangling man going in to bat. Rodney Williams. The high forehead, slight concavity of features that would no doubt show more clearly in profile, the thin mouth stretched in a grin, were unmistakable.

Gardner looked at it dolefully.

'He was a lot younger then,' he said. 'The company had a crack team in those days.' He made as if to take the photograph down, angered no doubt by the sight of the permanently grinning Williams, but seemed to change his mind. 'The whole thing's extraordinary. He was very keen on cars, you know, one of those car men. You don't think anything's happened to him, do you?'

The euphemism that always signified death . . .

'If you mean some sort of accident, I don't know but I don't think so. It's more what has he been up to, isn't it?'

Gardner looked mystified.

'It looks to me as if he may have been up to something he shouldn't have been, he's been on the fiddle. Either he decided he'd made enough out of it and was going to call it a day or else something happened to make him think discovery was imminent. Now, the most likely place for him to have been cooking the books is here. Do you have any thoughts on that one?'

'He wouldn't have had the opportunity. He never went near any books, so to speak. Do you want me to have our chief accountant up? I mean, as far as I can see, any fiddle he was up to would have to be an expenses fiddle and Ken Risby would be the man to tell you about that.'

Gardner made a call on the internal phone. While they waited for Risby Wexford said, 'There is nothing small, portable but of considerable value he could have stolen? No cheque coming into his hands he could have falsified? No forgery he could have perpetrated?'

Gardner looked simply bewildered. 'I don't think so. I'm sure not. I mean, I should know by now. Good God, the man's been gone over three weeks.' He jumped up. 'Here's Ken now. He'll tell us.'

But Risby was not able to tell them much. He was a thin, fair man in his thirties, with a nervous manner, and he seemed as shocked by Wexford's suggestion as Gardner had been. You'd think the pair of them lived in a world where fraud had never been heard of, Wexford thought impatiently, and every businessman was a sea-green incorruptible.

'He was a mite heavy on his expenses sometimes but that's all, that's positively all. He never had the handling of the firm's money. What makes you think he's done something like that?'

'You think about it. Look at it for yourself. For five

years the man's been lying to his wife about his position with this firm. What salary was he getting, by the way?'

'Twenty-five thousand,' said Gardner rather grudgingly.

More than Wexford had expected, £5000 more. 'And lying about that too. You can bet on it she thinks he was getting less than half that. One day he tells her he's going to Ipswich, a place he doubtless hasn't set foot in for five years, and off he goes, dumps his company car in the street, and disappears. Apart from getting the lady he's in cahoots with to phone here and say he's ill and apart from writing his resignation he's never heard from again. And you ask me why I think he's been up to something? Tell me about the man. If he's not a man who'd steal or forge, is there some other disgraceful thing he might have done?'

They looked at him. Having no imagination, they didn't know and couldn't hazard guesses. Wexford had plenty of imagination and very little knowledge of marketing.

'For instance, he couldn't have been selling this paint of yours at prices over the odds and pocketing the difference? Something like that?'

Gardner, who had looked as if he would never smile again, burst out laughing.

'He never actually *sold* anything, Reg. It doesn't work like that. He never handled money. He never handled money in any shape or form.'

'You make him sound like royalty,' said Wexford. 'Anyway, will you, Mr Risby, have a good look at your books for me, please? Do a supplementary audit or whatever.'

'Really not necessary, I assure you, not necessary at all. I'd go into court at this moment and swear there's not a squeak of a discrepancy in my books.'

'I hope you'll never have to go into court on this matter, but don't count on it.' Risby's eyes opened wide at that one. 'And do as I ask and check the books, will you? And now,' Wexford said to Gardner, 'I'd like to see that letter of resignation Williams wrote to you.'

Gardner called his secretary in to find it. Wexford noticed he called her Susan, and what was less expected, she called him Miles. The letter was typed and by someone not accustomed to frequent use of a typewriter.

Dear Mr Gardner,
This is to give you notice of my resignation from Sevensmith Harding from today. I am afraid it is rather sudden but is due to circumstances beyond my control. I shall not be returning to the office and would prefer you not to attempt to get in touch with me.

Yours sincerely,
Rodney J. Williams

PS. I will contact the Accounts Dept. about my superannuation refund in due course.

Wexford said, 'Everyone in this office calls each other by their Christian names but Rodney Williams called you Mr Gardner? Is that right?'

'No, of course not. He called me Miles.'

'He doesn't in this letter.'

'I took that to be because he thought the occasion demanded something more formal.'

'It's a possibility. Don't you find it odd when a man on three months' notice gives you one day's? Wouldn't you have expected a more detailed explanation for common courtesy's sake than "circumstances beyond my control"?'

'Are you suggesting someone else might have written that letter?'

Wexford didn't answer directly. 'I'll take it with me if I may. Maybe have some experts look at that signature. Can you let me have a specimen of his signature? One we *know* is his?'

Nine separate sets of fingerprints had been found on and in the car. These would presumably include the prints of whoever had vandalized it. The others would be Williams's, Joy's, Sara's, Kevin's. Early days yet to ask these people to let him check their own prints against those in the car. A lot of hairs, fair and grey, had been on the upholstery. No blood, of course, nothing dramatic. There was one odd thing, though. On the floor of the boot, along with the shovel, were some crumbs of plaster the lab had identified as either Tetrion or Sevensmith Harding's Stopgap.

It took a few more days to get a verdict on the letter.

A manual portable machine, the Remington 315, had been used to type it. There was a chip out of the apex of the capital A on this machine, a similar flaw in the ascender of the lower-case t and a smudging of the head of the comma. As to the signature, it wasn't Williams's. The handwriting expert was far more categorical than such people are usually willing to be. He was almost scathing in his incredulity that anyone could for a moment have believed that the signature was made by Williams.

When Joy had told Dora of her intention to phone Sevensmith Harding she had followed this up with a request to 'send' Wexford round to her house once more. This time Dora had said in quite a sharp way that her husband wasn't a private detective and Wexford, of course, hadn't gone. But Williams's disappearance had stopped being a private matter. At any rate, he thought, he wouldn't be unwelcome at 31 Alverbury Road. The answer to a prayer, in fact. He walked round there in the evening, at about eight.

This time the girl Sara let him in. She spoke not a word but closed the front door after him, opened the living-room door, left him and went back upstairs.

Joy Williams was watching television. The programme was one of those contests in which teams of people go through ridiculous or humiliating ordeals. Men in dress suits and top hats were trying to walk a tightrope over what looked like a lake of mashed potato. Just before the door was opened he had heard her laughing. She didn't turn the set off, only the sound. He thought she looked anything but pleased to see him. Her expression had very quickly become sullen.

Yes, she admitted, they had a joint bank account. Rod was away so much they had had to. Wexford asked her if he might see some recent bank statements.

She hunched herself, arms wrapping her thin body, right hand on left shoulder, left hand with the ugly showy rings on right. It was a habitual gesture with her which a psychiatrist might have said began as a way of protecting herself from assault. She had the green trousers on and a knitted jumper, its shoulders sprinkled with fallen hairs and dandruff.

'How often does your bank send you statements?'

'It's been once a month lately.' Her eyes strayed to the silent but tumultuous screen. A contestant had fallen into the mashed potato. 'They made a mistake over something and Rod complained, so they started sending statements once a month.'

Dr Crocker had told Wexford of a recent visit to one of his patients, a woman ill with bronchitis. The television had been on in her bedroom, all her six children sitting there watching it. When he tried to examine her she had protested angrily at his request that the set be turned off.

'I pull the plug out now without a by-your-leave,' said the doctor. 'If the TV's on or their video I don't ask any more, I pull out the plug.'

Wexford would have liked to do that. He would have done it if he had had just a fraction more evidence for disquiet over Rodney Williams. It was curious that Joy, who had come close to pestering Dora for his attention, was now making it plain she didn't want him there.

'Will you show me the statements?'

She turned her head reluctantly. 'OK, if you want.' He had put his request very politely as if she would be doing him a favour and she responded as if she was.

It didn't take her long to find the statements. She wasn't

going to miss more of her programme than she had to. As he began to look at the statements she leaned across and summoned a little sound out of the television, so that shrieks, exclamations and commentary were just audible. He wondered what could possibly distract her, what real event or shock, and then he knew. The phone bell. Somewhere, elsewhere in the house, the phone began to ring.

She jumped up. 'That'll be my son. My son always phones me on Thursday nights.'

Wexford returned to the monthly bank statements. Each one showed the sum of £500 paid into the account more or less at the beginning of the month. A salary cheque apparently. Several objections to that one. Williams's salary had been £25,000 a year and there was no way £500 a month, even after all possible deductions, could amount to as much as that. Secondly, the sum would vary, not be a set round figure. Thirdly, it would be paid in on the same day of the month, give or take a day each way, not sometimes on the first and sometimes on the eighth.

It was evident what had been going on. Williams had another account somewhere into which his salary was paid. From that account he transferred £500 a month into the account he had jointly with his wife. If this was so, and it must be, it was going to be useless asking Joy, as he had intended, if her husband had drawn on their joint account since his disappearance.

Sevensmith Harding would make no bones about telling him where this other account was. The problem would be the intransigent bank manager refusing to disclose any information about a client's account. He looked at the April statement again. Five hundred pounds had been paid in on 2 April. No May statement had yet been sent to Mrs Williams as May was only half over.

She came back into the room, looking brighter and younger, her face more animated than he had ever seen it. She had been talking to her son, her favourite.

'I'd like you to give your bank a ring,' he said, 'and ask

them if the usual five hundred was paid into the account at the beginning of the month. Will you do that?'

She nodded. He asked her to tell him about the last afternoon and evening Williams had spent at home. Rod had mowed the lawn in the afternoon, she said, and then he'd taken her shopping to the Tesco discount. She couldn't drive.

'We came back and had a cup of tea. Rod had a sandwich. He didn't want more than that. He said he'd get something on his way to Ipswich. Then he went upstairs and packed a bag and left. He'd be back on Sunday, he said.' She gave one of her dull laughs. 'And that was the last of him. After twenty-two years.'

'What did you do for the rest of the evening?'

'Me?'

'Yes, what did you do? Did you stay at home? Go out? Did anyone come here?'

'I went over to my sister's. She lives in Pomfret. I went on the bus. I had something to eat and then I went to my sister's.'

'And Sara?'

'She was here. Up there.' Joy Williams pointed to the ceiling. 'Studying for her A-levels, I suppose.' She made it sound an unworthy, even slightly disgraceful thing for her daughter to have been doing.

There was something wrong with this description of how the evening had been passed, something incongruous, only Wexford couldn't put his finger on what.

'I'd like to talk to Sara,' he said.

'Do as you like.'

She twisted round in her chair and looked fully at him, the television for the moment forgotten.

'She'll be in her bedroom but you can go up. She won't object.' The awful laugh came. 'Rather the reverse if I know her.'

4

So young Sara, who looked like one of Botticelli's girls, a Quattrocento virgin, had been caught in bed with a boyfriend. Or not in bed, most probably. On the yellow plastic settee or in the back of a car. It was difficult with daughters. You knew what your enlightened principles were but things looked different when it was *your* daughter. Still, that hardly justified Joy's snide insinuation. Wexford, going upstairs, decided that as well as disliking what he knew of Williams, he didn't care for Mrs Williams either. Not that it mattered whether he liked them or not. It made no difference. Perhaps the woman did have some justification. She was going through a bad time; she, who was surely in the process of losing her man, would feel bitter towards a daughter gaining one. And the discovery of Sara and the boy might have been made very recently.

He knew which bedroom it was because music was coming from behind the door. Rock music of some kind, soft with a monotonous drumbeat. She must have heard his feet on the stairs by now. He had taken care to make a bit of noise, not difficult on the linoleum covered with thin haircord. He knocked on the door.

She didn't say, 'Come in!' She opened it herself. Wexford had often noted reactions to a knock at the door. They offered indications of character and motivation. The woman, for example, who calls out 'Come in!' is more open, relaxed and easy-going than she who opens the door herself. The latter will be cagey and reserved. In the thirty seconds or so before she opens the door, what has she put away in a drawer or hidden under a magazine?

He could see that Sara had created the room herself. What attractiveness it had had nothing to do with the furniture, carpet and curtains provided by her parents. It was the smallest bedroom. Wexford had had an extension built on to his house when the girls were little but this house remained as it had originally been. There would be a large front bedroom for the husband and wife, a slightly smaller back bedroom – in this case for the son – and a tiny boxroom no more than nine feet by seven for the daughter. She had put posters all over the walls, one of a red horse galloping in the snow from the Yugoslav Naive school of painting, another of a thin naked black man playing a guitar. Between them hung a tennis racket, a corn dolly and a montage of Tarot cards. Perhaps the most striking poster was the one that faced the door. A harpy-like creature with the head and breasts of a woman and the body, wings and claws of a raven, clutched at an unfurling ribbon on which was painted the name – acronym? – ARRIA. Wexford remembered the tee-shirt Sara had been wearing when first they met. The raven woman had a face like Britannia or maybe Boadicea, one of those noble, handsome, courageous, fanatical faces, that made you feel like locking up the knives and reaching for the Valium.

Bookshelves that looked as if put up by Sara herself held a paperback *Life of Freud*, Phyllis Grosskurth's *Havelock Ellis*, Fromm, Laing, Freud on the *Wolf Man* and *Leonardo*, Erin Pizzey and Jeff Shapiro on incest and child abuse, but not a single work of fiction. With her tiny radio providing background music, she had been sitting at a dressing table that doubled as a desk, swotting for an exam. It was evidently chemistry. The textbook lay open at a page of formulae.

'We're trying to find your father, Sara. I wouldn't exactly say he's disappeared but he's making himself very hard to find.'

She had fixed him with her grave contained look. He noticed her skin, creamy and smooth like velvet, with a gold dusting of freckles on her small nose. When she opened the door to him she had been holding a green felt-tipped pen in her hand. On the back of the other hand she had drawn a green snake. Teenagers had always drawn on their hands, they had done so when he was in his teens and when his daughters were in their teens, but now some sort of specific fashion for it had sprung up. To have black and red and green drawings on your hands and arms and body was the 'in' thing. Sara had drawn with her green pen a spotted snake, not curled round itself but stretched out and slightly undulant, its forked tongue extended.

'Have you any thoughts about where he might be?'

She shook her head. She put the cap on the pen and laid it down.

'Would you like to tell me about the last time you were with your father? Were you here when he left?'

She hesitated, then gave a nod. 'It was the second day of term after the Easter holidays. I was late home because I went to the library. They'd got a book in for me, a new book I'd put my name down for and they'd sent me a card to say it was in.' She lifted two books off the stack and handed him one from underneath. She was out to impress and the book was a learned work: Stern's *Principles of Human Genetics*. He didn't take much notice of that but he did look at the date stamp in the back. 'I rang the library to renew it,' she said defensively. 'I couldn't read it in three weeks. It's very difficult.' She smiled at last and became at once a beauty. 'I'm not saying it's too difficult for me but genetics is an abstruse subject. I've got my A-levels and they have to take priority.'

'You're interested in this sort of thing?'

'I've been offered a place in medical school, St Biddulph's.' Crocker had trained there, Wexford recalled. 'I shall get it, of course, but in theory it depends on my A-level results.' Her tone was such as to show she was in no real doubt that these would meet the standard. 'I have to get at least three Bs but an A and two Bs would be better.'

She must be a bright girl. A year or two back statistics had been published showing an excess of medical students and that at this rate there would be a surplus of forty thousand doctors by the end of the century. Medical schools were being instructed to raise their standards and cut their intake. So if Sara Williams had been offered a place at the highly prestigious St Biddulph's . . .

'Your mother and father must be proud of you.'

The sweeping glance she gave him told him he had said something stupid or at least wide of the mark.

'I can see you don't know my parents.'

'They'd prefer something else for you?'

'I could be a shorthand typist, couldn't I? I could be a nurse. I'd get paid while I was being those things, wouldn't I?' Her voice was full of scorn and anger. 'I can't be stopped, though. I'll get a grant anyway. I don't know what I'd have done in olden times.'

By 'olden times' he supposed she meant the days of his own youth when your parents paid for your education or you borrowed the money or worked your way. Things were different now. A father couldn't put his foot down with the same effect. He could only persuade or dissuade.

'The last time you saw your father,' he reminded her.

Her anger had died. She was practical again, crisply reciting facts. But there was something derisive in the way she spoke of her father, as if he were a joke to her – or an organism under a microscope.

'I came in and he was just leaving. I heard him talking to Mum about the route he was going to take. The A26 for Tonbridge, then the Dartford Tunnel on to the M25 and the M25 to the A12 which would take him to Ipswich.'

'Why was he telling her the route? Would she be interested? I mean, wasn't it the route he normally took?'

'I said you didn't know my father. I'd say for a start he wouldn't be much concerned about the other person's *interest*. Dad talks a lot about cars and driving, roads, that sort of thing. I'm not interested but he talks to me about it. The car's a person to him, a woman, and she's got a 'hristian name. He calls her Greta. Greta, the Granada, you see.'

'So your father left and your mother went to Pomfret and you stayed here on your own studying?'

Was he imagining that hesitation, that brief wary flare in her eyes?

'That's right. I don't go out in the evenings at the moment. I haven't time.' She smiled again, this time with great artificiality. 'I heard they'd found his car.'

'In the process of being dismembered for its wheels and its radio.'

'Cannibalized,' she said, and she laughed the way her mother did. 'Poor old Greta.'

Could he have a look round the rest of the house? Notably through Williams's papers and clothes? Joy put up no objection. The television clack-clacked through the floor and the pop music thumped and droned through the wall. In the book of rules of human behaviour he kept in his head one of the first laws was the one about who got which bedroom. The British middle class mostly lived in three-bedroomed houses, one big bedroom, one slightly smaller, one little. In a family of parents, son and daughter, the daughter invariably got the second bedroom and the son the tiny one, irrespective of seniority. It was one aspect of life (the women's movement might have said if they'd noticed it) in which the female had the advantage over the male. Presumably it came about because girls from the first were conditioned into being more at home, more centred on home things and being confined within walls. In which case the women's movement wouldn't like it so much. But it was the girl in this household who had the smallest bedroom, even though her brother was now away most of the time. Of course, it might be that she had chosen this arrangement, but somehow he didn't think so.

He opened the door of the second bedroom and looked inside. There was a newish pine bedroom suite, two bright Afghan rugs, a fringed bedcover that was recognizably one of Marks and Spencer's designs. It looked as if someone with not much taste or money had done her best to make a 'nice' room of it and the sole personal touch its occupant had contributed was to hang a map of the world on the wall opposite the bed.

The main bedroom was like his own in size and proportions. The walls were even painted in the same colour as his own, Sevenstar emulsion Orange Blossom. There the resemblance ended. The Williamses slept in twin beds, each narrower than the standard three feet, he thought. He could tell hers was the one nearest the window by the nightdress case on it, quilted peach satin in the shape of a scallop shell. The rest of the furniture consisted of a wardrobe, dressing table, dressing-table stool, chest of drawers and two bedside tables all in some dark reddish wood with a matt finish and with rather bright gold chrome handles. There was also a built-in cupboard.

Wexford looked first in the drawer of the bedside cabinet between Williams's bed and the door. He found a box that had once held cufflinks but was now empty, a comb, a tube of antiseptic skin cream, an unused toothbrush, a packet of tissues, a tube of throat pastilles, two safety pins, several plastic collar stiffeners, a half-full bottle of nasal drops and an empty pill bottle labelled 'Mandaret. One to be taken twice daily. Rodney Williams'.

In the cupboard part of the cabinet were two paperback novels of espionage, an unused writing pad, a current British passport in the name of Mr R. J. Williams, a clean handkerchief initialled 'R' and two electric shavers.

The wardrobe contained Joy's clothes, a collection that had an unwashed, uncleaned smell about it with a whiff of camphor and some kind of disinfectant. Rodney Williams's clothes were in the cupboard. An overcoat, a sheepskin jacket, a plastic mac, two hip-length showerproof jackets, a shabby sports jacket and a new one, four suits, two pairs of slacks. All the clothes were good, all of much better quality than Joy's. Not a large wardrobe, Wexford thought, looking into the linings of coats and feeling in pockets. In the side compartments were underwear, pyjamas, on the floor three pairs of shoes and a pair of sandals. Whatever Rodney Williams had spent his surplus money on it wasn't clothes. Unless he had taken more with him than Joy or Sara knew. Maybe he had secreted a couple of bulging suitcases in Greta's boot during the course of the day.

The dining room, you could see, they hardly ever used. A light-coloured polished table stood in the dead centre of it with four light-coloured wood chairs with moquette seats around it. A sideboard with an empty Capo da Monte bowl on it nearly filled one wall and opposite this was a mahogany roll-top desk, perhaps a hand-down from a parent and certainly the nicest piece of furniture in the house. French windows, at which hung curtains of mustard-coloured rep – a favourite shade with Joy Williams – gave onto the back garden, a quarter acre of grass surrounded by close-board fencing and relieved by two small apple trees on which the blossom glimmered palely in the dusk. It didn't look as if the grass, several inches long now, had been mown since Williams did it five weeks before.

The desk wasn't locked. Wexford rolled back the top. There wasn't much inside. Writing paper, not the headed kind, envelopes, a bottle of ink in a cardboard box from which it had never been removed and never would be, a box of drawing pins, a glass jar of gum, a roll of Scotch tape. In one of the drawers was nothing but old Christmas cards, in the other a receipted electricity bill, a pocket calculator and a broken ballpoint pen.

If Williams had meant to go away for good wouldn't he have taken his passport?

He looked through the pigeonholes but found no cheque

books, used or in use. Joy probably kept hers in her handbag. He went back to her. She was still watching television and now the programme was the everlasting serial *Runway* in which his daughter Sheila played the stewardess heroine. Had, in fact, played her for the last time the previous week. But this was a secret known to no one but her own family as yet. No newspaper had so far got hold of the story that a major air disaster would in the autumn end the career of Stewardess Charlotte Riley for ever.

Joy Williams didn't know it. If she knew Sheila was his daughter – and surely she must – she gave no sign. He had the curious experience of standing beside her while they both watched his daughter attempting to placate an ill-tempered passenger. Then he did what Crocker recommended – or nearly so. If he didn't go so far as to pull out the plug he did switch off the set. She blinked at him.

'Does your husband possess a typewriter, Mrs Williams?'

'A typewriter? No.'

'Is he still taking Mandaret?'

She nodded, looking at the blank screen as if she expected it spontaneously and without benefit of electricity to spring into cinematic life.

'It's a form of methyldopa, isn't it? A drug for high blood pressure?'

'He's had blood pressure for two or three years.'

'I found an empty Mandaret container in his bedside cupboard. I suppose he took a supply with him?'

'He wouldn't forget them. He didn't like to miss a day on them. He always took one when he got up and one with his tea.'

'I take it he had a bag with him? A suitcase? Something to put his clothes in?'

Again she simply nodded.

'What was he dressed in?'

'Pardon?'

'What clothes was he wearing when he left here to drive to Ipswich?'

It was plain she couldn't remember. She looked blank – and she looked bored. Wexford understood in that moment that she didn't love Rodney Williams, hadn't perhaps loved him for years. His presence or absence as a life companion were matters of indifference to her but his financial support and the status he gave her were not. Or were her feelings more subtle and diffuse than that? Of course they were. Feelings always are. There is never a simple clear analysis of a woman's reaction to her husband or his to her.

He pressed the point he had made.

'Sort of fawn trousers,' she said, screwing up her face with the effort of it. 'Cavalry twill, they're called. A dark blue pullover. Is his raincoat upstairs?'

'A plastic mac?'

'No, he's got a good raincoat. It's nearly new. He must have taken that. I expect he had a jacket in his bag too. He's got a brown suede one.'

'Did he like a wet or dry shave?'

'Pardon?'

'Did he use a razor with shaving cream and water?'

'Oh, yes. He couldn't get on with those electrics. He'd tried but he couldn't get on with them.'

And that accounted for the Remington and the Phillips upstairs. She was staring miserably at the blank, grey, shiny screen. Wexford felt it was cruel to deprive her of her solace, like keeping a dumb hungry dog from its plate of Kennomeat. He asked her for her sister's name and address and then he switched the television on again. She looked at him as if she thought him completely mad but she said nothing and her eyes were compelled back to the screen and to Sheila, dressing now in a hotel bedroom for an evening out with the Boeing 747 captain in Hong Kong.

Wexford walked home, thinking about Williams and money. What had he done with all that money? Even after tax and other deductions, after the stingy allotment to his household of £500 a month, he would have been left with at least £12,000 a year. He'd had a company car. It didn't go on cars. The passport, which was seven years old, showed a single visit to Majorca. It didn't go on foreign holidays. Of course, he had to keep his son Kevin at Keele and pay for his keep. He wouldn't get much of a grant on his salary . . .

And then, suddenly, Wexford understood what had been bugging him for the past hour. It had been a Thursday evening when Williams had left. Kevin Williams always phoned home on Thursday evenings. And that Thursday was certainly the first since he had returned to university after the Easter vacation. Yet his mother, who plainly adored him, who waited excitedly for his call and spoke proudly of his devotion to duty in regularly phoning at that time, had gone out on that particular Thursday evening and for no more pressing or life-enhancing appointment than a visit to her sister.

If she had visited her sister.

And how about his clothes? Was she lying when she said he had taken only a jacket and a raincoat with him? Or didn't she know? Somehow he couldn't imagine Williams leaving his car in Arnold Road and then humping huge bulging suitcases the quarter of a mile to Myringham station. Why go to Myringham anyway when, if he wanted to catch a train to London, Kingsmarkham station was eight miles nearer?

The following week the clothes, or some of them, turned up.

5

A lonely country road links Kingsmarkham with Pomfret. Once Forest Road, Kingsmarkham, is past, the only houses to be seen are those few up on the hillsides crowned by Cheriton Forest. The forest is always rather dark and forbidding as coniferous forests are. On the horizon stands an obelisk, a needle of stone, placed there by some local magnate a hundred and fifty years ago.

Almost the last building in Kingsmarkham is the police station. On the other side of the High Street Cheriton Lane runs down to the buildings and courts of the Kingsmarkham Tennis Club, and half a dozen other narrow roads compose a small residential web. The gardens of houses in Forest Road back onto open fields, and fields traversed by a footpath lie between the club grounds and the town. The street lamps stop two hundred yards on the Pomfret side of the police station and after that there is an isolated one to light the bus stop.

Roughly halfway between the towns, at the point of no return, is the bus stop with bus shelter. The shelter was put there because there are no trees at this point to break the wind or provide cover from the rain. And on this night it was raining as it had been for many nights. The fine rain swept across the meadows in grey sheets.

The last bus from Pomfret to Kingsmarkham was due at 10.40. It came ten minutes late, rolling along not too fast through the rain, sending up fountains of spray onto the grass verges. The stop where the bus shelter was was a compulsory one, not a request, so the bus pulled in to make a token stop and prepared to pull out again, for there was no one waiting. A shout from a woman passenger sitting in a front nearside seat alerted the driver. He had already taken off the brake but he put it on again and the bus juddered to a halt.

'There's a person crawling on the pavement!'

Here, where the shelter was, the lay-by was bordered by a few yards of pavement. The driver got down. Two or three of the passengers, disobeying the driver – who was he to tell them? – got down. There was no conductor on those single deckers. The rain was coming down in torrents, needles of it pounding the surface of the lay-by, the kerb, and the sodden bundle that crawled and whimpered with blood coming from its chest.

At first the conductor had thought it a wounded dog. But the passenger was right, it was a man. It crawled up to the conductor and rolled over at his feet.

Next day, on the other side of Kingsmarkham, the Forby side, a firm called Mid-Sussex Waterways began dragging a pond. Green Pond Hall had stood empty for years but at the end of the previous January a buyer had been found for it and the purchase was completed by April. The grounds contained the pond and a stream and the new owner intended to turn the estate into a trout farm.

If the proper definition of a lake is a sheet of water covering the minimum of one acre, Green Pond was just too small to fit the requirement. But as a pond it was very large. It wasn't stagnant, for the small fast stream flowed through the middle of it, disappearing into a pipe which passed under a path and gushing out through a spout on the other side to fall away down to the Kingsbrook. In spite of this the pond was shallow and coated with the thick green slime of blanket weed. The purpose of the dragging was to clean it, increase its depth and rid the water of the algae Mid-Sussex Waterways believed might be caused by an influx of the nitrates which had been applied as fertilizer to the nearby meadows.

In the net, after the dragging, were found a wire supermarket basket minus its handle, a quantity of glass bottles, jars and light bulbs, the silencer part of a car exhaust system, wood in the form of twigs and chopped lengths, stones among which were flints and chalk pebbles, a rubber boot, a Pyrex casserole dish, chipped and cracked, a metal door handle and lock, a pair of scissors and a dark burgundy-coloured travelling bag.

The bag was coated with green slime and thin, fine-grained black mud, but when the clasps were undone and the zip unfastened it was seen that only water had penetrated the seams of the bag, soaking but hardly discolouring the clothes inside, the topmost of which was a brown suede blouson.

It was a piece of luck, Wexford thought, that William Milvey, the boss of Mid-Sussex Waterways, had found money inside the bag, £50 in fivers rolled up and fastened with a rubber band. If it had contained nothing but clothes, and damaged clothes at that, it was probable he would have tossed it into the pit which had been dug out by a mechanical digger for the purpose of receiving the rubbish caught in the dragnet. Money, Wexford had often noticed, has this kind of electric effect on people. Many a man who thinks himself honest, on finding an object bought with money will keep the object but not the money itself. It is as if the adage 'Finders keepers' applies to things but never to money, which has its own aura of sacredness, of being absolutely the preserve of him who has earned it.

But even so, Wexford might never have heard of the existence of the bag were it not for a kidney donor card which was in the breast pocket of the blouson and which was signed R. J. Williams.

William Milvey knew who R. J. Williams was. He lived next door but one to him in Alverbury Road.

* * *

This fact it took Wexford some half-hour to find out. He questioned Milvey thoroughly about the bag. Had he seen it in the pond before he saw it in the net? Well, yes, he thought he had, now Wexford came to mention it. He fancied he had. At any rate he thought he could remember seeing a brownish-red lump of something up against the bank of the pond nearest to the path and the Kingsbrook. No, he hadn't touched it or attempted to pull it out. The dragnet had pulled it out.

Milvey was a shortish thick-set man with the heavy build and big spread hands of someone who has done manual work for most of his life. He looked about fifty. The discovery of the bag seemed disproportionately to have excited him – or his excitement appeared disproportionate to Wexford at first.

'Fifty quid in it,' he kept saying, 'and that good jacket.'

'Did you see anyone about the grounds of Green Pond Hall?'

'Some fella up to no good, d'you mean?'

'I meant anyone at all.'

'We didn't have sight nor sound of no one.'

There might have been marks of car tyres on the drive in from the Forby Road or on the track that ran round the lower bank of the pond, the constant rain had turned these surfaces to mud, but any tracks there were had been obliterated by the heavy tyres of Mid-Sussex Waterways' mechanical digger.

Milvey simply couldn't remember if there had been any tyremarks on the track. They had the other man in and asked him, but he couldn't remember either.

'Fifty quid,' said Milvey, 'and that good jacket. Just chucked away.'

'Let me have your address, will you, Mr Milvey? I'll very likely want to talk to you again. Home or business.'

'They're one and the same. I operate from home, don't I?' He said this as if it were a fact he would have expected Wexford to know, and adding his address, used the same patient, mildly surprised tone. 'Twenty-seven Alverbury Road, Kingsmarkham.'

'Are you telling me you live next door but one to Mr Williams?'

Milvey's expression, though bland and innocent, had become a little uncomfortable. 'I reckoned you knew.'

'No, I didn't know.' Vaguely now Wexford recalled reading of a planning application made to the local authority for permission to erect a garage – more a hangar really – large enough to house a JCB in the garden of 27 Alverbury Road. The area being strictly residential, the application had naturally been rejected. 'You must know Mr Williams then?'

'Pass the time of day,' said Milvey. 'The wife has a chat with Mrs Williams. My girl's in the same class at school with their Sara.'

'Mr Williams is missing,' said Wexford flatly. 'He's been missing from home for the past month and more.'

'Is that right?' Milvey didn't look surprised but he didn't say he knew either. 'Fifty quid in notes,' he said, 'and a jacket worth three times that.'

Wexford let him go.

'It has to be coincidence,' Burden said.

'Does it, Mike? It would be a hell of a coincidence, wouldn't it? Williams disappears because he's done something or someone's done something to him. His overnight bag is dumped in a pond and who should find it but the guy who lives two doors down the street from him? I haven't read any John Buchan for – well, it must be forty-five years. But I can remember in one of his books the hero's car breaks down and the house he calls at for help just happens to be the home of the master anarchist. A bit later on the hit man who's sent to get him turns out to be a burglar he's recently successfully defended in court. Now that's fiction and strictly for persons below fifteen, I'd say. But this that you call coincidence is comparable to those.

Have you had any coincidences of that magnitude in your life?'

'Both my grandmothers were called Mary Brown.'

'Were they really?' Wexford was temporarily distracted. 'You never told me that before. And did they come from the same part of the country?'

'One from Sussex and one from Herefordshire. I bet you the odds against that happening are a lot longer than against Milvey finding Williams's bag. You look at it and you'll see it's not that much of a coincidence. If it had been buried, say, or stuck in a hollow tree and Milvey had found it, that would be something else. But it was in a pond and Milvey's in the pond-dragging business. Once it got in the pond and the pond was due to be dragged – which whoever put it there wouldn't know, of course – the chances would be that Milvey *would* find it. You want to look at it like that.'

Wexford knew there was more to it than that; he couldn't dismiss it in the easy way Burden did. Milvey's behaviour had been a shade odd anyway and Wexford was sure he hadn't told all he knew.

'How long do you think the bag's been in the pond?'

It was on the floor between them, deposited on sheets of newspaper, its contents, which Wexford had already examined, now replaced.

'Since the night he went, I suppose, or the next day.'

Wexford didn't go along with that either but he let it pass for the time being. As well as the brown suede blouson there was a raincoat in the bag, a trendy version of a Burberry, the fifty pounds, a toothbrush, tube of toothpaste and disposable razor wrapped up in a pair of underpants, a bottle of Monsieur Rochas cologne and a pair of brand-new socks with the label still on them. The underpants were a young man's Homs, pale blue and white, the socks dark brown, an expensive brand made of silk.

It was the kind of packing a man would do for an overnight stay somewhere, not for three nights, and the pants and socks and cologne seemed to indicate a night not spent alone. Or had there been more articles in the bag which had been removed? This could surely only have been done to prevent identification of the bag's owner. In that case why leave the donor card in the blouson pocket? 'I would like to help someone to live after my death', it stated somewhat naively in scarlet and white, and on the reverse side Rodney Williams had requested that in the event of his death any part of his body which might be required should be used in the treatment of others. Underneath this was his signature and the date a year past. The next of kin to contact was given, as might have been expected, as Joy Williams with the Alverbury Road phone number.

Men's natures were a mass of contradictions, there was no consistency, and yet Wexford marvelled a little that a husband and father could deliberately and ruthlessly deceive his wife over his income and pursue a course of skinflint meanness to her and his children yet want to donate his body for transplants. It would cost him nothing though, he would be dead after all. Was he dead?

'We're going to have to start looking for him. I mean really looking. Search the grounds of Green Pond Hall for a start.'

Burden had been pacing the office. He had taken to doing this lately and his restless pacing had a stressful effect on anyone he happened to be with, though he himself hardly seemed aware of what was going on. Twice he had been to the window, twice back to the door, pausing once to perch briefly on the edge of the desk. Now he had reached the window again where he stopped, turned and stared at Wexford in irritable incredulity.

'Search for *him*? Surely it's plain he's simply done a bunk to escape the consequences of whatever it is he's done.'

'All right, Mike. Maybe. But in that case what *has* he done? Nothing at Sevensmith Harding. He's as clean as a whistle there. What else could he have done? It's just possible he could be involved in some fraud that hasn't yet come to light but there's a strong case against that one. He got out. The only reason for that would be that discovery of the fraud was imminent. In that case why hasn't that discovery been made?'

Burden shrugged. 'Who knows? But it may just be a piece of luck for Williams that it hasn't been.'

'Why hasn't he come back then? If the outcome of this fraud has blown over why doesn't he come home? He hasn't left the country unless he's gone on a false passport. And why bother with a false passport when he'd got one of his own and no one started missing him till three days after he'd gone?'

'Doesn't it occur to you that leaving one's clothes on the river bank is the oldest disappearing trick in the world?'

'On the beach, I think you mean, not on the shores of a pond where the water's so shallow that to commit suicide you'd have to lie on your face and hold your breath. Besides, that bag has been in the pond only a couple of days at most. If it had been there since Williams went it'd be rotting by now, it'd stink. We'll send it over to the lab and see what they say but we can see what they'll say with our own eyes and smell it with our own noses.

'Williams is dead. This bag of his tells me he is. If he had put it into the pond for the purpose of making us think he was dead he'd have done so immediately after he left. And the contents would have been different. More identification, for instance, no scent and powder blue knickers. And I don't think the money would have been in it. He would have needed that money, he would have needed all the money he could lay hands on. There's no reason to think he could easily spare fifty pounds – whatever he's done he hasn't robbed a bank.

'He's dead and, letter and phone call notwithstanding, he was dead within an hour or two of when his family last saw him.'

* * *

Next day the searching of Green Pond Hall grounds began.

The grounds comprised eight acres, part woodland, part decayed overgrown formal gardens, part stables and paddock. Sergeant Martin led the search with three men and Wexford himself went down there to have a look at the dragged pond and view the terrain. It was still raining. It had been raining yesterday and the day before and for part of every day for three weeks. The weather people were saying it would be the wettest May since records began. The track was a morass, the colour and texture of melted chocolate in which a giant fork had furrowed. There were other ways of getting down to the pond but only if you went on foot.

At three he had a date at Stowerton Royal Infirmary. Colin Budd had been placed in intensive care but only for the night. By morning he was sufficiently recovered to be transferred to a side room off the men's surgical ward. The stab wounds he had received were more than superficial, one having penetrated to a depth of three inches, but by a miracle almost none of the five had endangered heart or lungs.

A thick white dressing covered his upper chest, over which a striped pyjama jacket had been loosely wrapped. The pyjama jacket was an extra large and Wexford estimated Budd's chest measurement at thirty-four inches. He was a very thin, bony, almost cadaverous young man, white-faced and with black, longish hair. He seemed to know exactly what Wexford would want to know about him and quickly and nervously repeated his name and age, gave his occupation as motor mechanic and his address a Kingsmarkham one where he lived with his parents.

'Tell me what happened.'

'This girl stuck a knife in my chest.'

'Now, Mr Budd, you know better than that. I want a detailed account, everything you can remember, starting with what you were doing waiting for a bus in the middle of nowhere.'

Budd had a querulous voice that always sounded mildly indignant. He was one of those who believes the world owes him elaborate consideration as well as a living.

'That's got nothing to do with it,' he said.

'I'll be the judge of that. I don't suppose you were doing anything to be ashamed of. And if you were what you tell me will be between you and me.'

'I don't know what you're getting at!'

'Just tell me where you'd been last evening, Mr Budd.'

'I was at snooker,' Budd said sullenly.

What a fool! He'd made it sound at least as if he was having it away with a friend's wife in one of the isolated cottages on the hillside.

'A snooker club?'

'It's on Tuesday evenings. In Pomfret, a room at the back of the White Horse. It's over at ten and I reckoned on walking home.' Budd shifted his body, wincing a bit, pulling himself up in the bed. 'But the rain started coming down harder, I was getting soaked. I looked at my watch and saw the ten-forty bus'd be along in ten minutes and I was nearly at the stop by then.'

'I'd have expected a motor mechanic to have his own transport.'

'My car was in a crunch-up. It's in dock having a new wing. I wasn't doing no more than twenty-five when this woman come out of a side turning . . . '

Wexford cut that one short. 'So you reached the bus stop, the bus shelter. What happened?'

Budd looked at him and away. 'There was this girl already there, sitting on the seat. I sat down next to her.'

The bus shelter was well known to Wexford. It was about ten feet long, the seat or bench inside two feet shorter.

'Next to her?' he asked. 'Or at the other end of the seat?'

'Next to her. Does it matter?'

Wexford thought perhaps it did. In England at any rate, for good or ill, for the improving of social life or its worsening, a man of honourable intent who goes to sit on a public bench where a woman is already sitting will do so as far away from her as possible. A woman will probably do this too if a woman or man is already sitting there, and a man will do it if another man is there.

'Did you know her? Had you ever seen her before?'

Budd shook his head.

'You spoke to her?'

'Only to say it was raining.'

She knew that already, Wexford thought. He looked hard at Budd. Budd said, 'I said it was a pity we were having such a bad May, it made the winter longer, something like that. She pulled a knife out of her bag and lunged it at me.'

'Just like that? You didn't say anything else to her?'

'I've told you what I said.'

'She was mad, was she? A girl who stabs men because they tell her it's raining?'

'All I said was that normally at this time I'd have had my vehicle and I could have given her a lift.'

'In other words, you were trying to pick her up?'

'All right, what if I was? I didn't touch her. I didn't do anything to frighten her. That was all I said, that I could have given her a lift home. She pulled out this knife and stabbed at me four or five times and I cried out or screamed or something and she ran off.'

'Would you know her again?'

'You bet I would.'

'Describe her to me.'

Budd made the mess of that Wexford thought he would. He didn't know whether she was tall or short, plump or thin, because he only saw her sitting down and he thought she had a raincoat on. A thin raincoat that was a sort of pale colour. Her hair was fair, he did know that, though she had a hat on or a scarf. Bits of blonde hair showed under it. Her face was just an ordinary face, not what you'd call pretty. Wexford began to wonder what had attracted Budd to her in the first place. The mere facts that she was female and young? About twenty, said Budd. Well, maybe twenty-five or six. Pressed to be more precise, he said she could have been any age between eighteen and thirty, he wasn't good on ages, she was quite young though.

'Can you think of anything else about her?'

A nurse had come in and was hovering. Wexford knew what she was about to say, he could have written the script for her – 'Now I think that's quite enough. It's time for Mr Budd to have his rest . . . ' She approached the bed, unhooked Budd's chart and began reading it with the enthusiastic concentration of a scholar who has just found the key to Linear B or some such.

'She had this sack with her. She grabbed it before she ran off.'

'What sort of sack?'

'The plastic kind they give you for your dustbin. A black one. She picked it up and stuck it over her shoulder and ran off.'

'I think that's quite enough for now,' said the nurse, diverging slightly from Wexford's text.

He got up. It was an extraordinary picture Budd's story had created and one which appealed to his imagination. The dark wet night, the knife flashing purposefully, even frenziedly, the girl running off into the rain with a sack slung over her shoulder. It was like an illustration in a fairy book of Andrew Lang, elusive, sinister and other-worldly.

6

What had Burden meant when he said this amniocentesis had discovered something to worry Jenny? Wexford found himself brooding on that. Once or twice he had woken in the night and the question had come into his mind. Sitting in the car, being driven to Myringham, he saw a woman on the pavement with a Down's Syndrome child and the question was back, presenting itself again.

He hadn't liked to pursue it with Burden. This wasn't the sort of thing you asked a prospective father about. What small defect was there a father wouldn't mind about but a mother would? It was grotesque, ridiculous, there was nothing. Any defect would be a tragedy. His mind ranged over partial deafness, a heart murmur, palate or lip deformities – the test couldn't have shown those anyway. An extra chromosome? This was an area where he found himself floundering in ignorance. He thought of his own children, perfect, always healthy, giving him no trouble really, and his heart warmed towards his girls.

This reminded him that he had the National Theatre's programme brochure for the summer season in his pocket. Sheila was with the company and this would be the first season she had top lead roles. Hence the disengagement from further work on *Runway*. He got out the programme and looked at it. Dora had asked him to decide which days they should go to London and see the three productions Sheila was in. For obvious reasons it always had to be he who made those kind of decisions.

The new Stoppard, Ibsen's *Little Eyolf*, Shelley's *The Cenci*. Wexford had heard of *Little Eyolf* but he had never seen it or read it, and as for *The Cenci*, he had to confess to himself that he hadn't known Shelley had written any plays. But there it was: 'Percy Bysshe Shelley' and the piece described as a tragedy in five acts. Wexford was making tentative marks on the programme for a Friday in July and two Saturdays in August when Donaldson, his driver, drew into the kerb outside Sevensmith Harding.

Miles Gardner had been watching for him and came rushing out with an umbrella. It made Wexford feel like royalty. They splashed across the pavement to the mahogany doors.

Kenneth Risby, the chief accountant, told him Rodney Williams's salary had been paid into the account Williams had with the Pomfret branch of the Anglian-Victoria Bank. From that account then, it would seem, Williams had each month transferred £500 into the joint account he had with Joy. Risby had been with the company for fifteen years and said he could recall no other arrangement being made for Williams, either recently or in the days when he was a sales rep. His salary had always gone to the Pomfret bank, never to Kingsmarkham.

'We've heard nothing,' Miles Gardner said. 'Whatever he meant by the PS to that letter he hasn't been in touch.'

'Williams didn't write that letter,' Wexford reminded him.

Gardner nodded unhappily.

'The first time we talked about this business,' Wexford said, 'you told me someone phoned here saying she was Mrs Williams and that her husband was ill and wouldn't be coming in. Would that have been on Friday, April the sixteenth?'

'Well, yes, I suppose it would.'

'Who took the call?'

'It must have been one of our telephonists. They're part-timers. I can't remember whether it was Anna or Michelle. The phone call came before I got in, you see. That is, before nine-thirty.'

'Williams had a secretary, I suppose?'

'Christine Lomond. He shared her with our assistant sales director. Would you like to talk to her?'

'Not yet. Maybe not today. It's Anna or Michelle I want. But which one do I want?'

'Michelle, I expect,' said Gardner. 'They tend to swop shifts a bit but it's usually Michelle on mornings.'

It had been, that Friday, and it was today. Michelle was a very young, very pretty girl with a vividly made-up face. The room where the switchboard was, not much more than a cupboard, was stamped with her personality (or perhaps Anna's) and there was a blue cineraria in a pot, a stack of magazines, a pile of knitting that had reached the bulky stage, and on the table in front of her, hurriedly placed face downwards, the latest diet paperback.

It was clear that Michelle had already discussed that phone call exhaustively. Perhaps with Anna or with Christine Lomond. Williams's disappearance would have been the talk of the office.

'I get in at nine,' she said. 'That's when the phone calls really start. But the funny thing was there weren't any that morning till Mrs Williams phoned at about twenty past.'

'You mean till someone phoned who *called* herself Mrs Williams.'

The girl looked at him. She shook her head quite vehemently. 'It was Mrs Williams. She said, "This is Joy Williams." '

Wexford let it go for the time being.

'What exactly did she say?'

' "My husband Mr Williams won't be coming in today." And then she sort of hesitated and said, "That's Mr Rodney Williams, I mean, the marketing manager." I said there was no one else in yet and she said that didn't matter but to give Christine the message he'd got flu and wouldn't be in.'

Whoever it was, it hadn't been Joy. At that time Joy didn't know her husband was Sevensmith Harding's marketing manager. Wexford had thanked Michelle and was turning away, diverting his mind to the matter of the firm's stock of typewriters, when he stopped.

'What makes you so sure the woman you spoke to was Mrs Joy Williams?'

'It just was. I know it was.'

'No, let me correct that. You know it was a woman who *said* she was Mrs Joy Williams. She had never phoned here before, had she, so you couldn't have recognized her voice?'

'No, but she phoned here afterwards.'

'What do you mean, afterwards?'

'About three weeks later.' The girl spoke with exaggerated patience now, as if to a very confused or simple-minded person. 'Mrs Joy Williams phoned here three weeks after her husband left.'

Of course. Wexford remembered that call. It was he who had advised Joy to make it.

'I put her through to Mr Gardner,' Michelle said. 'I was a bit embarrassed, to be perfectly honest. But I know it was the same voice, really I do. It was the same voice as the woman who phoned that Friday morning, it was Mrs Williams.'

He picked up the girl at the roundabout where the second exit is the start of the Kingsmarkham bypass. She was standing on the grass verge at the side of the roundabout, holding up a piece of cardboard with 'Myringham' printed on it. Brian Wheatley pulled in to the first exit, the Kingsmarkham town-centre road, and the girl got into the passenger seat. Then, for some unclear reason, perhaps because he had already pulled out of the roundabout and it would not have been easy to get back into the traffic, Wheatley decided to continue through the town instead of on the bypass. This wasn't such a bad idea anyway, the anomaly being that the bypass which had been built to ease the passage of traffic past the town was often more crowded than the old route.

Wheatley was driving home from London where he worked three days a week. It was about six in the evening and of course broad daylight. He had moved to Myringham only two weeks before and was still unfamiliar with the byways and back-doubles of the area. The girl didn't speak a word. She had no baggage with her, only a handbag with a shoulder strap. Wheatley drove through Kingsmarkham, along the High Street, and became confused by the sign-posting. Instead of keeping straight on he began to think he should have taken a left-hand turn some half a mile back. He therefore – on what he admitted was a lonely and secluded stretch of road – pulled into a lay-by and consulted his road map.

His intention to do this, he said, he announced plainly to the girl. After he had stopped and switched off the engine he was obliged to reach obliquely across her in order to open the glove compartment where the map was. He was aware of the girl giving a gasp of fright or anger, and then of a sharp pain, more like a burn than a cut, in his right hand.

He never even saw the knife. The girl jumped out of the car, slamming the door behind her, and ran not along the road but onto a footpath that separated a field of wheat from a wood. Blood was flowing from a deep cut in the base of Wheatley's thumb. He tied up his hand as best he could with his handkerchief but shock and a feeling of faintness made it impossible for him to continue his journey for some minutes. Eventually he looked at his map, found himself nearer home than he had thought, and was able to drive there in about a quarter of an hour. The general practitioner with whom he had registered the week before was still holding his surgery. Wheatley's wife drove him there and the cut in his hand was stitched, Wheatley telling the doctor he had been carving meat and had inadvertently pressed his hand against the point of the carving knife.

Whether or not the doctor believed this was another matter. At any rate he had made no particular comment. Wheatley himself had wanted to tell him the truth, though this would have meant police involvement. It was his wife who had dissuaded him on the grounds that if the police were called the conclusion they would reach would be that Wheatley had first made some sort of assault on the girl.

This was the story Wheatley told Wexford three days later. His wife didn't know he had changed his mind. He had come to the police, he said, because he felt more and more indignant that this girl, whom he hadn't touched, whom he had scarcely spoken to except to say he was going to stop and look at his map, should make an unprovoked attack on him and get away with it.

'Can you describe her?'

Wexford waited resignedly for the kind of useless description furnished by Colin Budd. He was surprised. In many ways Wheatley did not seem to know his way around but he was observant and perceptive.

'She was tall for a woman, about five feet eight or nine. Young, eighteen or nineteen. Brown hair or lightish hair, shoulder-length, sunglasses though it wasn't sunny, fair skin – I noticed she had very white hands. Jeans and a blouse, I think, and a cardigan. The bag was some dark colour, black or navy blue.'

'Did she give you the impression she lived in Myringham? That she was going home?'

'She didn't give me any sort of impression. When she got into the car she said thanks – just the one word "thanks", otherwise she didn't speak. I said to her that I thought I'd drive through the town instead of the bypass and she didn't answer. Later on I said I'd stop and look at the map and she didn't answer that either, but when I reached across her – I didn't touch her, I could swear to that – she gave a sort of gasp. Those were the only sounds she made, "thanks" and a gasp.'

The same girl as attacked Budd, one would suppose. But

if Wheatley were to be believed, while there was some very slight justification for the attack on Budd, there was none for this second stabbing. Could the girl possibly have thought that the hand which reached across to open the glove compartment intended instead to take hold of her by the left shoulder? Or lower itself onto her knee? There was something ridiculous about these assaults, and yet two meant that they were not ridiculous at all but serious. Next time there could be a fatality.

Or had there been one already?

The manager of the Pomfret branch of the Anglian-Victoria Bank bore an extraordinary resemblance to Adolf Hitler. This was not only in the small square moustache and the lock of dark hair half covering Mr Skinner's forehead. The face was the same face, rather handsome, with large chin and heavy nose and small thick-lidded eyes. But all that would have passed unnoticed without the moustache and the lock of hair, so that it was impossible to avoid the uncomfortable conclusion that Mr Skinner was doing it on purpose. He knew whom he looked like and he enhanced the resemblance. Wexford could only attribute one motive to a bank manager who wants to look like Hitler – a desire to intimidate his clients.

His manner, however, was warm, friendly and charming. All those, and implacable too. He could not consider either letting Wexford look into Rodney Williams's bank accounts or disclose any information about their contents.

'Did you say accounts plural?' said Wexford.

'Yes. Mr Williams has two current accounts here – and now I've probably said more than I should.'

'Two current accounts in the name of Rodney Williams?'

Skinner was standing up with his head slightly on one side, looking like Hitler waiting for Franco's train at Hendaye. 'I said two current accounts, Chief Inspector. We'll let it go at that, shall we?'

One for his salary to be paid into, Wexford thought as he was driven away, and the other for what? His Kingsmarkham household expenses were drawn from the Kingsmarkham account which he fed with £500 a month from Pomfret account A. Then what of account B? His wife didn't know of the existence of account A anyway. It alone was sufficient to keep his resources secret from her. Why did he need a third current bank account?

They were searching for him now on the open land, partly wooded, that lay between Kingsmarkham and Forby. But so far, since the discovery of the bag in Green Pond, nothing further had come to light. He's dead, Wexford thought, he must be.

Burden had been at Pomfret, talking to the Harmer family, Joy Williams's sister, brother-in-law and niece. John Harmer was a pharmacist with a chemist's shop in the High Street.

'They say Joy was with them that evening,' Burden said, 'but I wouldn't put that much credence on what they say. Not that they're intentionally lying – they can't remember. It was seven weeks ago. Besides, Joy often goes over there in the evenings. More or less to sit in front of their television instead of her own, I gather. But I suppose she's lonely, she wants company. Mrs Harmer says she was definitely there that evening, Harmer says it must be if his wife says so and the girl doesn't know. You can't expect a teenage girl to take much notice of when her aunt comes.'

Wexford told him what he had learned from the telephonist at Sevensmith Harding. 'Of course, the girl may be mistaken about the voices or she may have persuaded herself they were the same voice in order to get more drama out of the situation. But it's more than possible that the woman who phoned Sevensmith Harding the day after Williams left to say he was ill and the woman who phoned three weeks later to inquire as to his whereabouts are one and the same. And we know the second time was Joy. Now Joy was very keen to have me look for her husband when he first disappeared, but later on much less so – indeed, she was obstructive. That first time I talked to her she said nothing about having gone out herself that evening. That was only mentioned the second time. Joy is devoted to her son Kevin. Her daughter is nothing to her, her son everything . . . What on earth's the matter?'

Burden's face had set and he had gone rather pale. He had taken a hard grip on the arms of his chair. 'Nothing. Go on.'

'Well, then – her son always phones on Thursday evenings and that particular Thursday was the first one he had been back at college. Wouldn't a devoted mother have wanted to know all those things mothers worry about in such circumstances? Did he have a good journey? Was his room all right? Had he settled in? But this devoted mother doesn't wait in for his call. She goes out – not to some important engagement, some function booked months ahead, but to watch television at her sister's. What does all this suggest to you?'

Having struggled successfully to overcome whatever it was that had upset him, Burden forced a laugh. 'You sound like Sherlock Holmes talking to Watson.' Since his second marriage he occasionally read books, a change in him Wexford couldn't get used to.

'No,' he said, 'more "a man of the solid Sussex breed – a breed which covers much good sense under a heavy silent exterior".'

'I wouldn't say "silent". Was that from Sherlock Holmes?'

Wexford nodded. 'So what do you make of it?' he said more colloquially.

'That Joy is somehow in cahoots with her husband. There's a conspiracy going on. What for and why I wouldn't pretend to know but it's got something to do with giving everyone the impression Williams is dead. He left that evening and she went out later to meet him away from the house. Whatever they were planning was done away from the house because it had to be concealed from the daughter Sara as much as from anyone else. Next morning Joy rang Sevensmith Harding to say her husband was ill. Of course, it's nonsense to say she didn't know that he was their marketing manager and the extent of his income. Next he or she typed that letter on a *hired* typewriter. She probably did that, not knowing what he called Gardner and making the mistake of addressing him as 'Mr Gardner'. The abandoned car, the dumped bag of clothes were all part of a plan to make us think him dead. But the increased police attention frightened Joy, she wanted things to go more at her pace. Hence the obstructiveness. I said I didn't know why but it could be an insurance fiddle, couldn't it?'

'Without a body, Mike? With no more proof of death than a dumped travelling bag? And if you wanted people to think you were dead, aren't there half a dozen simpler and more convincing ways of doing it?'

'You feel the same as me then? You don't think he's dead?'

'I know he's dead,' said Wexford.

Next day he was proved right.

It looked like a grave. It was in the shape of a grave, as clearly demarcated as if a slab of stone lay upon it, though Edwin Fitzgerald did not at first see this. In spite of its shape he would have passed it by as a mere curiosity, a whim of nature. It was the dog Shep who drew his attention to it.

Edwin Fitzgerald was a retired policeman who had been a dog handler. He lived in Pomfret and had a job as a part-time security guard at a factory complex on Stowerton's industrial estate. The dog Shep was not a trained dog in the sense of being police-trained – as a 'sniffer', for instance. Fitzgerald had bought him after his last dog died – a wonderful dog that one, more intelligent than any human being, a dog that understood every word he said. Shep could only follow humbly in that dog's footsteps and was often the subject of unfavourable comparisons. He didn't understand every word Fitzgerald said, or at any rate behaved as if he didn't.

On this particular morning in June, a dry one, the first really fine morning of the summer, Shep disregarded all Fitzgerald's words, ignored the repeated 'Leave it, sir' and 'Do as you're told' and continued his frenetic digging in the corner of what his master saw as a patch of weeds. He dug like a dog possessed. Indeed, Fitzgerald informed him that he was a devil, that he didn't know what had got into him. He shouted (which a good dog handler should never do) and he shook his fist until he saw what Shep had unearthed and then he stopped.

The dog had dug up a foot.

Fitzgerald had been a policeman, which had the double advantage of having taught him not to be sickened by such a discovery and not to disturb anything in its vicinity. He attached Shep's lead to his collar and pulled the dog away. This took some doing as Shep was a big young German Shepherd intent on worrying at the protruding thing for some hours if possible.

As far as Fitzgerald could see, now he had got the dog clear, the foot was still attached to a limb and the limb probably to a trunk. It was inside a sodden, blackened, slimy shoe caked with mud, and about the ankle clung a bundling of muddy wet cloth, once the hem of a trouser leg. Shep had dug it out from one of the corners of this curious little plot of ground. All around, on this edge of the meadow, grew tall grass ready to be cut for hay, high enough to hide the dog when he plunged in among it, but the rectangle – seven feet by three? – which Shep had found in there and had dug into was covered closely and in a neat rather horticultural way with fresh green plants. Weeds they were, but weeds attractive enough to be called plants, red campion, clover, speedwell, and they covered the oblong patch as precisely as if they had been sown there in a seed bed.

The grass which surrounded it, gone to seed, bearing light feathery seed heads of brown and greyish-cream and silvery-gold, hid it from the sight of anyone who kept to the footpath. It took a dog to plunge in there and find the grave. A day or two of sunshine, Fitzgerald thought, and the farmer would have cut the hay, cut those weeds too without a thought. Shep was a good dog after all, even if he didn't understand every word Fitzgerald said.

He retraced his steps to the branch of the lane that led to Myfleet and hurried down the hill to his bungalow where he phoned the police.

7

From the Pomfret road a narrow lane winds its way up into the hills and to the verge of the forest. All down the hedges here grows the wayfarer's tree with its flat creamy bracts of blossom, and beneath, edging the meadows like a fringe of lace, the whiter, finer, more delicate cow parsley. There are houses, Edwin Fitzgerald's among them, approached by paths, cart tracks or even smaller narrower lanes, but the lane gives the impression of leading directly to the obelisk on the hill.

It is like downland up here, the trees ceasing until the forest of conifers begins over there to the east, chalk showing in outcroppings and heather on the chalk. And all the way the obelisk looming larger, a needle of granite with its point a tetragon. The road never reaches it. A quarter of a mile this side it swerves, turns east and divides, one fork making for Myfleet, the other for Pomfret, and soon there are meadows again and the heath is past. It was in one of these meadows, close to the overhang of the forest, traversed by a footpath leading from the road to Myfleet, that the discovery had been made. Over to the west the obelisk stabbed the blue sky, catching a shred of cloud on its point.

The grave was in a triangle formed by the wood, the lane and the footpath, in a slightly more than right-angled corner of the field. It was near enough to the forest for the air to smell resinous. The soil was light and sandy with an admixture of pine needles.

'Easy enough to dig,' said Wexford to Burden. 'Almost anyone not decrepit could dig a grave like that in half an hour. Digging it deep enough would have taken a little longer.'

They were viewing the terrain, the distance of the grave from the road and the footpath, while Sir Hilary Tremlett, the pathologist, stood by with the scene-of-crimes officer to supervise the careful unearthing. Sir Hilary had happened to be at Stowerton when Fitzgerald's call came in. By a piece of luck he had just arrived at the infirmary to perform a postmortem. It was not yet ten o'clock, a morning of pearly sunshine, the blue sky dotted with innumerable puffs of tiny white cloud. But every man there, the short portly august pathologist included, had a raincoat on. It had rained daily for so many weeks that no one was going to take the risk of going without; no one anyway could yet believe his own eyes.

'The rain made the weeds grow like that,' said Wexford. 'You can see what happened. It's rather interesting. All the ground here had grass growing on it, then a patch was dug to receive *that*. It was covered up again with overturned earth, the weed seeds came and rain, seemingly endless rain, and what grew up on that fertile patch and that patch only were broad-leaved plants. If it had been a dry spring there would have been more grass and it would all have been much less green.'

'And the ground harder. If the ground hadn't been soft and moist the dog might not have persisted with its digging.'

'The mistake was in not digging the grave deep enough. It makes you wonder why he or she or they didn't. Laziness? Lack of time? Lack of light? The six-foot rule is a good one because things of this kind do tend to work to the surface.'

'If that's so,' said Dr Crocker, coming up to them, 'why is it they always have to dig so far down to find ancient cities and temples and so forth?'

'Don't ask me,' said Wexford. 'Ask the dog. He's the archaeologist. Mind you, we don't have any lava in Sussex.'

They approached a little nearer to where Detectives Archbold and Bennett were carrying out their delicate spadework. It was apparent now that the corpse of the man that lay in the earth had been neither wrapped nor covered before it was buried. The earth didn't besmear it as a heavier clayey soil might have done. It was emerging relatively clean, soaking wet, darkly stained, giving off the awful reek that was familiar to every man there, the sweetish, fishy, breath-catching, gaseous stench of decomposing flesh. That was what the dog had smelt and liked and wanted more of.

'I often think,' said Wexford to the doctor, 'that we haven't much in common with dogs.'

'No, it's at times like this you know what you've always suspected, that they're not almost human at all.'

The face was pale, stained, bloated, the pale parts the colour of a dead fish's belly. Wexford, not squeamish at all, hardened by the years, decided not to look at the face again until he had to. The big domed forehead, bigger and more domed because the hair had fallen from it, looked like a great mottled stone or lump of fungus. It was that forehead which made him pretty sure this must be Rodney Williams. Of course, he wasn't going to commit himself at this stage but he'd have been surprised if it wasn't Williams.

Sir Hilary, squatting down now, bent closer. Murdoch, the scene-of-crimes officer, was beginning to take measurements, make calculations. He called the photographer over but Sir Hilary held up a delaying hand.

Wexford wondered how he could stand that stink right up against his face. He seemed rather to enjoy it, the whole thing, the corpse, the atmosphere, the horror, the squalor. Pathologists did, and just as well really. It wouldn't do if they shied away from it.

The body was subjected to a long and careful scrutiny. Sir Hilary looked at it closely from all angles. He came very close to touching but he did not quite touch. His fingers were plump, clean, the colour of a slice of roast pork. He stood up, nodded to Murdoch and the photographer, smiled at Wexford.

'I could have a poke-about at that after lunch,' he said. He always spoke of his autopsies as 'having a poke-about'. 'Not much doing today. Any idea who it might be?'

'I think I have, Sir Hilary.'

'I'm glad to hear it. Saves a lot of hassle. We'll smarten him up a bit before his nearest and dearest come for a private view.'

Joy Williams, Wexford thought. No, she shouldn't be subjected to that. He felt the warmth of the mounting sun kind and soft on his face. He turned his back and looked across the sweep of meadows to the Pomfret road, green hay gold-brushed, dark green hedgerows stitched in like tapestry, sheep on a hillside. All he could see was that face and a wife looking at it. This horrid image doth unfix my hair and make my seated heart knock at my ribs . . .

It occurred to him that the nearest point on the main road to this place was the bus stop where Colin Budd had been attacked. Did that mean anything? The lane that passed within yards of the burial place met the road almost opposite the bus stop. But Budd had been stabbed weeks after this man's death. The brother-in-law might do the identification instead. John Something, the chemist. John Harmer.

He seemed a sensible man. Younger than Williams by five or six years, he was one of those tailored people, a neat, well-made, smallish man with regular features and short, crisply wavy hair. He had closed up his dispensary and left the shop in the care of his wife.

Having taken a deep breath, he looked at the body. He looked at the face, his symmetrical features controlled in blankness. He wasn't going to show anything, not he, no shock, disgust, pity. You could almost hear his mother's voice saying to a small curly-headed boy: Be a man, John. Don't cry. Be a man.

Harmer remembered and was a man. But he might have said with Macduff that he must also feel it like a man, for his face gradually paled until it became as sickly greenish white as the corpse's. His stomach, not his will, had betrayed him. Or threatened to. He came out into the air, into the sunshine, away from charnel-house corpse rot, and smelt the summer noonday, and the bile receded. He nodded to Wexford, he nodded rather more and longer than was necessary.

'Is that your brother-in-law, Rodney Williams?'

'Yes.'

'You are quite certain of that?'

'I'm certain.'

Wexford had thought of asking him to be the bearer of the news to Joy but he had quickly seen Harmer wouldn't be a suitable, let alone a sympathetic, messenger. He went himself, walking to Alverbury Road, thinking as he walked. There wasn't much he personally could do until the pathologist's report came and the lab had been over Williams's clothes. With distaste he recalled the bloodied mass of cloth that had wrapped the wounds. He felt glad now he had had the lab go over that car so carefully and at a time when it looked as if Williams might have been guilty of some misdemeanour and have done a moonlight flit.

Those crumbs of plaster in the boot could be vital evidence. At first he had supposed they derived from some routine of Williams's work. But Gardner had told him there was never a question of Williams having handled the stuff he sold. More likely the truth was that those plaster crumbs had been caught up in the folds of that bloodstained cloth and the body itself had been in the boot of the car . . .

In the front garden of 31 Alverbury Road someone had mown the bit of lawn and cut the privet hedge. It looked as if both these tasks had been performed with the same pair of blunt shears. Rodney Williams had been in one respect domestically adequate – he had kept his garden trim.

Sara opened the front door to him. He hadn't expected her to be there and he was a little taken aback. He would have preferred breaking the news to her mother alone. The school term wasn't yet over but A-levels were and with those examinations behind her there was perhaps nothing for her to go to school for.

She had on a white tee-shirt, pure unrelieved white, short-sleeved and showing felt-tipped pen drawings on her arms and hands, the snake again in green, a butterfly with a baby face, a raven woman with aggressive breasts and erect wings, somehow obscene on those smooth golden arms, childish and rounded.

'Is your mother in, Sara?'

She nodded. Had the tone of his voice told her? She looked sideways at him, fearfully, as they went down the short passage to the kitchen door.

Joy Williams anticipated nothing. On the table at which she was sitting were the remains of lunch for two. She looked up with a mildly disagreeable inquiring glance. They had been eating fish fingers with baked beans – an infelicitous mixture, Wexford thought. He could tell the constituents of their lunch by the quantity of it Sara had left on her plate. Joy had been reading a women's magazine of the royalty–sycophantic–crocheted-tea-cosy kind which was propped against a bottle of soy sauce, pathetic import surely of Sara's. What does a daughter do for her mother in a situation such as this? Go to her and put an arm round her shoulders? At least stand behind her chair? Sara went to the sink, stood with her back to them, looking out of the window above it at the grass and the fence and the meagre little apple trees.

Wexford told Joy her husband had been found. Her husband's body. More than that he couldn't tell her, he knew no more. The girl's shoulders twitched. Mrs Williams leaned forward across the table and put her hand heavily over her mouth. She sat that way for a moment or two. The whistling kettle on the stove began to screech. Sara turned round, turned the gas off, looked at her mother with her mouth twisted up as if she had toothache.

'D'you want a coffee?' Joy said to Wexford.

He shook his head. Sara made the coffee, instant in two mugs, one with a big 'S' on it and the other with the head of the Princess of Wales. Joy put sugar into hers, one spoonful, then after reflection, another.

'Shall I have to see him?'

'Your brother-in-law has already made the identification.'

'John?'

'Have you any other brothers-in-law, Mrs Williams?'

'Rod's got a brother in Bath. "Had", I should say. I mean he's still alive as far as I know and Rod's not, is he?'

'Oh, Mum,' said Sara. 'For God's sake.'

'You shut your mouth, you little cow!'

Joy Williams screamed it at her. She didn't utter any more words but she went on screaming, drumming her fists on the table so that the mug bounced off and broke and coffee went all over the strip of coconut matting on the floor. Joy screamed until Sara slapped her face – the doctor already, the cool head in an emergency. Wexford knew better than to do it himself. Once he'd slapped a hysterical woman's face and later been threatened with an action for assault.

'Who can we get hold of to be with her?' he asked. Mrs Milvey? He thought of Dora and dismissed the thought.

'She hasn't any friends. I expect my Auntie Hope will come.'

Mrs Harmer that would be. Hope and Joy. My God, he thought. Although the girl was sitting beside her mother now, holding her hand, while Joy leaned back spent, her head hanging over the back of the kitchen chair, the tears silently rolling out of her eyes, he could see that it was all Sara could do to control her repugnance. She was almost shaking with it. The need to be parted, the one from the other, was mutual. Sara, no doubt, couldn't wait for those exam results, the confirmation of St Biddulph's acceptance of her, for October and the start of term. It couldn't come fast enough for her.

'I'll stay with Mum,' she said, and there was stoicism in the way she said it. 'I'll give her a pill. She's got Valium. I'll give her a couple of Valium and find something nice for her on the TV.'

The ever ready panacea.

It was too late for lunch now. He and Burden might have something in the office, get a sandwich sent down from the canteen. He had said he'd see the press at 2.30. Well, young Varney of the local paper who was a stringer for the nationals . . .

There was a van on the police station forecourt marked TV South and a camera crew getting out of it.

'They've been up at the forest getting shots of the grave and Fitzgerald and the dog,' Burden said, 'and they want you next.'

'Good. I'll be able to put out an appeal for anyone who may have seen that car parked.' A less encouraging thought struck Wexford. 'They won't want to make me up, will they?' He had never been on television before.

Burden looked at him morosely, lifting his shoulders in a shrug of total indifference to any eventuality.

'It's not the end of the world if they do, is it?'

There was no time like the present, even a present that would end in ten minutes with his first ever TV appearance.

'What's happened to end your world, Mike?'

Burden immediately looked away. He mumbled something which Wexford couldn't hear and had to ask him to repeat.

'I said that I supposed I should tell you what the trouble is.'

'Yes. I want to know.' Looking at Burden, Wexford

noticed for the first time grey hairs among the fair ones. 'There's something wrong with the baby, isn't there?'

'That's right.' Burden's voice sounded very dry. 'In Jenny's opinion, mind you. Not in mine.' He gave a bark of laughter. 'It's a girl.'

'*What?*'

Wexford's phone went. He picked up the receiver. TV South, the *Kingsmarkham Courier* and two other reporters were downstairs waiting for him. Burden had already gone, closing the door quietly behind him.

8

She was laying the table with their wedding present glass and silver. The lace cloth had been bought in Venice where they went for the first holiday after their honeymoon. Domesticity had delighted her when, as soon as she knew she was pregnant, she gave up teaching. It was the novelty, of course, being at home all day, playing house. Since then she had grown indifferent, she had grown indifferent to everything. Except to the child, and that she hated.

Sometimes, walking about the house after Mike had gone to work, pushing the vacuum cleaner or tidying up, the tears fell out of her eyes and streamed down her face. She cried because she couldn't believe that she who had longed and longed for a baby could hate the one inside her. All this she had told to the psychiatrist at their second session. She had listened to her in almost total silence. Once she said, 'Why do you say that?' and once 'Go on', but otherwise she simply listened with a kind interested look on her face.

Mike had suggested the psychiatrist. She had been so surprised because Mike usually scoffed at psychiatry that she said yes without even protesting. It was somewhere to go anyway, something different to do from sitting at home brooding about the future and her marriage and the unwanted child. And inevitably crying, of course, when she remembered as she always did what life used to be – when the days seemed too short, when she was teaching history to sixth formers at Haldon Finch, playing the violin in an orchestra, taking an advanced art appreciation course.

Jenny despised herself but that changed nothing. Her self-pity sickened her.

The sound of his key in the door – time-honoured heart stopper, test of love sustained – did nothing for her beyond bringing a little dread of the evening in front of them. He came into the room and kissed her. He still did that.

'How did you get on with the shrink?'

She resented the haste he was in. He wanted her cured, she felt, so that life could get back to normal again. 'What do you expect? A miracle in two easy lessons?'

She sat down. That always made her feel a little less bad because the bulge was no longer so apparent. And, thank God, the child was still, not rolling about and kicking.

'Don't let him give you drugs.'

'It's a woman.'

She wanted to scream with laughter. The irony of it! She was a teacher and this other woman was a psychiatrist and Mike's daughter Pat was very nearly qualified as a dentist, yet here she was reacting like a no-account junior wife in a harem. Because the baby was a girl.

He gave her a drink, orange juice and Perrier. He had a whisky, a large one, and in a minute he would have another. Not long ago he hadn't needed to drink when he got home. She looked at him, wishing she could bring herself to touch his arm or take his hand. An apathy as strong as energy held her back.

'Mike,' she said, and said for the hundredth time, 'I can't help it, I wish I could. I have tried.'

'So you say. I don't understand it. It's beyond my understanding.'

In a low voice, looking down, she said, 'It's beyond mine.' The child began to move, with flutters only at first, then came a hearty kick right under her lower ribs, giving her a rush of heartburn. She cried out, 'I wish to God I'd never had the thing done. I wish I'd never let them do it. They shouldn't have told me. Why did I let them? If I'd been ignorant I'd have gone on being happy, I'd have had the baby and I wouldn't have minded what it was, I'd have been pleased with any healthy baby. I didn't even specially want a son, or I didn't know I did. I didn't mind what it was, but now I know what it is I can't bear it. I can't go through all this and all through having it and the work and the pain and the trouble and a lifetime of being with it, having it with me, for a *girl*!'

He had heard it all before. It seemed to him that she said it every night. This was what he came home to. With slight variations, with modifications and changed turns of phrase, that was what she said to him on and on every evening. Until she grew exhausted or wept or slumped spent in her chair, until she went away to bed – earlier and earlier as the weeks passed. In vain he had asked why this prejudice against girls, she who was a feminist, a supporter of the women's movement, who expressed a preference for her friends' small girls over their small sons, who got on better with her stepdaughter than her stepson, who professed to prefer teaching girls to boys.

She didn't know why, only that it was so. Her pregnancy, so long desired, at first so ecstatically accepted, had driven her mad. The worst of it was that he was coming to hate the unborn child himself and to wish it had never been conceived.

The wine bar was dark and cool. The restoration of an old house in Kingsmarkham's Queen Street had revealed and then opened up its cavernous cellars. The proprietor had resisted the temptations of roof beams, medieval pastiches, flintlocks and copper warming pans and simply painted the broad squat arches white, tiled the floor and furnished the place with tables and chairs in dark-stained pine.

Wexford and Burden had taken to lunching at the Old Cellar a couple of times a week. It had the virtue of being warm on cold days and cool on hot ones like this. The food was quiche and salad, smoked mackerel, coleslaw, pork pie, quiche, quiche and more quiche.

'What did they serve in these places before quiche caught on? I mean, there was a time not long ago when an Englishman could say he'd never heard of quiche.'

'He's always eaten it,' said Wexford. 'He called it cheese and onion flan.'

He had the morning papers with him. The *Kingsmarkham Courier* was a weekly and wouldn't be out till Friday. The national dailies had given no more than a paragraph to the discovery of Rodney Williams's body and had left out all the background details he was sure Varney had passed on to them. The *Daily Telegraph* merely stated that the body of a man had been found in a shallow grave and later identified as Rodney John Williams, a salesman from Kingsmarkham in Sussex. Nothing about Joy, his children, his job at Sevensmith Harding or the fact that he had been missing for two months. True, they had put him, Wexford, on TV but only on the regional bit that came after the news and then only forty-five seconds of the half-hour-long film they'd made.

The corpses of middle-aged men weren't news as women's were or children's. Women were always news. Perhaps they would cease to be when the day came that they got their equality as well as their rights. An interesting speculation and one which reminded him . . .

'You were going to tell me but we were interrupted.'

'It's not that she's anti-girls usually,' Burden said. 'For God's sake, she's a feminist. I mean, it's not some stupid I-must-have-an-heir thing or every-woman's-got-to-have-a-son-to-prove-herself. In fact I think she secretly thinks women are better than men – I mean cleverer and more versatile, all that. She says she doesn't understand it herself. She says she had no feelings about the child's sex one way or the other, but when they told her, when she knew, she was – well, dismayed. That was at first. It's got worse. It's not just dismay now, it's hatred.'

'Why doesn't she want a girl?' Wexford remembered certain sentiments expressed by his daughter Sylvia, mother of two sons. 'Is it that she feels women have a raw deal and she doesn't want to be responsible for bringing another into the world?' By way of apology for this crassness, he added, 'I have heard that view put.'

'She doesn't know. She says that ever since the world began sons have been preferred over daughters and now it's become part of race memory, what she calls the collective unconscious.'

'What Jung called it.'

Burden hesitated and then passed over that one. 'She's mad, you know. Pregnancy has driven her mad. Oh, don't look at me like that. I've given up caring about being disloyal. I've given up damn well caring, if you must know. Do you know what she says? She says she can't contemplate a future with a daughter she doesn't want. She says she can't imagine living for twenty years, say, with someone she hates before it's born. What's my life going to be like with that going on?'

'At the risk of uttering an old cliché, I'd say she'll feel differently when the baby's born.'

'Oh, she will? You can be sure of that? She'll love it when it's put into her arms? Shall I tell you what else she says? That she never wants to see it. We're to put it up for adoption immediately without either of us seeing it. I told you she was mad.'

All this made Wexford feel like a drink. But he couldn't start drinking at lunchtime with all he'd got ahead of him. Burden wasn't going to drink either. Judging by the look of him some mornings, he saved that up for when he got home. They paid the bill and climbed up the stone steps out of the Old Cellar into a bright June sunshine that made them blink.

'She's seeing a psychiatrist. I pin my faith to that. Me of all people! I sometimes wonder what I've come to, saying things like that.'

Sir Hilary Tremlett's report of the results of the post-mortem had come. To decipher the obscurer bits for Wexford, Dr Crocker came into the office as Burden was departing. They nearly passed each other in the doorway, Burden long-faced, monosyllabic. The doctor laughed.

'Mike's having a difficult pregnancy.'

Wexford wasn't going to enlighten him. The other chair had been pushed under the desk. He shoved it out with his toe.

'He says here he found three hundred and twenty milligrammes of cyclobarbitone in the stomach and other organs. What's cyclobarbitone?'

'It's an intermediate-acting barbiturate – that means it has about eight hours' duration of effect – a hypnotic drug, a sleeping pill if you like. The proprietary brand name would be Phanodorm, I expect. Two hundred milligrammes is the dose. But three hundred and twenty wouldn't kill him. It sounds as if he took two tablets of two hundred each.'

'It didn't kill him, though, did it? He died of stab wounds.'

Wexford looked up to see the doctor looking at him. They were both thinking the same thing. They were both thinking about Colin Budd and Brian Wheatley.

'What actually killed him was a wound that pierced the carotid.'

'Did it now? The blood must have spouted like a fountain.'

'There were seven other wounds in the neck and chest and back. A lot of stuff here's about fixed and mobile underlying tissues.' Wexford handed the pages across the desk, retaining one. 'I'm more interested in the estimate he makes of the proportions of the knife. A large kitchen knife with a dagger point, it would seem to have been.'

'I see he suggests death occurred six to eight weeks ago. What d'you reckon? He took two sleeping pills and someone did him in while he was away in the land of nod?

If it happened as you seem to think soon after he left his house at six that evening, why would he take sleeping pills at that hour?'

'He might have taken them,' said Wexford thoughtfully, 'in mistake for something else. Hypertension pills, for instance. He had high blood pressure.'

While the doctor was reading Wexford picked up the phone and asked the telephonist to get him Wheatley's number. Wheatley had said he worked in London on only three days a week so there was a chance he might be at home now. He was.

'I didn't think you showed much interest,' he said in an injured way.

That one Wexford wasn't going to answer. It was true anyway. They hadn't shown all that much interest in a man getting his hand scratched by a girl hitchhiker. Things had taken on a different aspect since then.

'You gave me a detailed description of the girl who attacked you, Mr Wheatley. The fact that you're a good observer makes me think you may have observed more. Will you think about that, please, and try and remember everything that happened? Principally, give us some more information about what the girl looked like, her voice and so on. We'd like to come and see you.'

Mollified, Wheatley said he'd give it some thought and tell them everything he could remember and how about some time that evening?

The doctor said, 'It couldn't have happened inside a car, you know, Reg. There'd have been too much blood.'

'Perhaps in the open air?'

'And tied his neck up in a Marks and Spencer's floral-printed teatowel?'

'It doesn't say that there!'

'I happened to notice it when the poor devil was resurrected. We've got one like it at home.'

The phone rang. The telephonist said, 'Mr Wexford,

there's a Mrs Williams here wanting to talk to someone about Mr Rodney Williams.'

Joy, he thought. Well.

'Mrs Joy Williams?'

'Mrs Wendy Williams.'

'Have someone bring her up here, will you?'

The sister-in-law? The wife of the brother in Bath? When you don't know what to do next, Raymond Chandler advised writers of his sort of fiction, have a man come in with a gun. In a real-life murder case, thought Wexford, what better surprise visitor than the mysterious Wife of Bath?

He looked up as Burden re-entered the room. Burden had been going through the clothes found on Williams's body: navy blue briefs – very different from the white underwear in the cupboard in Alverbury Road – brown socks, fawn cavalry-twill slacks, blue, brown and cream striped shirt, dark blue St Laurent sweater. The back pocket of the slacks had contained a cheque book for one of the accounts with the Anglian-Victoria at Pomfret (R. W. Williams, private account), and a wallet containing one fiver, three £1 notes and two credit cards, Visa and American Express. No car keys, no house keys.

'He probably kept his house key on the same ring as his car keys,' Burden said. 'It's what I do.'

'At any rate, we'll get at that bank account now. The doctor here says there was a teatowel wrapped round his neck. To staunch the blood presumably.'

There came a knock at the door. Bennett came into the room with a young woman, not anyone's idea of a Wife of Bath.

'Mrs Wendy Williams, sir.'

She looked about twenty-five. She was a pretty girl with a delicate nervous face and fair curly hair. Wexford asked her to sit down, the doctor having sprung to his feet. She slid into the chair, gripping the arms of it, and jumped as

Crocker passed behind her on his way to the door. Burden closed the door behind him and stood there.

'What did you want to see me about, Mrs Williams?'

She didn't answer. She had fixed him with a penetrating stare and her tongue came in and out, moistening her lips.

'I take it you're Rodney Williams's sister-in-law? Is that right?'

She moved her body back a little, hands still tight on the chair arms. 'What do you mean, his sister-in-law?' She didn't wait for a reply. 'Look, I . . . I don't know how to say this. I've been so . . . I've been nearly out of my mind.' Mounting hysteria made her voice ragged. 'I saw in the paper . . . a little bit in the paper and . . . Is that, that *person* they found . . . ? Is that my husband?'

9

It was seldom he could give people reassuring news. He was tempted to say no, of course not. The body has been identified. She was holding on to the arms of the chair, rubbing her fingers up and down the wood.

'What is your husband's name, Mrs Williams?'

'Rodney John Williams. He's forty-eight.' She spoke in short jerky phrases, not waiting for the questions. 'Six feet tall. He's fair going grey. He's a salesman. It said in the paper a salesman.'

Burden stared, then looked down. She swallowed, made an effort against panic, an effort that concentrated on tensing her muscles.

'Could you . . . please, I have a photo here.'

Her hands, unlocked from the chair, refused to obey her when first she tried to open her bag. The photograph she handed to Wexford fluttered, she was shaking so. He looked at it, unbelieving.

It was Rodney Williams all right, high domed forehead, crack of a mouth parted in a broad smile. It was a more recent picture than the one Joy had and showed Williams in swimming trunks (flabby hairless chest, spindleshanks, a bit knock-kneed) with this girl in a black bikini and another girl, also bikini'd but no more than twelve years old. Wexford's eyes returned to the unmistakable face of Williams, to the head you somehow wanted to slap a fringed wig on and so transform it.

She was waiting, watching him. He nodded. She brought a fluttery hand up to her chest, to her heart perhaps, froze for a moment in this tragic pose. Then her eyelids fell and she sagged sideways in the chair.

Afterwards he was to think of it as having been beautifully done but at the time he saw it only as a genuine faint. Burden held her shoulders, bringing her face down onto her knees. Picking up the phone, Wexford asked for a policewoman to come up, Polly Davies or Marion Bayliss, anyone who was around. And someone send a pot of strong tea and don't forget the sugar basin.

Wendy Williams came out of her faint, sat up and pressed her face into her hands.

'You are the wife of Rodney John Williams and you live in Liskeard Avenue, Pomfret?'

She drank the tea sugarless and very hot, at first with her eyes closed. When she opened her eyes and they met his he noticed they were the very clear pale blue of flax flowers. She nodded slowly.

'How long have you been married, Mrs Williams?'

'Sixteen years. We had our sixteenth wedding anniversary in March.'

He could hardly believe it. Her skin had the clear bloom of an adolescent's, her hair was baby-soft and the curl in it looked natural. She saw his incredulity and in spite of her emotion was flattered, a little buoyed up. He could tell she was the sort of woman to whom compliments, even unspoken ones, were food and drink. They nourished her. A faint, tremulous smile appeared. He looked again at the photographs.

'My daughter Veronica,' she said. 'I got married very young. I was only sixteen. That picture was taken three or four years back.'

A bigamist he had been, then. Not a common or garden wayward husband with a girlfriend living in the next town, not a married man with a sequence of pricey mistresses, but your good old-fashioned true blue bigamist. There was no doubt in Wexford's mind that Wendy Williams had as good-looking a marriage certificate as Joy's and if hers happened not to be valid she would be the last to know it.

That, then, was why he had taken no change of clothes with him. He had those things in his other home. And more than that, much more. Wexford now saw the point of those bank accounts: one for his salary to be paid into and two joint accounts to be fed from it, one for each household, R. W. Williams and J. Williams; R. W. Williams and W. Williams. There had been no need to assume a different name on his second marriage – Williams was common enough to make that unnecessary. He had been like a Moslem who keeps strictly to Islamic law and maintains his wives in separate and distinct dwellings. The difference here was that the wives didn't know of each other's existence.

That Williams had had another wife, what one might call in fact a chief wife, was something this girl was going to have to be told. And Joy was going to have to be told about her.

'Can you tell me when you last saw Mr Williams?' Not calling him 'your husband' any more was the beginning of breaking the news.

'About two months ago. Just after Easter.'

This wasn't the time to ask her to account for that eight week gap. He told her he would come and see her at home that evening. Polly Davies would look after her and see she got home safely.

Something had at last happened to distract Burden temporarily from his private troubles. His expression was as curious and as alerted as a little boy's.

'What did he do at Christmas?' he said. 'Easter? What about holidays?'

'No doubt we shall find out. Other bigamists have handled it. He probably had a Bunbury as well.'

'A *what*?'

'A nonexistent friend or relative to provide him with alibis. My guess is Williams's Bunbury was an old mother.'

'Did he have an old mother?'

'God knows. Creating one from his imagination wouldn't have been beyond his capacity, I'm sure. You know what they say, a mother is the invention of necessity.'

Burden winced. 'That night he left Alverbury Road, d'you think he went to his other home?'

'I think he set off meaning to go there. Whether he reached it is another matter.'

Fascinated by Williams's family arrangements, Burden said, 'While Joy thought he was travelling for Sevensmith Harding in Ipswich he was with Wendy and while he was with Joy Wendy thought he was where?'

'I don't suppose she knew he worked for Sevensmith Harding. He probably told her a total lie about what he did.'

'You'd think he'd have got their names muddled – I mean called Wendy Joy and Joy Wendy.'

'There speaks the innocent monogamist,' said Wexford, casting up his eyes. 'How do you think married men with girlfriends manage? Wife and all get called "darling".'

Burden shook his head as if even speculating about it was too much for him. 'Do you reckon it was one of them killed him?'

'Carried his body and stuck it in that grave? Williams weighed a good fifteen stone or two hundred and ten pounds or ninety something kilos or whatever we're supposed to say these days.'

'It might have been Wendy made that phone call.'

'You reckon her voice sounds like Joy's?'

Burden was obliged to admit that it didn't. Joy's was monotonous, accent-free, uninflected; Wendy's girlish, rather fluting, with a faint lisp. Wexford was talking about voices, about the rather unattractive but nevertheless memorable quality of Joy's voice when his phone rang again.

'Another young lady to see me,' he said to Burden, putting the receiver back.

'Bluebeard's third wife?' It was the first attempt at a joke he had made in two months.

Wexford appreciated that. 'Let's say a fan, rather. Someone who saw me on the telly.'

'Look, why don't I take Martin and get on over to Wheatley? Then I'll be able to come to Wendy's with you tonight.'

'OK, and we'll take Polly along.'

The girl walked into his room in a breeze of confidence. She was seventeen or eighteen and her name was Eve Freeborn. Apposite names of the Lady Dedlock–Ernest Pontifex–Obadiah Slope kind that Victorian novelists used are in real life less uncommon than is generally supposed. That Eve Freeborn was aptly named Wexford came quickly to understand. She might have been dressed and cast for the role of Spirit of Freedom in a pageant. Her hair was cropped short and dyed purple in parts. She wore stretch jeans, a check shirt and thongs.

The story she told Wexford, sitting with legs wide apart, hands linked, forearms making a bridge from the chair arms to rest her chin on, was delivered in a brisk and articulate way. Eve was still at school, had come there straight from school. President of the debating society no doubt, he thought. As she turned her hands outwards, thumbs on her jaw, he noticed the felt-tipped pen drawing on her wrist, a raven with a woman's head, and then as she moved her arm the shirtsleeve covered it.

'I realized it was my duty as a citizen to come to you. I delayed just long enough to discuss the matter with my boyfriend. He's at the same school as me – Haldon Finch. In a way he's involved, you see. We have the sort of relationship where we believe in total openness.'

Wexford gave her an encouraging smile.

'My boyfriend lives in Arnold Road, Myringham. It's a single-storey house, number forty-three.' Opposite Graham

Gee who had reported the presence of poor old Greta, Wexford thought. 'His mother and father live there too,' said Eve in a tone that implied enormous condescension and generosity on the part of the boyfriend in allowing his parents to live in their own house. 'The point is – and you may not believe this but it's the honest truth, I promise you – they don't like him having me to stay the night with him. I mean, not me personally, you could understand that if they didn't like me, but any girl. So what we do is I come round after he's gone to bed and get in the window.'

Wexford didn't gape at her. He merely felt like doing this. He couldn't resist asking, 'Why doesn't he come to you?'

'I share a room with my sister. Anyway, I was telling you. I went round to his place around ten that Thursday night. There wasn't all that much space to park and when I was reversing I went into the car behind. I just bashed the wing of it a bit, not much, it wouldn't have had to have a new wing or anything, but I did think it was my duty to take responsibility and not just leave it, so I . . . '

'Just a moment. This was the night of April the fifteenth?'

'Right. It was my boyfriend's birthday.'

And a charming present he must have had, Wexford thought.

'What was this car you went into?'

'A dark blue Ford Granada. It was the car you asked about on TV. I wrote a note and put it on the windscreen, under a wiper. Just with my name and address on and phone number. But it blew away or got lost or something because the car was still there a long while after that and the driver never got in touch with me.'

At ten that night. Greta the Granada had been there at ten but how long had it been there?

'Just as a matter of curiosity, whose car were you driving?'

'My own,' she said, surprised.

'You have your own car?'

'My mother's technically. But it comes to the same thing.'

No doubt it did. They were amazing, these young people. And the most amazing thing about them was that they had no idea previous generations had not behaved as they did. People got old, of course, became dull and staid, they knew that, but in their day surely teenage girls had slept with their boyfriends, appropriated their parents' cars, stayed out all night, dyed their hair all colours of the spectrum.

He thanked her for her help and as she got up he saw the little drawing or tattoo again. He realized that he didn't know which of the local schools Sara Williams attended. And there remained the as yet unknown quantity, Veronica Williams . . .

'Do you know a girl of your own age called Sara Williams? Is she perhaps at school with you?'

He was positive she hadn't made the connection before, was making it now for the first time. 'Do you mean Sara is the daughter of this man who was murdered?'

'Yes. You go to the same school?'

'No, we don't,' she said carefully, 'but I know her.'

Wheatley lived on an estate of new houses on the Pomfret side of Myringham. They had been built, Burden recalled, by a company so anxious to sell their houses that 100 per cent mortgages had been guaranteed with them and a promise given to buy a house back for its purchase price if after two years the occupier were dissatisfied. The place had a raw look, oddly cold in the June sunshine. Wheatley's pregnant wife came to the door. A child of about three, a girl, was behind her, holding on to her skirt. Burden registered the fact of the pregnancy and the sex of the child with his heightened sensitivity to such matters and then he thought that his wife's pregnancy might have affected

Wheatley's attitude to the girl he picked up. For instance, he might be sexually frustrated. Burden knew all about that. Wheatley too might have exaggerated the purity of his attitude towards the girl because he dared not risk the possibility of his pregnant wife finding out he was capable of putting his hand on other women's knees – or, in this instance no doubt, on other women's breasts.

The third bedroom of this very small house had been turned into a study or office for Wheatley. He was on the phone but rang off within seconds of Burden's and Martin's arrival. Yes, he had remembered some more about the girl. He was sure he could give them a more detailed description. There was no question of his remembering more of what the girl had said to him because she hadn't said any more. 'Thanks' and a gasp had been the only sounds that had come from her.

'I told you she was tall for a woman, at least five feet nine. Still in her teens, I'm sure. She had dark brown shoulder-length hair with a fringe, very fair skin and very white hands. I think I can remember a ring, not a wedding or engagement ring or anything, but one of those big silver rings they wear. I wouldn't call her pretty, not a bit.' Was that a sop to the wife who had come quietly into the room, carrying the little girl? 'Sunglasses, a dark leather shoulder bag. She had blue denim jeans on and a grey cardigan. She was thin – really skinny, I mean.' Another matrimonial sop. 'And underneath the cardigan she had a tee-shirt on. It was a white tee-shirt with a crazy picture on it – some sort of bird with a woman's head.'

'You didn't mention that before, Mr Wheatley.'

'I didn't mention the ring before or what colour her clothes were. You asked me to think about it and I thought about it and that's what I remember. You can take it or leave it. A white tee-shirt with a bird on it with a woman's face.'

* * *

'I don't believe it!'

She stared at Wexford, her mouth open in an appalled sort of way, her eyelids moving. She brought her hands up and scrabbled at her neck.

'I don't believe it!' Now there was defiance in her tone. Then, by changing one word, she showed him she accepted, she understood that what he had told her was true. 'I *won't* believe it!'

Polly Davies was with him, sitting there like a good chaperone, silent but attentive. She glanced at Wexford, got a nod from him.

'I'm afraid it's true, Mrs Williams.'

'I don't – I don't have a right to be called that, do I?'

'Of course you do. Your name doesn't depend on a marriage certificate.' Wexford thought of Eve Freeborn. There was a world between her and Wendy Williams, though a mere fourteen years, less than a generation, separated them. Would Eve know such a thing as a marriage certificate existed?

'Mrs Williams,' said stalwart Polly, 'why don't you and I go and make some coffee? We'd all like coffee, I'm sure. Mr Wexford will want to ask you some questions but I know he'd like you to have time to get over the shock of this.'

She nodded and got up awkwardly as if her bones were stiff. A glazed look had come across her face. She walked like a sleepwalker and no one now would have mistaken her for a twenty-five-year-old.

Burden shrugged silently as the door closed behind them and subsided into one of his typical morose reveries. Wexford had a look round the room they were sitting in. The house was newer than the Williams home in Kingsmarkham, a small 'town house' with an integral garage, built probably in the late 1960s. Wendy was a thorough, meticulous and perhaps fanatical housekeeper. This was a through room with a dining area and it had very recently been redecorated in gleaming white with an undertone of palest pink. One of the colours in the Sevensmith Harding 'Ice Cream' range? The carpet was deep strawberry pink, some of the furniture mahogany, some white canework, cushions in various shades of pink and red. It was tasteful, it was a far cry from the stereotyped shabbiness of Joy's home, but somehow it was also uncomfortable, as if everything had been placed there – hanging baskets, little tables, red Venetian glass – for effect rather than for use.

He remembered that a young girl also lived here. There were no signs of her. But what sign did he expect or would he recognize if he saw it? She had been twelve in the picture . . .

'My daughter is sixteen now,' Wendy said when the coffee was brought. A slightly defiant note came into her voice as she added, 'She was sixteen three weeks ago.'

Her gaze fell. He did some calculations, remembering what she had said about her wedding anniversary taking place in March. So Williams had 'married' her three months before the child was born. He had had to wait until she reached the legal age for marriage.

'Where were you married, Mrs Williams?'

'Myringham Registry Office. My mother wanted us to have a church wedding but – well, for obvious reasons . . .'

Wexford could imagine one very obvious reason if she had been six months pregnant. The nerve of Williams, a married man, 'marrying' this child, as she had been, a mere dozen miles from his home town! The wedding to Joy, Dora had told him, had been at St Peter's, Kingsmarkham, the bride in white slipper satin . . .

Wendy was thrusting a paper at him. He saw it was her marriage certificate.

In the Registration District of Myringham, at the Registry Office. Rodney John Williams, aged thirty-two. In some respects, at any rate, he had been honest. Though he could hardly have distorted those facts. They had been on his birth certificate. A Bath address, his brother's probably, his occupation sales representative. Wendy Ann Rees, aged sixteen, Pelham Street, Myringham, shop assistant. The witnesses had been Norman Rees and Brenda Rees, parents presumably, or brother and sister-in-law.

He handed it back to her. She looked at it herself and her tongue flicked out to moisten her lips. For a moment, from the way she was holding it, he thought she was going to tear the certificate across. But she replaced it in its envelope and laid the envelope on the low white melamine table that was close up against the arm of her chair.

She pressed her knees together and folded her hands in her lap. Her legs were very good with elongated slim ankles. To come to the police station she had worn a grey flannel suit with a white blouse. He had a feeling she was a woman who attached importance to being suitably dressed. The suit was changed now for a cotton dress. She was the type who would 'save' her clothes, not sit about in a straight skirt or risk a spot on white silk. In her sad wistful look youth had come back into her face.

'Mrs Williams,' he began, 'I'm sure you won't mind telling me how it was you weren't alarmed when your husband was away for so long.'

She did mind. She was reluctant. Patience, simply waiting quietly, succeeded with her where pressing the point might not have.

'Rodney and I . . . ' She paused. It was always 'Rodney' with her, Wexford noted, never 'Rod'. 'We – we quarrelled. Well, we had a very serious quarrel. That must have been a few days after Easter. Rodney spent Easter with his mother in Bath. He always spent Christmas and Easter with her. He was an only child, you see, and she's been in an old people's home for years and years.'

Wexford carefully avoided looking at Burden. Wendy said, reminded by her own explanation, 'Has she been. . . ? I mean, has anyone *told* her?'

Enigmatically, Wexford said that had been taken care of. 'Go on please, Mrs Williams.'

'We quarrelled,' she went on. 'It was a very private thing

we quarrelled about. I'll keep that to myself if you don't mind. I said to him that – well, I said that if he – if *it* didn't stop, if he didn't promise me faithfully that never – well, I said I'd take Veronica away and he'd never see us again. I – I struck him, I was so angry, so distressed, I can't tell you – well, he was angry too. He denied it, of course, and then he said I needn't trouble about leaving him because he'd leave me. He said he couldn't stand my nagging any more.' She lifted her head and looked Wexford straight in the eye. 'I did nag him, I'll be honest about it. I couldn't bear it, never seeing him, him always being away. We'd never had a single Christmas together. I always had to go to my parents. We hardly ever had a holiday. I used to *beg* him . . . ' Her voice faltered and Wexford understood that realization was dawning. She was beginning to see what the real reason was for those absences. 'Anyway,' she said, making an effort at control, 'he – he calmed down after a while and I suppose I did too. He was going away again and he was due back on the Thursday – the fifteenth, that is. I was still very sore and upset but I said goodbye to him and that I'd see him on Thursday and he said maybe I would and maybe he'd never come back, so you see, I – when he didn't come back I thought he'd left me.'

It wasn't a completely convincing explanation. He tried to put himself in her shoes. He tried to think how he would have felt years ago when he and Dora were young if they'd had a row and she, going away to visit her sister, say, had told him maybe she wouldn't come back. Probably such a thing had actually happened. It did happen in marriages, even in excellent ones. But if she hadn't come back on the appointed day, if she'd been a couple of hours late even, he'd have started going out of his mind with worry. Of course, much depended on the seriousness of the quarrel and on the reasons for it.

'Tell me what happened that Thursday.'

'In the evening, do you mean?'

'When he didn't come.'

'I was at work. Thursday's our late night. I didn't tell you, did I? I'm manageress of the fashion floor at Jickie's.'

He was surprised. Somehow he had taken it for granted she didn't work. 'In Myringham?' he asked. 'Or the Kingsmarkham branch?'

'Oh, Kingsmarkham. In the Precinct.'

Jickie's was Kingsmarkham's biggest department store and the largest area of the Kingsbrook Shopping Precinct was given over to it. Doubtless Rodney Williams had taken care never to accompany Joy when she went shopping there for a jumper or a pair of tights on a Saturday afternoon. Had he risked walking arm in arm down Kingsmarkham High Street during shopping hours? With his son or daughter in the car, had he risked parking in the precinct car park? It was a tightrope he had walked and no doubt, for such is the nature of people like him, he had enjoyed walking it, but he had fallen off at last. Because of the tightrope or for some entirely different reason?

'We stay open till eight on Thursdays but I can never get away till nine and it takes me a quarter of an hour to get home. When I did get back Veronica was here but Rodney hadn't come. I thought there was still a chance he might come but he didn't and then I knew. Or I thought I knew. I thought he'd left me.'

'And in all the weeks that followed,' Burden put it, 'you weren't anxious? You didn't wonder what could happen to you and your daughter if he didn't come back?'

'I'd be all right financially without him. I've always had to work and now I'm doing quite well.' There was a note of self-esteem in the little soft voice now. Inside the white and pink and fair curls and underneath the lisp and diffidence, Wexford thought there might be a core of steel. 'We had a ninety per cent mortgage on this house and up till five years ago it was all Rodney could do to keep us. He got promotion then and things were easier but I kept on working. I needed a life of my own too, he was away so much.'

'Promotion?' hazarded Wexford, feeling his way.

'It's quite a small company and they haven't been doing too well lately – bathroom fittings and furniture, that sort of thing. Rodney was made sales manager for this locality.'

Polly Davies picked up the tray and took it away into the kitchen. Wexford thought how easy it was to imagine Rodney Williams – or his idea of Rodney Williams – in his other home but next to impossible to imagine him here. Seated at that glass-topped dining table, for instance, with its bowl of pink and red roses or in one of those pink chintz armchairs. He had been a big coarse man and everything here had a daintiness like a pink shell or the inside of a rose.

'I have to know what you quarrelled about, Mrs Williams.'

Her tone became prissy, very genteel. 'It has nothing whatsoever to do with Rodney's death.'

'How do you know?'

She looked at him as if this were unfair persecution.

'How could it be? He got killed because he picked up someone hitching a lift and they killed him. Something like that . . . It's always happening.'

'That's an interesting guess but it's only a guess, isn't it? You've no evidence for it and there's plenty of evidence against it. The car being returned to Myringham, for instance. A phone call was made to your husband's employers and a letter of resignation sent to them. Do you think that phone call was made by some homicidal hitch-hiker?'

She sat rigid, keeping her eyes obstinately averted. Polly came back.

'Are you all right, Mrs Williams?'

A nod. An indrawn breath and a sigh.

'What did you quarrel about?'

'I could refuse to tell you.'

'You could. But why take a stand like that when what you tell us will be treated in the strictest confidence? Ask yourself if it's so awful that we won't have heard it before. And don't you think that if you don't tell us we may come to think it something worse than it really was?'

She sat silent. She wore an expression like someone who expects at any moment to see something nasty and shocking on television. It was an anticlimax when she said almost in a whisper, 'There was another girl.'

'You mean your husband had a woman friend he'd been seeing?'

' "Seeing",' she said, 'I like that expression – "seeing". Yes, he'd been seeing a woman friend. That's one way of putting it.'

'How would you put it?'

'Oh, like that. The way you do. What else does one say? Something crude, I suppose.' The repressive lid suddenly jumped and let out a dribble of resentment, of bitterness. 'I thought no one else but me would ever matter to him. I look young, don't I? I'm pretty enough, I don't look my age. People say I look eighteen. What was the matter with him that he . . . ? Yes, we quarrelled about that. About a girl. I wanted him to promise me it would never happen again.'

'He refused?'

'Oh, he promised. I didn't believe him. I thought it would start up again when he got the chance. I couldn't stand it, I didn't want him if he was going to do that. I was glad when he didn't come back. Don't you see? I was *glad*.'

'I'll have to have this girl's name.'

Quick as a flash: 'I don't know her name.'

'Come now, Mrs Williams.'

'I don't know it. He wouldn't tell me. Just a girl. What does it matter?'

She had said too much already, she was thinking. He could read that, plain in her face, the look in her eyes of being appalled at her own indiscretion. At that moment, before he could say any more, the door opened and a young girl came in. Just before this happened there had been a sound downstairs and footsteps on the stairs – the living room was on the middle floor – but it had all taken place very quickly, within a few seconds. And now, without warning, the girl was here among them.

What first struck Wexford was that although she was not so tall and her hair was shorter she looked exactly like Sara Williams. They might have been twins.

10

Her hair was the same pale fudge colour, not curly but not quite straight either, the tips just touching her shoulders. Brown eyes, ellipse eyebrows, small straight nose, fine white skin sprinkled with freckles. Rodney Williams's high domed forehead and his small narrow mouth. But instead of jeans she wore a summer dress with white tights and white sandals. She stood in the doorway looking surprised at the sight of them, a little more than just startled.

Wendy Williams was taken aback.

In a flustered way she said, 'This is my daughter Veronica,' and to the girl, 'You're home early.'

'Not much. It's after nine.'

The voice was her mother's, soft and slightly affected but without the lisp. It was quite unlike Sara's abrupt uninflected tones. Recovering poise Wendy said to her, 'These are police officers. They'll only be a few minutes.' She lied fluently, 'It's to do with trouble at the shop. You won't mind leaving us alone for a bit, will you, darling?'

'I'm going to have a bath anyway.'

Closing the door with the sort of precision her mother might use, she went off up the spiral staircase that was the core of this house.

'I don't know why she's so offhand with me lately. This past year . . .'

Wexford said, 'You haven't told her?'

'I haven't seen her. She always goes to her friend's straight from school on a Tuesday. Or so she says, she's so secretive . . .'

'Which school, Mrs Williams?'

'Haldon Finch Comprehensive. I'll tell her about her father after you've gone. I suppose I shall have to tell her what he was – a bigamist, with another wife somewhere. It won't be easy. I don't know if you appreciate that.'

Wexford, when interrogating, would allow any amount of digression but never total distraction. Those he questioned were obliged to come back to the point sooner or later. It was hard on them for often they believed they had escaped. The leash had snapped and freedom was surely there for the taking, but the hand always came down and snatched up the broken end.

'We were talking about this woman friend your husband had. He may have gone to her on the night he died.'

'I don't know any more about her!'

Fear had come into her voice now. It was what many would have called caution or apprehensiveness but it was really fear.

'You called her a girl. You implied a young girl.'

A panicky jerky rapid way of speaking – 'A young single girl, very young, that's all I know. I told you, I don't know any more!'

Wexford recalled the overtures Williams had once made to Sylvia. When Sylvia was fifteen. Was it something like that that Wendy had implied when she asked so pathetically if she didn't still look young? That she at thirty-two to his forty-eight might not be young enough for him?

'Do you mean she's young enough to live at home with her parents?'

A nod, painful and perplexed.

'What else do you know of her, Mrs Williams?'

'Nothing. I don't know any more. Do you think I wanted him to talk to me about her?'

That was reasonable enough. At first he thought she was lying when she said she was ignorant of the girl's name. Now he was less sure. How often had he heard people say, 'If my husband (my wife) were unfaithful to me I wouldn't want to know', and when they were forced to know, 'I don't want to hear anything about it'? The knives of jealousy are honed on details.

The question he sensed she would hate but which must be asked he had saved till last.

'How did you know it was happening at all? How did you know of her existence?'

He had been wrong. She didn't mind. She didn't mind because her answer was a lie that she had been rehearsing in her mind, silently and busily while they talked, waiting for the past half-hour for the question to come.

'I had an anonymous letter.'

Eventually he would get at the truth. It could wait.

'Now, Mrs Williams, your daughter . . .'

'What about her?' Very quick and defensive.

'I shall want to talk to Veronica.'

'Oh no, not that. Please.'

'When you have told her and she has had a day or two to get over the shock.'

'But why?'

'Her father has been murdered. He was due to come here and she was here, alone here. It's possible he did come and she was the last person to see him alive.'

'He didn't come here. She would have told me.'

'We'll see, Mrs Williams. We shall also want to look over this house, particularly at any of your husband's personal property.'

'We keep coming back to these young girls,' Burden said.

'And to ravens with women's faces.'

'That too. Budd and Wheatley were both attacked by a young girl – not very seriously, either of them, but they were attacked and the assault was with a knife. Rodney Williams liked young girls – I mean, he seems especially to have liked them very young – and he had a very young girlfriend. He died as the result of a knife attack, he was stabbed to death. Now Wheatley says the girl who attacked him was wearing a white tee-shirt with a design on it of a sort of bird with a woman's head . . .'

'And Sara Williams,' said Wexford, 'possesses just such a tee-shirt and has a poster with a similar motif on her bedroom wall.'

'Does she? You're kidding.'

'No. It's true. And Eve Freeborn has a raven with a woman's head tattooed or drawn on her left wrist, and since the sun came out, Mike, and women aren't bundling themselves up in cardigans and jackets I've seen no less than five girls around Kingsmarkham and Pomfret wearing white tee-shirts with ravens with women's faces on them. How about that?'

'God, and I thought we were really getting somewhere. It's like that bit in Ali Baba and the Forty Thieves when the woman says he'll know the right oil jar because it'll have a cross on it and when he gets there someone's put crosses on all the oil jars.'

'You've been reading again. Or going to pantomimes. It looks to me as if these raven-harpy pictures are the motif or symbol of some sort of society or cult. Latter-day anarchists or some sort of spurious freedom fighters.'

'Animal Rights?' said Burden doubtfully.

'It could be, I suppose. The implication being that the animal – or in this case bird – has the feelings and rights of a human being? The poster Sara Williams has in her bedroom has some letters on it as well as the picture. An acronym, I think, a, r, r, i, a, Arria.'

'Animal Rights something or other?'

'There was a woman called Arria, in Roman history, I seem to remember. I'll try and find out. If it's animal rights, Mike, you would expect its members to make their attacks on people who in their view were being cruel to animals. Factory farmers, for instance, or masters of foxhounds. I don't suppose Wheatley keeps calves chained up in boxes in his back garden, does he? We'll ask Sara.

But first I want to leave her and Joy to get over the shock of Williams having another wife and another child.'

'You've told them?'

'Yes. It was the money aspect that seemed to mean most to Joy. She had been deprived in order that he could maintain another household. She gave that bitter laugh of hers. If I'd had to live with that laugh it would have got horribly on my nerves.'

'How's Martin getting on with his typewriter inquiries?'

Wexford threw the report across the desk. It was no Sevensmith Harding machine that had been used to type Williams's letter of resignation. All the typewriters in use in the Myringham office were of the sophisticated electronic kind. Neither of the Williams households contained a typewriter of any sort. The Harmers had a typewriter in the two-storey flat over the shop where they lived and both Hope Harmer and her daughter Paulette used it. It was a small Olivetti, an electric machine.

'His new young lady typed that letter,' Burden said. 'Find her and we find the typewriter.'

'Find her and it won't matter whether we find the typewriter or not.'

Sergeant Martin had also been to Bath.

There, it seemed, Rodney Williams had had his origins. On an estate of houses some few miles outside the city, in a house very like the one Rodney had bought for his second bride, lived his brother Howard. It was Howard's address that appeared on Wendy's marriage certificate.

His parents had also once lived in Bath but his father had died when he was a child and his mother when Rodney was twenty-seven. That dead mother Rodney in his calculating way had used to his advantage. No doubt he had told Wendy that old Mrs Williams disapproved of his marriage to a young girl, would never wish to meet her, but the good son would be obliged to pay the occasional duty visit . . .

The brother seemed honest and straightforward. There

was very little contact between him and Rodney. Years ago, fifteen or sixteen at least, some of Rodney's mail had been sent to his address by mistake. He had simply sent it on. Communications from the registrar at the time of the marriage to Wendy, Wexford thought. Howard Williams was also a salesman and on 15 April he had been in Ireland on business for his firm.

Joy hadn't told him of his brother's death. He had seen it in the papers and seemed to have reacted with calm indifference.

Wendy Williams's home was on the outskirts of Pomfret and a mile from the Harmers' shop. Had the relative nearness of his in-laws to his second and bigamous home worried Williams? Had he only agreed to buy a house there to placate Wendy or gratify some wish of hers? Or did he see this sort of risk as just part of the tightrope walk?

Between the estate and the nucleus of the town, that which not long ago *was* the town, lay the sports grounds of the Haldon Finch Comprehensive School, playing fields, tennis courts, fives courts, running track. The Haldon Finch, though new and an example of the new education with its two thousand pupils of both sexes housed in no less than six buildings, was as much 'into' games as any public school of the past. You might get ten O-levels but you were nothing if you weren't good at games.

At 5.30 in the afternoon twelve girls were playing tennis on the courts adjacent to Procter Road.

'It must be a match with another school,' Burden said. 'They start after school's finished.'

He and Wexford were in the car, on their way to see Veronica Williams. Donaldson had taken a short cut, or at least a traffic-avoiding cut, and they had found themselves amid this complex of sports fields.

'We'll get out and watch for a minute or two.'

Burden got out, though demurring.

'It makes me feel funny standing about watching girls.

I mean, you ask yourself – *they* ask *them*selves – what sort of blokes would do that?'

'What would you think if you saw two middle-aged women watching young men playing squash?'

Burden looked sideways at him.

'Well, nothing, would I? I mean, I'd think they were their mothers or just women who liked watching sport.'

'Exactly. Doesn't that tell you something? Two things? One is that, whatever the women's movement says, there is a fundamental difference between men and women in their attitude to sex, and the other that this is an area in which women might claim – if it's occurred to them – to be superior to us.'

'It's changing though, you have to admit. Look at all those clubs up north where men do strips for women audiences.'

'The attitude is still different. Men go to strip shows and gawp in a sort of seething silence.'

'Don't women?'

'Apparently women laugh,' said Wexford.

One of the tennis players was Eve Freeborn. He spotted her from the purple slick in her hair. Her partner was a thin dark girl, their opponents a big heavily built blonde and another thin dark girl, this one wearing glasses. This four was on the court nearest to the road. Wexford could see enough of the other two courts and the other four couples only to be sure that Sara Williams was not among them. Sara didn't attend the Haldon Finch, of course – that would have been too great a risk even for Rodney Williams – but if this was a match six of the girls must come from another school. Seated on the three umpire chairs were three young women who had the look of games teachers.

He was aware at once that no one was playing very well. Had the standard deteriorated since the days when he had watched Sylvia and Sheila playing tennis? No, it wasn't that. It was television. These days you saw tennis played on TV. Top championships week after week, it seemed, here or in Europe or in America, and it spoiled you for the real thing, the local article. A pity really. It made you irritated at how often they missed the ball. Eve Freeborn had a good hard service. She would have served aces – only they were always on the wrong side of the line. Her opponent in the glasses was the worst player of the twelve, slow on her feet with a weak service and a way of scooping the ball up into the air, making it easy prey for Eve's slamming racket.

'Two match points,' said Burden, who had been attending more closely to the progress of the set.

Eve served a double fault. One match point. She served again, weakly, and the blonde shot it back like an arrow down the tramlines. The umpire announced deuce. Eve served another double fault.

'Van out,' said Wexford.

'My God, but that shows your age. That's what they said at tennis parties in the thirties.'

The umpire corrected him by saying crisply that the score was 'advantage Kingsmarkham'. So it was Kingsmarkham High who were the visitors here, once a grammar school, now private and fee-paying, no longer state-aided.

Kingsmarkham won the game. They changed ends, the girls paused by the umpire's chair and wiped faces and arms, drank Coke out of cans. Eve was standing only a few yards from Wexford. The little flame-coloured badge he had till now seen only as an orange spot near the neckline of her white tee-shirt showed itself at closer quarters to be a badge. He could make out spread wings on it and the letters ARRIA. Eve didn't or wouldn't look at him. Perhaps he wasn't recognizable out of his office, in shirt-sleeves. He peered more closely. The umpire got down from her chair and came to the wire fence. She was a stocky, muscular young woman with a cross face and flashing eyes. In a voice full of crushed ice she said, 'Was there something you wanted?'

Wexford inhibited all the possible replies, improper, provocative, even mildly lecherous, that sprang to mind. He was a policeman. Anyway, Burden got in first with the flasher's classic caught-before-the-act answer.

'We were just looking.'

'Well, perhaps you'd like to get on with whatever you're supposed to be doing.'

'Move along, Mike,' said Wexford.

They went quickly to the car. The games mistress glared after them.

'Do they still call them that?'

'Call them what? Games mistresses?' Burden was silent for a moment. Then he said, screwing up his face, 'I'll tell you when my new daughter's eleven. If she gets to exist. If she gets to be eleven. If she and I are together when she does.'

'It's not as bad as that.'

'No? Maybe not. Maybe it's she and I that'll be together and not Jenny and I.'

Things must be bad with Burden for him to burst out with that in Donaldson's hearing. Not that Donaldson would say a word. But he would hear and he would think. Wexford said nothing. He watched Burden's face close up, the eyes grow dull and the mouth purse, the frown that was hardly ever absent re-establish itself in a deep double ridge. The car drew away. He looked behind him and saw Eve leaping to achieve her best volley of the match.

'Veronica was supposed to be playing in a tennis match,' said Wendy Williams, 'but of course she was too upset. She hasn't been to school today and I had to take the day off. I had to tell her her father had another wife and family. It was bad enough telling her he was dead.'

The second Mrs Williams, whom Wexford had at first

thought of as rather sweet and gentle, he now saw had other sides to her nature, among them a rather unpleasant habit of laying the blame for her misfortunes on whomsoever else might be present.

'I told her everything and at first she wouldn't speak and then she became very distressed.' The soft little voice trickled round the phrases. The eyes opened wide and wistful, like a Pear's Soap child seeing distant angels. Wexford had the disturbing thought that perhaps she had cultivated all this because Williams had fancied little girls. 'You'll be gentle with her, won't you? You'll remember she's only sixteen? And it's not just that she's lost her father, it's worse than that.'

No question here of being sent up to the girl's bedroom. Veronica would come down. And Wendy would be there. He supposed Veronica must have been the missing tennis player for whom the dark girl not wearing glasses had substituted. While he was speculating Veronica came in, walking diffidently, a dead look still on her face. She had been crying but that was a long while ago now. Her eyes wre dry and the lids pale, but a puffiness remained. Nevertheless she had dressed herself carefully for this encounter, as had her mother. Such things, which would have been lost on many men, never escaped Wexford. Wendy was in a black cotton dress with big sleeves that was a little too becoming to qualify as true mourning and Veronica in a pink pleated skirt, sweat shirt with a gold V on it and pink and white running shoes. Probably Wendy got their clothes from Jickie's at a discount.

'This is Chief Inspector Wexford and Inspector Burden, darling. They want to ask you one or two questions. Nothing difficult or complicated. They know what a bad shock you've had. And I shall be here all the time.'

For God's sake, she's not ten, Wexford thought. The girl's dull staring look disconcerted him.

'I'm sorry about your dad, Veronica,' he began. 'I know you're feeling unhappy and you'd probably like to be left alone. But your mother's told you what's happened. Your father isn't simply dead. He was killed. And we have to find out who killed him, don't we?' A not unfamiliar doubt assailed him. Did they? *Cui bono?* Who would be satisfied, avenged, recompensed? He was a policeman and it wasn't for him to think such thoughts. Not a hint of them was in his tone. He looked at the girl and wondered what had been going on in her mind all those weeks her father was missing. Had she believed, like her mother, that he was with another woman? Or had she accepted his absence as she must have accepted all his other absences when he was allegedly away travelling for his firm or paying filial visits in Bath? She was no longer looking at him but down at the floor, her head drooping like a tired flower on a stalk.

'Do you think we could go back to April the fifteenth?' he said. 'It was a Thursday. Your mother expected your father home that evening but she had to stay on late at work. You were here though, weren't you?'

The 'yes' came very quietly. He might not have understood it for what it was if she hadn't nodded as well.

'What did you do? You came home from school when – at four?' He too was talking to her as if she were ten, but something in her attitude, her bowed head, feet crossed, hands in lap, seemed to invite it. Again that nod, the head lifted a little to make it. 'And then what happened? What sort of time did you expect your father to come?'

She murmured that she didn't know.

'We never knew what time to expect him,' Wendy said. 'We never knew. It might have been any time.'

'And did he come?' said Wexford.

'Of course he didn't! I've told you.'

'Please, Mrs Williams, let Veronica answer.'

The girl was shy, nervous, perhaps also unhappy. She was certainly in shock still. But suddenly she made an effort. It was as if she saw that there was no help for it, she was going to have to talk, she might as well get it over.

Sara's tortoiseshell brown eyes looked into his and Sara's Primavera lips parted with a quiver.

'I had tea. Well, a Coke and some stuff Mummy left me in the fridge.' Yes, Wendy for all her own youth was the kind of woman who would be smotheringly protective, even to the extent of preparing meals in advance for a sixteen-year-old as if she were an invalid. Veronica said, 'I'd asked my friend round – the one whose place I was at when you came before – but she rang up and said she couldn't come. She said I could go to her.'

'But you wanted to wait in for your father?'

She was no Sara, no Eve Freeborn. She turned her head and looked to her mother for help. It came, as no doubt it always did.

'Veronica had no need to wait in for Rodney. I've told you, we never really thought he'd come at all.'

' "We", Mrs Williams?'

'Well, I don't really know what Veronica thought. I hadn't said anything to her then about the possibility of our splitting up. I was waiting to see what would happen. But the point is Veronica had no need to wait in for him and I wouldn't have . . . well, she's got her own life to lead.'

What had she been going to say when she broke off and made that extraordinary statement about this little creature's obviously nonexistent independence?

'You went out then?'

'I went to my friend's. I didn't stop there long. We played records. I wanted her to come out for a coffee but she couldn't, she was baby-sitting with her brother. She's got a brother who's only two. That was why she couldn't come over to me.'

'So you went back home. What time?'

'I didn't go straight home. I had a coffee on my own at Castor's. I got home about nine and Mummy came in ten minutes after.'

'You must have been disappointed your father wasn't there.'

'I don't know,' she said. 'I didn't think about it,' and surprisingly, for this wasn't really at issue, 'I don't mind being alone. I like it.'

'Well, my goodness,' said Wendy, not letting that one pass, 'you're never left alone if I can help it. You needn't talk as if you'd been neglected.'

Wexford asked the name of the friend and was told it was Nicola Tennyson and given an address that was between here and the town centre. No objection was put up by Wendy to their examining such of his personal property as Rodney Williams had in this house. It left Wexford with the feeling that this was because she rather wanted them to see over her house, its cleanliness, its elegant appointments and the evidence of her skill as housekeeper.

Here, at any rate, was the rest of Williams's wardrobe. It was interesting to observe how he had kept his more stylish and 'in' clothes for this household. Jeans hung in the gilt-decorated white built-in cupboard, Westerner shirts, a denim suit and another in a fashionably crumpled stone-coloured linen mixture. There were two pairs of half-boots and a pair of beige kid moccasins. And the underwear was designed for a younger man than the part-time occupant of 31 Alverbury Road.

'He was two different men,' Wexford said.

'Perhaps three.'

'We shall see. At any rate he was two, one middle-aged, set in his ways, bored maybe, taking his family for granted, the other young still, even swinging – take a look at these underpants – making the grade with a young wife, living up to this little bandbox.'

Wexford looked around him at the room, thinking of Alverbury Road. There were duvets on the beds here, blinds at the windows, a white cane chair suspended from the ceiling, its seat piled with green, blue and white silk cushions. And the bed was a six-foot-wide king-size.

'He probably called it the playpen,' said Burden pulling a face.

'Once,' said Wexford.

In this house Williams had had no desk, only a drawer in the gilt-handled white melamine chest of drawers. This had been Wendy's house, no doubt about it, the sanctum where Wendy held sway. Girlish, fragile, soft-voiced though she might be, she had made this place her own, feminine and exclusive – exclusive in a way of Rodney Williams. He had been there on sufferance, Wexford sensed, his presence depending on his good behaviour. And yet his behaviour had not been very good even from the first. There had always been the travelling, the Bunbury of a mother, the long absences. So Wendy had made a home full of flowers and colours and silk cushions in which he was allotted small corners as if – unconsciously, he was sure it was unconsciously – she knew the day would come when it would be for herself and her daughter alone. Wexford looked inside the drawer but it told him little. It was full of the kind of papers he would have expected.

Except for Williams's driving licence with the Alverbury Road address.

'He was taking a risk leaving that about,' said Burden.

'Taking risks was his life. He took them all the time. He enjoyed the high wire. Anyway, suspicious wives read letters not driving licences.'

There were bills in the drawer, the counterfoils from credit-card chits, an American Express monthly account. Which address had that gone to? Yes, this one. It fitted somehow. Visa and Access were the workaday cards, American Express more cosmopolitan, more for the playboy. No doubt it was Wendy who paid the services' bills from the joint account. There was none in the drawer, only a rates demand, a television rental account book, an estimate from Godwin and Sculp, builders, of Pomfret, dated 30 March, for painting the living room, and an invoice from the same firm (stamped *Paid*) for renewal of a bathroom cistern.

Under this lot lay Rodney's joint account cheque book, a paying-in book for the joint account, and a small glass bottle, half full of tablets, labelled 'Mandaret'.

On this the top floor of the house were two more bedrooms and a bathroom. Veronica's room was neat as a pin, white with a good deal of broderie anglaise about it and owing much to those magazine articles prevalent in Wendy's own childhood on how to make a dream bedroom for your daughter. No doubt poor Wendy had never had a dream bedroom of her own, Wexford thought, and he sensed that her youth had been nearer to that of Sara. No posters here, no home-made mobiles and no books either. It was designed for a girl who would do nothing in it but sit in the window seat looking pensive and wearing white socks.

The spiral staircase, a contraption of hideous discomfort and danger to all but the most agile, went through the middle of the house like a screw in a press. Down on the ground floor was a shower room, a separate lavatory, the third door on that side opening into the integral garage, and at the end of the passage a room the width of the house that opened through french windows onto patio and garden roughly the size of a large dining table. The room, that might have been for dining in or a study for Rodney Williams if he had been allowed one, was plainly devoted to Wendy's interests. She had a sewing machine in it and a knitting machine, an ironing board set up with two irons on it, one dry and one steam, and there were clothes everywhere, neatly hung or draped, sheathed in plastic bags.

Mother and daughter were still sitting upstairs at the glass-topped table. Wendy had taken up some sewing, a handkerchief or possibly a traycloth into which she was inserting tiny stitches, her little finger crooked in the way it used to be said was vulgar to hold a teacup. Veronica nibbled at dry roasted peanuts out of a foil packet. The dry kind it would be, the other sort tending to leave grease spots. They were both as tense as compressed springs, waiting for the police to go and leave them alone.

'Have you heard of a society or club called ARRIA?' Wexford said to Veronica.

The spring didn't leap free of its bonds. There was no shock. Veronica merely nodded. She didn't screw up the empty peanut packet but flattened it and began folding it very carefully, first into halves, then quarters.

'At school?'

She looked up. 'Some of the girls in the sixth and seventh years belong to it.'

'But you don't?'

'You have to be over sixteen.'

'Why girls?' he said. 'Haldon Finch is co-ed. Don't any boys belong?'

She was a normal teenager really. Underneath the prissy looks, the shyness, the Mummy's girl air, she was one of them. The look she gave him seethed with their scorn for the cretinous incomprehension evinced by adults.

'Well, it's all women, isn't it? It's for women. They're – what d'you call it? – feminists, militant feminists.'

'Then I hope you'll keep clear of it, Veronica,' Wendy said very quickly and sharply for her. 'I hope you'll have nothing to do with it. If there's anything I really hate it's women's lib. Liberation! I'm liberated and look where it's got me. I just hope you'll do better than I have when the time comes and find a man who'll really support you and look after you, a nice good man who'll – who'll *cherish* you.' Her lips trembled with emotion. She laid down her sewing. 'I wasn't enough of a woman for Rodney,' she said as if the girl wasn't there. 'I wasn't enough of a girl. I got too hard and independent and – and *mature*, I know I did.' A heroic effort was made to keep the tears in, the break out of the voice, and a victory was won. 'You just remember that, Veronica, when your turn comes.'

* * *

Sergeant Martin was handling the complaint though, as he told Wexford, he hadn't much to go on. Nor had any harm been done – yet.

'A Ms Caroline Peters who's a physical education instructor at the Haldon Finch Comprehensive,' Martin said. 'Miz not Miss. She got very stroppy, sir, when I called her Miss. I called her an instructress too and had a job getting my tongue round it but that wasn't right either. She says two men were hanging about watching the girls playing a tennis match. Acting in a suspicious manner, she says. Came in a car which was parked for the express purpose of them getting out to watch. Voyeurs she called them. Afterwards she asked the girls if any of them knew the men but they denied all knowledge.'

Thank you Miss Freeborn, thought Wexford.

'Leave it, Martin. Forget it. We've better things to do.'

'Leave it altogether, sir?'

'I'll handle it.' A note to the woman or a phone call explaining all, he supposed. She had a right to that. She was a good conscientious teacher acting in a responsible manner. He mustn't laugh – except later perhaps with Burden.

There had been much food for thought picked up on his visits to Liskeard Avenue. And there had been something to make him wonder, something that was neither a piece of information nor the germ of an idea but entirely negative.

Wasn't it extraordinary that during those visits, those long talks, and during his initial interview with her, Wendy Williams had shown not the slightest interest in Rodney's other family? She had asked not a single question about the wife she had supplanted but not replaced, nor about the children who were siblings by half-blood of her own Veronica. Because she was inhibited by intense jealousy? Or for some other reason more germane to this inquiry?

11

Kevin Williams looked more like his mother than his father. He wouldn't have been recognizable as Veronica's half-brother. The genetic hand-down which was so distinctive a feature in Sara and Veronica had missed him and his forehead was narrow with the hair growing low on it. His manner was laconic, casual, indifferent.

Wexford, who had Martin with him, had interrupted what seemed to be a family conclave. For once the television was off, sight and sound. Joy Williams introduced no one but her son and this introduction she made proudly and with abnormal enthusiasm. Wexford was left to deduce that the woman and the girl who sat side by side on the yellow sofa must be Hope Harmer and her daughter Paulette.

Mrs Harmer, though plumper, fairer and better cared for than her sister, looked too much like her for her identity to be in doubt. She was a pretty woman and even in the present crisis she looked pleased with life. But the girl – to use an expression favoured by Wexford's grandsons – was 'something else again'. She was beautiful with a beauty that made Sara and Veronica merely pretty young girls. She reminded Wexford of a picture he had once seen, Rossetti's portrait of Mrs William Morris. This girl was dark and her face had the same dark glow as the face in the picture, her features the same symmetry and her large dark eyes the same other-worldly soulfulness. When he asked her if she was who he thought she was she raised those dark grey dreaming eyes and nodded, then returned to what she had been looking at, a magazine that seemed entirely devoted to hairstyles.

Kevin's term had ended the day before and he had come straight home. Not to stay, though, he made clear to Wexford when they were alone in the stark dining room. He owed it to his mother to stay a few days, but next week he intended to stick to the plan he had made months before of going down to Cornwall to stay with a friend and later he would be camping in France. He seemed astonished when Wexford asked him for the address of the Cornish friend.

'We'd rather you didn't leave the country at present.'

'You can't keep me here. My father's death has nothing to do with me.'

'Tell me what you did on the evening of Thursday, April the fifteenth.'

'Was that when he died?' The casual manner had grown sullen. He was his mother in truculent mood all over again.

'I'll ask the questions, Kevin.'

It wasn't said roughly, but nevertheless the boy looked as if no one had spoken like that to him before. His low forehead creased and his mouth pouted.

'I only asked. He was my father.'

In his tone, that of contrived, badly acted sentiment, Wexford suddenly understood that no one in this household had cared a damn for Rodney Williams. And they hadn't in the other household either. People didn't care for him for long. In this area he had, at any rate, got his deserts.

'What happened that evening? What did you do?'

'Phoned home, I suppose,' he said, careless again. 'I always do on Thursdays or my mother goes bananas.'

'You phone from college?'

'No, the phones are always out of order or it's a hassle finding one that's free.' Kevin seemed to have decided he might as well give in to Wexford's questioning if not with a good grace. 'I go out to phone. Well, two or three of us do. To a pub. I phone home and transfer the charge.'

'You'll remember that Thursday if I tell you it was the first Thursday after you got back to college from the Easter vacation.'

The boy thought about it, seeming to concentrate. Wexford had no doubt he had known perfectly well all along.

'Yeah, I do remember. I phoned home around eight, eight-thirty – I don't reckon you want to know to the minute, do you? My mother was out. I talked to Sara.'

'That must have surprised you, your mother being out when you phoned.'

'Yeah, it was unusual. She thinks the sun shines out of my arse, as you've maybe noticed.' He jerked his shoulders in an exaggerated shrug. 'Unusual,' he said, 'but not unknown.'

More indignation came when Wexford asked for the names of Kevin's companions on the trip to the pub where the phone was. But it was hot air, pointless obstructiveness. The names were forthcoming after some expostulation.

'How did you get on with your father?'

'There was no communication. We didn't talk. The usual sort of situation, right?'

'And your father and Sara?'

The reply came sharply. It was incredible. It was exactly the reply a boy of Kevin's age might have made a hundred years before – or, according to literature, might have made.

'You can leave my sister out of this!'

Wexford tried not to laugh. 'I will for now.'

He found Joy and her sister questioning Martin in depth about Wendy Williams. The girls, the two cousins, had gone. Martin was answering in monosyllables and he looked relieved when Wexford came in. Joy broke off at once and, having seen he was alone, said, 'Where's my son?' as if Wexford might have arrested him and already stowed him away in a police car.

* * *

This would be his first encounter with Miles Gardner since the discovery of Rodney Williams's body. He and Burden waited for him in the managing director's office. The panelled room was dim and shadowy in spite of the bright day outside. A copper pot filled with Russell lupins stood on the windowsill. Wexford picked up the desk photograph of Gardner's family and looked at it dubiously.

'I suppose I'm sensitized to adolescent girls,' he said. 'I see them everywhere.'

'Just remember what the games mistress said.'

'I don't think I'm in danger, though they're a very pretty lot we're in contact with. One can almost see Williams's point of view.'

'He was just a dirty old lecher,' said Burden, apparently forgetting Williams had been a mere three years his senior.

'The primrose way to the everlasting bonfire.'

Gardner came in, apologizing for having kept them waiting. He began on some insincere-sounding expressions of sorrow at Williams's demise which Wexford listened to patiently and then cut short.

'If you're free for lunch we might all go over to the Old Flag.'

But this was something Gardner, regretfully, couldn't manage. 'I've promised to give my daughter lunch, my youngest one, Jane. She's got the day off school to go for an interview at the university here. A bit of an ordeal, she's a nervous kid, so I bribed her with the offer of a slap-up lunch.'

The University of the South was situated at Myringham. Another eighteen-year-old then . . .

'She should get a place,' Gardner said, and with a kind of rueful pride, 'There go our holidays abroad for the next three years.'

Wexford said he would like to talk to Christine Lomond, and in the room that had been Williams's if possible. Gardner took him there himself, up in the small slow lift. There were two desks and two typewriters, a Sierra 3400 and an Olympia ES 100. But this place was 'clean' as far as typewriters went. Martin had seen to that. The girl who came in was fresh-paint glossy in a suit of geranium-red linen, dark green cotton blouse, green glass rhomboid hanging on a chain and on her left wrist a watch with a red and green strap. Her hair had been touched with what his daughter Sylvia assured him were called 'low lights', though Wexford couldn't quite believe this and thought she must have been having him on. Christine Lomond's fingernails were the brilliant carmine of the latest Seven-shine front-door shade Pillarbox ('A rich true red without a hint of blue, a robust high gloss that stands up ideally to wind and weather'). They scuttled over the filing cabinet like so many red beetles.

Wexford had asked her to see what she could find him as samples of Williams's own typing, any report, assessment, rough notes even, he might have brought to the office with him. She said she was sure anything of that sort would have been handwritten, and it was two or three handwritten sheets that she produced for him, and then several more which she told him had probably been typed on the Olympia machine but using a different daisywheel, thus altering the typeface. Wexford was particularly interested because there seemed to him to be a flaw in the apex of the capital A.

The experiment, however, showed nothing but his own ignorance of typewriters or at any rate of recent technological advances made in typewriters. The red-tipped white fingers whipped a sheet of paper into the machine, switched it on, switched it off, whipped out the daisywheel, inserted another, and rapidly produced a facsimile of the first four lines of Williams's sales forecast for the first three months of the year.

'It's getting a bit ragged,' Christine Lomond said. 'We need a new wheel,' and she pulled the damaged one out and dropped it into the wastepaper basket.

'Where do you live, Miss Lomond?'

'Here. In Myringham. Why?' She had a rather abrupt manner, of the kind that is usually called 'crisp'.

'Did you like Mr Williams?'

She was silent. She seemed affronted, having anticipated perhaps nothing more than an investigation of papers and machines. How old was she? Twenty-six? Twenty-seven? She could be a good deal less than that. The heavy make-up and elaborate hairstyle aged her.

'Well, Miss Lomond?'

'Yes, I liked him. Well, I liked him all right. I didn't think about liking or disliking him.'

'Would you think back, please, and give me some idea of what you were doing on the evening of April the fifteenth?'

'I can't possibly remember that far back!'

Her eyelids flapped. They were a gleaming laminated sea blue ('Delicate turquoise with a hint of silver, ideal for that special ceiling, alcove or display cabinet').

'Try and pinpoint it,' said Burden, 'by thinking of what you were doing next day. That was the morning someone phoned to say Mr Williams was ill and wouldn't be in. Does that help?'

'I expect I was at home on my own.'

She didn't sound defensive, guilty, afraid. She sounded sullen, as if the clothes and the make-up, the 'grooming' had not been effective.

'Do you live on your own or with someone?'

Surely the most innocent of questions. She pounced on it as surely as if those red nails had seized and clutched.

'I certainly do not live with someone! I was at home on my own watching the TV.'

Another one. What had they done in the old days before the cathode conquest? He ought to be able to remember pre-television alibis but he couldn't. I was reading, sewing, putting up shelves, fishing, listening to the radio, out for a walk, in the pub, at the pictures? Maybe.

Unwillingly, even grudgingly, she gave them her address. She admitted to possessing a typewriter, an old

Smith Corona, though not a portable, and insisted it was in her parents' house in Tonbridge and she had never had it with her in the Myringham bedsit.

Downstairs in the reception area they encountered a young girl undressing. Or so to Wexford's astonished eyes it at first appeared. She was talking to the telephonist (Anna today) and in the act of pulling a cotton dress off over her head. Long slim legs in white tights, pale blue pumps with curly heels, and yes, a skirt which dropped to its former just-above-the-knee length when the garment, evidently a middy blouse, was off. Underneath it was a white tee-shirt. Her back was to Wexford. She kicked off the blue pumps, sending one flying across the room and leaving no doubt in the mind of an observer that this was a cathartic shedding of a hateful costume after an ordeal was over.

'Jane,' said Anna in a warning tone, 'there are some . . .'

She spun round. On the front of the tee-shirt were printed the letters ARRIA.

The first thing that struck Wexford about the house in Down Road, Kingsmarkham, was that there was no question of any of its occupants being obliged to share a bedroom. It was a very large, castellated, turreted, balconied Edwardian pile. Most houses like it had been converted into flats but not this one. A single family inhabited it and its (at least) eight bedrooms. Yet Eve Freeborn had given him the reason for going to her boyfriend in Myringham instead of his coming to her that she shared a bedroom with her sister. Perhaps she hadn't a sister either. He would soon see.

At first he thought the girl who opened the front door to him *was* Eve. After all, the fact that this one had green hair meant nothing. They changed their hair colour these days as fast as they used to change their lipstick. A second look told him they weren't even identical twins. Twins, yes, fraternal twins with the same build of body and the same eyes. That was all. God knew what colour their hair really was. They had probably forgotten themselves.

The house smelt faintly of marijuana. An unmistakable smell that was like woodsmoke blended with sweet cologne.

'Eve?' Eve's sister said with incredulity. 'You want to see Eve?'

'Is that so difficult?'

'I don't know really . . . '

He had shown her his warrant card. After all, she was a young girl and it was evening. She shouldn't admit unidentified men into the house. But she was looking at it as if it were a warrant for her arrest. He felt impatient.

'Perhaps I should fill in a form or produce a sponsor.'

'Oh, no, come in. I'm sorry. It's just that . . . '

She had an irritating way of leaving her sentences unfinished. He followed her into the hall, darkly panelled like the offices of Sevensmith Harding, and up a big elegant winding staircase with a gallery at the top. The marijuana smell was fainter but it was still there. What astonished him about the house was the aura of the sixties that pervaded it. On the wall here was a poster (albeit a glazed and framed poster) of John Lennon seated at a white grand piano. A vase stood on a side table filled with dried grasses and shabby peacock's tail feathers. And hanging up as an ornament, not because it had been left there by chance, was an antique red silk dress embroidered with gold, its red and its gold tattered and shredded by time and moths. He said, 'Are your parents at home?'

'They've got a flat in London. They're there half the time.'

Impossible to tell if she minded or was glad. Those parents need not be more than forty themselves, he thought, and Mother might be less. Eve's twin said, 'Perhaps you'd better wait here. I'll just see if . . .'

All the bedroom doors were open. Only they weren't bedrooms, not exactly. Each one, as far as he could see, had the look rather of a bedsit, with chairs and tables and floor cushions and a couch or divan with an Indian bedspread flung artlessly over it, posters on the walls and postcards pinned up higgledy-piggledy. He sat down to wait in a rocking chair that had its rockers painted red, black and white and a dirty lace veil draped over its back, and wondered how to explain this mysterious house.

Then he understood. It wasn't the girls who were living in the past, who were twenty years out of date, or purposely living in an anachronism. Those parents had been young in the sixties, had revelled probably in that new inspiring freedom, and now the spirit of the sixties, the flavour, the mores would never leave them. Not the girls but the parents were the marijuana users. He would have to do something about that . . .

How long was she going to keep him waiting?

He got up and went out into the passage. There was no one about. But from somewhere he could hear the sound of female voices – a sound that was not in the least like the twittering of birds, strong earnest talk rather than a murmuration. A staircase led to the attic floor but it wasn't from up there that the voices came.

There was a burst of laughter, some sporadic clapping. He walked down the passage towards the sound, came out into another smaller, squarer landing, a map of the heavens painted on its ceiling by a trained but unsure hand. An amateur astrologer who had been to art school, he thought, which brought the sixties once more to mind. As he stood there, doubtful of the wisdom of bursting into a room full of women, the door opened and two girls came out. They stopped in the doorway, looking at him in astonishment. One was unknown to him, the other was Caroline Peters, physical training instructor.

Before anyone spoke Eve Freeborn came out of the room, shouldering her way past the two who blocked the doorway. She was once more in the pelvis-crusher jeans but this time with a purple satin blouse to match her hair. Caroline Peters, on the other hand, was dressed exactly like a boy

– or like boys used to dress before punk apparel came to stay: blue jeans, brown leather jacket, half-boots; no make-up, hair cropped in a crewcut.

'Sorry,' Eve said. 'Have you been waiting long?'

'*They* kept *us* waiting,' said Caroline Peters with the maximum venom, 'for four thousand years.'

She had recognized him and wasn't pleased. Or had he been recognized for what he was in addition to being a policeman – a man? Wexford had never before personally encountered the kind of militant feminist who advocates total separatism. Enlightenment broke upon him.

'Have I by any chance interrupted a meeting of ARRIA?'

'It's over,' said Eve. 'It's just over.'

'We wouldn't have permitted interruption.'

Wexford looked at Caroline Peters. 'Don't go yet, please. I'd like to talk to you too.'

She lifted her shoulders, went back into the room. Eve waved a hand at the other girl, a pretty, sharp-faced redhead.

'This is Nicky.'

Inside the room, another, larger, bedsit hung with striped bedspreads on ceilings and walls like a Bedouin tent, half a dozen more girls were standing about or preparing to leave. Sara Williams was there and her cousin Paulette, the two of them talking to Jane Gardner, and all of them wearing ARRIA tee-shirts. A black girl, thin and elegant as a model, sat crosslegged on a floor cushion.

Eve said to the company, 'I don't remember what he's called,' as if it hardly mattered, 'but he's a policeman.' She pointed at one girl after another: 'Jane, Sara, Paulette, Donella, Helen, Elaine, and Amy, my sister, you've met.'

Caroline Peters pushed her hands into the pockets of her leather jacket.

'What is it you want?'

'I'd like to know more about ARRIA for a start.'

'For a *start* it was *started* by me and a like-minded woman, a classical scholar now at Oxford.' She paused. 'Arria

Paeta,' she said, 'was a Roman matron, the wife of Caecina Paetus. Of course she was obliged to take his name.' Wexford could tell she was one of those fanatics who never miss a trick. 'Ancient Rome was known for its gross oppression and exploitation of women.' Teacher-like, she waited for his comments.

They came – perhaps to her surprise. 'The Emperor Claudius,' said Wexford who had done his homework, 'ordered Paetus to commit suicide but he proved too cowardly, so his wife took the sword and plunging it into her own heart, said, "See Paetus, it does not hurt . . ." '

'You've been reading Graves!'

'No. *Smith's Classical Dictionary.*' The girl called Nicky laughed. 'But I don't know what the letters stand for,' he said.

'Action for the Radical Reform of Intersexual Attitudes.'

'A case of making the nym fit the acronym? Or is it a deliberate obscuration?'

'Perhaps it is.'

'How many schools are involved?'

It was Eve who answered him. 'Kingsmarkham High, Haldon Finch, St Catherine's . . . ' but Caroline Peters interrupted her.

'I teach at Haldon Finch. ARRIA had its inception just over a year ago at St Catherine's. We admitted as members only those women over sixteen, those in fact in the sixth and seventh years. I'm glad to say it had an immediate appeal – how could an organization designed expressly for women, designed to give men no quarter – be otherwise?' She turned on him a glacial look of distaste and it gave him a most unpleasant feeling. He didn't belong to a minority, there was no way he could be categorized into a minority, yet the sensation she gave him was of doing so and of an oppressed one at that. 'Our very well-organized propaganda machine,' she said, 'spread the good news through the other schools in the area and we soon had considerable cells at Pomfret College of Further Education and Kingsmarkham High.' The good news, he thought, the 'gospel' no less. She astonished him by saying, 'We now have a membership of just over five hundred women.'

He suppressed the whistle he wanted to give. What must the local population of seventeen- and eighteen-year-old girls be? All of them, including those who had left school, could surely hardly amount to more than a couple of thousand and that meant 25 per cent in ARRIA. Why, they could almost start a revolution!

'All right, you've got badges, you've had tee-shirts printed, you hold meetings, but what do you *do*?'

Caroline Peters answered readily. 'Basically, have as little contact with men as possible. Defy men by intellectual and also by physical means.'

He pricked up his ears at that. She wasn't carrying a bag but she had pockets. Most of the other girls had bags. He hadn't got a warrant and, almost more to the point, hadn't a woman with him to carry out a search.

'We have a constitution and manifesto,' she said. 'I expect there's a copy about and I see no objection to your having one. Would you women agree to that?' There was a murmur of assent, some of it amused. 'But I must point out that our aim isn't to meet men on equal terms. It isn't to come to a truce or compromise with them nor to reach that uneasy détente which in past revolutions has sometimes come into being between a proletariat and a bourgeoisie. As Marx said in another context: Philosophers have tried to explain the world. The point surely is to change it. Good night, everyone.' She went out of the room, closing the door with a somewhat sinister quietness behind her.

Silence. The black girl, Donella, cast up her eyes, rolling sloe-brown pupils in moon-white whites. Eve said, 'By physical means, she only meant self-defence stuff. It's compulsory when you join to take a self-defence course, karate or judo or tai chi or whatever.'

'Personally,' said Donella, 'I think that's one of the things that attracts people – the sport, you know.'

'You may have noticed, there've been three times as many evening courses in martial arts started since ARRIA began. That's in response to increased demand, that's ARRIA.'

Nicky had spoken with pride, not aggressively. She made a swift chopping movement with one arm. Wexford, a large man over six feet tall, felt relieved he wasn't on the receiving end of that blow. It was true about the judo and karate courses, he had remarked on it himself to Burden, pleased that women were at last taking steps to defend themselves against the muggings and rapes which in the past few years had so disproportionately increased.

'All right,' he said, 'that's for self-defence. How about aggression? I don't suppose anyone's going to admit to carrying an offensive weapon?'

Nobody was. They didn't look scared or guilty or even alert. He fancied he saw wariness in one or two faces.

'I'll give you a copy of the constitution,' Eve said. 'There's nothing private about it. Everyone's welcome to know what we do, men as well as women. Do you have daughters?'

'They're a lot older than you.'

She looked at him in a not unkindly way, assessing. 'Well, they would be, wouldn't they? You can't be too old for ARRIA, though.'

The constitution was typed and photocopied. He noted that there were no flaws in the apexes of the capital As or the ascenders of the lower-case ts. It went into his pocket to be read at leisure. Sara Williams, he observed, was watching his every movement. The big fair girl called Helen he now realized had been Eve's partner in the tennis match. He said to Eve, 'If everyone is in fact going I'd like to talk to you alone for five minutes.'

The brisk policeman's tone replacing the one of easy jocularity seemed to jolt her. She pushed fingers through the purple crest of hair.

'OK, if that's the way you want it. Everybody out, right?' She gave a hiccuping giggle. 'Home, women!'

Amy said, 'Well, I think I'll just . . . ' and drifted vaguely towards the door.

They all began to take their leave in ways peculiar to young girls, whether feminists or reactionaries. Helen and Donella closed in upon each other with a tight bear hug which ended in giggles and heads subsiding on each other's shoulders. Sara wrapped her arms round herself and moved across the floor with vague dancing steps. Jane humped her bag, filled with ARRIA constitution sheets, as if it weighed a ton, making agony faces. Nicky was lost in a dream that seemed to turn her into a sleepwalker so that she neither paused in her exit nor spoke but merely raised a languid flapping hand in farewell as she passed through the doorway.

Alone with Eve, Wexford said, 'You've been telling me lies.'

'I have not!'

'Why did you tell me your boyfriend couldn't come here because you had to share a bedroom with your sister? This is an enormous house and as far as I can see your parents mostly aren't here anyway. But you told me lack of space – and you implied lack of privacy – stopped him coming here.'

'Well,' she said, a sly look in her eyes, 'I can explain that. You'll see the answer in our constitution actually. Rule 4.'

He pulled the constitution out of his pocket. Here it was, Rule 4. 'Women' – not ARRIA members, he saw, but always 'women' as if the society contained the world's entire female population – 'Women shall avoid the company of men wherever possible but should their presence be required for sexual, biological, business or career purposes, it is expedient and desirable for women to go to them rather than permit them to come to us.'

'But why?'

'Caroline and Edwina – she's the classical one who's at Oxford – they said it smacked of the sultan visiting his harem. You've got to think it through, you know. When you do you can see what they mean.'

'So that's why you went to your boyfriend in Arnold Road? You required his presence for sexual or even biological purposes?'

'Isn't that why women usually require men?'

'There are other ways of putting it. More aesthetic ways, I'd say. Maybe more civilized.'

'Oh, *civilized*. Men made civilization and it's not up to much, is it? It's no big deal.'

He left it. 'Did you know Sara Williams was the daughter of the murdered man whose car you saw in Arnold Road?'

'Not then I didn't. I do now. Look, I only know her through ARRIA and I didn't know her father. For all I knew, she mightn't have had a father.'

He accepted that. 'Miss Peters didn't tell me much about this society of yours, did she? Only that it's a wildfire movement, it's caught on in all the local schools. How about the – what shall I call it? – esoteric stuff? How do you join? Do you pay a subscription? Is there any sort of ritual – like freemasons, say?'

'We don't need money,' she said, 'so there's no sub. Where would they get it from anyway? Most of our members are still at school. They'd have to get it from their fathers and that's out. See Rule 6 and dependence. The only thing that costs us is the photocopying, only it doesn't because Nicky does it on her dad's Xerox in the night, when he's asleep.'

There was an irony there but Wexford didn't point it out. 'Anyone can join?'

'Any woman over sixteen who's not married. Obviously a married woman has already capitulated. Anyway, it wouldn't be possible for her to keep to the rules.'

'That would let my daughters out.'

She ignored him. 'I'm a founder member. When we

started there was a lot of really wayout stuff going on. Edwina wanted initiation ceremonies, sort of baptisms of fire if you can imagine.'

'What sort?'

He was deeply curious. At the same time he was afraid she would soon realize she was spending too much time unnecessarily in the society of a man. She considered his question in thoughtful silence. She was not a pretty girl. But perhaps this didn't matter in these days when beauty was no longer at a premium. She had one of those chinless faces, long-nosed, full-lipped, but with creamy delicate skin. A frown creased, or rather crumpled, her forehead. Creasing was for older people. Eve's frown was like the bunching of a piece of cream velvet.

'Some of the others went along with her ideas,' she said. 'I mean, she was a radical feminist. For instance, she used to say we couldn't make revolution on Marxist principles on account of Marx having been a man. She said sexuality was politics and the only way to get freedom was for all women to be lesbians. Any hetero behaviour was collaborating with the enemy. Even Caroline Peters never went as far as that.'

'You were going to tell me about initiation.'

Eve seemed reluctant to reach the subject. 'They actually formed a splinter group over it. Sara, the one whose father was murdered, she was one of them and Nicky Anerley was another. One of the things they objected to was being educated along with the other sex. They wanted schools and colleges run by women and with women teachers. Of course, it would be best, it's the ideal if you know what I mean, but it's a bit fantastic.'

'Particularly as it's only in very recent years that women have gained admission to certain men's colleges, notably at Oxford.'

'That's beside the point. This would be a question of getting the men out altogether. Edwina and the rest of them who were at mixed schools wanted to go on strike until they agreed not to admit boys. But Caroline wouldn't have that. I suppose she was afraid of losing her job.'

'And that's what caused the rift in the party?'

'Well, partly. This was all last summer and autumn. It more or less stopped when Edwina went up to Oxford in October and the others drifted back. I may as well tell you. It was all a sort of fantasy anyway. Edwina said in order to prove herself a true feminist a woman ought to kill a man.' Eve looked at him warily. 'I don't mean everyone who joined ARRIA was to have to kill a man to get to be a member. The idea was for groups of three or four to get together and . . .

'But that's not an initiation ceremony really, is it? I could tell you about some of those if you want.'

12

With inscrutable face Jenny Burden sat reading ARRIA's manifesto. She was past the stage now of prettifying disguises of her pregnancy. It was beyond disguise and her condition didn't flatter her. Younger than her years though she had always looked, she now appeared too old to be having a baby. Her face was not so much lined as lacking in its former firmness, caverns hollowed out under the eyes and chin muscles sagging. She had no lap now so she held the flimsy sheets against a book propped up on the table in front of her.

But Wexford could tell by Burden's pleased expression that he was content to see his wife making even this small effort to escape from the apathy that had settled on her as the psychotherapy she was having progressed. No longer in revolt, no longer violent in her hatred of the child, she had become resigned. She waited in hopeless passivity. When Wexford arrived she had taken his hand, put up her face for a kiss, inquired in a limbo voice after Dora and the girls. And he had thought: when the baby is born she could go completely mad, enter a schizophrenic world and pass the rest of her life in hospital. She wouldn't be the first to whom such a thing had happened.

Still, now she was reading ARRIA's constitution, and apparently reading every word with care. Wexford wouldn't talk about the Williams case in her presence and Burden knew that. Suddenly she began reading aloud.

'Rule 6: With certain limited exceptions, no woman shall be financially dependent on a man. Then they list the exceptions. Rule 7: All women shall take a course in some martial art or self-defence technique. Rule 8: All women shall carry a permitted weapon for self-defence, i.e. ammonia spray, pin, penknife, pepper shaker, etc. Rule 9: No member shall marry, participate in the bourgeois concept of becoming 'engaged' or share accommodation with a man in a cohabiting situation. Rule 10 . . . Do you want Rule 10?'

'Oh, I have read it,' Wexford said. 'It is heresy!'

She didn't recognize the quotation. 'You're bound to think that way, aren't you? Perhaps I should have read all this before I met you, Mike.'

He took the blow with a physical flinch.

'ARRIA didn't exist then. It was around earlier this year before I gave up work, though. I always wanted to get hold of their manifesto but no one would even talk to me about it. I was a married woman, you see.'

'I suppose I was lucky to get it,' Wexford conceded.

Burden was making an effort to recover from the pain she had given him. 'I want to hear Rule 10.'

'All right. Rule 10: Women wishing to reproduce should select the potential father for his physique, health, height, etc., and ensure impregnation in a rape or near-rape construct.'

'In a *what*? What the hell does it mean?'

Wexford said, 'Margaret Mead says men of the Arapesh fear rape by women just as women in other cultures fear rape by men.'

'The mind boggles.' By this, Wexford knew, Burden meant he would dearly have loved to inquire further into the mechanics and techniques but was hampered by inhibition. 'The trouble is surely that most of this was written by lesbians like Edwina Klein and Caroline Peters. It doesn't seem to cater for women who actually *love* men – and those are surely in the vast majority.'

Jenny looked coldly at her husband. 'In the sort of explanation bit that comes after the rules it says the authors realize woman may feel affection for men and even – I quote – "what is termed sexual love" but it is necessary that something must be given up for the cause. Other women in the past have denied themselves this indulgence and been amply compensated. It goes on: "After all, what does this so-called 'love' amount to when a woman sets it against its concomitants: gross exploitation, pornography, degradation, career prohibition or curtailment, rape, father–daughter incest and the still-persisting double standard?" '

'It doesn't seem to bear much relation to our own home lives, does it?' said Burden.

Jenny had tears in her eyes, Wexford saw. They shone there, unshed. 'Revolutionaries are always extreme,' she said. 'Look at the Terror of 1793, look at Stalinism. If they're not, if they compromise with liberalism, all their principles fizzle out and you're back with the status quo. Isn't that what's happened to the broader women's liberation movement?'

The men looked at her with varying expressions of doubt and dismay. Burden had gone rather pale.

'If these girls,' said Jenny, 'can accomplish just a fraction of what they're setting out to do, if they can begin to make people see what "inequitable arbitration" really amounts to, perhaps – perhaps I shan't so much mind my daughter being born.'

This time she didn't break down into tears. 'I know you want to talk. I'll leave you.' She turned to her husband, kissed his forehead, carried herself clumsily to the door. There was no dignity there and no beauty because the child that made her heavy was unwanted . . . Burden put out one finger to touch the ARRIA manifesto like someone steeling himself to make contact with something he has a phobia about.

'I feel it threatens me, all this. I'm frightened of it.'

'It's good that you're honest enough to admit it.'

'Do you really think there's anything in this killing a man stuff?'

He had done so at first. It had seemed the obvious answer and for a moment or two the only possible answer. At that point his whole tone towards Eve had changed. He had been dancing lightly with her and then, suddenly, the music stopped and he seized hold of her. That was what it was like. Of course, he had frightened her with his quick rough questions . . .

'But nobody ever did it! It was a fantasy – like group sex or something. Like an orgy. You think about what it would be like, you fantasize, but you don't *do* it.'

'Many do.'

'Well, OK, that wasn't a very good comparison. The point is fantasy doesn't become reality, the two don't mix.'

'Don't they? Isn't that what a psychopath is? Someone who confuses fantasy with reality?'

She had insisted, with the panic of someone who realizes she has said too much, that Edwina Klein's idea had been hers alone, even the splinter group had opposed it. Knives next. He had gone on to ask her what was meant by 'permitted weapons'. Did this category include knives? Not *real* knives, she said, and she had looked at him as a child might, round-eyed, afraid of something it doesn't understand.

'It's tempting,' he said to Burden, 'to think of a group of those ARRIA girls grabbing hold of poor old Williams like the Maenads with Orpheus and doing him in on the Lesbian shore.'

Burden looked at him, mystified. 'Shall we have a beer?' he said.

'Good idea.

> ' "Malt does more than Milton can
> To justify the ways of God to man." '

'You're right there,' Burden said feelingly.

He came back with two cans and two tankards on a tray. Poor chap, Wexford thought, he's had enough. And how curious it was that all these dramatic things happened to Burden, who was such an ordinary, unimaginative, salt-of-the-earth person. The prototype surely of Kafka's man to whom who, though he shut himself up in his room, hid himself, lay low, life nevertheless came in and rolled in ecstasy at his feet. Whereas for him, Wexford, nothing much came along to disturb his private peace. Thank God for it!

'Just the same,' he said, 'we're going to have our work cut out checking out every one of ARRIA's members. There are said to be five hundred of them, remember.'

'The girl who stabbed Budd may not be the same girl who stabbed Wheatley who may not be the same girl as the one that killed Williams, but on the other hand they may be one and the same.'

'Right,' said Wexford. 'But don't let's talk of the "one" that killed Williams. No girl on her own could have carried his body into that car and then carried it out again and buried him.'

'The way I see it, we have to think of it along these lines. On the one hand we have the radical feminists of whom we know (a) that the notion of killing a man was at any rate considered by them and (b) that they are required by their own rules to carry offensive weapons. We also know that Wheatley certainly and Budd probably were stabbed by ARRIA members. We've been told too that Williams, pursuing his well-known tastes, had a very young girlfriend. Now is this girlfriend a member of ARRIA?'

'Whatever the ARRIA rules may say,' said Wexford, 'we know members do have to do with the opposite sex. Look at Eve climbing in through her boyfriend's window. She hasn't made the supreme sacrifice of giving up men. And if you want to kill a man what better way of doing it than in what ARRIA would probably call a libido-emotional construct – in other words a love affair?'

Burden finished the last of his beer. In the next room

Jenny had put a record on, Ravel's *Pavane on a Dead Infanta*. 'Who said that about malt and Milton?'

'Housman. His life was ruined by an unrequited love.'

'Blimey. Why ravens?'

'In ARRIA's logo, d'you mean? They're predatory birds, aren't they? No, I suppose not. Harsh-tongued? I really don't know, Mike. At any rate, they're not soft and submissive. The collective noun for them is an "unkindness". An Unkindness of Ravens. Appropriate, wouldn't you say? In their attitude to the opposite sex anyway. They stab at us with knives rather than beaks.'

'Not without provocation, of course.'

'That's true. Budd on his own admission tried to get fresh with the girl who attacked him. He may have got fresher than he says. Wheatley says he didn't get fresh at all but I'm not inclined to believe him. They made passes and got themselves stabbed. Makes you wonder what Williams did, doesn't it?'

As Wexford walked home he thought about what he had had to do as a result of his visit to the Freeborns' house. Sergeant Martin and Detective Bennett had paid a follow-up call and this morning Charles Freeborn, the girls' father, had appeared at Kingsmarkham Magistrates' Court charged with possessing cannabis and with permitting cannabis to be smoked upon his premises. Bennett, who detected the stuff in a positively cat-and-mouse way – or cat-and-catmint way – had begun a methodical search of the big overgrown garden, starting at the conservatory, following the crazy-paving path through a copse of unpruned dusty shrubs. This path curved all round the perimeter of the garden, winding its way between ghosts of flowerbeds where a few attenuated cultivated plants thrust their heads through a matting of bindweed, ground elder and thistles. A gate in the fence at the garden's foot afforded a shortcut into a path to the High Street. Bennett had been wondering if he was getting obsessional imagining *Cannabis sativa*, which requires sunlight and space, might ever flourish here when he suddenly came upon the only tended flowerbed in the whole half acre.

He was nearly back at the house again, the stifling, shadow-spreading trees behind him. A neat rectangular clearing had been made in the shaggy grass here, the soil well watered, weeded, and the bed bordered with bricks. Martin had declared the vigorous young plants to be seedling tomatoes but Bennett knew better. Infra-red light is essential to the Indian hemp if its effect when ingested is to be the characteristically hallucinogenic one, and these plants were basking in it, for their bed was in the only part of the garden to enjoy day-long uninterrupted sunshine.

Wexford pondered, not for the first time, on the ethics of going into someone's house for a check and a chat, while there detecting a forbidden drug and immediately, scarcely with a qualm, taking steps to prosecute the offender. One's host *in absentia*, so to speak. Of course he was right, *it* was right. He was a policeman and that came first. That must always come first or chaos would come instead . . .

By the time the schools broke up towards the end of July Wexford's men had vetted and cleared something like 50 per cent of the ARRIA membership. Tracking them down was the difficulty, for Caroline Peters denied the existence of a list of members. Why should a list be needed when there was no subscription, and dates and venues of meetings were passed on by grassroots?

Paulette Harmer, Williams's niece, a sixth-form-college student, was cleared. She had been out with her boyfriend, to whom she would become engaged at Christmas – thereby abrogating ARRIA membership? – on the evenings Budd and Wheatley were stabbed, and at home with her parents and her aunt Joy on 15 April. Eve Freeborn, before going to her boyfriend in Arnold Road, had spent the evening at home with her parents and her sister. This alibi also accounted for Amy. Neither could be cleared of the Budd and Wheatley stabbings. Nor could Caroline Peters who, however, had been at a meeting in London on the evening of the 15th. The redheaded Nicky turned out to be Nicola Anerley and not the Nicola Tennyson who was Veronica Williams's friend. She had been at a party on 15 April, Helen Blake's eighteenth birthday party, which had also been attended by another twelve members of ARRIA, all of whom Wexford was able to discount as far as the murder of Williams was concerned.

Jane Gardner he questioned himself. She was the right age, pretty and lively, an active member of ARRIA. He owed it to the cordial relationship he had had with her father to go himself and not send Bennett, say, or Archbold.

Miles was at home, had made a point evidently of being at home. He was affronted and preparing to be bitterly offended. He and his tall wife were in the drawing room (walls of Sevenstar Chinese yellow, black carpet, *famille jaune* porcelain) and Wexford was shown in by the cleaning lady masquerading as a maid. They spoke to him, he thought, in the aghast tones of parents asking a headmaster why he intends to expel their daughter from his school. Pamela Gardner called him 'Mr Wexford' though it had been 'Reg' in the past. Since she had no means of summoning the cleaning lady except by shouting, she went to fetch Jane herself.

'This is so entirely unnecessary,' Gardner said in a hard voice.

Wexford said it was routine and felt like a cop in an ancient Cyril Hare detective story.

The girl came in smiling and perfectly at ease. Then he had to ask the parents to go. They did but with a very ill grace. At first Pamela Gardner pretended she didn't understand what he meant. Light dawned, then came incredulity, lastly disgusted acceptance. She took her husband's arm as if the very cornerstones of their home life had been threatened.

'Did you get a university place?' Wexford asked Jane as soon as they were alone.

'Oh yes, thanks. We met before, didn't we? At Dad's office? I never thought I would actually. I'd even enrolled at secretarial college in London just in case. My school doesn't have a commercial department.'

There came back to him a recollection of this girl changing her clothes in full view of the street. In 'Dad's office'. And when she had turned round to see him looking at her she hadn't turned a hair.

'Did you know Rodney Williams, Jane?'

'I'd met him. At the office. Dad introduced us. He had a lot of charm, you know.' She smiled, reminiscently, a bit sadly. 'He could make you feel you were the only person there worth talking to.'

It struck Wexford that this was the first person he had spoken to with a good word to say for Rodney Williams. She spoiled it a little.

'I expect he was like that with all girls of my age.'

Was she an enthusiastic member of ARRIA? Had she been in the splinter group? Did she carry a weapon? Where had she been when Budd was stabbed, when Wheatley was stabbed, when Williams was killed? Yes to the first and second questions, an indignant no, wide-eyed and law-abiding, to the third. A baby-sitting alibi for 15 April, a visit to her newly married sister for a Budd alibi, no memory of what she had been doing on the evening of the Wheatley stabbing. Apropos of none of this, surprising her with what seemed inconsequential, he said, 'Which schools do have commercial departments?'

'Haldon Finch, Sewingbury Sixth Form.' She gave him an earnest look. 'Dad's really upset that you suspect me.'

'There's no question of that. This is routine.'

'Well . . . ' Suddenly she was the good daughter, dutiful,

compliant, obedient. 'He and Mummy are dead against you taking my fingerprints.'

'You' presumably implied the Mid-Sussex Constabulary or did she think he had come armed with pads and gadgets? The cleaning lady showed him out, her apron changed for rather smart dungarees. There was no sign of Miles or Pamela. Donaldson drove him back to Kingsmarkham and dropped him outside his own house. Dora, dressed up, was on the phone to Sylvia.

He passed close by her and touched her cheek with his lips. She responded to the kiss, mouthed something about getting a move on, went on talking to Sylvia. He went upstairs, changed into what he called his best suit, grey like the others but the latest and least shabby. When he retired he would never wear a suit again – not even to the theatre.

In the train he told Dora about the Gardners and said he had a feeling they wouldn't be asked to any more garden parties. She said that didn't matter, did it? She didn't care. And he shouldn't care either, he should relax, especially tonight.

'I wish I'd read the play.'

'You haven't had time.'

'You can always make time for things you want to do,' he said.

As it was he didn't even know what *The Cenci* was about and of its history only that it had for a long time been banned from the English stage. He and Dora, on holiday in Italy, had seen Guido Reni's portrait of Beatrice Cenci in the Galleria Nazionale in Rome, though he wouldn't have connected that with the play but for Sheila's saying it would be reproduced in the programme. It would have been a good idea to have read the play – or to have read Moravia's *Beatrice Cenci*, a novel that might be more entertaining.

The play threatened at first not to entertain at all. Shelley, Wexford thought to himself while aware he was no informed critic, wasn't Shakespeare. And wasn't he, in writing this sort of five-act tragedy in blank verse, some two hundred years out of date? Then Sheila came on, not looking like the portrait but with a small cap on her golden hair and dressed in white and grey, and he forgot everything, even the play, in his consuming pride in her. She had a peculiar quality in her acting, which critics as well as he had remarked on, of bringing clarity to obscure or periphrastic lines, so that her entrances always seemed to let light in upon the arcane. It was so now, it continued to be so . . . He saw and understood. The plot and purpose of the play began to unfold themselves for him and Shelley's style ceased to be an anachronism.

The effect on Dora was less happy.

She whispered to Wexford while they were having a glass of wine during the interval, 'There's more to it than I can see, I know that. It's not just that they can't stand the old man's harshness any longer, is it? I mean, why did Sheila come tearing in screaming about her eyes being full of blood?'

'Her father raped her.' Wexford realized what he had said and corrected himself. 'Count Cenci raped his daughter Beatrice.'

'I see. Oh yes, I do see. It's not made very clear, is it?'

'I imagine Shelley couldn't afford to spell it out. As it was, it must have been the incest theme that got the play banned.'

While waiting for the curtain to go up on Act Four he read the essay on the historical facts on which the play was based which had been written for the programme by an eminent historian. Beatrice, her stepmother and her brother had been put to death for the murder of Count Cenci. They really had. It had all happened. Guido had painted the portrait while Beatrice was in prison. Later they had tortured her to extract a confession.

It wasn't the kind of piece, he decided, that one would ever want to see again or read or remember a line from.

When it was over they went backstage. They always did. Sheila, though in jeans and sweater now, still had a mask of gleaming white paint on her face and her hair top-knotted for execution as when she had cried:

'. . . Here, Mother, tie
My girdle for me . . . My Lord,
We are quite ready. Well, 'tis very well.'

Going home, Dora fell asleep in the train. Wexford found his mind occupied with the prosaic subject of typewriters.

It was the caretaker of the Haldon Finch Comprehensive School, primed by a phone call from the County Education Department, who showed them round. Wexford had been inside the school before, years ago when the nucleus of these buildings had been the old county high school. Incorporated into it now were the buildings next door, a former clinic and health centre, as well as a vast new assembly hall and the glass, concrete and blue-slate complex of classrooms, music room and concert hall, with the sports centre a gilt-roofed rotunda that the sun set ablaze.

'It reminds me,' Wexford said to Burden, 'of a picture I once saw of the Golden Temple at Amritsar.'

But the commercial department had no new building to house it. It was pushed away into three rear classrooms at the top of the old high school, as if the education authority had half-heartedly accepted the recent remark of a government minister that shorthand and typing were no part of education and should not be taught in schools. Wexford followed Burden and the caretaker up a remarkable (and remarkably battered) Art Deco marble staircase and along a wide vaulted passage. The caretaker unlocked and opened the double doors into the commercial department. These too were Art Deco, with parabolas and leaves in green ironwork on their frosted glass. The old high school had been built in 1930 and the classrooms inside looked as if they had received no more than one coat of paint since then. They were shabby, typically green and cream, with a view of rooftops and a brick well full of dustbins.

It was in the farthest room that the typewriters were. Wexford asked himself what he had expected. The latest in word processors? Obviously here the country's resources were mainly devoted to science and sport. Nor presumably would ARRIA encourage its members towards a secretarial career. There was not an electric typewriter among the machines and some of them looked older than the building itself. Burden, walking between the tables, had a piece of paper in his hand, probably with the faults of the typewriter they were looking for written on it. As if he couldn't remember without that! A break in the head of the upper-case A and the ascender of the lower-case t, a comma with a smudged head.

He felt a small flicker of excitement when he spotted the first of the Remington 315s.

'Can you type?'

'Enough to test these,' said Burden and impressed Wexford by getting to work and using all his fingers.

Nothing wrong with the A, the t and the comma on the first one. Burden slipped his paper into the roller of the second. The capital A wasn't all it might have been but neither was the B or the D or a lot of others. The lower-case faces and the comma seemed unflawed. He tried the third machine, the caretaker watching with the fascinated awe of one who expects the litmus paper to turn not red but all the colours of the spectrum. This typewriter, however, seemed without faults. It produced the best-looking copy so far. There was only one more. Burden slipped his paper in and this time, instead of 'Now is the time for All good men to come to the Aid of the party', typed 'A thousand ages in Thy sight are like an evening gone'. If he had been a Freudian, Wexford thought, he would have wanted to know why. Perhaps it was just done to astonish the caretaker. Anyway, whatever the reason, this wasn't the machine Rodney Williams's letter of resignation had been typed on.

'That's it then.'

'Show my four samples to the experts. We could be wrong.'

'We're not wrong. These are all the typewriters the school has?'

'Apart from them as has gone away to be serviced.'

'Now he tells me,' said Wexford.

'There's always some go away in the summer holidays. It's never the lot of them. They go in, like, rotation.'

'Do you know how many have gone and where?'

The caretaker didn't know the answer to either question. No more than, say, five, he thought. He had never heard the name of any firm which might be servicing the machines or seen a van arrive to take them away.

'We must be thankful,' Wexford said as they came out of the school, 'that at least it's an old manual portable we're looking for and not one of the modern kind with a golfball or daisywheel.'

'A what or a *what*?'

'Let's say with a detachable typeface that our perpetrator could simply have taken out and thrown away.'

School might have broken up but sport went on. Half a dozen boys in shorts and tee-shirts were running laps round the biggest playing field and on the tennis courts a doubles game and a singles were in progress. The umpire seats were empty but Caroline Peters was there in the role of coach, and as they approached the wire fencing Wexford saw that what he had supposed to be a singles match was in fact instructor and instructed, the pupil here being Veronica Williams.

The four doubles players were Eve and Amy Freeborn, Helen Blake and another girl he had never seen before. So there were actually seventeen- and eighteen-year-olds in this corner of Sussex he had never seen before? He was beginning to think he knew them all by sight and usually by name too. He and Burden went over to the fence and watched, as they had done that previous time. Caroline Peters glared but didn't come over to admonish. She knew who they were now.

It was clear from the first that Veronica was streets ahead of the other players, though two years younger than any of them. She was the best tennis player Wexford had ever seen on a local court. This time the discrepancy between what he saw on TV and what he saw at home did not seem quite so wide. She was a strong, lithe, fast player with a hard accurate backhand and a powerful smashing action. When Caroline Peters made her serve her service was as hard as Eve's but the balls struck the court well inside the line.

The doubles players changed ends. Eve looked in Wexford's direction and then ostentatiously away. Loyalty to the father he had had charged with possessing cannabis, he supposed. He had been getting a lot of stick of that kind lately. All part of a policeman's lot, no doubt. Veronica returned Caroline Peters's lob with a hard transverse drive which Caroline ran for but couldn't reach. It was a mystery, Wexford thought, where somebody got that kind of talent from. You couldn't imagine that finicking Wendy playing any sort of game or even walking more than half a mile, while Rodney Williams had been out of condition for years. Did the other Williams family play games? There had been a tennis racket up on Sara's bedroom wall, he remembered. Of course, the probable answer was that any healthy young girl keen on tennis could be coached to the standard of Veronica Williams. She was already sixteen. It was already too late for her to begin competing in anything much more significant than inter-school matches.

The girl whose face and name he didn't know served a double fault. One more of those and the set would be lost. She served one more of those and threw her racket down in the kind of petulance she wouldn't have known about if she hadn't watched Wimbledon on TV. Wexford and Burden walked back to the car.

'Have we got anything on the fingerprints found in Williams's car yet?' Burden asked.

'They took about sixty prints,' Wexford said, 'all made by nine people. By far the greater proportion were made by one man and they've more or less established that man was Williams.'

'I don't suppose his fingers were in very good shape after being in the ground for nine weeks.'

'Exactly. They matched the car ones to prints in his bedroom – well, bedrooms – of course. The other prints were made by two unknown men, and may well belong to whoever began the dismantling of Greta, by Joy, Wendy, Sara, Veronica, and two more women or girls who might be friends of the wives and daughters – or who might not. The steering wheel had been wiped.'

'Much what you would expect really,' said Burden.

Nicola Tennyson, Veronica's friend, was thrilled to have her fingerprints taken. She was unable to remember much about 15 April. Certain it was that she had been baby-sitting her brother that evening and Veronica had come in, but she couldn't remember times. Veronica and she were often in each other's homes, she said.

One of the two unidentified sets of fingerprints on Greta turned out to be hers.

13

Wheatley said that the woman who stabbed him had been more than commonly tall. Budd said that because he had only seen her sitting down he couldn't tell her height. That wasn't strictly true. He had seen her running off with the sack over her shoulder. The sack was the only thing he could really remember, that and the fact she had blonde hair. The girl who attacked Wheatley had 'brown or lightish' hair. She was eighteen or nineteen. Budd thought his assailant was twenty. Or twenty-five or -six. Or any age between eighteen and thirty.

In each case their wounds had been made with the blade of a large penknife. Not necessarily the same penknife, though. Not necessarily the same woman. Wexford asked himself what had been in the sack. He didn't think Budd had invented the sack. Budd wasn't endowed with enough imagination for that. There had been a sack all right, a black plastic dustbin liner. What had she been carrying it for and why?

It had been pouring with rain. Those plastic sacks were very good for keeping things dry. Keeping what dry? The bus stop was the nearest one to the place where they'd found Rodney Williams's body. But he had been dead six weeks by the night Budd was attacked. Wendy Williams wasn't particularly tall but she was blonde and she looked much younger than she was. To Budd she might seem in her early twenties.

She had begun a fortnight of her annual holiday. Wexford

thought to himself that she might be spending the major part of it at Kingsmarkham Police Station. He went with the car to fetch her.

Veronica was in the raspberry-ice-cream living room, seated at the glass-topped table, turning the pages of *Vogue*. He thought she looked like a teenage girl in a French film of the sixties. He hadn't seen many French films of the sixties but nevertheless the impression was there in Veronica's bandbox look, the beautifully cut, newly washed, pageboy hair, the clothes – primrose pinafore dress, starched white blouse, blue bootlace tie, white ankle socks, sky-blue sandals – that were just a little too young for her, the expression on her face that was 99 per cent innocence and 1 per cent calculation.

'I saw you playing tennis the other day.'

'Yes, I saw you too.'

Why the wary look suddenly, the shade of unease across that naivety?

'You're very good.'

She knew that already, she didn't need to be told. A polite smile and then back to *Vogue*. Wendy Williams came down the spiral staircase, walking slowly, giving him a voyeur's look if he had wanted it of shapely legs in very fine pale tights all the way up to a glimpsed border of cream lace. He wasn't looking, but out of the corner of his eye he saw her hold her skirt down as if he had been.

She had dressed up. Women these days didn't bother with fancy dressing except for special occasions, except when it was fun. That was general, not just the ARRIA view of things. For going down the cop shop, Wexford thought, you went in the jeans and shirt you wore around the house. But this was something that hadn't yet got through to Wendy Williams and maybe never would. She probably didn't possess a pair of jeans. And Veronica's would be the designer kind with Vidal Sassoon or Gloria Vanderbilt on the backside. Wendy had a pretty cotton dress on, the kind that needs a lot of ironing, a wide black patent belt to show she still had an adolescent waist and red wedge-heeled shoes that pinched where they touched.

The car filled with her perfume. Estée Lauder's White Linen, decided Wexford, who was good on scent. He made up his mind to take her up to his office, not into one of the interview rooms.

'You haven't told me much about this girlfriend of your husband's, Mrs Williams,' he said when they were there.

'I've told you all I know. I've told you it was a very young girl and that's all I know.'

'I don't think so,' he said. 'There's more if you search your memory.'

A secretive look was closing up her face. Why? Why should she want to conceal this girl's identity from him?

'I wish I'd never mentioned any girl to you!' Exasperated. The tone of a mother to a child who keeps nagging her about a treat she has promised him.

'You had an anonymous letter, you said.'

She hesitated. She opened her mouth to begin an explanation. He cut her short.

'You didn't keep it though. You burned it.'

'How did you know?'

'Mrs Williams, let me tell you what I do know. First, it's only in books that people burn anonymous letters. In real life they may not care much for them, they may even recoil from them in disgust, but they don't burn them. Most people don't have fires any more, for one thing. Where would you burn something?'

She didn't say anything. A sullen crushed look made her almost ugly.

'People who get anonymous letters may not like looking at them. Usually they put them away in a drawer in case or until we want to see them. Or there's the dustbin. You read somewhere that the requisite thing to do with an anonymous letter was burn it, didn't you? In a detective story probably. The truth is you never received one.'

'All right, I didn't.'

'Hasn't anyone ever told you you musn't tell lies to the police?'

He hadn't spoken harshly. His tone was almost bantering. It was mockery, even as mild as this, she couldn't stand. She flushed and her mouth set mulishly.

'I didn't tell lies. There was a girl.' Perhaps she could see he wasn't going to say anything for a moment or two. 'He was perverted about young girls, that's what it amounted to and it ruined my life.' Her voice rose, edgy and plaintive. 'I thought he was in love with me when we first met. I thought he loved me but now I know he just fancied me because I was young. And when Veronica was coming he had to marry me. Well, *marry*. It's easy to marry, isn't it? You can do it over and over again.

'I never had any life, I never had any youth. Do you know something? I'm thirty-two and I've never so much as been taken out to dinner in a decent restaurant by a man. I've never been abroad. I've never had a thing to wear that didn't come discount from Jickie's. I never even had an engagement ring!'

He asked her how she knew of the girl's existence. Just at this point Marion came in with coffee on a tray, three unprepossessing cheese sandwiches and three custard-cream biscuits. Wendy looked at the sandwiches and shook her head in a shuddery genteel sort of way.

He repeated the question.

'Rodney confessed.'

'Just like that? Out of the blue? You didn't suspect anything but he confessed to you he had a young girlfriend?'

'I told you.'

'Why did he confess? Was he intending to leave you for her? As in fact you thought he had done?'

That made her laugh in the way someone does who has knowledge of a secret you will never guess. He persisted and she looked exasperated, answering that she had told him already. She ate nothing, he ate a sandwich, leaving the rest for Marion, who had a hearty appetite. Afterwards, he thought, Wendy Williams would probably tell people she was kept at the police station for hours and not given a thing to eat or drink.

He asked her once more about 15 April. The evening. What time had she left Jickie's to drive home to Pomfret? All the staff at Jickie's had been questioned by Martin and Bennett and Archbold. They had forgotten. Why should they remember that particular evening? One of the girls on the fashion-floor pay desk said that if Mrs Williams hadn't actually left the building before nine, that would have been very late for her. On Thursdays she usually left as soon after eight as possible and had been known to leave at 7.30.

Wendy insisted she left at nine. She stuck to that. He left it. He said there was something he had to ask her. Seeing that her husband consistently neglected her and for two months she believed he had finally left her, had she formed a friendship with any other man?

'It would be a natural and normal thing to you. You're a very young woman still. You said yourself that you felt life and youth had been denied you.'

'Are you suggesting I was having a – a relationship with someone?'

'It would be very understandable.'

'I think that's disgusting! That's really immoral. I've got my daughter to think of, haven't I? I've got Veronica to set an example to. Just because Rodney behaved in that horrible way, that's no reason for me to do the same. Let me tell you, I've always been absolutely faithful. I've never looked at another man, it would never have entered my head.'

He was beginning to know her and her protests. He said not another word on that one but thought the more. It was afternoon now and Burden would be setting in motion their prearranged plan. It might not work, of course – and if it did what would it show or prove? He didn't even know if he expected it to work.

In the meantime he questioned her about her life, her feelings, her reactions. Still she hadn't said a word about the other Williams family. She was prepared to acknowledge Rodney Williams had married her bigamously while ignoring the existence of his first or true wife. You would have expected her natural curiosity to get the better of her. Was she rising above such human failings? That was a possible explanation.

'Mrs Joy Williams,' he said deliberately, 'has a son and daughter. Her daughter and Veronica are very much alike. Do you have any feelings about these people?' He was aware he sounded like a psychotherapist, though any interrogating policeman was one of those. But nevertheless he made a slight correction. 'Aren't you interested in knowing something about them?'

'No.' Once more she had flushed. She looked mulish. 'Why should I be? They're nothing to me. Rodney can't have cared much for them.'

'Why do you say that?'

She made a little gesture with her hands to indicate that the answer was obvious. Wexford said that was enough for today and he'd organize a car to take her home. They went down in the lift, timing it perfectly, for as the lift came to a stop and the doors opened Burden came walking across the black and white checkerboard floor towards it with Joy Williams beside him. Wexford spoke to Burden for the sake of stopping and saying something. The two women stood there, Joy staring at Wendy, Wendy contemplating the wall ahead of her as if it were the most fascinating example of interior decor since the cave paintings of Trois Frères.

They presented a contrast, pathetic and grotesque. It was almost too marked to be quite real. They were like a cartoon for an old-fashioned advertisement, the wife who doesn't use the face cream, floor polish, deodorant, stock cubes, and the wife who does. Joy had a cardigan on over a cotton dress with half its hem coming down. All her shoes had a curious way of looking like carpet slippers though they weren't. Wendy swayed a little on her high heels, craning her neck and putting on a winsome look. Wexford smelt a gush of White Linen from her, perhaps because she was sweating. The irony was that both these women had been rejected.

Burden and Joy went into the lift. The doors closed.

'Do you know who that woman was?'

'What woman?' said Wendy.

'I'm not talking about Detective Bayliss. The woman who has just gone up in the lift with Inspector Burden.'

She raised her eyebrows, moved her shoulders.

'That was Mrs Joy Williams.'

'His wife?'

'Yes,' said Wexford.

'She looked about sixty.'

Upstairs Burden was asking Joy about the phone call, the letter of resignation. Why had she gone out on the evening of 15 April instead of remaining at home to await her son's phone call?

'I can't be always at his beck and call,' she said, her voice full of bitterness. 'It's all one to him whether I'm there or not. He's his father all over again – indifferent. I've done everything for him, worshipped the ground he walked on. Might as well not have bothered. Do you know where he is now? In Cornwall. On holiday. That's all it means to him that his mother's a widow.'

It could just be true. It could just be that she had at last seen the results of spoiling a son. A quarrel, Burden thought, the day before Kevin returned to university. He could hear the things that would have been said – all right, just wait till next time you want something; you phone, my lad, but don't count on me being here . . . Yet there had been no sign since then of adoration flagging.

'Do you know who that woman was with Chief Inspector Wexford?'

'I can guess.' The harsh clattering laugh. 'Cheap little tart. I don't admire his taste.'

He asked her if Sara had a boyfriend. Incredibly, she said she didn't know. It was plain she didn't care. Hatred came into her eyes when her daughter's name was mentioned.

'And after all I've done for her,' said Joy as if their discussion had been on the subject of the host of services she had performed for Sara and the girl's ingratitude. Burden had her driven home. He felt as if he had been brought up against a wall, the solid brick an inch from his face.

Carol Milvey was not a member of ARRIA but she was eighteen years old and lived next door but one to Joy Williams. And it was her father, the boss of Mid-Sussex Waterways, who had found Rodney Williams's travelling bag in Green Pond, a coincidence which had never been explained. Sergeant Martin saw her. The interview was a brief one, for Carol Milvey had been ill in bed with tonsillitis on 15 April and had taken two days off school.

A further ten members of ARRIA were cleared, both for 15 April and the evening on which Brian Wheatley had been stabbed in the hand. It was August now and people were beginning to go away on holiday, ARRIA members surely included. The Anerley family and their daughter, the redheaded Nicola, had been in France since the end of the school term and were not expected back until 12 August. On this date too Pomfret Office Equipment Ltd were due to reopen after two weeks' holiday closure, a southern version of North Country wakes weeks, as Wexford remarked. If the typewriters missing from Haldon Finch were serviced in the neighbourhood it was with Pomfret Office Equipment they had to be. No other firm of typewriter engineers admitted to knowledge of their whereabouts.

The commerce department at Sewingbury Sixth Form College had been checked out. They had microcomputers, ACT Apricots, as well as four dedicated word processors, and their typewriters were ten highly sophisticated Brother machines. Kingsmarkham High School had one typewriter only in the building and that in the school secretary's office.

Kevin Williams came back from Cornwall and left again with six like-minded students to camp in the Channel Islands. The Harmers with Paulette's boyfriend went to North Wales for a week, leaving an Indian pharmacist and his wife, both highly qualified but jobless, in charge of shop and dispensary. Sara went nowhere. Sara stayed at home, awaiting no doubt the A-level results due the second or third week of the month, after the degree results and before the O-levels.

'I can't help wondering if there'll still be A-levels when this new baby of ours grows up,' said Burden. Nowadays he talked gingerly and awkwardly about the coming child but as if its birth were a certainty and its future more or less assured. 'I'll be an old man by the time she wants to go to university. Well, I'll be in my sixties. I'll be retired. Do you remember filling in those grant forms? Getting one's employer to vouch for one's earnings and all that? Still, by then they'll do it all on a computer, I suppose, a kind of twenty-first-century Apricot.'

'Or an Apple,' said Wexford. 'Why do computer makers call their wares after fruit? There must be some unexpected Freudian explanation.' A glazed look of boredom blanked Burden's face. 'Talking of unexpected explanations,' Wexford said quickly, 'do you realize there's one aspect of this case we've given no thought to? Motive. Motive has scarcely been mentioned.'

Burden looked as if he were going to say that the police need not concern themselves with motive, that perpetrators in any case often stated motives that seemed thin or incredible. But he didn't say that. He said hesitantly, 'Aren't we concluding Williams was killed in what ARRIA would call self-defence?'

'Surely the difficulty there is that if we assume – which we are doing – that the woman or girl who made the phone call and wrote the letter was Williams's girlfriend, why should she need to defend herself against him? Budd and Wheatley were attacked because they made sexual advances. But this girl, being his girlfriend, presumably welcomed his sexual advances.'

Burden said in his prudish way, 'That might depend on their nature.'

'You mean they were sadistic or he wanted to wear one of her nightdresses? We've no evidence Williams was funny in that way. And aren't you forgetting something? It looks as if this murder was somewhat premeditated. Williams was given a sleeping drug before he was stabbed. I don't see my way to accepting a theory that one day Williams suggested to his girlfriend that they have sex in this new naughty way, whereupon she substitutes a sedative for his blood-pressure pill and when he's asleep stabs him eight times with a French cook's knife.'

'Then what motive do you suggest?'

'I don't. I can't see a girlfriend killing him to be rid of him because surely all she had to do was give him the out, tell him to go back to his wife or wives. And although a girl could have killed him on her own, she couldn't have disposed of his body on her own. A girl with a jealous husband or boyfriend? ARRIA members don't have husbands. ARRIA members aren't supposed to get sufficiently involved with men for a triangular jealousy situation to arise. But is she an ARRIA member? Does she exist?'

'If one could only read the book of fate,' said Burden, unaware that he was quoting and no longer thinking about the Williams case anyway.

'If this were seen,' said Wexford, 'the happiest youth,

viewing his progress through, would shut the book and sit him down and die . . . '

He went home to fetch Dora and the two of them went to see Sheila in *Little Eyolf* at the Olivier.

14

Pomfret Office Equipment Ltd was open for business by 9.30 on the morning of 12 August. It was a shopfront with a big storage shed behind. The business was run by two men called Ovington, father and son. Edgar Ovington, the father, acknowledged at once that his firm serviced typewriters for the Haldon Finch Comprehensive School. The machines were usually attended to during the long summer holiday. His son had fetched the Haldon Finch machines the day before term ended, 26 July.

Wexford and Burden followed him into the shed at the back. It was full of typewriters, manuals, electric and electronic machines. They stretched away, rows of them ranked on slatted shelves, all labelled with tie-on luggage labels. Ovington pointed out the Haldon Finch typewriters, three on the lower shelf, two on the upper. The label on each said: H. Finch. Three portable Remington 315s, two Adler Gabrielle 5000s. Burden gave Ovington a condensed explanation of why they were looking for a particular typewriter and what made it particular. He asked for a sheet of paper. Ovington broke open a packet of 70-gramme white bond and peeled off two sheets from the top.

A flaw in the upper-case A, the ascender of the lower-case t and the head of the comma smudged. Burden slipped a sheet of paper into the roller of the first machine and typed a few lines from 'O God Our Help in Ages Past', the only hymn he knew by heart. No flaws. No flaws in the second machine either.

'You haven't put a new typeface on any of these machines?' Wexford asked.

'I haven't so much as touched them yet,' said Ovington.

Burden tried the third Remington. It was perfect, a better face than the others had, its need of servicing apparent only in the tendency of one or two of the keys to stick.

'These were the only typewriters fetched from the Haldon Finch Comprehensive School?'

'That's right. I label everything the minute it comes in to be on the safe side.'

'Yes, I see. So there's no possibility one of these machines could accidentally have been returned to a private customer?'

'It wouldn't go to a private customer if it was labelled Haldon Finch, would it?' said Ovington truculently.

He was a dour, prickly, suspicious man, always on the lookout for slurs anyone might cast on his ability or efficiency. Burden's request to try out any other Remington 315s there might be among the two hundred or so machines in the shed started him arguing and might have held them up but for the arrival, smiling and anxious to please, of the son, James Ovington. He was a tall, big-built young man with a toothy smile and a head as bald as an egg.

'Help yourselves. Be my guest.' The big white teeth glared as the lips stretched. 'Would you like me to have a sample of typing done from every machine here?' He meant it too, there was no sarcasm.

'We'll do it,' said Burden. 'And it's only the 315s we're interested in.'

Two more stood on the shelves besides the three he had tested. 'Sufficient is Thine Arm alone,' he typed, 'And our defence is sure'. Nothing wrong with that one. 'The busy tribes of flesh and blood With all their cares and fears, Are carried downward by the flood, And lost in following years.' No flaws.

'Thanks for your help,' said Wexford.

James Ovington said it was his pleasure and smiled so

widely that his dragon-seed teeth threatened to spill out. His father scowled.

'It's going to be in a ditch somewhere or a pond,' said Burden.

'Not in Green Pond, anyway. Or Milvey would have found it.' Wexford was reminded again of the as yet unexplained coincidence. The connecting link between Milvey and Rodney Williams wasn't Carol Milvey, for Carol Milvey had been ill with tonsillitis on the evening of Williams's death. So what was it? Connecting link there must be. Wexford refused to believe that it was by pure chance that Milvey had discovered his neighbour's overnight bag in Green Pond.

And coincidence became remarkable beyond any possible rational explanation, entering the realms of magic or fantasy, when a call came in from Milvey himself next day to say he had found not the typewriter but a long kitchen knife, a French cook's knife, in a small ornamental pond on the Green Pond Hall estate.

The three ponds in the old water garden, now a wilderness, had been silted up with soil and fine sand washed down by springs from Cheriton Forest. Wexford's men had cleaned out those ponds during their search of the estate but since that time a further silting-up had taken place. The prospective trout farmer had called Mid-Sussex Waterways in once more to attempt to find a solution to the problem of the clogged water course.

Had the knife been placed there since the police search? Or had it been washed down from a hiding place upstream? It was a large knife, the handle of ivory-coloured plastic six inches long, the blade nine inches, a right-angled triangle with the hypotenuse the cutting edge. It had a sharp and vicious-looking point. There were traces of grey mud in the rivet sockets of the handle but not a streak or pinpoint of rust anywhere. Wexford had the knife sent to

Forensics at Stowerton. The Milvey link was still a mystery to him. He confronted Milvey across his desk, at a loss for what to ask him next. The wild thought entered his head that Milvey and Joy Williams might have been lovers. It was too wild – not fat dull Milvey and draggle-tailed Joy. And if Milvey were involved in Williams's death, why should he produce the weapon?

He found himself reduced to saying, 'You do see, don't you, Mr Milvey, that this situation and your position in it is a very mystifying one. The man who lives next door but one to you is murdered. You find first the bag he had with him when he disappeared, then a knife that in all probability is the murder weapon.'

'Somebody,' said Milvey who didn't seem to see the point, 'had to find them sooner or later.'

'The population of Kingsmarkham is somewhere in the area of seventy-eight thousand souls.'

Milvey stared at him with bull-headed stupidity. At last he said with truculence, 'Next time I find something I reckon will help the police with their inquiries I'll keep quiet about it.'

While Forensics were testing the knife against Williams's wound measurements Sergeant Martin with Bennett and Archbold made inquiries as to its provenance. They listed thirty-nine shops and stores in the area where similar knives were sold. Only Jickie's, however, stocked that particular brand of French cook's knife.

'Wendy Williams may work there,' Wexford said, 'but everyone shops there. We do. You do. Martin's asking the staff in the hardware department if they can remember anyone recently buying a French cook's knife. You know how far that'll get us. Besides, they've stocked the things for the past five years. There's no reason to believe the knife was bought specifically to kill Williams. In fact, the chances are it wasn't.'

'Yes, we're still at square one,' Burden said.

'You're being faint-hearted. Come and spend an afternoon among the typewriters. I've a hunch I want to put to the test.'

Ovington senior was on his own. He tried at first to fob them off with pleas of pressure of work. Wexford suggested gently that this might be construed as obstructing the police in the course of their inquiries. Ovington, grumbling under his breath, led them once more into the shed at the back of the shop.

Walking between the rows, Wexford examined the labels tied to the machines.

'You always use this method of labelling?'

'What's wrong with it?'

'I didn't say there was anything wrong with it. I don't think it's very clear, that's all. For instance, what does "P and L" stand for?' He pointed to the labels on a pair of Smith Corona SX 440s.

'Porter and Lamb on the estate,' said Ovington gruffly. He meant the industrial estate at Stowerton.

'And TML?'

'Tube Manipulators Limited.'

'And you know absolutely what those initials – I might say codes – mean when you're returning machines? You know that "P and L" stands for Porter and Lamb and not, for instance, for Payne and Lovell, the hardware people in the High Street here?'

'We don't do any work for Payne and Lovell.' Ovington looked astonished.

'I think you understand me though. With this system of labelling mistakes could be made. I'll come to the point. "H. Finch" is rather a rough and ready way of indicating the Haldon Finch Comprehensive School.'

'It serves its purpose.'

'Suppose you had a customer called Henry Finch. What would stop his machine getting mixed up with the Haldon Finch ones?'

'We don't have a customer called Henry Finch, that's what.'

Burden said sharply, 'D'you have any customers called Finch?'

'We might have.'

It was the curious reply, or a version of it, Wexford had so often heard witnesses give in court when they did not want to commit themselves to a positive 'yes'. 'I might have', 'I may have done'. Ovington, in his greasy old suit, open-necked shirt, his chin pulled back into his neck and his lips thrust forward, looked shifty, guilty, suspected and suspicious, truculent for the mere sake of truculence.

'I'd like you to check, please.'

'Not Henry,' said Ovington. 'Definitely not. A lady. Not an H at all.'

'You're wasting my time, Mr Ovington.'

He was enjoying it, with sly malice. 'We did some repairs on a Remington for her a while back. Not a 315 though.' At last, scratching his head, 'I could look in the book.'

'This could be it,' Wexford said when he and Burden were alone for a moment. 'They could have got mixed up and sent the wrong one back.'

'Wouldn't she have noticed?'

'She might not be a regular typist. She might not have used the machine since its return.'

He began looking at labels on all the typewriters on the lower shelf on the left-hand side. P and L, E. Ten (what could that mean?), TML, HBSS, H. Finch, J. St G, M. Br . . . Ovington came back with a ledger.

'Miss J. Finch, 22 Bodmin Road, Pomfret. She collected the machine herself on July the twenty-sixth.' He slammed the book shut as if he had just proved or disproved something to his triumphant satisfaction.

July 26. The day the Haldon Finch machines were collected and brought here, Wexford thought. Did all this mean anything or nothing? Were the girlfriend and the girlfriend's typewriter after all sitting pretty somewhere in London or Brighton?

Neither he nor Burden knew where Bodmin Road was.

'You know something?' Burden said. 'Wendy Williams lives in Liskeard Avenue and Liskeard's a place in Cornwall. Bodmin's the county town of Cornwall. It may be just round the corner.'

'We'll look it up as soon as we get back.'

It was just round the corner. Liskeard Avenue, Falmouth Road, Truro Road, with Bodmin Road running crossways to connect them all.

'She was practically a neighbour of his,' Burden said, sounding almost excited. 'An ARRIA member, I bet you. Here she is on the Electoral Register. Finch, Joan B.'

'Wait a minute, Mike. Are we saying – are we assuming rather – that a Haldon Finch typewriter was collected by her in error or that it's her own typewriter she has, that this is the machine we're looking for, and we've stumbled upon her not by deduction but by pure luck?'

'What does that matter?' Burden said simply.

Twenty-two Bodmin Road was a small purpose-built block of four flats. According to the doorbells, J. B. Finch lived on the first floor. However, she was not at home either in the afternoon or at their two further calls at seven and eight in the evening. Wexford had been home an hour when a call came through to him to say a fourth man had been stabbed, this time in the upper arm, not a serious wound, though there had been considerable loss of blood.

The difference was that this time his cries were heard by two policemen sitting in a patrol car in a lay-by on the Kingsmarkham bypass. It was after sunset, the beginning of dusk. They had found the victim of the attack lying half across a public footpath, bleeding from a wound near his shoulder. While they were bending over him a girl came out from among the trees of the woodland on the north side of the path, announced her name as Edwina Klein and handed them a penknife from which she had wiped most of the blood.

15

ARRIA expected a show. Its members were in Kingsmarkham Magistrates' Court in force. Wexford had never seen the small wood-walled area that passed for a public gallery so full. Caroline Peters was there and Sara Williams, redhaired Nicola Anerley, Jane Gardner and the Freeborn twins, Helen Blake and Donella the black girl, the tennis player who wore glasses and the tennis player who did not.

It was to be a test case, of course. Wexford had guessed all of it pretty well before he talked to Edwina Klein. She had not exactly been an *agent provocateur*. It was a terrible world we lived in if a woman who chose to walk alone along a field path at dusk could be called that. But the truth was that Edwina had set out to walk there, and to do so evening after evening since she came down from Oxford at the end of June, in the expectation of being attacked. She had been frank and open with him, hiding nothing, admitting, for instance, that it was she who while home for a weekend had been Wheatley's assailant. For this reason he had decided not to oppose bail. She would talk freely to him again, she had promised and, with a faith that would have set the Chief Constable's hair standing on end, he believed her.

With Caroline Peters a founder member of ARRIA, she was a thin straight girl of medium height, fiercely intelligent, a pioneer and martyr. She was dressed entirely in black, black trousers, black roll-neck sweater, her hair invisible under a tightly tied black scarf. A raven of a woman, the only colour about her the tiny orange ARRIA badge pinned on near her left shoulder.

What did the girls in the public gallery expect? Something like the trial of Joan of Arc, Wexford supposed. All were ignorant of magistrates' court procedure, all looked disbelieving when in five minutes it was all over and Edwina committed for trial to the crown court. The charge was unlawful wounding. She was released on bail in her own surety of £1000 and for a similar sum in that of an elderly woman, her great-aunt, not old enough to have been a suffragette but looking as if she might regret having missed the chance.

The ARRIA contingent filed out, muttering indignantly to each other. Helen Blake and Amy Freeborn picked up the orange banner with a woman-raven on it that they had been obliged to leave outside. The others fell in behind them and what had been a group became a march. 'We shall overcome,' they sang, 'we shall overcome some day.' They marched behind the banner up to the police station forecourt and across it and out into the High Street.

Joan Finch was sixty-five years old, perhaps more. Wexford wasn't surprised. There must be few women called Joan under fifty, and even fifty years ago Joan was becoming an old-fashioned name. It was Burden who had built so much on the chance of her being the girl they were looking for.

She took them into the poky little den, designed for surely no more than luggage storage, where she worked, and showed them the typewriter, a big manual Remington at least as old as herself. Fingers today would flinch at that iron forest of keys that took so much muscle power to fell it.

As Ovington had told them, she had collected it from Pomfret Office Equipment on 26 July. There was no doubt at all that it was hers. It had been her mother's before her and seemed as much of a family heirloom as any clock or piece of china.

Of sole significance to Wexford and Burden was the fact

that it wasn't a Remington 315 portable machine. This was something Miss Finch seemed unable to grasp. She insisted on sitting down at the typewriter and producing for them a half page of men coming to the aid of the party and quick brown foxes. The Ovingtons had done a good job. There wasn't a flaw or an irregularity to be seen.

They had lunch at the little bow-fronted wine bar two doors away. Pamela Gardner was at a corner table lunching with a woman friend. She looked through Wexford with a contemptuous stare. Her daughter had bounced along that morning, singing as heartily as anyone and a good deal more loudly, waving to him as if they were old friends. Edwina Klein was coming to the police station at 2.30 to talk to him. It was no part of the conditions of her bail that she should do this but he felt sure she wouldn't fail him. Burden said, 'Only three weeks to go now.' He was talking of the coming baby. 'They say it'll be on time. They don't really know though.'

'There's more they don't know than they ever let on.'

Burden picked at his quiche. 'She had the heartburn at the beginning and I'm getting it now.' He was pale, bilious-looking.

'We'll see if the Harmers can supply you with an indigestion remedy.'

The Pre-Raphaelite head of Paulette could be seen through the window of the dispensary where she was evidently helping her father. It was Hope Harmer who served Burden. She seemed discomfited by their visit, unable perhaps to realize that policemen too have private lives and are as liable to bodily ills as anyone else.

'Did you have a good holiday?' Wexford asked her.

'Oh yes, thank you, very nice. Very quiet,' she added as people do when describing their Christmas celebrations as if to admit to liveliness and merriment were to deny respectability. 'All good things come to an end though, don't they? We could have stayed away another week only my daughter's expecting her A-level results. They're due any day.'

Sara Williams must also be on tenterhooks then . . . 'Another would-be doctor in the family?'

'No, no. Paulette's hoping to follow in her Daddy's footsteps.'

She was all bright placatory smiles, accompanying them to the door when they left like an old-fashioned shopkeeper. Wexford walked into the police station just before 2.30. Edwina Klein was waiting for him, shown upstairs to his room, and he felt relief at the sight of her in spite of his confidence that she would keep her word. With her, seated in the other visitor's chair, like a chaperone, was the aunt.

Wexford was surprised. He had seen Edwina as the very epitome of independence, of self-reliance.

'I happen to be a solicitor as well as an aunt.'

'Very well,' said Wexford, 'but this won't be an interrogation, just a talk about various aspects of this case.'

'That's what they all say,' said the aunt whose name was Pearl Kaufmann. In appearance she was rather like Virginia Woolf in her latter days, tallish, thin, long-faced, long-nosed, with a full mouth. She wore a navy blue silk dress, mid-calf length, and clumpy white sandals that made her feet look large.

Edwina was still in the black she had worn in court but with the roll-necked sweater changed for a sleeveless black tee-shirt that was better suited to the heat of the day. The ARRIA badge had been transferred to this. Edwina had sunglasses on which turned her face into an expressionless mask.

'He treated me exactly as if I was a prostitute,' she had said to him of Wheatley at that earlier conversation. The black glasses hadn't covered her eyes then. They had been bright with eagerness, with earnestness, with the zeal of youth. 'Not that there's anything wrong with being a prostitute. That's OK, that's fine if that's where you're at. It's just the way men *assume* . . . '

'Only some men.'

'A lot. He didn't even talk to me. I tried to talk to him. I asked him where he worked and where he lived. When I asked him where he lived he gave a strange sort of laugh as if I'd said something *wrong*.'

'Why did you ask him for a lift? To provoke exactly the sort of situation that arose?'

'No, I didn't. Not that time. I admit I did last night but it was different with the man in the car. I'd had a lift from London to Kingsmarkham and the guy couldn't take me any farther.' She seemed to consider. 'It was because of what happened in the car that I decided to try walking in the forest and see.'

'You'd better tell me what happened in the car, hadn't you?'

'He pulled into a lay-by. He did talk then. He said, "Come on, we'll go in the wood." I didn't know what he meant, I really didn't. Do you know what he thought? He thought I wanted paying first. He said, "Will ten pounds do?" And then he touched me.' Edwina Klein laid her right hand on her left breast. 'He touched me like I'm doing now. Like it was a tap or a switch. He didn't try to put his arms round me or kiss me or anything. It was just offering to pay and feeling the switch. I took out my knife and stuck it in his hand.'

There had been no aunt present when she talked to him then and no black circles to take the character from her face. Her manner now was more subdued, less indignant. Her experience of the court had perhaps chastened her. She waited almost meekly for him to begin questioning her. Miss Kaufmann sat looking at Wexford's wall map with simulated interest.

'Have you stabbed any other men?' he said abruptly, knowing the remark would be objected to.

Edwina shook her head.

'We won't mind about that, Mr Wexford.' It seemed highly suitable to the aunt's manner and appearance that she should use this obsolete Victorian phrase. She elucidated with something more contemporary. 'We'll forget you said that.'

'As you please,' said Wexford. 'When the police use *agents provocateurs* – as, for example, in the case of a policewoman sitting in a cinema where a member of the audience is suspected of assaulting women – the public, particularly the public of your sort of persuasion, gets up in arms. There's an outcry when a young policeman deliberately uses a public lavatory frequented by homosexuals. In other words, it's not all right for them to do this in the interests of justice but it's all right for you to in the mere interest of a principle. There's rather a crude name for what you did and were, isn't there?'

He had been too mealy-mouthed, too gentlemanly, he quickly saw.

'A pricktease,' she said flatly. The aunt didn't move an eyelid. 'I didn't do that. I didn't do anything but go for a walk in a wood. I wasn't provocatively dressed.' Scorn came into her voice now and she lifted up her head. 'I wouldn't be! I had jeans on and a jacket. I never wear make-up, not ever. The only thing I did to provoke anyone was *be* there and be a woman.'

'I think my niece is saying,' said Miss Kaufmann dryly, 'that it isn't possible to be a woman in certain places with impunity. She was out to prove this and she did prove it.'

He let it go. He left it. He felt the force of what the two women said and he knew it was true, and that this was an instance of a policeman knowing that the opposing argument is sounder than his own but of having to stick to his own just the same. That all women who intended to go about by themselves at night should learn self-defence techniques seemed to him the best answer. The alternative was that men's natures should change and that was something which might slowly happen over centuries but not in years or even decades. He wrote busy nothings on the sheet of paper in front of him to fill thirty seconds of time and keep them temporarily silent. At last he lifted his head and looked at Edwina Klein. For some reason, perhaps because his eyes were naked, she took off her glasses. Immediately she looked earnest again and very young.

'You know the Williams family, I think?'

She was prepared for this. Somehow she knew that this was what she was really there for. Her answer surprised him.

'Which Williams family? There are two, aren't there?'

'There may be two hundred in this neighbourhood for all I know,' he said sharply. 'It's a common name. I'm talking about the Williams family that live in Alverbury Road, Kingsmarkham. The girl is called Sara. She was in court this morning. I think you know her.'

She nodded. 'We were at school together. She's a year younger than I am.'

'Did you know Rodney Williams, the dead man?'

She was very quick to reply. Miss Kaufmann looked up as if warningly. 'Him and Mrs Williams, yes. Sara and I used to do ballet together.' She smiled. 'Believe it or not.' Miss Kaufmann cast up her eyes as if she could hardly believe it. 'They'd come for Sara or one of them would. I remember him because he was the only father who ever came. Sometimes he'd come and sit through the whole class.'

Watching pubescent girls in little tutus, thought Wexford, or more likely leotards these days.

'You asked me which family I meant,' he said.

'I slightly know the other one.' She lifted her shoulders. 'Veronica Williams looks exactly like Sara.'

He felt a tightening of nerves. She might be a link between the two families. She was the only person he had yet talked to who knew – or admitted to knowing – both sets of Williamses.

'You were aware that they were half-sisters then? You knew Williams was their father?'

'No. Oh no. I suppose I thought – well, I didn't think

about it. I honestly don't know, really. Perhaps that they might be cousins?'

'When did you last see Rodney Williams?'

'Years ago.' She was becoming nervous, frightened. It meant nothing, it was evidence only of her realization that she had been brought here to face one sort of ordeal and, that over, was being subjected to another of an unexpected kind. 'I haven't seen him for years.'

'Then how do you know Veronica?'

No dramatic *crise de nerfs* and no hesitation either. 'I played tennis against her. When I was at school.'

'She's three years younger than you.'

'OK. Sure. She was a sort of child prodigy. She was in Haldon Finch's first six when she was under fourteen.'

It was all reasonable, more than plausible. She had been in Oxford the night Rodney Williams died, having gone up early, a week before her term began. She had told him so last evening and told him, in grave and careful detail, whom to check this with. Bennett was in Oxford checking now but Wexford had little doubt Edwina hadn't lied to him.

'You knew both families,' he said now, 'but you didn't know, so to speak, they were one family? You didn't know Rodney Williams was the father of Veronica as well as of Sara and Kevin?'

'Kevin? I've never even heard of him before.'

'Sara's older brother.' He decided to be entirely frank with her. Miss Kaufmann sat watching him, an acid twist to her mouth. 'They didn't know of the existence of the others,' he said. 'The Pomfret family didn't know of the existence of the Kingsmarkham family and the Kingsmarkham family didn't know of the existence of the Pomfret family until quite a while after Rodney Williams was dead. So if you knew, that must mean you also knew Rodney Williams was a bigamist or at least a married man maintaining two households. And if you knew that how did you know it?'

'I didn't.'

The cool negative disappointed him. He had felt on the brink of a breakthrough. But she qualified it.

'I didn't know. I said they looked alike, I'd noticed that, and I remember once saying to my aunt that they must be cousins.' Edwina looked at Miss Kaufmann and Miss Kaufmann nodded in a rapid impatient way. 'I didn't know either of them well,' Edwina said. 'You've got to remember that. I'd never spoken more than a few words to Veronica. And Mrs Williams, that's the real wife, I've seen her about but she's forgotten who I am or something, and as far as the other one goes I was just a customer.'

He had nothing else to ask her. She had stabbed Brian Wheatley and Peter John Hyde, her assailant in the wood, but he was certain she hadn't killed Williams. If a woman had done that she would have needed a second to help her.

'That's all then, thank you, Miss Klein.'

She got up and walked slowly and gracefully to the door, holding herself erect but with her head slightly bowed. They had the same figure, the same walk, this aunt and niece, though fifty years separated them. What would become of Edwina Klein now? It was inevitable she would be found guilty. Would her college have her back? Or was her whole future spoiled? Had she blown it for the sake of a lost cause? At the door, just before he opened it for her, she said, 'There's one thing. You said the Pomfret Williamses and the Kingsmarkham Williamses didn't know about each other. For the sake of setting the record straight, that's not right.'

The excitement was back, drying his throat. 'What do you mean?'

'What I say. They did know about each other.'

He took his hand from the door and leaned against it like someone barring egress. But Edwina Klein stood there willingly, looking a little puzzled, the aunt bored but patient.

'How do you know that?'

'Because I've seen them together,' she said.

Relief ran over him like sweat. He felt cool and lightheaded with it. She was aware now that she had told him something revelatory, unguessed at, and her face, close to his, was full of alert inquiry.

'Whom did you see together?' he asked her.

'Those two women. I saw them in the Precinct Café in Kingsmarkham having coffee together.'

'When? Can you remember when?'

If it were a week ago or even a month ago it meant nothing.

'Last Christmas, I think. It must have been Christmas or Easter for me to have been home. The only weekend I've been home was when *Wheatley* gave me that lift.' Edwina put infinite scorn into the pronunciation of his name. 'It wasn't then and it wasn't Easter. I know it can't have been because there was snow on the ground.'

'Snow fell,' said Miss Kaufmann, helpful now her niece was not directly threatened, 'during the first week of January.'

'It must have been then,' said Edwina.

She smiled, as if pleased to have been of help at last. He knew she hadn't lied.

16

As Wexford opened the gate of 31 Alverbury Road the postman was coming down the path, a wad of mail fastened with a rubber band in his left hand. None of it apparently was for 29 and his next call was at Milvey's, two doors down. Watching him, Wexford suddenly understood how Milvey came into the case. There was no coincidence at all, it was all simple and logical, only he had been putting the cart before the horse . . .

He rang the bell. As he did so St Peter's clock struck nine. It was Sara who opened the door and so quickly he knew she must have been standing directly behind it. She was holding a paper.

'Two As and a B,' she said, and smiled with gratification.

She had spoken as if the sole purpose of his call had been to hear about her A-level results. Before she closed the door she must have seen the police car outside with Donaldson at the wheel and Marion Bayliss in the back.

'Congratulations,' Wexford said. 'Where's your mother?'

She didn't answer. She might not have heard for all the notice she took.

'St Biddulph's told me they'd take me with three Bs or two Bs and an A, so this is rather better.'

Frenetic excitement was in the girl's eyes, an excitement that was manic and all the more disconcerting for being under such tight control. He had seen her as a Botticelli girl, mild-faced, tranquil, with a spring-like innocence. Primavera should not tremble with triumph nor Venus's eyes glitter.

'I'm going to phone my cousin Paulette, find out how she did.'

To crow a little? Or to be kind? Joy Williams came out from the kitchen, dressed as he had never seen her before. He hadn't told her but perhaps she had guessed she would be meeting Wendy again. Or Wendy herself had told her the evening before? He was prepared for that. He rather hoped they realized he knew of their prior acquaintance. Joy wore a clean, tidy skirt and blouse. She had washed her hair and smudged lipstick on her mouth, in the uncertain slapdash way women do who seldom wear it and somehow feel ashamed to do so. Probably she always dresses up when she and Wendy meet, he thought. There would be rivalry there even if they were allied in a common hatred of Williams. Besides, an alliance would not mean they actually *liked* each other . . .

Sara could be heard on the phone. 'Have they come? Well?'

Not much of a bedside manner. He imagined her talking in that hectoring way to a patient. A hard, neurotic little go-getter, he thought her, without an atom of concern for the mother whom the police suspected of murdering her father.

'That's not bad though, is it?' she was saying. 'It's not as if you need As or even Bs.'

Patronizing. Somewhat lofty. The pharmacist, of course, was the poor man's doctor, or the doctor for the faint-hearted. 'I'll ask the chemist to give me something for my throat.' Or my head, back, cystitis, bleeding, lump in the breast . . . He took Joy out and closed the front door behind them.

Sergeant Martin and Polly Davies brought Wendy in. The evening before she had been in tears of vexation at missing a day's work but that she could have refused to come – that the police were still in a position only to ask and persuade – seemed no more to have occurred to her than to Joy. They were not blessed with lawyers for aunts. The senior wife – the Sultana Valideh – was already seated in the interview room when Wendy was brought in, the expressionless face averted, the dark brown animal eyes staring past her at the window.

Wendy wore a printed smock dress, Kate Greenaway-like, in a Laura Ashley print, at the neck and wrists frills tied with bows. She had white tights on and white shoes. While the sergeant and Polly stood by (Polly told Wexford later) Wendy had taken her daughter Veronica in her arms and hugged her in a highly emotional way, bringing a fresh rush of tears. Veronica had looked very taken aback. But Wendy had pressed her close to her, stroking her hair, almost as if she expected never to see her again. And Polly, who was a reader of romantic period fiction, said it was like Marie Antoinette setting off in the tumbril.

'Farewell, my children, for ever! I am going to your father.'

Now all that remained as evidence of this scene was the swollen pinkness of Wendy's face. She gave Wexford a piteous look. She would have preferred Burden to interrogate her, she found him more sympathetic than this elderly, hard, sardonic man, but Burden wasn't there. He was in Alverbury Road in conversation with Mrs Milvey.

Wexford said, and he seemed to be addressing either or both of them, 'Which of you first found out the other existed?'

It was Wendy who answered. Her voice was even more fretful than usual. 'I don't understand what you mean.'

'I'll put it another way. When did you first discover Rodney Williams had a wife? And you, Mrs Williams, when did you find out your husband had "married" again?' He put very audible inverted commas round that past principle. 'Well?' he said. 'I know you haven't been truthful with me. I know you knew each other. The question is when did you first know?'

'I never knew she existed till you told me.' Joy spoke in her weary lifeless way. 'When you told me my husband was a bigamist on top of all the rest.'

'All what "rest", Mrs Williams?'

'Lying to me about his job for a start.'

Wendy murmured something.

'I'm sorry, Mrs Williams, I didn't catch that.'

'I said "having other women". I meant that's what the rest was, having other women.'

'He never had other women,' said Joy. She was responding to Wendy's prompting but she wasn't speaking to her. It was Wexford she was addressing. 'He had *her* but he never had others.'

'Let her delude herself if she wants,' said Wendy to no one in particular, lifting her shoulders and smiling very faintly.

'When did you first meet her, Mrs Williams?' Wexford was finding it a shade awkward, their both sharing the name. He got up and came round the table to address the words specifically to Wendy. Joy burst out, 'You've no business to call her that! She's no right to that name. She's Miss Whatever-she-used-to-be. You call her that!'

'The manners of a fishwife,' said Wendy. 'She's as common as dirt. No wonder he came to me.'

'Nasty little bitch! Look at her, dressed up like a kid!'

They're staging it, Wexford thought, they must be. It's all set up for my benefit, rehearsed as like as not. He called the two women quietly to order.

William Milvey was at home that day. The offices of Mid-Sussex Waterways were in his house and he was awaiting the visit of the VAT inspector. That was who he thought Burden was and for some moments they talked at cross-purposes, having one of those conversations so amusing to hearers and so frustrating to the participants.

Their hearer in this case was Mrs Milvey, a big-built

lady, very ready with her laughter. She laughed merrily at their discomfiture. But Burden's troubles were quickly over. After that all went smoothly and it turned out to be as Wexford had supposed.

'The wife's a director of our company just as much as me,' Milvey said importantly. 'And naturally she knows the ins and outs of the business equally to what I do.'

'I have to know where he's going to be every day in case there's phone calls,' said Mrs Milvey, who was less pompous than her husband. 'The fifteenth of April? I'll have a look in the book, shall I, Bill?'

At this point the VAT inspector did arrive, a man in his early twenties by the look of him, carrying a briefcase. Milvey seemed reluctant to absent himself from the more interesting (and perhaps less alarming) examination but he was obliged to go. He took the VAT man into his office and closed the door. Mrs Milvey smiled comfortably at Burden.

'From Easter right up till the end of April they was working up Myringham way,' she said, referring to the ledger she was holding. 'They never started on Green Pond till a month later.'

'Are you sure?'

'Positive. No doubt about it. It's down here in black and white. Green Pond, May the thirty-first. Besides, I remember it all now. Bill had a job lined up for the end of May, a big drainage job over to Sewingbury, and the chap cancelled at the last minute. But as luck would have it, this trout farm chap at Green Pond had been given his name and he rung up and said could he drag the pond? Well, Bill happened to be free on account of the cancellation. Must have given the trout farm fella a bit of a surprise, him saying yes, I'll start prompt on Monday.'

The office door opened again and Milvey put a hand out for his book. His wife gave it to him.

'Did you tell anyone?'

'I expect so. There was no secret about it, it was open

and above board. You like to have a bit of news to tell folks, don't you? Now you're wanting to know if I told my neighbour Mrs Williams, aren't you?'

'Did you?'

'I never knew a thing about her husband then, mind you. I met her going down to the shops. Bill was getting the van out. I said something like, Monday he'll be doing a job at Green Pond Hall. There's going to be a trout farm, did you know? Something like that.'

'But you definitely told her your husband would be dragging the pond on Monday, May the thirty-first?'

'I couldn't see it would do any harm, could I?'

Had it? Wexford hadn't been entirely correct in his supposition, which was that Mrs Milvey had told Joy the pond had already been dragged or was not to be dragged until a much later date. But this gave a different – and incomprehensible – look to things. If Joy had known Green Pond was to be dragged on the following Monday, the pond into which she had dumped her husband's travelling bag, wouldn't she have retrieved it during the weekend? The alternative possibility was that she had hidden it elsewhere and only put it in Green Pond when *she knew it was to be immediately dragged*. Why should she do such a thing, why behave so absurdly?

This was a hunch of Wexford's that had gone awry. Burden was on his way to put the second one to the test. They seemed no nearer, as far as he could see and in spite of Edwina Klein's revelation, to breaking the case. Next week he would probably start his paternity leave . . .

Bald-headed James Ovington, the son, was alone in charge of Pomfret Office Equipment. His ingratiating smile was as broad as ever. Burden noticed a new mannerism, a nervous way he had of rubbing his hands together. At any rate, the dour and obstructive father was nowhere around.

'Now can I help? Tell me what I can do.'

'You have a method of labelling your machines here,' said Burden. 'Not exactly a code, a kind of speedwriting.

Last time we were here we noticed one labelled "E. Ten". I wondered what that stood for. It wasn't a Remington 315, of course, we'd have pounced on it if it had been. This is a kind of shot in the dark and I daresay I'm not making myself too clear.'

'It's clear enough you want to know what "E. Ten" stands for and that's easy.' Nevertheless, he hesitated and Burden wondered why a shade of unease seemed to cross his face.

'Eric Tennyson,' Ovington said. 'That's who it is, that's who "E. Ten" stands for.'

Second time lucky . . . 'I don't suppose you know if he has a daughter called Nicola?'

'Well, I do know as a matter of fact. The answer's yes.'

Veronica Williams's friend, her home the house to which Veronica regularly went on Tuesdays. But the typewriter labelled 'E. Ten' wasn't a Remington 315. Unless . . .

'An Olivetti,' said Ovington. 'They've got another machine. I don't rightly remember what. She types stuff for people, I mean does it for a living.' The uneasy look was back again. 'I may as well tell you,' he said as if about to make a confession of something that for a long while had weighed heavily on him. 'They're friends of mine. I knew I ought to tell you last time you were here.'

'But why shouldn't they be friends of yours, Mr Ovington?'

'Well . . . They're friends of Mrs Williams too. I mean the Mrs Williams whose husband got killed, the one you're making inquiries about. I mean that's where I met her, in their house.'

'Are you trying to tell me something, Mr Ovington?'

This fresh smile, a forced straining of the muscles, turned his face into a gargoyle. He rubbed his hands briskly, then clasped them behind his back to prevent a repetition of the gesture. Light from the shallow overhead lamps in the shed shone with a yellow gleam on the hairless head. Why were the heads of bald men compared to eggs?

Ovington's head more than anything resembled a polished pebble.

'What is it you're saying, Mr Ovington?'

'I've been getting friendly with her. With Mrs Williams. There was nothing wrong, I don't mean that. I met her at Eric's and we'd have a drink sometimes, go for a walk, that sort of thing. When it looked as if that husband of hers had finally – well, when it looked as if he'd gone for good, I – I hoped things could get more serious.' He spoke jerkily, floundering, hopelessly unable to handle the situation he had got himself into. 'There was nothing *wrong*. I'd like to repeat that.'

Burden thought irrelevantly that Wendy Williams must be attracted by bald men, first Rodney with his exaggerated forehead, naked as an apple, then this pebble-head.

'But I thought,' Ovington said earnestly, 'that it would be wrong of me – disloyal, you know – to deny the relationship at this juncture, sort of deserting the sinking ship when you hear the cock crowing, if you get my meaning.'

More or less Burden did get it. He thought of the joy Wexford would have in that gloriously mixed metaphor. Now for the Tennysons. Half an hour later he was in their house on the Haldon Finch side of Pomfret, being told by Mrs Tennyson that her daughter was camping in Scotland till the end of the month but could she help him?

Her husband had fetched the repaired and serviced Olivetti from Pomfret Office Equipment three days before. Yes, she had her small portable for use when the other one was away for its annual overhaul. She showed it to him: a Remington 315.

Burden stuck the sheet of paper she gave him into the roller. 'A thousand ages in Thy sight, Are like an evening gone . . .' A flaw in the apex of the capital A, the ascender of the lower-case t, the head of the comma . . .

'I'd never seen her in my life till you had us meet here.'

That was Wendy. Joy said nothing.

'I put it to you that you'd known each other for a long time. I suggest it was like this: Mrs Joy Williams came into Jickie's as a customer one day and in conversation you discovered the link between you. This happened a year ago. You've been in touch with each other ever since.'

Joy gave one of her cold rattling laughs that had something in it of the cackle of a game bird.

'If I'd known about her why should I pretend I didn't?' said Wendy.

Joy answered. She didn't exactly address Wendy, she hadn't yet done that except to abuse her, but she made her first statement not inimical to the other Mrs Williams.

'If her and me knew each other he thinks we might have murdered Rod.'

'I'm more likely to have murdered *her*,' said Wendy in a lofty voice. She looked down and noticed a ladder in her pale milk-coloured tights. It crept up the outside of her right leg like a millipede. Joy noticed it too. She fixed her eyes on the slowly mounting run and her mouth moved. It was nearly a smile.

Wexford said, looking at Joy, 'Someone phoned Sevensmith Harding on Friday, April the sixteenth, to say Rodney Williams was ill and wouldn't be coming to work. The girl who took the call isn't in much doubt that it was your voice, Mrs Williams.'

'She doesn't know my voice. How could she, whoever she is? Aren't you forgetting, I didn't know Rod worked there?'

The door opened and Burden put his head round. Wendy was licking her finger and dabbing at the ladder with her wet fingertip, dabbing as it happened in vain, for the ladder quite suddenly crept another half-inch. It was this which might have occasioned Joy's rattle laugh. Wexford got up and went out of the room, leaving the two women with the two women detectives.

Burden had sent his typing sample to the forensics lab.

He told Wexford the substance of his interview with Mrs Tennyson. She had typed no letter of resignation herself and no one had asked her to do such a thing. Wendy Williams she had known for years, though her acquaintance with Rodney had been slight. Their daughters were the same age, were at school together, were 'best friends'.

'Could Wendy have typed it?' Wexford asked him. 'I mean, could she have had access to this machine? If this killing was premeditated, and it looks as if it was, she could have typed that letter days or even weeks before.'

'The Tennyson woman shuts herself up in a room she uses as an office and types for three or four hours a day. As a regular thing she uses the Olivetti and the Remington isn't even kept in there. It's usually in a cupboard in the hall unless the husband Eric wants it or the daughter Nicola uses it to type a school essay. Apparently, they're allowed to do that at the Haldon Finch. Could you credit it?'

'It seems a sensible and harmless practice,' said Wexford. 'Was Wendy ever alone in that house?'

'Early in April she came to call for Veronica, take her home or something. It was dark or late or she was passing. Anyway, the two girls were still out and Mrs Tennyson was typing something. She left Wendy alone for at most ten minutes, she says, until she finished off what she was doing.'

'Wendy would have to know the machine was there. She would have to have paper. But I agree it goes a long way to answering the question of how and where the letter was typed. As to typewriters, what better than to use one that was normally kept shut up in a cupboard? It was by the merest luck that we got on to it.' He listened while Burden told him about Ovington. 'Is that a motive, Mike? We keep coming back to that, the lack of motive. But if Wendy wanted to marry Ovington . . .'

'Who did Joy want to marry?'

'Yes, OK, I see your point. If they did it they did it together and Joy wouldn't be likely to help murder Rodney so that Wendy could marry someone else.' Wexford brought his fist to his forehead and drummed against it. 'I'm a fool! There's no motive. If Wendy knew about Joy she also knew she wasn't married to Rodney, so there was no legal bar to her marrying someone else . . . What about the knife, the weapon we're never going to prove *was* the weapon beyond a doubt? It could have been Joy's or Wendy's.'

'Wendy works at Jickie's and Jickie's stock those knives.'

'Wendy works there but the whole neighbourhood shops there.' Wexford thought for a moment. 'Among the stuff we found in Rodney Williams's bedroom in Liskeard Avenue,' he said, 'was an estimate from a firm of decorators for painting Wendy's living room. When we saw that room it had obviously been painted very recently. By that firm? By another? By Wendy herself? I think we ought to find out, don't you?'

Burden looked at him. They were both thinking that Rodney Williams had been stabbed to death. One of the knife thrusts had pierced the carotid. 'Yes, I do,' he said.

The day was very warm and close, a heavy, sultry, almost sunless day of the kind that only comes as August wanes. For the few moments he and Burden were in his office, the window open and the half-closed blinds swaying slightly in a hint of breeze, he had kept his jacket off. Now he put it on again and went back downstairs to the interview room where the two women were.

17

A picture of Joy and Wendy leaving Kingsmarkham Police Station was on most front pages of the national press next day. The more sensational of the newspapers managed to give the impression that they were not leaving but entering and that readers would not be too wide of the mark in concluding they had never left. Joy had her hand up over her face, Wendy looked piteously into the cameras, a distraught waif in her little-girl smock. The ladder in her tights was cruelly evident. Burden stood by, cool and rather aloof in a newish suit.

'You look young and handsome,' said Jenny at the breakfast table. 'You look so thin!' She shifted her huge weight, pushing back her chair.

'It's the worry.'

'I expect it is, poor Mike.' She put up her arms and hugged him. It was now only possible for her to do this while sitting down. He held her and thought, It may still be all right, we may still survive.

He went out before nine into a morning that was anything but fresh, a grey, sultry, sticky day. The sky was a flat, very pale grey with the sun a puddle of white glowing through it. This was the kind of day, he thought, that only England knows. Fifty of them can compose a summer.

How many builders and decorators were there in Pomfret? In Kingsmarkham? Not just the established firms but the one-man bands, the man who works in his spare time for money in the back pocket? With luck the Pomfret Williamses had availed themselves of the services of the firm who sent Rodney the estimate.

He didn't go to the police station first, so he was not present when Hope Harmer phoned to say her daughter was missing, had not been home all night or reappeared that morning.

John Harmer was in his dispensary and business was as usual. That is, when customers wanted soap or disposable razors instead of a prescription made up he came out and served them. He refused to believe anything had happened to his daughter. She was a grown woman well able to take care of herself as her prowess at that judo stuff evinced. Her absence probably had something to do with this women's movement nonsense.

Paulette's mother had come to work but only perhaps because of the pressures put on her by her husband. It was from there that she had phoned, the culminating act of a scene between them, Wexford guessed. She was in a piteous state. Hope Harmer was a woman whom it suited only to be happy. She was easily content and in contentment her plump, fair good looks bloomed. Unease affected her as it does an animal, drawing her face, freezing her features, mysteriously making bright hair lank and placid eyes stark with fear.

Wexford had Martin with him, the two of them top brass for the mere matter of a missing girl – but circumstances alter cases.

'My husband says what do I expect when I let her go out with her boyfriend at all hours and stay the night at his place. But they all do it these days and you can't be different. Besides they're engaged and I always say if you really love each other . . . '

She was talking for the sake of talking but her voice faltered. She began twisting her hands.

'Did Paulette go out with her fiancé last night?'

'No, he's in Birmingham. He had to go to Birmingham for his firm.'

Not for the first time Wexford marvelled at how illogical human thinking can be.

'But she did go out? Where did she go?'

'I don't know. She didn't say. She just went out at about seven.'

Martin said, 'You didn't want to know where she was going?'

'Want to know! Of course I wanted to know. If I had my way I'd know where she was every minute of the day and night. I mean I didn't ask her, I'd forced myself to that. When she was younger her father used to say: I want to know where you're going and who with but once you're eighteen you're legally grown-up and you can do what you like. Well, she's eighteen and she remembered that and my husband remembers it and he stops me asking and Paulette wouldn't answer anyway.'

The poor woman was wretchedly caught between husband and daughter, and bullied, doubtless, by both – or had she been happy to have decision-making taken out of her hands?

'Tell me what happened later on. Of course you didn't wait up for her?'

'I would have. I knew Richard was in Birmingham, you see. John said he wasn't having me get in a hysterical state. He took a sleeping pill and he made me take one.'

Presumably sedatives were unlimitedly on tap *chez* Harmer . . .

'This morning I – well, I left her bedroom door open before I went to sleep. That way – if it was shut, you see, I'd know she'd come in. I – I had to make myself open my own bedroom door and look. Her door was still open, it was such a shock, I . . . Well, I went to look, in case she'd come in and left her door but, of course, she hadn't. John still wasn't alarmed. Somehow I couldn't make him see that if Richard was in Birmingham Paulette couldn't have been with him . . . '

Mrs Harmer burst into raging tears. Instead of falling

forward onto her arms to cry she lay back, let her head hang back and wailed. Martin went into the dispensary and fetched John Harmer. He came in looking cross and harassed. The noise his wife was making had the effect of causing him to put his hands over his ears in the manner that does nothing to block out sound but indicates that the sound is in some way distasteful or irritating.

'She'd better have a Valium. That'll help her pull herself together.'

'What she had better do, Mr Harmer,' said Wexford, 'is get off home. And you had better take her. Never mind the shop.'

Godwin and Sculp had not done Wendy Williams's decorating but they knew who had – a man who had once worked for them, who had left to set up in business on his own and who undercut them, Burden was told, at every opportunity. Running Leslie Kitman to earth was less simple. He had no wife and his mother was no Mrs Milvey to have his precise location at her fingertips. She gave Burden five possible addresses at which her son might be found: a farmhouse between Pomfret and Myfleet, a block of flats in Queen Street, Kingsmarkham, a cottage in Pomfret, and two houses on new estates outside Stowerton. Kitman was at none of them but the second Stowerton household told Burden he might just be lucky and find him in – Liskeard Avenue.

And it was there, three houses away from Wendy Williams's, that Burden discovered Kitman on top of a ladder. The house was like Wendy's, grey bricks and white weatherboard and picture windows. Kitman was painting a top-floor window frame. When Burden, standing at the foot of the ladder, shouted up who he was, Kitman launched immediately into a catalogue of reasons for not renewing his car tax. Burden hadn't even noticed his car, still less that the tax disc showed an expiry date of the end of June. At last, though, Kitman was made to understand and he came quickly down the ladder, his brush dripping white paint onto the lawn beneath.

The evening before Wendy Williams had spent in bed where she had retired, worn out, as soon as she returned from the police station. Veronica had brought her tea and bread and butter. It was all she ever seemed to fancy when upset. Joy Williams had also been at home with her daughter. At any rate they had been in the same house, Sara in her room as usual, Joy watching television and intermittently struggling to complete the form of application for a grant that would take Sara through medical school. And although it was a Thursday evening there had been no phone call from Kevin who extended this courtesy to his mother only when he was at college and not while junketing around holiday resorts.

These were the alibis Wexford was given by his two principal suspects. Richard Cobb came back from Birmingham in the course of the afternoon and furnished Wexford with a very detailed and apparently satisfactory account of where he had been the night before. Police in Birmingham would help with a check on that. By six Paulette hadn't come home and Wexford knew she never would, he felt in his bones she wouldn't.

The day was sultry and overcast. For hours the thunder had been growling and rumbling and gradually a wind had risen, a dry gusty wind that did nothing to lower the temperature. It still remained hot and stuffy. Wexford and Burden sat in Wexford's office. A search for Paulette hadn't begun yet. Where would one search?

'The lines I'm thinking along,' said Wexford, 'are that Paulette Harmer procured the Phanodorm with which Rodney Williams was sedated. She was in a position to do that, she could easily have done it. I'm wondering if she lost her nerve and told someone – well, Joy – she was going to admit it before we found out.'

'Of course, there's another possibility . . . ' Burden left the suggestion suspended.

Wexford looked abstractedly out of the window. It was time to go home but he had no inclination to go. The weather, the atmosphere, the late day, hung heavy with expectation. The thunder, of course, was a threat in itself, a sign of imminent storm, yet it seemed to contain some kind of emotional menace as well, as of looming tragedy.

'Tell me about Kitman,' Wexford said. 'In detail.' Burden had already given him an outline of his talk with the painter.

'He started doing that job for Wendy on April the fourteenth. There was paper on the walls, he said, and he had a job stripping it off. He was doing it all through the fourteenth and the fifteenth and he still hadn't finished by the time he knocked off on the fifteenth.'

'Should have used Sevensmith Harding's Sevenstarker, shouldn't he?' said Wexford and quoting, ' "The slick, sheer, clean way to strip your walls." '

'Maybe he did. He says the room was still furnished but he had covered the pieces of furniture up with his own dustsheets. When he came back in the morning – the morning of Friday the sixteenth, that is – some of the sheets were off and folded up. But that was also on the morning of the fifteenth and other mornings, I gather. Wendy and Veronica were to some extent still living in that room.'

'Did he notice anything else that Friday morning?'

'A stain on the wall is what we want, isn't it? A great bloodstain? And blood all over his dustsheets? There wasn't anything like that or if there was he didn't notice or can't remember. The walls were splashed and marked and patchy anyway, you can imagine. And on the sixteenth he covered up whatever might have been there by putting his first coat of paint on. Sevenstar emulsion, no doubt. One thing he did notice, though, and I didn't ask him about this, he volunteered it. Apparently it's been vaguely preying on his mind ever since. One of the dustsheets wasn't his.'

'*What?*'

'Yes. I thought that'd make you sit up. He has a few dustsheets he takes about with him. Some of them are old bed sheets and there are a couple of curtains and a candle-wick bedspread too. Well, according to him, when he left on the fifteenth all seven of his sheets were covering the furniture and part of the carpet. Next morning he came in to find that three of the sheets had been taken off the furniture and were folded up on the floor. He thought nothing much of it but later he noticed that one of the folded sheets wasn't his. It was newer than his and in better condition.'

'Did he ask Wendy about it?'

'He says he did. On the Saturday. She told him she knew nothing about it. And what did it matter to him, after all? He had the right number of dustsheets. You don't go to the police because someone has taken one of your dust-sheets and substituted another. But he wondered about it, he says. It niggled him is the way he puts it. Are we going to have those two women back?'

'Of course we are.'

It was Friday, the last Friday in the month. ARRIA met on the last Friday of the month, Wexford thought. No, the last Thursday. It was two months ago yesterday that he had gone to the Freeborns' house and interrupted a meeting.

He picked up the phone and spoke to John Harmer. Paulette's father was anxious now, no longer calm and scathing. He said his wife was asleep. Heavily sedated, Wexford guessed.

'The place is crawling with police,' said Harmer.

Wexford replied dryly, 'I know.'

He thought it an unfortunate way of describing the initial search he had mounted in the environs of the Harmers' home. The man's breathing at the other end of the line was audible. His voice had been rough and shaky. If insulting the police helped him, well . . .

'I can't tell you I don't think this a serious cause for concern, Mr Harmer. I'm very sorry. I think you should prepare yourself for bad news. Perhaps it would be best to say nothing to your wife as yet.'

'I'm not likely to wake her up and tell her you think her only child's dead, am I?'

Wexford said a polite goodbye and rang off. Harmer's rudeness gratified him a little. It was more than excusable in the circumstances and at least it showed Harmer wasn't the unfeeling husband he had thought him. Tomorrow morning they would widen the search for Paulette. By then he might have some idea of where and how to widen it.

A few drops of rain struck the windows, needles on the glass. The thunder thudded and cracked over Myringham way. Martin and Marion Bayliss brought the two Mrs Williamses in and Wexford went down to the interview room to confront them. Wendy in her Jickie's suit, hair freshly set – in Jickie's hairdressing department? – was in tears, dabbing at her eyes with a pink tissue. Joy had never looked so down at heel, broken sandals on her bare feet, a button missing from her button-through creased cotton dress, a scarf tied round her head. She looked like a refugee, such as have passed in streams across Europe at frequent times in modern history. Her face was grey and drawn.

Burden came in and sat beside him. The room had got so dark they had to have the light on. Still it wasn't really raining. When no one attempted to comfort Wendy and no offers of cups of tea were made she stopped crying. Rather defiantly, she produced the box of pink tissues from her bag and set it on the table in front of her.

'Was Paulette Harmer the girl your husband was seeing?'

Wexford addressed the question to both women. It was awkward. It seemed to treat polygamy as a legal state. Joy gave a dry cackle, more than usually scornful. Wendy said she didn't know who Paulette Harmer was, she had never heard of her.

'Who was it then?'

'He didn't have a young girlfriend,' said Joy. 'He didn't have any girl.' She nodded at Wendy. 'Unless you count her. And that's not the word I'd use for her.'

Wendy sniffed and pulled a tissue out of the box.

'Well, Mrs Williams?' Wexford said to her.

'I told you, I don't know.'

'On the contrary, you told me you knew there was one. This very young girl living around here with her parents – you never heard of her, she doesn't exist?'

Wendy looked at Joy. Their eyes met. For the first time Wexford thought he sensed a rapport between them. Then Wendy turned sharply away and shook her head violently.

'Rodney Williams was attracted by young girls,' Wexford said. 'You're an example yourself, Mrs Williams. How old were you when you and he met? Fifteen? Is that why you invented a young girlfriend for him? You knew it was in his nature?'

'I didn't invent it.'

He was suddenly aware of a change taking place in Joy. She was shaking with emotion. Her hands held the table edge. Rain had begun to patter on the windows. Burden got up and closed the fanlight. Joy leaned forward.

'Has Sara been talking to you?' she said.

It was on the tip of his tongue to say he would ask the questions. But he didn't say it. He felt his way. 'It's possible.'

'The little bitch!'

How was it he sensed that the two women were at last united by some common bond? And that bond wasn't the dead man. The noise of the rain was intense now, a crashing cloudburst. He thought, they did know each other. The Klein girl was telling me the truth. They were close in a conspiracy and they're back in it again, the acting is over

. . . He turned to Joy and it was as if his approaching, ultimately fixed gaze lit the fuse.

She spoke in a raucous throaty voice.

'You may as well have it. It wasn't young girls he was attracted to, not *any* young girls. It was his own daughter.'

18

It happened, it wasn't even uncommon. Lately it had been the modish subject for the pop sociology paperback. Yet that father–daughter incest might be a motivating factor in this case had not crossed Wexford's mind. Afterwards he was to ask himself *why* it hadn't crossed his mind, knowing his mind and the way it worked, but now in the interview room with the two women across the table from him he could only recall *The Cenci* and Beatrice – his own daughter playing Beatrice – running onto the stage crying:

'O world! O life! O day! O misery!'

That should have told him. Wendy had covered her face with her hands. Joy stared at him, her lips sucked in. A bead of saliva had appeared at the left corner of her mouth. She put her hand out for one of Wendy's tissues, tentatively, cautiously, watching Wendy, like an old dog approaching the food bowl but uncertain as to what the young dog will do. Wendy took her hands down. She didn't speak. She gave the tissue box a little push in Joy's direction. Burden sat, wearing his stony, contemptuous look.

Wexford was framing a question. Before he could utter it Joy spoke.

'She came and told me. Her own mother! His own wife! She said he'd come into her bedroom in the middle of the night. He said he was cold, he never seemed to get warm since we'd slept in twin beds. That's what he said to her. He said she could make him warm. Why didn't she scream out? Why didn't she run away? He got into bed with her and did it to her. I'm not going to repeat the word she used, they all use it for *that*. It was while I was asleep. I was asleep and he was doing that with his own daughter.'

She laughed. The sound was drier than ever with more of a rattle in it but it was a laugh. She looked at Wendy and directed the laugh at her. And, Wexford thought, she may have been in cahoots with her, she may have told her all this before in womanly confidence, in sisters-under-the-skin conspiracy, but she enjoys telling it now – in our presence, a public triumphant putdown.

Like the therapist to whom he had compared himself, he would let her talk without interruptions, without breaking in to question. If she would talk. The pause endured. Wendy looked away and at the screen of water, curiously claustrophobic, the rain was making down the panes. She had pushed her fingers so hard into the skin of her face that they left pink pressure marks. Without prompting, Joy went on.

'She waited till he'd gone to work and then she told me. I was ironing her a blouse for school.' Insult had been thus added to injury, she implied. The father's rape would have been less offensive to the mother if the news had been imparted to her while she was ironing a shirt for Kevin. 'She burst right out with it. There wasn't a question of being tactful, mind, of – well, breaking it gently. He was only my husband. It was only my husband she was telling me about being unfaithful to me.' The laugh came again, but a ghost of it this time. 'I wouldn't listen to her. I said, don't tell me, I don't want to hear. I put my hands over my ears.'

A rejecting gesture not unknown in the Harmer–Williams families, Wexford thought. He nodded at Joy, feeling it was necessary to give some sign.

'I put my hands over my ears,' she said again. 'She started shouting at me. Didn't I care? Wasn't I upset? I answered her then. I said of course I was upset. No mother wants to hear her daughter's like that, does she? I said to her, You spread that about and you'll split us all up, your father'll go to prison and what are people going to think of me? What's Kevin going to say to them at college?'

Burden said quietly, 'What did you mean by that, Mrs Williams, your daughter was "like that"?'

'It's obvious, isn't it? I'm not saying he wasn't weak.' A glance for Wendy and a quick withdrawal of the eyes. 'Well, we know he was. But he'd never have done that without . . . '

She stopped and looked at Wexford. He remembered when he had first talked to Sara and her mother had sent him up to her bedroom saying she wouldn't object – 'Rather the reverse if I know her.'

'Encouragement?' he said flatly.

She nodded impatiently. 'Putting her arm round him, trying to get his attention. She wasn't *ten*. I said to her, you're not ten any more. Sitting on his knee – what did you expect? Now the least you can do is keep quiet about it, I said, think of my feelings for a change.'

'When did all this happen?'

'It was before Christmas. I know it was because I remember saying that she'd picked a fine time, hadn't she, just when we were all going to be together for Christmas.'

Wendy, whose face had been impassive, winced slightly. Had she realized at last where and how Rodney Williams spent his Christmases? It was soon after that, probably in the first week of January, Wexford recalled, that Edwina Klein had seen the two women together.

'Did you tell anyone?' Burden asked.

'Of course I didn't. I wasn't going to broadcast it.'

He turned on Wendy. 'When did she tell you? Or should I say warn you?'

Wendy had looked shocked by none of this. Not even surprised. But she shook her head. 'She never did.'

'Come on, Wendy . . . ' Wexford had solved the names problem at last. 'Joy found out you existed, sought you out especially to tell you what Rodney was really like. To tell you, in fact, to have a care to your own daughter.'

'Tell her?' said Joy. 'Why should I care?'

'Wendy,' Wexford said more gently, almost insinuatingly, 'you're not going to tell us you didn't know about Rodney and his daughter Sara. You're not going to make believe what we heard just now was all news to you. You couldn't have looked less surprised than if I told you it was raining. Joy came into Jickie's, didn't she, and told you who she was? I'll make a guess at the week before Christmas. How did she know who you were? She'd seen Veronica in the street and spotted the resemblance to Sara – a likeness no one could mistake . . . '

That they were surprised now, both of them, he couldn't doubt. He had been wrong there then. Never mind. There were other ways – following Rodney, seeing him and Wendy together, a host of ways.

'You met at Jickie's, went on to meet again after Christmas. No doubt there were many meetings . . . '

Wendy jumped up, eyes full of tears, grabbing a handful of tissues.

'I want to talk to you alone! Just you and me quite alone!'

'Surely,' said Wexford.

He got up. Burden didn't wait for them to leave the room before starting on Joy with his questions. When did she first suspect Rodney had a second home? Did she ever ask him? Joy was laughing at this second suggestion when Wexford closed the door. He took Wendy upstairs to his own office. The rain had abated, was now merely trickling, slipping, spilling, down the washed gleaming glass. Twilight hadn't yet begun and the sky was a clear grey, light from cloud-coated sunshine. Wendy stumbled a little going into the room. He thought it might be unwise to touch her, even to the extent of steadying her. She held on to the door frame and shot him a look of grievance.

In the chair he held out for her she sat down gingerly,

treating herself as if she had become fragile. She had turned into a convalescent, tentatively putting out feelers to the world. Her shoulders she was keeping permanently lifted.

'What did you want to say to me, Wendy?' He had dropped the 'Mrs Williams' altogether now.

She whispered it, sustaining the invalid image, a broken woman, wan-faced, such as might fittingly inhabit the Castle of Petrella and be called Lucretia.

'The same as what she said.'

'I'm sorry, Wendy. You must make yourself plainer than that.'

'It was the same for us. The same as what she said. Or – well, it would have been. I mean, he would have done but he went away and got himself killed.'

Light penetrated. 'You mean Rodney also made advances to Veronica? Only, if I interpret what you're saying correctly, it was merely advances?'

She nodded, tears splashing now, wads of tissues held to her eyes like swabs.

'Before Joy warned you or afterwards?'

A shrugging, then a shaking, of the whole body. Make-up scrubbed off with that cheapest and most readily available cleanser, tears, Wendy presented to Wexford a youthful, naked, desperate face.

'He had been a little more attentive to her, had he, than we in our society expect of a father to a teenage daughter? Did she tell you or did you see? Kissed her and said it was good to be alone with her and you out of the way?'

She jumped up. 'Yes, yes, yes!' she shouted.

'So on April the fifteenth, although you didn't think there was much chance of Rodney coming back, you encouraged your daughter to go out so as not to be alone with him? You told her not to run the risk of being alone with him but to stay out until you came home?'

Guilt was heavy on her face now, driving away indignation. He felt she was on the brink of a confession.

'Or did you send her out so that *you* could be alone with Rodney – you and Joy?'

The air was sharply clear, the rain past, the sky two shades of blue, a dark clean azure and the smoky blue of massed cloud. Nine o'clock and growing dark. Water lay in glassy pools, reflecting the sky. There was an unaccustomed coolness, almost a nip in the temperature. Before morning there would be more rain. Wexford could see it in the clarity and smell it in the atmosphere. He walked from the police station and kept on walking, just to get away from the enclosing four walls, the stuffiness, the millions of uttered words, the weariness of lies.

People used to tell him when they needed an alibi – now they cited television – that they had been for a walk. They didn't know where, just for a walk. He hadn't believed them. Everyone knew where they had been on a walk. Now he thought he might not be able to say where he had been tonight. His progress was aimless, though not slow, a fairly brisk marching in the fresh cold air, a thinking walk to dwell on what had passed.

So inconclusively. So unsuccessfully. He had wrung those two women, turned the handle and ground them through the rollers. Joy had laughed and Wendy had wept. He had kept on repeating over and over to himself: Edwina Klein saw them together. Why should she lie? Why should she invent? He had to let them go at last. Wendy was near collapse – or feigning it beautifully.

It was clear, the whole case, Burden said. A motive had at last emerged. Joy killed out of bitterness and jealousy, Wendy out of fear Rodney would serve Veronica the same way as he had served Sara. An unfortunate verb in the circumstances, but perhaps not inept . . . A conspiracy laid just after Christmas, brooded over through the early spring, hatched out in April. Murder in the room that would be decorated tomorrow. Staunch the blood with Kitman's dustsheet, realize too late what you have used.

It must have happened that way, there was no other. Perhaps they hadn't intended to kill, only confront him jointly, threaten and shock. But the French cook's knife had been handy, lying on the table maybe. That didn't explain drugging him with Phanodorm. The knife Milvey had found? Its blade matched the width and depth of the wounds. So would a thousand knives.

He was in Down Road, under the dripping lime trees. Perhaps, all along, he had known he was making his way here. The big old houses, houses that could justly be called 'piles', seemed sunken tonight in dark, still, sodden foliage. A dark green perfume arose from grass and leaf and rain-bathed flowers. Somewhere nearby a spoilt dog, left alone for the evening, vented its complaints in little bitter whimpering wails. Wexford opened the gate to the Freeborns' house. Lights were on, one upstairs and one down. The dustmen had been that morning, long before the rain started, and left the scattering of litter they didn't bother to remove from places where the occupants failed to tip lavishly. A sodden sheet of paper, pasted by rain onto the gravel, bore the ARRIA logo and a lot of printing it was too dark to read.

Both twins came to the door. He approved their caution. Once more they were alone in the house, left to their own devices, the switched-on parents far away at some veteran hippies' haunt. Both had pale blue hair tonight, pink stuff on their eyelids, otherwise the nearly identical faces were bare. And identical on both faces was dismay at the sight of him. Eve spoke.

'Do you want to come in?'

'Yes, please.' The house no longer smelt of marijuana. That was one thing he had achieved, a dubious success. The girls seemed not to know where to take him. They stood in the hall. 'There was a meeting of ARRIA last night,' he said. 'Where was it? Here?'

'They're mostly held here,' said Amy.

'And it was here last night?'

'Yes.'

He pushed open a door and switched a light on. It was a huge living room, floor cushions making islands on parquet that hadn't been polished for two decades, a divan with thrown over it something that might have had its origin in Peru, the only chair a wicker hemisphere hanging from the ceiling. French windows, uncurtained, gave onto what seemed an impenetrable wood.

He sat in the hanging chair, refusing to be alarmed by its immediate swinging motion.

'Who was at the meeting?'

They exchanged glances, looked at him. 'The usual crowd,' said Amy, and conversationally, 'It's always the same lot that turn up, isn't it?'

The names he ran through got a nod at every pause. 'Caroline Peters? Nicola Anerley? Jane Gardner? Paulette Harmer?' Eve nodded. She nodded in the same way as she had at the other names. 'Edwina Klein?'

There must have been a note of doubt in his voice.

'Yes, Edwina was here. Why not?'

'Why not indeed. And why not Sara Williams, come to that?'

'Sara didn't come,' said Amy. 'She had to stay home with her mother.'

So John Harmer hadn't been so far out when he suggested his daughter's disappearance had something to do with this 'women's movement nonsense'.

'What time did the meeting end?'

'About ten,' said Amy. 'Just about ten.' She had forgiven him if her sister never would. She had altogether put off that distant manner. 'Someone told me today that Paulette didn't go home all night and . . . ' She left the sentence hovering.

'You never told me,' Eve said sharply.

'I forgot.' Amy turned her eyes back on Wexford. 'She

was a bit late. She didn't say why. Edwina brought her aunt – not to join, just to see what went on, though she's eligible of course, never having married. It was good seeing someone old who'd had principles and stuck to them.'

'I have fought the good fight,' said Wexford. 'I have run a straight race. I have kept the faith.'

'That's right. That was exactly it. How did you know?'

He didn't answer her. The Authorized Version was unknown to them, lost to their generation as to the one before, a dusty tome of theology, in every way a closed book.

'Was Paulette alone when she left?'

'The meeting was upstairs.' Eve was chilly and unbending but she had spoken. 'We didn't see people out. They went downstairs and let themselves out. Paulette left with Edwina and her aunt.'

'They may have left together,' said Amy, 'but they didn't go off together. I looked out of the window and saw Edwina and her aunt getting into the aunt's car and Paulette wasn't with them.'

'What's out there?' Wexford said abruptly. He pointed at the long windows beyond which was visible only a mass of foliage.

'The conservatory.'

Amy opened the doors, swung them open and put her hand to a switch. Unconventional the Freeborn family might be; they were not feckless. The old domed conservatory, its upper panes of stained glass, claret and green in an Art Nouveau design of tulips, was full of dark green leafy plants, some of which looked subtropical, all demanding ample water and getting it. It must cost a fortune to heat in winter, Wexford thought, coming closer, entering the conservatory and spotting an orchid or two, the velvety mauve trumpet of a *brunfelsia*.

Eve, without being asked, flooded the garden beyond with light. Touching another switch brought on arc lamps, one on the conservatory roof, another in the branches of an enormous ilex. The garden, so-called, hardly deserved floodlighting. It was a wilderness of unmown grass, wild roses, brambles, the occasional hundred-year-old tree. And it was huge, the kind of garden whose owners might justly say they were never overlooked. Shrubs that appeared dense black at this hour made an encircling irregular wall round its perimeter.

'We don't any of us go in it much,' said Amy. 'Except as a shortcut to the High Street. And when it's muddy or whatever . . . ' Another sentence was left hanging. She went on vaguely, 'Dad's keen on the conservatory. It's him that grows the plants.'

The *Cannabis sativa*, thought Wexford, but hardly in here. You needed infra-red light for that and plenty of it. He opened the door into the garden, a glass door of slender green and white panels. The cold damp air breathed water in suspension at him. He noticed a path among the grass, pieces of crazy paving let into what had once been turf, was now wet hay. The girls weren't coming with him. Eve wound her arms round her body, hugging herself against the cold. Amy breathed on the glass and with her fingertip began drawing a raven with a woman's face. Wexford went down the path. The arc lamps reached no further than thirty feet or so. He took his torch out of his pocket and switched it on.

The path led to the gate in the far fence, he thought. That was what Amy meant by a shortcut to the High Street. First it wound through a copse of dark shrubs, laurels, rhododendrons, all glistening and dripping with water. He was curiously reminded of walking in a cemetery. Cemeteries were like this, untended often, places of ornamental shrubs, funereal trees, like this without flowers, unlike this with gravestones.

He came upon the fence and the gate quite suddenly, almost bumping into the gate which was in a break in the untrimmed hedge that followed the line of the close-boarding. From here the backs of other big houses could just be seen, two of them with yellow rectangles on black that were lights in their windows. The light didn't reach here and no moon had appeared. The path curved its way all round the garden. He followed its ellipse, returning on the right-hand side. Bamboo here, half dead most of it, a mass of canes. Then something prickly that caught at his raincoat. He pulled and heard the tearing sound. Turn the torch on it to see what had happened . . .

Turn the torch into the midst of this circle of briar roses, brambles with wicked thorns – onto an outflung arm, a buried face, a logo and acronym, red on white cotton – ARRIA and the raven-woman.

It was more like a cemetery here than he had supposed . . .

19

The scene-of-crimes officer. Dr Crocker. Sir Hilary Tremlett fetched out of his bed and wearing a camelhair coat over pyjama top and grey slacks. Burden as neat and cool as at mid-morning. And the rain coming down in summer tempests. They had to rig a sort of tent up over the body.

She had been strangled. With a piece of string or cord perhaps. Wexford himself could see that without reference to Dr Crocker or Sir Hilary. The photographer's flash going off made him blink. He didn't want to look at her any more. It sickened him, though not with physical nausea, he was far beyond that. No pharmacology degree now, no marriage to Richard Cobb, no full flowering of that strange beauty that had been both sultry and remote.

The girls worried him, Eve and Amy, alone in that house with a young girl, a contemporary, dead in the garden. Marion Bayliss had tried to reach their parents but they were at none of the phone numbers the twins could produce. Neighbours shunned the Freeborns. With the families immediately next door they weren't even on speaking terms. Eve thought of Caroline Peters and it was she who came to the house in Down Road and stayed for the rest of the night. Wexford crawled into bed at around three. There was a note for him from Dora which he read but did not mark or inwardly digest: 'A man called Ovington keeps phoning for you.' She was deeply asleep and in sleep she looked young. He lay down beside her and the last thing he remembered before sleeping himself was laying his hand on her still-slender waist.

* * *

'She'd been dead about twenty-four hours,' said Crocker, 'which is about what you thought, isn't it?'

When you don't get enough sleep, Wexford thought, it's not so much tired that you feel as weak. Though perhaps they were the same thing. 'Strangled with what?' he asked. 'Wire? Cord? String? Electric cable?'

'Because it's easily obtainable and pretty well impossible to break I'd guess the kind of nylon cord you use for hanging pictures. And where were your suspects – ' Crocker looked at his watch ' – thirty-six hours ago?'

'At home with their daughters, they say.'

Wexford began going through the statement Burden had taken from Leslie Kitman, the painter. A description of the missing dustsheet was gone into in some detail. Useless now, of course. It was four months since that dustsheet, concealed in a plastic bag, had been removed by the council's refuse collectors. And the knife as likely as not with it. Somehow he couldn't believe in Milvey's knife, he couldn't take two Milvey coincidences . . .

The walls had been stained and pitted, Kitman said. He couldn't remember if the stains had looked any different on the morning of 16 April from the afternoon of 15 April. Some of the holes, he thought, might have been filled in by someone else. He had made good some of the cracks and holes with filler which, when it dried, left white patches. On 16 April and the morning of the 17th he had lined the walls with wood-chip paper and on the Monday following begun painting over the paper.

Was he going to have those women in again? One of them had killed the girl the night before last. To keep her from confirming their guilt in the matter of the Phanodorm. Only one of them or both? Joy could easily have known where she would be and that she left by the shortcut to the High Street where she would catch the Pomfret bus.

Burden was late. But then he too had been up and on the go since early yesterday morning, finally getting to bed even later than Wexford. To be up after midnight, thought

Wexford, is to be up betimes. He had always liked that, only no one knew what 'betimes' meant any more, which rather spoiled the wit of it. Thinking of going to bed reminded him of Dora's note and he was about to pick up the phone and get hold of Ovington when Burden walked in.

He didn't look tired, just about ten years older and a stone thinner. He was wearing his stone-coloured suit with a shirt the same shade and a rust tie with narrow chocolate lines on it. Might be going to a wedding, thought Wexford, all he needed was a clove carnation.

'Jenny's started,' he said. 'I took her to the infirmary this morning at eight. There's not going to be anything doing much yet awhile but they wanted her in promptly.'

'You'd better start your leave as from now.'

'Thanks. I thought you'd say that. I must say these babies do pick their moments. Couldn't she have waited a week? She's going to be Mary, by the way.'

'After your grandmothers, no doubt.'

But the coincidence he had related to Wexford had slipped Burden's memory. 'Do you know that never crossed my mind? Perhaps Mary Brown Burden then?'

'Forget it,' said Wexford. 'It sounds like an American revivalist preacher. Keep in touch, won't you, Mike?'

Later in the day, with luck, the pathologist's report on Paulette Harmer would come and also perhaps something from Forensics on the murder weapon. He had Martin go to a magistrate and swear out a warrant to search the Williams home in Liskeard Avenue, and he wasn't anticipating any difficulties in getting it. In the meantime he had himself driven to the other Williams home. He didn't feel up to walking, whatever Crocker might advise.

Sara was mowing the front grass with one of those small electric mowers that cut by means of a line wound on a spool and are principally intended for trimming edges. As he got out of the car the motor whined and stopped cutting and the girl, crimson with bad temper, up-ended the flimsy machine and began tugging furiously at the line. He heard a hissed repetition of the word Joy disliked so much that she had used of her father's assault.

'Fuck, fuck, fuck, fuck!'

'If you do that with the current switched on,' Wexford said, 'one day you're going to cut your hand off.'

She cooled as rapidly as she had become incensed.

'I know. I've promised myself I'll always switch it off before I fiddle with it. But these god-damned things never work for long.' She pulled prongs out of socket to oblige him and smiled. An ARRIA tee-shirt today, identical to the one on dead Paulette. 'This is the fourth of these spools we've had this summer. Do you want to see my mother?'

As yet she couldn't know about Paulette. He remembered her thinly veiled boasting to her cousin on the phone and he didn't think she would much care. Nor would she much care when her mother was arrested for the murder. But perhaps it was natural for victims of incest not to care much about anything. He felt a wrench of pity for her.

'I want to talk to you first.'

The garage, now there was no car to occupy it, had become a toolshed and repository for rather battered garden furniture. Sara indicated a deckchair to Wexford. For her part she sat down on an upturned oil drum and set about struggling with the stubborn spool. This looked as if it might go the way of its fellows, three of which lay on a shelf next to a dozen half-used Sevenstar paint tins. He supposed she was busying herself so as not to have to look at him while he talked to her about her father.

At his first mention of incest, a tactful broaching of what her mother had told him, she didn't flush but turned gradually white. Her skin, always pale, grew milk-like. And he noticed a phenomenon, perhaps peculiar to her. The fine gold down on her forearms erected itself.

He asked her gently when it had first happened. She kept her head bent, with her right hand attempting to rotate the spool while with her left forefinger and thumb she tugged at the slippery red line.

'November,' she said, confirming his own ideas. 'November the fifth.' She looked up and down again quickly. 'There were only two times. I saw to that.'

'You threatened him?'

She hesitated. 'Only with the police.'

'Why didn't you tell your brother? Or did you? I have a feeling you and your brother are close.'

'Yes, we are. In spite of everything.' She didn't say in spite of what but he thought he knew. 'I *couldn't* tell him.' Like a different girl speaking, her face turned away, 'I was ashamed.'

And she hates her mother, so it was a pleasure to tell *her*? She gave a final tug and the line came through, far too much of it, yards of loosely-coiled scarlet flex.

Kevin was indoors, having unexpectedly arrived that morning by means of some comfortless and inefficient transport. He was lying spent, exhausted, dirty and unkempt, on the yellow sofa, his booted feet up on one of its arms. Joy had answered Wexford's knock with refreshments for Kevin in her hands, a trayful of sandwiches, coffee, something in a carton that was ice cream or yogurt. Wexford shut the door on him, hustled Joy into the kitchen. She was dressed exactly as she had been the day before, even to the headscarf – had she tied it on to run to the shops for Kevin-provender? – and gave the impression of having never taken her clothes off, of sleeping in them. He told her, quite baldly, about Paulette, but she knew. John Harmer had phoned her while Sara was in the garden. Or that was the explanation she gave Wexford for knowing. He said he would want her later at the police station, she and Wendy. He would send a car for her.

'What's my son going to do about his evening meal?'

'Give me a tin opener,' said Wexford, 'and I'll teach him how to use it.'

She didn't observe the irony. She said she supposed he could have something out of a tin for once. At least she didn't suggest his sister might cook for him, which was an improvement (if that was the way you looked at things) on twenty years ago.

The next stop was Liskeard Avenue, Pomfret. Martin had got his warrant and was there with Archbold and two uniformed men, PC Palmer and PC Allison, Kingsmarkham's only black policeman. A tearful Wendy was trying to persuade them it wouldn't be necessary to strip the paper off her living-room walls.

At the glass table sat Veronica. Evidently she had been at work on the hem of a white garment that lay in front of her but had laid down her needle when the policemen arrived. Wexford thought of the girl in the nursery rhyme who sat on a cushion and sewed a fine seam, feeding on strawberries, sugar and cream. It must have been her dress which suggested it to him with its pattern of small wild strawberries and green leaves on a creamy ground. Tights again, dark blue this time, white pumps. Another thing that made those girls look alike was the way neither of their faces showed their feelings. They were the faintly melancholy, faintly smug, nearly always impassive faces of madonnas in Florentine paintings.

Wexford's daughter Sylvia had a cat which uttered soundless mews, going through the mouth-stretching motion of mewing only. Veronica's 'hello' reminded him of that cat, a greeting for a lip-reader, not even as audible as a whisper. Wendy renewed her appeals as he came in, now making them to him only.

'I'm sorry, Wendy. I understand your feelings. We'll have the room redecorated for you.' Or for someone, he thought but didn't say aloud. 'And there'll be as little mess as possible.'

And it really was Sevensmith Harding's Sevenstarker they intended to use for the job, four large cans of it, each labelled in red italic script that this was the slick, sheer, clean way to strip your walls. Wexford found himself hoping this wasn't too gross an exaggeration.

'But what for?' Wendy kept saying, at the same time,

curiously enough, picking up ornaments and pushing them into a wall cupboard, loading a tray.

'That I'm not at liberty to say,' said Wexford, falling back on one of the stock answers of officialese. 'But there's plenty of time. Please clear the room yourself if you want to.'

In silence Veronica picked up her sewing. She threaded her needle, using a small device manufactured for that purpose, and slipped a pink thimble onto her forefinger.

'She's doing the hem of her tennis dress. She's playing in the women's singles final at the club this afternoon.' Wendy spoke in tragic tones, only slightly modified by a faint proud stress on the word 'club'.

Kingsmarkham Tennis Club, presumably, or even Mid-Sussex. 'We shan't stop her,' Wexford said.

'You'll upset her.' She drew him into the kitchen, through the already open doorway. 'You're not going to say anything to her about you-know-what? I mean you're not going to go into it?'

'I'm not a social worker,' he said.

'Nothing actually happened anyway. I saw to it nothing happened.'

Impossible, though, not to see Rodney Williams, hitherto no more than liar and con-man, as some sort of monster. To make a sexual assault on one daughter was heinous enough, but almost immediately to have designs on her younger half-sister?

'Of course, you wouldn't have suspected anything *might* happen if Joy hadn't warned you.'

'How many times do I have to tell you I never saw the woman till you – introduced us?'

'Something you haven't told me is how you knew Rodney made sexual advances to Veronica. He didn't tell you but you knew. Veronica was the young girl living at home with her family you led us a wild goose chase about, wasn't she?' He closed the door between the rooms and leaned against it.

Wendy nodded, not looking at him.

'How did you know, Wendy? Did you see something? Did you notice something in his behaviour when he thought you weren't looking? Was that after or before Joy warned you?'

She mumbled, 'I didn't see anything. Veronica told me.'

'*Veronica?* That innocent child in there who's more like twelve than sixteen? That child you've very obviously sheltered from every exposure to life? She interpreted her father's affectionate kisses, his arm round her, his compliments, as sexual advances?'

A nod. Then a series of vehement nods.

'And yet you say "nothing actually happened". By that I take it you mean there was no more than a kiss and a touch and a compliment. But she – *she* – saw this as an incestuous approach?'

Wendy's response was characteristic. She burst into tears. Wexford pushed up a stool for her to sit on and found a box of tissues, never a difficult task in that house. He returned to the living room where the carpet was now covered with sheets and from which Veronica had disappeared. Allison was daubing the walls with Sevenstarker, Palmer already at work with a metal stripping tool. The hunch he had about what was under that paper was probably crazy, but besides that it was just possible an analysis of old plaster might show traces of Rodney's blood. And might not. Anyway, it was work for Leslie Kitman. He could come in next week and put it all back again at the expense of the Mid-Sussex Constabulary.

The rain had started again. That would put paid to Veronica's match in the afternoon as neither the Kingsmarkham Tennis Club nor the Mid-Sussex County at Myringham had covered courts. Wexford, back in his office though it was Saturday, noted the time. Twelve-thirty. Getting on for three hours since Mike had been in and announced the imminence of his new daughter. Well, it was too soon yet to expect much, early days.

Something kept nagging at the back of his mind, something Wendy had said. About the tennis match, he thought it was. But she hadn't said anything except that Veronica would be playing that afternoon. Why did he have this curious feeling then that in what she said lay the whole answer to this case? He often had feelings like that about some small thing when a case was about to break, and the small thing always turned out to be vital and his hunch seldom wrong. The difficulty was that he didn't know what he had a hunch about.

All the available men he had were either at Wendy's taking her room apart or else, the far greater number of them, conducting a house-to-house in Down Road and interrogating every girl who had been at the ARRIA meeting. A mood of loneliness and isolation enclosed him. Dora had gone to London and to stay the night with Sheila in Hampstead. His elder grandson Robin would be nine today, his birthday party due to begin three hours from now. Crocker played golf all day on Saturdays. Wexford would have liked to sleep but he found it hard to sleep in the daytime. What the hell was it Wendy had said? What *was* it? Tremlett was probably still at work on that poor girl's body . . . She had got Phanodorm for Joy and threatened to tell that she had. Well, not threatened, warned rather that she would have to, she would be scared not to. Joy had given Rodney the Phanodorm, substituting it for his blood-pressure pills, and it took just the time of a drive to Pomfret to act. Follow him by bus to Wendy's. He's asleep when you get there and you look at him and remember what he's done to you by way of what he's done to your daughter. Married another woman too, like a bloody sheikh. And the other wife goes along with you, though you hate her. It's her daughter at risk now since you told her where his tastes lie. Why let him ever wake up again? If there's a mess she says the room's going to be decorated tomorrow. And if you hide the body for long enough . . .

In the morning phone the office, say he's ill, disguising your voice a bit. She'll type his letter of resignation for you, she's got access to a typewriter in a friend's house that no one's going to trace. You're both in it equally, you and she, the two wives of Rodney Williams, for better for worse, till death parts you. She stabbed him too, though you gave him the sleeping pill. You and she together carried the body down that crackpot spiral staircase, through the doorway into the integral garage. Laid him in the car with his travelling bag. She drove because you never learned, but you did most of the grave digging. Soiling your hands never bothered you the way it did her. Two wives, in it together equally, and whom murder has joined let no man put asunder.

Wexford had got himself under Joy's skin and he very nearly finished this internal monologue with one of her awful laughs. The chances were Burden wouldn't phone before evening. And then surely he'd phone him at home. He drove to the Old Cellar and had himself a slice of quiche, broccoli and mushroom, a pleasant novelty, one small glass of Frascati to go with it – it was Saturday, after all, though with nothing to celebrate – and then back again to the estate where the streets were named for Cornish towns, Bodmin, Truro, Falmouth, Liskeard. A cold grey rain fell steadily. They were back to the weather they had had between Rodney Williams's disappearance and the discovery of his body.

In Wendy's living room considerable progress had been made. Three walls were more or less stripped. It wasn't what Wexford would have called slick, sheer and clean but it wasn't bad. Martin had got hold of someone from Forensics, a shaggy girl in navy all-in-ones, who nevertheless had the air of an expert and was painstakingly scraping samples of brownish plaster off the walls.

Wendy was downstairs in her sewing-ironing-laundry

room or whatever, cutting patterns out of magazines. For therapy, no doubt. Veronica was with her, Miss Muffet on a velvet pouffe. No match for her today as he had predicted. He suddenly remembered his threat to send a car for Joy 'later' and the crisis over Kevin's dinner this had precipitated. Well, it would have to be much later . . . Or tomorrow. Or every day on and for ever. No, he mustn't think that way.

Wendy had changed her dress for a linen suit. Perhaps she had been going to watch her daughter play, for Veronica, as though not resigned to cancellation until the last moment, was in her tennis whites, pleated miniskirt – who could imagine her in shorts? – and a top almost too well finished to be called a tee-shirt.

'I suppose they'll postpone it till Monday night,' said Wendy in a high rather mad voice, 'and that means half the spectators won't come.'

Down the spiral staircase came the expert with her case of samples, the scraper still in her hand.

'I think I'm going to be sick,' whispered Veronica.

Her mother was all care, all solicitude, jumping up, hastening her to the ground-floor bathroom.

Wexford went back upstairs. Archbold had gone. The expert had gone. Martin was drinking tea from a flask and the other two Coke from cans while they waited for the Sevenstarker on the fourth wall to do its stuff. Wexford felt something very near a qualm. The room, which had been a shell-pink sanctuary, was a nasty mess. A shambles, Martin called it, but a shambles, meaning a slaughter house, was just what Wexford thought it had been used for, the reason for this destruction. Suppose he was wrong? Suppose the killing of Rodney Williams had taken place elsewhere?

Too late now.

The police's loss would be Kitman's gain. It is the business of the thinking man, he paraphrased, to give employment to the artisan.

'Let me have one of those, will you?' he said to Martin, pointing to the scrapers. The white patches of plaster among the brown were the areas Wendy herself had filled before Kitman began papering.

It wouldn't budge the white plaster.

'Want me to have a go, sir?' Allison produced what Wexford thought might be a cold chisel.

'We'll all have a go.'

It made Allison's day. He had never before distinguished himself in any way since joining the force two years before. Sometimes he thought – and his wife – that they had only taken him on because he was black and not because he was suitable or any good. They were inverted race snobs. For weeks everyone had bent over backwards to treat him with more kindness, courtesy and consideration than they would show, for instance, to a millionaire grandfather on his deathbed. That had worn off after a while. He was a bit lonely too in Kingsmarkham where only his wife, his kids and two other families were West Indian like him. But today paid for all that. It was what made him in his own eyes an officer of the law.

'Sir, I think I've found . . . ' he began.

Wexford was there beside him like a shot. Under his eyes Allison dug in carefully, thanking his stars he'd remembered to put his gloves on. The object was stuck in the fissure wrapped up in newspaper, plastered over. He chipped and dug and then put his hand to it, looking at Wexford, and Wexford nodded.

The knife didn't clatter out. It was unveiled as reverently as if it were a piece of cut glass. They all looked at it lying there on its wrappings, clean as a whistle and polished bright as a long prism in a chandelier.

20

Wexford had them with him all day Sunday and Monday morning's papers said an arrest was imminent. But Wexford wanted the two women, not just one, Joy as well as Wendy. Charging Wendy with Rodney Williams's murder was an obvious act. The knife buried in her living-room wall had a blade which exactly matched the knife wounds on the body and it was wrapped in part of the *Daily Mail* of 15 April. Still, he wanted Joy as well and Joy had no apparent connection with the crime. The only evidence he had was a witness who claimed to have seen the two women together and a voice on the phone that was probably hers.

Joy also had an alibi. Wendy didn't. All day long nails were going into Wendy's coffin, or at least the shades of the prison house were closing about her. Until Ovington came. That is, until Ovington's second visit.

Alone in the house, eating a junk food supper, Wexford got a call from Burden late on Saturday evening. Jenny's labour hadn't exactly been a false alarm but it had gradually subsided during the day. They were keeping her in, though, and considering some method of induction . . .

'You wanted her to wait a week,' said Wexford nastily. 'You'd better come back to work.'

He phoned Ovington first thing in the morning. Never mind about Sunday and all that. By the time Ovington arrived at the police station he and Sergeant Martin and Polly Davies had Joy and Wendy in an interview room, the demented refugee and the broken doll. The curious thing was they had come closer to each other. In appearance, that is. There had been a sort of blending, and he thought of Kipling's hedgehog and tortoise, combining to make an armadillo. Joy and Wendy hadn't gone that far, but anxiety and harassment had done their work on the younger woman and the older had smartened herself up, perhaps because her son was back. At any rate the headscarf was gone and she had proper shoes on. But Wendy's make-up was stale, she had hairs all over the shoulders of her black cotton dress and the ladder that sprang in her tights didn't fidget her.

He left them to go and talk to Ovington. Smiling as usual, absurdly ingratiating, he could hardly have persuaded even the most gullible to believe him, certainly not a hard-headed policeman.

'She was with you on April the fifteenth?' Wexford said. 'She came to your place after work for a drink? Why hasn't she so much as mentioned this to me?'

'She doesn't want anyone to know she was seeing me while her husband was still alive.'

That was in character. Wifely virtue was one of the aspects of the image Wendy liked to present. That didn't mean Ovington's story was true. Ovington was trying it on, a kind, stupid man with a misplaced idea of duty. Absently Wexford thanked him for coming. Then, as he was going back to the Williams wives, it occurred to him Ovington might have been in it with Wendy instead of Wendy with Joy. In that case who had made the phone call?

Wendy was crying. She said she was cold. It was true that the weather had turned very cold for the time of year but she should have been prepared for that, sacrificed vanity and brought a coat. He thought of all the places in the world and all the policemen in them where Wendy would have been allowed to shiver, where the temperature would have been lowered if possible, a little hypothermia encouraged. You couldn't call it torture, cooling someone into admissions . . .

'Get her something to put on,' he said to Polly.

He took them through the incest again and he got more stories full of holes. Joy hadn't believed Rodney would do that, yet she insisted Sara had led him on, insisted too that he would have gone to prison if she had breathed a word. Wendy now said Veronica had told her Rodney had started coming into her bedroom to kiss her good night and it wasn't 'nice'. That, said Joy, forgetting her former statement, was just how it had begun with Sara. Polly came back into the room with a grey knitted garment, something from Marks and Spencer's range for old ladies – God knows where she found it – which Wendy put on with a show of reluctance.

Sandwiches were brought in to them at lunchtime, one lot corned beef, the other egg and cress. Not exactly the Sunday joint, two veg and Yorkshire pudding. By that time Wexford had taken them through 15 April and was getting on to last Thursday night. Wendy had forgotten her coat but not her box of tissues, shades of peach this time. She sat snivelling into handfuls of them.

Just before three Joy broke at last. She started to howl like a dog. She rocked back and forth in her chair, howling and drumming her fists on the table. Wexford stopped the proceedings and sent for a cup of tea. He took Wendy into the interview room next door and asked her about Ovington. Rather to his surprise she agreed without much reluctance that she had been in Ovington's flat on 15 April from about 7.45 until about 9.15. Why hadn't she said so before? She gave the reason Ovington had given for her. They had hatched this up together, Wexford thought.

'I thought I might as well tell you,' she said with an aplomb that almost staggered him. 'I didn't before because you've all got minds capable of anything. But there's been so much real dirt dug up I don't think my innocent little friendship amounts to much.'

What did any of it weigh against that knife in the wall?

* * *

Late in the afternoon Burden walked in, looking a hundred years old.

'For God's sake,' said Wexford. 'I wasn't serious.'

The truth was Burden didn't know how otherwise to pass the time. He started on Joy, trying to break her alibi. But the tea had done wonders for her. She stuck to her story about watching television at the Harmers' and after half an hour of that had the brainwave that might have struck her days ago. She didn't have to talk at all if she didn't want to. Nobody had charged her with anything.

Unfortunately, by this time Wendy was back in the room with her and heard what she said.

Through her tears she smiled quite amicably at Joy. 'Good idea. I'm not talking either then. Pity I didn't think of it before.'

Joy uttered one last sentence. 'It was me thought of it, not you.'

United in silence, they stared at Wexford. Why not charge them both? With murdering Rodney Williams and, if he couldn't make that stick, with murdering Paulette Harmer? Special court in the morning, a remand in custody . . . Archbold came in and said there were three people to see him. He left the silent women with Burden and Martin and went down in the lift.

James Ovington was sitting there with his taciturn father and an elderly woman he introduced as his mother. Somehow Wexford had never thought of Ovington *père* as having a wife but, of course, he would have; James Ovington must have come from somewhere. He only looked like a waxwork. More so than ever this afternoon, his complexion fresher, his cheeks pinker, his smile flashing.

'My parents want to tell you something.'

That was one way of putting it. They didn't look as if they had any desire beyond that of going home again. Wexford asked them to go up to the first floor with him to his office but Mrs Ovington said she'd rather not, thank you, as if any suggestion of going upstairs in the company of men was indecent. They compromised with an interview room. Mrs Ovington looked disparagingly about her, evidently thinking it wasn't very cosy. James Ovington said, 'What were you going to tell the chief inspector, Dad?'

Nothing, apparently.

'Now you know you were willing to come here and tell him.'

'Not willing,' said Ovington senior. 'If I must I must. That's what I said.'

'Is this something about Mrs Wendy Williams, Mr Ovington?' prompted Wexford.

Very slowly and grudgingly Ovington said, 'I saw her.'

'We both did,' said Mrs Ovington, suddenly brave. 'We both saw her.'

Wexford decided patience was the only thing. 'You saw her, yes. When was this?'

James opened his mouth to speak, wisely shut it again. His father pondered, at last said, 'She's got a car. She'd parked it outside the shop on the yellow line. That don't matter after half six. We never saw her go in.'

Silence fell and endured. Wexford had to prompt.

'Go in where?'

'My son's place, of course. What else are we talking about? He's got the bottom flat and we've got the top, haven't we?'

'Up four flights,' said his wife. 'Wear the old ones out first, that's what it is.'

'We saw her come out,' said Ovington. 'Out of our front window. Round a quarter past nine. Tripped over and nearly fell in them heels. That's how Mother come to see her. I said, Here, Mother, look at this, them heels'll have her over.'

'It was April the fifteenth!' said James, unable to contain himself any longer.

'I don't know about that.' His father shook his head. 'But it was the first Thursday after Easter.'

* * *

That night he went to bed early and slept for nine hours. He didn't let himself think about the two women, Joy with no evidence against her, Wendy exonerated by the Ovingtons. They had been sent home with the warning that he would very likely want them back again on Monday morning. Old Ovington hadn't been lying but still his story didn't militate against the possibility that while Joy had done the deed in Wendy's house Wendy had later met her in time to help her dispose of the body, the clothes and the car.

In the morning he awoke clear-headed and calm. Immediately he remembered what it was Wendy had said to him. It had been when she told him Veronica was to play in a tennis singles final. The significance was in what it reminded him of, and now he remembered that too and as he did so everything began to fall gently and smoothly into place, so that he felt like one recalling and then using the combination of a safe until the door slowly swings open.

'But what a fool I've been,' he said aloud.

'Have you, darling?'

'If I'd got on to it sooner maybe that poor girl wouldn't have died.'

'Come on,' said Dora. 'You're not God.'

The phone was ringing as he left the house. It was Burden but Wexford wasn't there to answer it and Dora spoke to him.

A report on the postmortem, rushed through by Sir Hilary Tremlett, was awaiting Wexford. He went through it with Crocker beside him. Strangling had been with a fine powerful cord and whatever this was had left a red staining in the deep indentation it had made around the victim's neck.

'The nylon line from the spool of an electric edge trimmer,' said Wexford.

Crocker looked at him. 'That's a bit esoteric.'

'I don't think so. Joy Williams has three such spools in

her garage and one of them, unless I'm much mistaken, will be empty.'

'Are you going to go there and check that?'

'Not just at the moment. Maybe later. Do you think it wrong to encourage a child to inform against its immediate family?'

'Like what happens in totalitarian societies, d'you mean? Or what I suppose happens. Extremists always believe the means are justified by the end. It depends what you mean by immediate family too, I mean, against a parent is a bit grim. That sticks in one's throat.'

'Drugging a man and stabbing him and burying the knife in a wall sticks in one's throat too.' Wexford picked up the phone and put it down again. 'I've got two women to arrest,' he said, 'and the way things are I'll never make the charges stand up. When do the schools go back?'

Crocker looked a little startled at this apparent *non sequitur*. 'The state schools – that is, the older kids – sometime this week.'

'I'd better do it today if I'm to catch her without her mother.' He lifted the phone again, this time asked for an outside line. It rang for so long he began to think she must be out. Then at last Veronica Williams's soft, rather high voice answered, giving the number in all its ten digits. Wexford spoke her name, 'Veronica?' then said, 'This is Chief Inspector Wexford of Kingsmarkham CID.'

'Oh, hello, yes.' Was she afraid or did she always answer the phone in this cautious breathless way?

'Just one or two things to check with you, Veronica. First, what time is your match tonight and where is it?'

'Kingsmarkham Tennis Club,' she said. 'It's at six.' She gathered some courage. 'Why?'

Wexford was too old a hand to answer that. 'After that's over I'd like to talk to you. Not you and your mother, just you alone. All right? I think you have quite a lot of things you'd like to tell me, haven't you?'

The silence was so heavy he thought he'd gone too far.

But no. And it was better than he had hoped. 'I have got things to tell you. There are things I've *got* to tell you.' He thought he heard a sob but she might only have been clearing her throat.

'All right then. When you've finished your match come straight here. D'you know where it is?' He gave her directions. 'About ten minutes' walk from the club. I'll have a car to send you home in.'

She said, 'I'll have to tell my mother.'

'By all means tell your mother. Tell anyone you like.' Did he sound too eager? 'But make sure your mother knows I want to see you alone.'

The enormity of what he was doing hit him as he put the phone down. Could anything justify it? She was a sixteen-year-old girl with vital information for him. The last teenage girl with vital information for him had been strangled before she could impart it. Was he sending her to the same death as Paulette Harmer? If Burden had been there he would have told him everything but with the doctor he had reservations.

'You're not going round there, then?' Crocker said, a little mystified as much by Wexford's expression as by the cryptic phone conversation.

'That's the last thing I must do.'

Later, when the doctor had gone, Wexford thought, I hope I have the nerve to stick it out. Pity it's so many hours off. But the advantage of an evening match was that afterwards it would soon be dark . . . Advantage! She would be phoning her mother now at Jickie's to tell her, he thought, and somehow – hopefully – persuading Wendy not to come with her. He would have that girl watched every step of the way.

The phone rang.

He picked it up and the telephonist said she had a Miss Veronica Williams for him. What a little madam she was giving her name as 'Miss'!

'I could come and see you now,' the childish voice said.

'That might be easier. Then I wouldn't have to upset Mummy. I mean I wouldn't have to tell her I don't want her with me.'

He braced himself. He hardened his heart. 'I'm too busy to see you before this evening, Veronica. And I'd like you to tell your mother, please. Tell her now.'

If she called back, he thought, he'd relent and let her come. He wouldn't be able to hold out. Would she recognize Martin? Archbold? Palmer? Certainly she'd know Allison. But would it matter if she did recognize them? He'd be there himself anyway. There was no way he was going to let her take that ten-minute walk in the half-dark from the club down a lane off the Pomfret Road to the police station, especially in the case of her following his directions and taking the footpath across one and a half fields.

The phone rang again. That's it, he thought. I can't keep it up. I'll go round there and she'll tell me and that'll be evidence enough . . . He picked up the receiver.

'Inspector Burden for you, Mr Wexford.'

Burden's voice sounded strange, not really like his voice at all.

'It's all over. Mother and baby are doing fine. Jenny had a Caesarean at nine this morning.'

'Congratulations. That's great, Mike. Give my love to Jenny, won't you? You'd better tell me what Mary weighed so that I can tell Dora.'

'Eight pounds nine ounces, but it's not going to be Mary. We're changing just one letter in the name.'

Wexford didn't feel up to guessing. Jenny's persuaded him into something fancy against his better judgement, he thought.

'Mark, actually,' said Burden. 'I'll see you later. Cheers for now.'

21

A woman had once been found murdered on that very footpath.* They would all have that in their minds, even Palmer and Archbold who hadn't been there at the time, who had probably still been at school. As Veronica Williams still was. Had she ever heard of the murder? Did people still talk about it?

That woman had lived in Forest Road, the last street in the area to bear the postal address Kingsmarkham. The Pomfret boundary begins there, though it is open country all the way to Pomfret in one direction and nearly all the way to Kingsmarkham Police Station in the other. The tennis club, however, is not in Forest Road but in Cheriton Lane which runs more or less parallel to it on the Kingsmarkham side. Smallish meadows enclosed by hedges cover the few acres between the club and the town, and the footpath runs alongside one of these hedges, at one point skirting a little copse. It emerges into the High Street fifty yards north of the police station and on the opposite side.

Wexford had Martin and Palmer in a car in Cheriton Lane, would station himself and Archbold in the copse, Loring among the spectators at the match, Bennett to start walking from the High Street end, Allison to follow her at a discreet distance.

'One black man'll look very like another to her, sir,' Allison had said. 'That mightn't be so in a city but it is out here.'

'Don't tell me Inspector Burden and I look alike to you.'

* See *A Sleeping Life*.

'No, sir, but that's a question of age, isn't it?'

Which puts me firmly in my place, thought Wexford. Burden was in his office, sitting beside him, anxious to take part in the protection-of-Veronica exercise. Can't keep away from the place for more than five minutes, Wexford had grumbled at him. At least Burden had supplied a diversion in the lull of the long afternoon.

'I don't understand how they could make a mistake over the sex like that. God knows I don't know much about it, but if a man has an XY chromosome formula and a woman XX surely they must always have it from embryo to old age?'

'It's not that. It's like this. In an amniocentesis they extract cells from the amniotic fluid the foetus is in. But occasionally they make a mistake and once in about ten thousand times they take cells from the mother not the child. And even then they aren't always going to know their error. Because if the child does happen to be a girl . . . In this case, though, I gather someone's head is going to roll.'

'It caused a lot of unnecessary misery.'

'Misery, yes,' said Burden, 'but maybe not unnecessary. Jenny says it's taught her a lot about herself. It's taught her she's not what you might call a natural feminist and now she has to approach feminism not from an emotional standpoint but from what is – well, right and just. We didn't know, either of us, what a lot of deep-rooted old-fashioned prejudices we had. Because I felt it too, you know, I also wanted a son though I never said. It's taught us how much we've concealed from the other when we thought we were frank and open. All this has been – well, not far from – what does Jenny call it? – Guided Confrontation Therapy.'

With difficulty Wexford kept a straight face. 'So long as now you've got a son you don't wish it was a girl.' He said 'you' but he meant Jenny whom he thought the kind of woman for whom the unattainable grass might always be the greener.

'Of course not!' Burden exclaimed, looking very sour. 'After all, as Jenny says, what does it really matter so long as it's healthy and has all its fingers and toes?'

This was a cliché Wexford didn't feel he could compete with. Now Burden was here how would he feel about taking part in the Veronica watch? Not much, said Burden, he had to be back at the hospital. Then Wexford thought it might start raining. If it rained the match would be cancelled and in all probability Veronica would simply take the bus to the police station from Pomfret.

But the sky lightened round about 5.30. He wondered what those two women were thinking. How had they reacted to being left all day to their own devices? Unless the match was over in two straight sets Veronica could hardly expect to leave the club before seven. Should he fill in the time by seeing what he could get out of Kevin Williams? But he didn't really want to get anything out of him. He knew it all already. Why not simply go and watch the match?

It hadn't occurred to him to ask himself – or anyone else for that matter – if the tournaments of the Kingsmarkham Tennis Club were or were not open to the public. And it wasn't until he walked through the doors of the clubhouse that the question came into his mind. But a hearty elderly man with the air of a retired Air Force officer who said he was the secretary welcomed him with open arms. They loved spectators. If only they could get more spectators. It provided such encouragement for the players.

He had already spotted Martin and Archbold sitting in the car a discreet distance from the gates. Now if Veronica saw him, as it was most likely she would do, his best course would be to leave. Then, later, she wouldn't fail to follow. The great thing was not to give her a chance to speak to him. Therefore, to the bar, a refuge which was also the last place to which a sixteen-year-old competitor was likely to retreat before a match. The secretary, seeing him headed in that direction, trotted up to say that as a non-member he wasn't allowed to purchase a drink but if he would permit a drink to be bought *for* him . . . ? Wexford accepted.

The bar was semicircular, with a long curved window offering a view of three of the club's nine hard courts. Wexford had a half of lager, the club like most places of its kind being unable to provide any sort of draught beer or 'real ale'. The secretary talked rather monotonously, first about the bad public behaviour of certain international tennis stars, then their own disappointment at Saturday's rain and the enforced cancellation of this singles final. There would have been more spectators on a Saturday, he said sadly. In fact, nine people had actually come along – he had counted – but had had to be turned away. Of course, they were most unlikely to come back tonight. Wexford had the impression that if any of them had turned up the secretary would have bought them drinks too.

It got to six, to ten past. She's not going to come, Wexford thought. Then an umpire arrived and climbed up into the high seat. Five canvas chairs and a wooden bench had been arranged for a possible audience. It looked as if they would remain empty but after a while two elderly women with white cardigans over their tennis dresses came and sat down and at the same time, approaching by the path that led from the farther group of six courts, Loring sauntered up. In sound English fashion the women sat in the canvas chairs on the left-hand end of the row and Loring at the extreme right-hand end of the bench. Colin Budd should have been so wise.

Veronica and a taller, older, altogether bigger girl appeared outside the court and let themselves in by the gate.

'Well, best get out there and give them some moral support,' said the secretary, rubbing his hands together.

It was certainly cold. A gust of wind whipped across the court, tearing at Veronica's short pleated skirt. In classic style they began with a knock-up.

'I don't think I will,' said Wexford. 'D'you mind if I watch from in here?'

The secretary was terribly disappointed. He gave him a look of injured reproach.

'You mustn't buy any drinks, you do know that, don't you? And you're not to serve him, mind, Priscilla.'

Loring, his jacket collar turned up, was smoking a cigarette. The secretary appeared, running up to the two women, and sat beside them. The knock-up, in which Veronica had had the best of it, was over and the match began.

Dark would come early because the day had been so dull. Wexford wondered if the light would hold long enough for the match to be played to the finish. Veronica, whose service it was, won the first game to love but had a tougher time when her opponent came to serve.

'You can have a drink if you like,' said Priscilla. 'I work it like this. I give it to you for free and next time a member buys me a drink I'll charge yours up to him. I'm a total abstainer actually but I don't let on to this lot.'

Wexford laughed. 'Better not, thanks all the same.'

'Suit yourself.' She came over and stood beside him and watched.

Three games all. It looked as if it would go on and on and then quite quickly it was all over, Veronica having won her own two service games and broken her opponent's.

'She's a little cracker, that kid,' said Priscilla. 'Strong as a horse. She's got arms like whipcord.'

It was twenty to seven and the edge of dusk. Veronica won the first two games but the other girl was fighting back for all she was worth. Perhaps she had never played against Veronica before. At any rate, it had taken her all this time to find her weakness but she had found it at last. Veronica couldn't handle long swift diagonal drives to her forehand, though backhand presented her with no problems. It was half a dozen of those forehand drives that won her opponent the next game and the next and the next two until she was leading 4–2. The light had grown bluish but the white lines on the court were still clearly visible, seeming to glow with twilight luminosity.

And then it was as if Veronica mastered the craft of dealing with those hard cross-court strokes. Or, curiously, as if some inspiration came to her from an external source. Certainly it was not that she had spotted him or had recognized Loring, whom she had never previously seen. But a charge of power came to her, a gift of virtuosity she had not known before. She had never before played like this, Wexford was sure of it. For a brief quarter of an hour she played as if she were on the centre court at Wimbledon and was there not by a fluke but by a hard-won right.

Her opponent couldn't withstand it. In that quarter hour she gained only four points. Veronica won the set by 6 games to 4 and thus secured the match. She threw her racket into the air, caught it neatly, ran to the net and shook hands with her opponent. Wexford said good night to Priscilla and left the way he had come, having watched the players go into the pavilion where the changing rooms were. Loring was still sitting on the bench.

Allison he spotted as soon as the footpath entered the field. He was lying very still in the long grass by the hedge and mostly covered by it. But Wexford saw him without giving any sign that he had done so. He was pretty sure Veronica wouldn't. The path wound on parallel to the hedge, then began to skirt the copse.

The false dusk hung still, suspended between light and dark. If it had been much darker no prudent young girl would have dared walk this way. Veronica Williams, of course, in spite of the impression she gave, was not a prudent young girl.

The air was still and damp and the grass moist underfoot. Wexford made his way along the path, under the high hedge, certain as he had been all along that Veronica's assailant would wait for her in the copse. Archbold had been there since 5.30 to be on the safe side. It was too late now for Wexford to join him without taking the risk of being seen. As it was, by staying to watch the match, he was taking a chance of spoiling the whole plan. Ahead of him a maple tree in the hedge spread its branches in a cone shape, the lowest ones almost touching the ground. He lifted them, stood against its trunk and waited.

By now it was 7.30 and he had begun to wonder if she would come after all. Though members had been thin on the ground there might have been some plan to fête her in the clubhouse. Hardly with drinks though. And she would have got out of it, she needed to see him as much as he her. Then he remembered she was her mother's daughter; it would take her longer than most girls to change her clothes, do her hair. She might even have a shower. Wendy was the sort of woman who would get a dying person out of bed to change the sheets before the doctor comes.

He stood under his tree in the silent dusk which was growing misty. Occasionally it was possible to hear in the distance a heavy vehicle on the Kingsmarkham to Pomfret road. Nothing else. No birds sang at this season and this hour. He could see the path about ten yards behind only and perhaps fifty yards ahead and it seemed to him then the emptiest footway he had ever contemplated. Allison would get rheumatism lying there on the damp ground, the cold seeping into his bones. Archbold, wrapped in his padded jacket, had probably fallen asleep . . .

She appeared quite suddenly. But how else could she have come but noiselessly and walking quite fast? She didn't look afraid though. Wexford saw her face quite clearly for a moment. Her expression was – yes, innocent. Innocent and trusting. She had no knowledge that there was anything to fear. If Sara, her half-sister, was a Florentine madonna, she was a Medici page, her small face grave and wistful in its gold-brown frame of bobbed hair and fringe. She wore her pink cotton jeans, beautifully pressed by Mother, her pink and white running shoes, a powder blue and white striped anorak that hung open over a white fluffy pullover, and she was carrying her tennis racket in a blue case. Wexford took all this in as she passed him, walking quickly.

He didn't dare come out. She might look back. Instead he dropped down into the field at the other side of the hedge. There had been a crop growing here, wheat or barley, but the grain had been cut and all that remained was a stubble that looked grey in this light. He ran along the hedge side, some few feet above the footpath. A long way ahead now he could just see the top of her head bobbing along. She had reached the corner of the copse.

There was a barbed-wire entanglement here that threatened to bar his passage, the spaces between the wires too narrow to squeeze through, the top wire too high to sling a leg over without terrible detriment to trousers. There was nothing for it but to retrace steps, pass through the hedge and clamber up the bank onto the footpath. She was too far away to see him even if she did look back. He jumped down, rounded the bend in the path, but now, though the copse was in full view, he couldn't see her at all.

His heart was in his mouth then. If she had met her assailant and gone into the wood, if Archbold truly had gone to sleep . . . He left the path and plunged into the copse. It was dark and dry in there, a million needles underfoot from the firs and larches. He ran through the trees and met Archbold head on.

'There's no one here, sir. I haven't seen a soul in three hours.'

'Except her,' said Wexford breathlessly.

'She just walked past. She's on her own, heading for the High Street.'

He came out of the wood on the Kingsmarkham side,

Archbold behind him. She was nowhere to be seen, the hedges too high, the foliage on the trees too thick and masking. And then he forgot discretion and catching a murderer and ran along the path in pursuit of her, afraid for her and for himself. A moment before he had been praying Bennett wouldn't appear, walking from the Kingsmarkham end, and spoil it all. Now he hoped he would.

There was one more field and that low-lying, the path passing diagonally across it and then running beside a hedge at right angles to the road. No sign of Bennett. Because he had seen her? Or seen her attacker? Would he be capable of that in this fast-fading light? The meadow was grey and the hedges black and the air had the density of fallen cloud. Through the mist you could just see a light or two from cars on the Pomfret road, behind that an irregular cluster of pale lights that was probably the police station.

She was nowhere. The meadow was empty. There was a movement just discernible on the far side of it, where the path met the hedge. She had crossed the diagonal and come to the last hundred yards, her pale clothes catching what light there was so that she gleamed like a night moth. And like a night moth fluttered along against the dark foliage.

Wexford and Palmer didn't take the diagonal. They dared not risk being seen. They kept to the boundary hedge, though there was no path here, and Palmer, who was thirty, outran Wexford who felt that he had never run so hard in his life. All the time he could see the pale fluttering moth moving down there, homing on the stile that would bring her to the wide grass verge of the Pomfret road.

She never reached it. The fluttering stopped and there was something else down there with her at the bottom of the field where the dead elms stood, their roots a mass of underbrush, of brambles and nettles and fuzzy wild clematis. The something or someone else had come out of that and barred her way. He thought he heard a cry but he couldn't be sure. At any rate it was no scream but a thin shriek of – surprise perhaps. He cut the corner, running hell for leather, his heart pounding fit to burst, running the way no man of close on sixty should run.

And Archbold got there only just first. It was strange that the knife should catch a gleam on it even in this near darkness. Wexford saw the gleam and then saw it drop to the ground. Archbold was holding Veronica who had turned her face into his chest and was clinging to his coat. He went up to the other himself. She made no attempt to run. She clasped her hands and hung her head so that he couldn't see her face.

In that moment Bennett materialized, so to speak. He came out of the dark, running. Sara Williams looked up then with an expression of faint dull surprise.

'Take them both,' said Wexford. 'They'll be charged with the wilful murder of Rodney Williams.'

22

'It was they, not their mothers, who knew each other,' Wexford said. 'Edwina Klein told me but I misinterpreted what she said. "Those two women knew each other," she said to me. "I saw them together." I took her to mean Joy and Wendy. Joy and Wendy were women and Sara and Veronica were girls. Except that to a militant feminist founder member of ARRIA all females are women. Just as they are,' he added, 'to organizers of sports events. It's the women's singles even if both players are fifteen.'

Burden and the doctor said nothing. They were all sitting in Burden's grass widower's house, drinking Burden's grass widower's instant coffee. It was over. A special court for one and a special juvenile court for the other and the two girls had been committed for trial. Afterwards the press had caught Wexford, a camera crew springing out of their van with the agility of the SAS, and once again he would be on television. Looking a hundred years old, he thought, after being up half the night talking to Sara Williams. People would phone in suggesting it was time he retired.

'They met at a tennis match, of course. The second time I met Sara I noticed she had a tennis racket up on her bedroom wall. She wasn't anywhere near Veronica's standard, not in the high school's first or second six. She just scraped into their reserve. Still, one day she was called on to play and she met Veronica as her opponent. What happened then? I don't know and she hasn't told me. I'd guess that one of the other girls there commented that they looked alike and seeing they had the same surname, were they cousins? It was up to one of them to probe further and one of them did. Sara, probably. After that it wouldn't have been hard to find out, would it? "Look, I've got a photo, this is my mum and dad . . . " '

'Something of a shattering experience, wouldn't you say?' said the doctor.

'Also I think an exciting one.'

'That's a superficial way of looking at it,' said Burden. 'I'd almost say unfeeling. Both those girls were lonely, Veronica sheltered and smothered, Sara neglected, no one's favourite. Wouldn't it have been both shattering and immensely *comforting* to find a sister?'

The sensitivity which had developed in Burden late in life always brought Wexford a kind of affectionate amusement. It was so often misdirected. It resembled in a way those good intentions with which hell is paved.

He picked his words carefully. They were strong words but his tone was hesitant.

'Sara Williams doesn't have normal feelings of affection, need for love, loneliness. I think she would be labelled a psychopath. She wants attention and she wants to impress. Also she wants her own way. I imagine that what she got from her half-sister was principally admiration. Sara has an excellent brain. Intellectually, she's streets ahead of Veronica. She's a strong, powerful, amoral, unfeeling solipsist with an appalling temper.'

Crocker's eyebrows went up. 'You're talking about an eighteen-year-old who was raped by her own father.'

Wexford didn't respond. He was thinking about what the girl had said to him, presiding at the table in the interview room with Marion Bayliss at one end, himself opposite and Martin facing Marion. But Sara Williams had presided, holding her head high, describing her feelings and actions without a notion of defending herself.

'My sister looks just like me. I used to feel she was another aspect of me, the weaker, pretty, feminine part, if you like. I wanted ultimately to be rid of that part.'

Solipsism, according to the Oxford dictionary, is the

view or theory that self is the only object of real knowledge or the only real thing existent.

'Why didn't you tell your parents you and Veronica had met?'

'Why should I?'

Her cool answers took the breath away.

'It would have been the natural thing to confront your father with what you had found out.'

She was honest in her way. 'I liked having the secret. I enjoyed knowing what he thought I didn't know.'

'So that you could hold it over him?'

'Perhaps,' she said indifferently, bored when the discussion was not totally centred on herself.

Was that what she had had to threaten him with in the matter of the incest? Was that how she had stopped it?

'You prevented Veronica from telling her mother?'

'She did what I told her.'

It was uttered the way a trainer speaks of an obedient dog. The trainer takes the obedience for granted, so effective are his personality and technique, so unthinkable would an alternative reaction be. Wexford thought Crocker and Burden would have had to hear and see Sara to appreciate all this. He couldn't even attempt to put it across to them. 'The two girls met quite often,' he went on. 'Sara even went to Veronica's home when Wendy was at work. Veronica came to admire her extravagantly. She followed her, she would have obeyed her in anything.'

'Would have?'

'Did. Psychiatrists call what overtook them *folie à deux*, a kind of madness that overtakes two people only when they are together and through the influence of each on the other. But in all such cases you'll always find one party who is easily led and one who is dominant.' Wexford digressed a little before returning to the point. 'Looking back, I don't think Sara Williams has ever addressed a sentence to me that didn't begin with "I" or wasn't about herself.'

He went on, 'The coming and going between the

Williams homes led to a pooling of information. For instance, Sara had believed her father was a sales rep with Sevensmith Harding for the Ipswich area. Veronica thought he was a rep with a bathroom fittings company. They took steps to find out the truth and did. It's over a year now since they found out what Rodney really did, what his position was, and discovered – via some research into marketing managers' earnings on Sara's part – what his actual salary was.

'Sara also warned Veronica of their father's – proclivities. That, of course, is how Wendy came to fear an incest attempt. Not because she witnessed anything herself or because Veronica put two and two together from a kiss and a cuddle but because Sara told Veronica what to expect and Veronica passed it on without disclosing her source. One way and another Sara made Veronica into a very frightened girl. A very bewildered and confused girl. Think of her situation. First she discovers her father has a legal wife and a grown-up family, next that he could never have in fact married her mother and she must be illegitimate. Necessarily, therefore, he's deceitful and a liar. He doesn't even have the job he says he has. Worst of all, he has raped his other daughter and will certainly have the same designs on her. No wonder she was frightened.

'Telling Wendy her fears of a sexual attack had the effect only of causing trouble between her mother and father. Did Wendy accuse Rodney and Rodney hotly deny it? Almost certainly. The quarrel was at any rate bad enough to make Wendy believe Rodney would leave her but fear that if he didn't Veronica would be in danger. So we see that the reason she didn't want Veronica to stay in on the evening of April the fifteenth was that if Rodney did come back she would be alone with her father – and this would be the first time she would be alone with him after the disclosure was made.

'But Veronica had another confidante and friend now, apart from her mother. She had Sara. And Sara absolutely justified the faith she put in her. Sara had a good idea for diverting Rodney's attention from his daughter, diverting his attention from everything, in fact. Substitute sleeping pills for his blood-pressure tablets. It was something that could only be done once though and in an emergency.

'Now on April the fifteenth, however much their mothers may have been in ignorance, Sara and Veronica knew that when Rodney left Alverbury Road he would drive straight to Liskeard Avenue. So Sara herself made the exchange of tablets, two only remaining in the container. Don't forget we found an empty Mandaret container in Alverbury Road and a half-full one in Liskeard Avenue. Rodney took his two Mandaret as he thought, leaving the empty container in his bedroom, and drove to Pomfret. No doubt he began to feel drowsy on the way.'

'But these were Phanodorm, supplied by Paulette Harmer?' said the doctor.

'I suppose they were supplied by her. It seems most likely. But Paulette didn't die because she illicitly provided a sleeping drug. She died because the turn events were taking made her concentrate her mind on the evening of April the fifteenth, made her remember in fact what had really happened. What she remembered was her mother speaking to her aunt Joy on the phone that evening and making some remark about being glad Kevin had settled in back at college. And she was going to tell us because she knew from the papers and television and her parents' conversation how strong was the suspicion against her aunt. She knew very well her aunt had been at home that evening, in at eight to receive Kevin's phone call and still in at eight forty-five to receive her mother's.'

The girl should have been strewing flowers or rising from the waves in a cockleshell. The face was bland, innocent and somehow secretive. Even now there was a tiny self-satisfied smile. Her hair was scraped back tight from that high forehead but wisps had come free and lay in gold tendrils on the white skin.

'I got a phone call from Veronica. It was just to tell me he'd gone to sleep like I said he would. I said I'd come over.'

He had interrupted her to ask why.

'I just thought I would. I wasn't going to get a chance like that again, was I?'

He stopped himself asking her what she meant. Her eyes seemed to enlarge, her face grow blanker.

'I saw him sleeping there and I thought, I've got him in my power. I thought of the power he had over *me*. I started to get angry, really angry.'

'And Veronica?'

'I didn't think about Veronica. I suppose she was there. Well, I know she was. I said to her, "We could kill him and stop all of it." I told her to get me a knife. I wasn't serious then, it was fantasy. I was angry and I was excited – high like when you've had a drink.'

Folie à deux. Was Veronica excited too? He wouldn't get much about another's feelings out of this girl.

'I took the knife out of her hands and took off the cardboard guard that was on it. I went up to my father who was lying on the settee and I started playing around, waving the knife over him, pretending to stick it in him. I could tell he was sound asleep. I was making Veronica laugh because I was doing all this stuff and he was just oblivious of it. I don't remember what made me stop playing. I was so excited and high I don't remember. But that's how it was. One minute it was fantasy and the next it was for real.'

She looked down the table at Marion and then the other way at Martin. It was as if she were gathering the attention of her audience. Once more her eyes met Wexford's in a steady gaze.

'I raised the knife and stuck it in his neck, right in hard with both hands. I'd made him wake up then and make noises, so I stabbed him a few more times to stop the blood spraying like that. I'm going to be a doctor so I knew the blood would stop when he was dead . . . '

It took Wexford, hardened as he was, a moment or two to collect words.

'Did Veronica stab him?'

'I gave her the knife and told her to have a go. I'd made a big wound in his neck and she stuck it in there and then she went off and was sick.'

'Completely mad,' said Burden. 'Bonkers.'

'Perhaps. I'm not sure. Let's not get into defining psychosis.'

'What happened next?' said the doctor.

'The room was covered for the most part in dustsheets. Rodney had come in half asleep, climbed the stairs and lain down on the settee which had a dustsheet over one end. The end, incidentally, where he laid his head. It was this sheet, the property of Leslie Kitman, which received most of the blood. Some went on an area of wall from which the paper had been stripped that day. Sara washed the wall and wrapped Rodney's head up in the dustsheet. Veronica, recovered and very much under orders from Sara, washed the knife and then had the idea of plastering it into the wall. This was the first weird too-clever thing the girls did. There were others. There were fissures in the walls needing to be filled in and in the garage was a packet of filler. Also in the garage was Rodney's car, Greta the Granada, which Sara, though not Veronica, was able to drive. They rolled up the dustsheet and wrapped two of Wendy's Marks and Spencer's teacloths round Rodney's neck. Having cleaned up the room, they carried Rodney down the spiral staircase, through the door from the hall into the garage and put him into the boot of the car. On their way out in the car they deposited the dustsheet in the dustbin. It was about seven-thirty.'

'Then,' said Burden, 'how did Kevin manage to speak to his sister when he phoned Alverbury Road at eight o'clock?'

'He didn't. He spoke to his mother. And, of course, he and Joy were both well aware it was his mother he had spoken to. They lied to protect Sara. Oh, I know Joy hasn't much affection for Sara but she was her daughter. Once she began to think about it she saw that Sara might have had something to do with Rodney's disappearance. At first she genuinely thought he had left her and she got me in to advise her. But then things changed. I think I know why. On my advice, she phoned Sevensmith Harding and they told her *she* had spoken to them on Friday, April the sixteenth, to explain Rodney was ill. Now Joy no doubt at first thought this a mere mistake but they had been so sure it was her voice. Joy knew someone whose voice sounded very like hers – her own daughter.

'Don't forget that she knew how Sara felt towards her father on account of the incest. She also knew Sara had been out of the house for hours on the evening of April the fifteenth. So she told us and got Kevin to agree – no difficulty there, he distrusts the police and is close to his sister – that it was she who had gone out and Sara who had been at home to take the phone call. Was there collusion with Sara? I doubt it. There was no real communication between her and her mother. My guess is Joy said it might be wiser to arrange things this way and Sara agreed with just a nod and a "yes" probably.'

'You're painting a picture of a self-sacrificing maternal type,' said the doctor, 'which doesn't at all accord with our concept of Joy Williams. Rather like the old story of the mother pelican tearing at its own breast to feed its young – and just as much of a myth.'

'No. Joy quite rightly believed there was no real risk in it for her. She thought it impossible we could arrest the wrong person. Her trust must have been sorely put to the test these past few days.'

Always happier on circumstantial details, Burden said, 'So the two girls took Williams's body up to Cheriton Forest and dug a grave for him with his own snow shovel?'

'A shallow grave because, having killed him, Sara didn't want it to be too long before the body was discovered. She wanted a couple of weeks to pass only, rightly believing that this was the sort of time which would be just about right to blur the evidence. In fact, things didn't go her way and it was two months before the body was found.

'I turned over and over in my mind the complication of the Milvey coincidence. But now it has come out quite clearly. There is no coincidence. Sara and Veronica hid Rodney's travelling bag – in the forest probably – hoping it would be found within, say, the next few days. But as it happened, no one found it. Then one day Mrs Milvey happened to say to Joy in Sara's hearing that Milvey would be at Green Pond next day, dragging the pool. Sara retrieved the bag and dumped it in the pool in time for Milvey to find it next day.'

'But why did she want the body found? What difference could it make to her?'

'I'll come to that later.'

'I don't see why go to all the trouble of phoning Sevensmith Harding and forging a letter to delay discovery, and then later try to accelerate it. Incidentally, I take it it was Sara who made the phone call? Her voice is very like Joy's.'

'She made the phone call and Veronica typed the letter. At her friend Nicola Tennyson's house, on Nicola's mother's typewriter.

'They buried the body, hid the travelling bag, and Sara drove Veronica back to Pomfret to be sure she got home before Wendy did. That was at about nine. Wendy, of course, didn't get home until nine thirty, being out doing some mild courting with James Ovington. Sara drove to Myringham and dumped the car in Arnold Road where no more than half an hour later it was seen and indeed bumped into by Eve Freeborn. If Sara had been a bit later and Eve a bit earlier those two members of ARRIA would have encountered each other and made our task a lot easier. But by the time Eve came Sara was on the bus for home.

'In the morning she shut herself in the living room and made the phone call before she went to school. Of necessity it was a very early call and she was lucky there was someone there to receive it. And that, I think, accounts for all the circumstances of the murder of Rodney Williams.'

Burden picked up the tray.

'Does anyone want more coffee?'

Neither did. Wexford said it was nearly beer time, wasn't it? The doctor frowned at him and he deliberately looked away, out into Burden's bright, neat garden, the flower borders like chintzy dress material, the lawn a bit of green baize. The sunshine was making Jenny's yellow chrysanthemums nearly too bright to look at. Burden opened the french windows.

'The sad thing,' said Crocker, 'is that all this is going to make it next to impossible for Sara Williams to make a career in medicine.'

Burden looked at him. He said sarcastically, 'Oh, surely St Biddulph's will overlook a little matter like stabbing her father to death with a carving knife.'

'You don't think it justification then, and more than justification, for a girl to make a murderous assault on the father who has raped her and shows signs of meting out the same treatment to her younger half-sister? Don't you think any judge or jury would see this as an extenuating circumstance?'

It was Wexford who answered him. 'Yes, I do.'

'Right, then there's not going to be any question of years of imprisonment, is there? She'll never have the dubious distinction of being a GP like your humble servant here, but at least there won't be punishment in the accepted sense.'

'I wouldn't be too sure of that.'

'On account of the planning and the covering of tracks, do you mean?'

'She killed Paulette Harmer,' Burden said.

'She did indeed but that wasn't what I meant. You see, Rodney Williams never committed incest with his elder daughter. He never showed signs of committing incest with his younger daughter. And I very much doubt if he ever sexually assaulted anyone, even in the broadest meaning of that term.'

23

Crocker had caught on quickly. Wexford left it to him to explain. The doctor began outlining Freud's 'seduction theory' as expressed in the famous paper of 1896.

Thirteen women patients of Freud claimed paternal seduction. Freud believed them, built on this evidence a theory, later abandoned it, realizing he had been too gullible. Instead, he concluded that little girls are prone to fantasize that their fathers have made love to them, from which developed his stress on childhood fantasy and ultimately his postulation of the Oedipus Complex.

'You're saying it was all fantasy on Sara's part?' Burden said. 'She's not exactly a *little* girl.'

'Nor were Freud's patients little girls by the time they came to him.'

Wexford said, 'I think Sara had a daughter's fantasy about her father. When she was older she read Freud. She read books on incest too – they're all there in her bedroom. There's a mention of father–daughter incest in the ARRIA constitution. Did she read that too or did she write it? At any rate, *in her mind* she was heavily involved with her father, far more involved with him than he was with her.'

'How do you know the seduction didn't really take place? Men do commit incest with their daughters. I mean, how could Freud have known one of those thirteen wasn't fantasizing but telling the truth?'

'I can't answer that,' Wexford said, 'but I can tell you it never happened to Sara. She isn't the kind of girl to whom it happens. She isn't ignorant or obtuse or cowed or dependent. This seduction, or apparent seduction, followed a classic pattern as laid down in the books. The girl doesn't struggle or fight or scream. She doesn't want to make a disturbance. At the first opportunity she tells her mother and mother reacts with rage, reproaches, accusations of the girl's provocative behaviour. Now Joy, as we might expect, fitted beautifully into the classic pattern. But Sara? If it had really happened wouldn't Sara, a leading member of ARRIA, a militant feminist, have fought and screamed? She was very handy with a knife, wasn't she? And she's the last person to care about making a disturbance in a household, either emotional or physical. As for telling her mother – Sara tell her mother? There's been no real communication between them for years. She despises her mother. If she'd told anyone it would have been her brother Kevin. No, there was no seduction, for if there had been she would have kept the experience secret to use against her father, not come running with it to Joy.

'It was Sara who stabbed Colin Budd, of course. It happened, if you remember, the night before Milvey started dragging Green Pond. Sara retrieved the bag after dark, went up to the forest to do it and put the bag inside a plastic sack. When Budd came along she was waiting to catch the bus that would take her to the other end of Kingsmarkham, near enough to the Forby road and Green Pond Hall. The last thing she wanted was Budd taking an interest in her. Besides, she had indoctrinated herself to be always on the watch for sexist approaches. What was she doing but going about her private business? And this man has to treat her as if her primary function in this world was to be an object for his diversion and entertainment. No doubt she also lost her nerve. She stabbed him with a penknife.'

'If it was all fantasy,' said Burden, reverting to the analysis of Sara Williams's character, 'why did she warn Veronica? Why warn her of something that would never happen?'

'You're supposing fantasy is something "made up", so therefore something the fantasizer herself doesn't believe in?'

'Well, does she? Did Sara convince herself?'

'Yes and no. She's admitted to me nothing ever happened. On the other hand, I wouldn't be surprised if tomorrow she says it did and believes it herself. Having this secret to communicate, this awful and horrifying secret, must have much increased her ascendancy over Veronica. It enhanced her power. Veronica was very frightened of her, you see, full of admiration, awe almost, but even before the killing of Rodney becoming unnerved by the whole set-up.'

Wendy had been sent for and for once had been calm, sensible, steady. He had considered the atmosphere of his office more relaxing than one of those stark interview rooms. Marion and Polly were seated side by side and Veronica a little apart from everyone until Wexford came in. Little Miss Muffet and the great spider who sat down beside her. Only there was no frightening her away. It would be a long time now before Veronica Williams could get away.

She was very pale. Her hair, he noticed, was a couple of inches longer than when he had first seen her, six inches longer than the crop of the beach photograph. Had she been growing it in imitation of her idol and model Sara? He had asked her when she first met her half-sister.

'It was September.' Her voice was so soft he had to ask her to repeat it. 'September – a year ago,' she said.

'And you met how often after that? Once a week? More?'

Very quietly, 'More.'

He extracted from her the information that they constantly spoke on the phone. It was like a game sometimes, Sara phoning and saying she would be in Liskeard Avenue in five minutes, she phoning Sara to say if Sara was careful not to be seen she could come and watch Rodney and Wendy watching *her* play tennis.

'It stopped being a game, though, didn't it? On April the fifteenth it stopped?'

She nodded and her body convulsed in an involuntary shiver. Wendy said, 'Why did you always do everything she said? Why did you tell her everything?'

How could she answer that?

'You told her you were coming here to confess your part in it, didn't you, Veronica?' Wexford spoke very gently.

Her eyes went to Wendy. 'I thought the police would arrest my mother.'

A small spark of triumph on Wendy's doleful face. In these unbelievable circumstances her years of devotion were rewarded . . .

Wexford surfaced from his reverie to see Burden depositing three beer cans in front of them from a tray laden with the kind of junk food he lived on while Jenny was away.

'Wake up!'

'Sorry.'

'Look, if there was no incest and therefore no renewed assault from Rodney to be feared, if there was no threat to Veronica, what was the motive for killing him? All through this case we could never come up with any sort of solid motive. Or are you saying a psychopath doesn't need a motive – at any rate not a motive understood by normal people?'

Wexford said slowly, 'I've suggested to you that there was a good deal of calculation in Sara's behaviour, some of it of an apparently incomprehensible kind. Her original concealment of the body, for instance, and later her anxiety for it to be found. I've also made it clear – rather to your joint disapproval, I think – that I don't feel much sympathy towards Sara. And this is because I feel she had no justification for what she did.

'She had a motive all right, and as calculated and cold-blooded a motive as any poisoner polishing off an old relation for his money.'

'But Rodney didn't have any money to leave, did he?' Burden objected.

'Not so's you'd notice, though the manager of the Anglian-Victoria has shown me how a nice little bit was accumulating in the account from which the two joint accounts were fed. Enough, anyway, for him to recommend that Rodney put it into investments. Still, it wasn't for a possible inheritance that Sara killed him, though money was her motive.'

'Not a cash gain though, I think,' said the doctor.

Wexford turned to Burden. 'You raised this very subject not long ago, Mike. That was when you thought you were going to have a daughter – and that's relevant too. You talked about her going to university and applying for government grants. Do you remember?'

'I suppose so. I don't see where the relevance comes in.'

'Sara wants to be a doctor,' said Wexford. 'Well, *wanted* to be, I should say. It was a driving ambition with her. And increasingly hard though this is becoming, she knew she had the ability to get into medical school. Her parents, however, discouraged her. And it must have looked to her at that stage as if this was a classic case of opposition to daughter's ambitions simply because she was a daughter and not a son, because in fact she was a woman. On Joy's part it probably was. Very likely she wouldn't have cared for Sara to achieve greater success and have a more prestigious profession than Kevin.

'At first this parental opposition didn't much worry Sara. I'm speaking, of course, about this time last year. Sara remembered her brother getting a place at Keele and the form of application for a grant coming from Sussex County Council Education Committee to her father. At the time she didn't take much notice. Certainly she didn't see the completed form. But she knew that the greater the parental income the smaller the grant would be and that with the form there came a form of certificate of parental employment the parent's employer had to complete detailing his gross salary, overtime, bonus or commissions and his taxable emoluments. Now, Mike, you'll recall that certificate in your own case and sending it to the Mid-Sussex Constabulary when you applied for grants for John and Pat?'

Burden nodded. 'I'm beginning to see the light here.'

'Twelve months ago Sara met Veronica. Gradually, when the shock of that encounter began to recede, when it provided the solution to certain unexplained anomalies, shall we say, Sara saw the cold reality for what it was. Her father might talk about not wanting his daughter to be a doctor for aesthetic reasons, for reasons of suitability, she would get married and her education be wasted, et cetera. He might talk that way but the reason behind the talk was very different. Finding that he had lied both to her mother and Veronica's about what his position and his earnings were, she had taken steps to discover what he did and what he earned. Now she understood. If he filled in the grant application form for her he would have to declare to the Sussex County Council that his income was not £10,000 a year but two and a half times that, and there would be no way he could deceive the authority as he had deceived her mother because his employers, Sevensmith Harding, would have to complete the certificate of parental income from employment.

'Now according to the grants department's contribution scales, a parent earning £10,000 per annum would have to contribute to medical school costs only something in the region of £470 but a parent earning £25,000 a sum of nearly £2000. Rodney had two homes and two families, he was already paying out this sort of sum for Kevin at Keele – remember he had to tell the grants department the truth, whatever he told his wives – and Sara could see the way the wind was blowing. She could see there was no way he would part with £2000 a year for her benefit. And when she asked him point blank if he would fill in the form when it came he told her he wouldn't – she would never make a doctor and he was doing her a kindness in not encouraging her.'

'What a bastard,' said Crocker.

Wexford shrugged. 'The mistake is ours when we deceive ourselves about parent–child relationships. When we keep up the belief that all parents love their children and want what's best for them.'

'Surely, though, if Sara had talked about this at school or discussed it with some sympathetic officer at the grants department, a way could have been found for her to get a grant, bypassing Rodney? There must be many cases where a parent withholds consent and won't complete a grant application.'

'Probably. But Sara is only eighteen. And remember that to have done what you suggest she would have to reveal that her father was a liar and a cheat, that he deceived her mother, that he was a bigamist. And how long would all this take? Would it mean her waiting a year? And what of her place at St Biddulph's, a teaching hospital where places are like gold dust and where they keep a reserve list bursting with applicants dying to be accepted? What she decided on instead was, first, persuasion and if that failed, blackmail.'

'She told him that if he didn't consent to fill in the form she'd tell Joy about Wendy and get Veronica to tell Wendy about Joy?'

'She was *going* to tell him that. She had a bit of time though. She hadn't even sat her A-levels. The grant form wouldn't come till July. And she also had the incest. Of course, it had never taken place but Joy thought it had, Veronica was scared stiff it had. If all else failed she might be able to use it as another weapon in the blackmail stock-pile. That was why she was pleased to see how effective her warnings had been in Veronica's case. Veronica was beginning to be afraid of the affectionate attention Rodney paid her. Veronica didn't want to be alone with him and if she had to be she wanted him disarmed and immobilized.

Sara saw to that with the Phanodorm, and increased Veronica's fear by the seriousness of taking such a step.

'But how much simpler, after all, to kill him! And there he was, lying asleep, the potential destroyer of her future. Kill him now, in this room which will soon be made pure and immaculate, cleansed of all signs of violent death. Rid the world of him, seize your opportunity. And perhaps it would also be a heroic act. Hadn't there almost been a clause in the ARRIA constitution demanding a man's death as qualification for entry? Veronica will help because Veronica also hates him now and is mortally afraid of him . . .

'But suppose they never find the body? Suppose the weeks go by and July comes and August and with them the grant application and you can't fill in the section that says "Father, if deceased the fact should be stated . . . " because only you and Veronica know he is deceased? You have finished your A-levels and the time is going by – the moment has come to take steps for that body to be found without more delay.'

'You might say,' said Crocker, 'that the murder was both coolly premeditated and carried out on an impulse.'

'You might. Because of what Sara is, a highly complex personality, this was all kinds of a murder. A ritualistic killing – remember that Veronica was required to stab him too. A revenge killing – Sara had more than half-convinced herself and wholly convinced Veronica of the reality of the incest. When she stabbed Rodney she was a woman out of classical myth, she was Beatrice Cenci. It was an *experimental* killing, a kind of vivisection, carried out by Sara the scientist, to see if it would work, to see if it could be done. It was murder from disgust, from disillusionment. Rodney, whom she had once worshipped, was just a squalid bigamist with another daughter, a copy of herself, he loved as much as or more than he had ever loved her. But above all, in spite of all those other factors, it was murder for gain, carried out so that she might satisfy her ambition at all costs. All in all, I don't think that's the sort of person I'd care to have as my family physician, still less performing surgery on me and mine. So perhaps Rodney was right when he told Sara she was an unsuitable candidate for medical school. Who knows? Perhaps it wasn't simply meanness with him, he wasn't quite the bastard you make out. Perhaps he sensed in that daughter of his, without ever examining his conclusions, traits in her character that were abnormal, that were destructive, and it was to these he referred when he said she would never make a doctor.'

Wexford got up.

'I shall call it a day,' he said. 'I shall go to the wife of my bosom the same as I ought to go.'

Burden began tidying the room, putting things on a tray. 'And tomorrow the wife of my bosom comes home to me.' He looked pleased, satisfied, hopeful, as if there had been no five months' long disruption of his happiness. 'One of her old pupils at Haldon Finch went in to see her and the baby. An ARRIA member. She told Jenny the raven bit means they're cleaning up the carrion men have left behind in the world. We did wonder.'

'Ah,' Wexford paused in the doorway. 'Something I nearly forgot to tell you. About Williams's young girlfriend . . .'

They looked at him. 'Williams didn't have a young girlfriend,' Burden said.

'Of course he did. She had nothing to do with his death, nothing to do with this case, so she hardly concerned us. But a man like Williams – it was in his nature, inevitable. Both his wives knew it, they sensed it. Probably he'd always had a young girlfriend, a succession of them.

'This one – hers were the other set of prints on the car. No wonder she said her dad didn't want me to take them. They met at Sevensmith Harding, of course. In the office.'

'Jane Gardner . . . '

'That's who he had his date with on April the fifteenth in Myringham. Join her for her baby-sitting, then spend the night together at the Cheriton Forest Hotel. Why else did he have a bag with him with a single change of underwear and a toothbrush and toothpaste? But the sleeping pills overcame him as he was driving through Pomfret, and instead of going on to meet Jane he was just able to make it to his own house. What she thought was that he'd stood her up. Then, when he disappeared, that he'd gone off with another woman. I had a word with her this morning and she admitted it – no more need to conceal it now we'd made an arrest.'

'What put you on to her?'

'I don't know. Guesswork. She was the only person I ever spoke to who had a good word for Rodney Williams.'

Wexford let himself out, closing Burden's blue front door behind him.

Also in Arrow by Ruth Rendell

THE FALLEN CURTAIN
and other stories

A wife drives her husband to alcoholism and plots first his psychological destruction – then his murder.

A son is ruined by his mother's obsession.

A man marries a girl he has rescued from a suicide attempt – only to be destroyed by her frightening possessiveness.

A family feud culminates in horror beyond imagination.

Master storyteller Ruth Rendell lays bare the dark recesses of the human psyche in this haunting, memorable and chilling collection of moral tales.

Awarded an Edgar by The Mystery Writers of America

'Ruth Rendell leads the field'
OBSERVER

'A natural Story-teller'
THE TIMES LITERARY SUPPLEMENT

MASTER OF THE MOOR

The bleak expanse of Vangmoor was a dark, forbidding place. One victim had been found there, blonde, her face disfigured, her head shorn close to the scalp – killed without motive or mercy. Then a second woman went missing on the moor, and a sense of utter dread gripped the fifty local men who searched for her. Someone watched them in that treacherous place. Was he a killer? Or was he merely angry that a killer had usurped him? For he, and only he, was Master of the Moor . . .

'Our leading lady "whydunnit" writer'
H. R. F. KEATING, SUNDAY EXPRESS

'A splendidly sinewy tale'
GRAHAM LORD, THE TIMES

'Arresting . . . Credible . . . A very good book indeed'
LONDON EVENING STANDARD

'Powerful, intriguing . . .'
TIMES LITERARY SUPPLEMENT

RUTH RENDELL BESTSELLERS AVAILABLE IN ARROW

☐	Road Rage	£5.99
☐	The Keys to the Street	£5.99
☐	The Bridesmaid	£5.99
☐	The Copper Peacock	£4.99
☐	A Guilty Thing Surprised	£5.99
☐	A Judgement in Stone	£5.99
☐	Shake Hands For Ever	£5.99
☐	No More Dying Then	£5.99
☐	The Fallen Curtain and other stories	£4.99
☐	Master of the Moor	£5.99
☐	Blood Lines	£4.99
☐	Simisola	£5.99

ALL ARROW BOOKS ARE AVAILABLE THROUGH MAIL ORDER OR FROM YOUR LOCAL BOOKSHOP.

PAYMENT MAY BE MADE USING ACCESS, VISA, MASTERCARD, DINERS CLUB, SWITCH AND AMEX, OR CHEQUE, EUROCHEQUE AND POSTAL ORDER (STERLING ONLY).

☐☐☐☐☐☐☐☐☐☐☐☐☐☐☐☐

EXPIRY DATE .... SWITCH ISSUE NO. ☐☐

SIGNATURE ....

PLEASE ALLOW £2.50 FOR POST AND PACKING for the first book and £1.00 per book thereafter.

ORDER TOTAL: £................................ (INCLUDING P&P)

ALL ORDERS TO:

ARROW BOOKS, BOOKS BY POST, TBS LIMITED, THE BOOK SERVICE, COLCHESTER ROAD, FRATING GREEN, COLCHESTER, ESSEX, CO7 7 DW, UK.

TELEPHONE: (01206) 256 000
FAX: (01206) 256 914

NAME ....

ADDRESS..

....

Please allow 28 days for delivery. Please tick box if you do not wish to receive any additional information. ☐

Prices and availability subject to change without notice.